Praise for *Obsession*

'Thrilling, unputdownable, a fabulous rollercoaster of a read.'
B A Paris, bestselling author of *Behind Closed Doors*

'Compelling and thoroughly addictive.'
Katerina Diamond, No.1 bestselling author of *The Teacher*

'A welcome addition to the domestic noir bookshelf. Robson
explores marriage, jealousy and lust with brutal clarity, making
for a taut thriller full of page-turning suspense.'
Emma Flint, author of *Little Deaths*

'Amanda Robson has some devastating turns of phrase
up her sleeve and she expertly injects menace into
the domestic. A dark and disturbing journey.'
Holly Seddon, author of *Try Not to Breathe*

'A compelling psychosexual thriller, Amanda Robson is a
new name to look out for in dark and disturbing fiction.
High quality domestic noir.'
Paul Finch, *Sunday Times* bestseller

'A compelling page-turner on the dark underbelly of
marriage, friendship and lust. (If you're considering an affair,
you might want a rethink.)'
Fiona Cummins, author of *Rattle*

D0916530

About the author

After graduating, Amanda Robson worked in medical research at The London School of Hygiene and Tropical Medicine, and at the Poisons Unit at Guy's Hospital where she became a co-author of a book on cyanide poisoning. Amanda attended the Faber Academy novel writing course in 2011 and now writes full-time. *Obsession* is her debut novel.

AMANDA ROBSON

OBSESSION

avon

HarperCollins
PUBLISHERS
Since 1817

AVON

A division of HarperCollins*Publishers*
1 London Bridge Street,
London, SE1 9GF

www.harpercollins.co.uk

A Paperback Original 2017

2

First published in Great Britain by
HarperCollins*Publishers* 2017

Copyright © Amanda Robson 2017

Amanda Robson asserts the moral right to
be identified as the author of this work

A catalogue record for this book is
available from the British Library

ISBN-13: 978-0-00-824883-3

Set in Bembo by Palimpsest Book Production Limited,
Falkirk, Stirlingshire

Printed and bound in the United States of America

Find out more about HarperCollins and the environment at
www.harpercollins.co.uk/green

To my close family.
To my husband, Richard Gillis. My sons, Peter and Mark Gillis.
My parents Shirley and Peter Robson, and my brother and his
wife, Chris and Carol Robson.

There is a sharp intake of breath as the jurors are shown a photograph of the crime scene. Oh, the strange, strange fascination of death. The acrid smell of death that will never go away.

ONE

~ Carly ~

I am drunk; liquid-limbed, mind-pumping drunk, and so is my husband, Rob. Craggy features, softened by shadows, move towards me across the mosquito candle placed in the middle of the camping table, as he smiles at me and tops up my glass. I shiver a little and zip up my jacket. The low sky of this Breton night has brought the sort of chill that predicates frost. But although frost won't happen in July in the south of Brittany, during this camping holiday, I have not felt warm enough. Not once. Not at night, curled up beneath my inadequate blanket, or in the day when I'm supervising our children around the unheated swimming pool. The extra layer of body fat, cultivated after the arrival of our third child, is not protecting me from the cold.

Our children are asleep in the tent behind us. I feel their silence and the exhalation of their breath, deep rooted and satisfying. At least I don't have to watch their every movement until morning, as I do during the days. Holidays aren't holidays any more. We just take our children to a different place to look after them. A place that is harder work.

Everything about this camping holiday is exhausting. Standing by the pool for hour after hour, checking that they're not drowning. The boredom of watching and waiting for the occasional sight of a familiar head coming out from behind a plastic palm tree or poolside dolphin. Holding giggling toddlers as we are tossed down knotted plastic tubes, sliding along until we're spewed out into the water, the movement almost breaking our backs. The endless cooking of barbecues – washing burnt gunk off the griddle. As far as I am concerned this is the best part of the day; the children are in bed and I have Rob to myself.

For this is what I like. Rob to myself. We married just over ten years ago, so we were alone for several years before our children were born. We met at the training hospital when I was a trainee nurse and he was a junior doctor. I will never forget the sight of him walking down the ward towards me, that first cracked smile. No doubt someone looking in would consider our relationship argumentative. Some of our friends say that they never have a cross word. How do they achieve that? Why do we argue? My mother says it is because we care. Whatever. It isn't really a satisfactory day without the rumblings of a discussion.

Tonight, sitting opposite my husband, a surfeit of alcohol pounding through my veins, I am filled with a new kind of mischief.

'Who else would you go for, if you could?' I hear myself slur.

'No one,' he slurs back.

'I don't believe you. You tell me and I'll tell you,' I push.

Rob sits in silence.

'Come on,' I say. 'Let's be really honest – to compound our relationship.'

He looks at me and puts his plastic wine glass on the metal table.

'But Carly, we don't need to compound our relationship.'

4

'I think we do.'

Green eyes burn to emerald.

'I don't want to know who you fantasise about.'

'But I want to know about you.'

A jawline held taut.

'I don't fantasise about anyone.'

'I don't believe you.' I pause. 'Anyway, I don't need to know who you fantasise about. We're just playing a game. Give me a name, someone you quite like.'

He shrugs his shoulders.

'I quite like Jenni.'

'Jenni?'

Jenni. NCT Jenni. Placid and peaceful with doe-like eyes. Endlessly, endlessly kind.

'What about you?'

I don't reply.

The camping holiday continues but it doesn't improve. Our two-day conjugal hangover doesn't help. The swimming pool and the weather are growing colder. Cloud gathers and hangs along the coastline, releasing a clinging sea mist which sticks to the headland, making our nightly walk along the cliff path to the nearest restaurant border on suicidal. The rain starts on Tuesday evening. On Wednesday morning I wake up and hear its soft drum beat still pounding against the canvas. At first the sound is comforting. A 'let's stay in bed and make love because it's cold and wet outside' sort of sound. I snuggle up to Rob and then reality hits me. Camping. Rain. Bored children about to wake up. I escape to the shower block.

By the time I reach the shower block I am so wet I'm not sure why I'm bothering to have a shower. The lukewarm dribble of water from the showerhead slightly raises my body temperature, but not my mood as I struggle to pull my clothing back across my damp skin and worry about my weight. I shouldn't have eaten pizza yesterday. Or chips the day before. And what about the beer? Soft and delicious and brimming with calories.

Forget about alcohol. It's the only thing I'm enjoying about this holiday.

At least I am not like Jenni, so thin after childbirth that her breasts have disappeared. I look at myself in the mirror, cup my breasts with my hands, think of her boyish figure, and laugh. Jenni.

Rob and Jenni. Who would have thought of that?

When I return to the tent it has come to life. Rob is starting to prepare breakfast and the children are playing a shouting game, or, as I listen harder, a roaring game. Our seven-year-old daughter, Pippa, is crawling on the floor on all fours, head back and growling. She's trying to frighten her younger brothers, Matt and John, shaking her long blonde hair and attacking them with fingernail claws. They are crawling away from her and laughing, too innocent to realise that if she could, she would hurt them. Rob, seemingly deaf to the noise, is putting cereal on the table.

As soon as I enter the tent, Rob's face lights up and he moves towards me, kisses me on the lips.

'Hey you. Do you want to play?' he asks.

'Mummy, Mummy,' Pippa roars. 'You can be a tiger.'

'A tiger that needs morning coffee before it can growl,' I say, planting myself firmly on a chair.

'The swimming pool closes when it rains. What are we going to do today?' Rob asks as the kettle whistles.

'Go home?' I suggest hopefully.

Being back home has many advantages, warmth being one of them, temperature control at the touch of a button preferable to the vagaries of weather. Regular sex without worrying that the children can hear is another positive. But the biggest advantage is sitting at the breakfast bar on Monday morning sipping coffee, waiting for my mother, knowing I have a child-free day in front of me.

My triangular-shaped mother, Heather, arrives, straight from her flat just around the corner. She steps into the hall, wearing her favourite floral dress and her M&S cardigan. Her shoulder-length curly hair looks as if it needs combing. It always looks as if it needs combing, but it's just the way her curls frizz. Some remaining brown hair peppers her grey like drizzled dirt. Mother, when are you going to improve your appearance? It doesn't seem to make any difference to how much our children love her. Pippa thunders down the stairs, two at a time, and falls into her grandmother's arms.

'Gwandma, Gwandma,' John shouts, bumbling downstairs in his Gruffalo pyjamas which Gwandma has bought him, launching himself into the hug. Before long Matt has joined the love-in too. I tip the rest of my coffee down the waste disposal, place my mug in the dishwasher and sidle towards the front door. I manage to kiss my mother as I pass her; the children have left a patch of skin on her cheek accessible.

'I hope you don't mind, but I'll be late tonight.'

'That's fine, dear. I won't be in any hurry to leave. Are you working late?'

'Going for a drink with Jenni.'

I close the front door and step into watery sunshine. My mother looks after the children for us three days a week, so that I can work for Rob in Riverside Surgery. Rob. The most popular GP in Stansfield. I hear it from our receptionists, from the school-gate mums, from the neighbours, and have no reason to doubt that it's true. Our surgery list is full. I can't compete with his popularity. Why would I want to? I'm just one of his practice nurses. All I do is give injections, take blood, and perform breast and gynae checks. Although aspects of my job are boring, I enjoy my three days at work more than my weekdays at home with the children. Weekends at home are fine because Rob is so very helpful. But my weekdays with the children are just plain hard work. Stopping fights, making too many peanut butter sandwiches (Matt's favourite), wading through burial mounds of laundry. The worst part is Pippa's school-gate pick-up. Mother seems to relish it, enjoys talking to the school-gate mafia. She fits in. But I don't. The school-gate mafia; women who are living through their children. Women who don't have anything else.

I walk towards the surgery. Left at the end of our road, along Stansfield High Street, past the Chinese restaurant, past the fish shop. I cross the road at the traffic lights and enter the surgery through the side door, away from the receptionists and the patients. I hang up my raincoat and open the door to the nurses' station. Sitting at my desk, I switch the computer on to check my patient list. Eight patients this morning. Two breast checks. Three blood tests. Three sets of travel injections. As I press the buzzer for my first patient, the shadow that started following me on holiday begins to darken.

The shadow is no lighter when I finish at the surgery and am on my way to meet you, Jenni. You are waiting for me after work at the coffee shop, by the bus stop in the centre of town. I see you through the window as I move past the bus queue – sending a text from your iPhone, your glossy hair tumbling across your face. As soon as I enter the coffee shop you look up and beam at me, as if seeing me is the most important part of your day. Jenni, you always try to make people feel like that. As if they are important. It is one of your tricks. I know that now. When we first met, I fell for it.

We knew each other at nursing college, didn't we, Jenni? But only from a distance. You weren't really my type. Christian

Union. No make-up. Didn't look men in the eye. Rumour had it you didn't go out on Saturday nights, stayed in to prepare your mind for the Lord on Sunday. Jenni. What were you like?

Our paths crossed again on a couples' night nearly six years ago at our local NCT co-ordinator's house, stranded together like beached whales on a low-slung sofa, so heavily pregnant that we could hardly change positions. Mark and John incubating inside us, almost ready to be born. I was the expert because I already had Pippa. You were stick thin except for your bump, which overwhelmed you, looking so worried as the NCT co-ordinator droned on about Braxton Hicks contractions and TENS machines and whether they worked. I looked at you as you listened, chocolate brown eyes closed in fear, and wanted to protect you. To hold you against me and tell you it's not as bad as it sounds. (Even though with Pippa it was far worse.)

At the end of the meeting we went to the pub, I can't remember which one of the four of us suggested it, but we all thought it was a good idea. We went to the White Swan, down by the river at the end of our road. A cold October night, sitting by the fire drinking orange juice and tonic water whilst the men cradled their pints. We were so engrossed in our own conversation, we didn't talk to them much. It took me so long to find you, Jenni, the first female friend I really cared about. All through school and university, men had been my companions. Women can be so bitchy, don't you think? So temperamental. Men are kinder. Simpler. I had up to this point socialised with them more as a rule. But then came the female-dominated world of pregnancy and early childhood that led me to you.

Today, with Mark and John at school, and another birth behind each of us, we hug clumsily across a small wooden table in the coffee shop opposite the surgery. Across the coffee you are already halfway through drinking. Across the crumbs of someone else's cake. I sit down on an uncomfortable wooden stool, which scrapes across the floor as I position it.

'How was your holiday?' you ask.

'Awful.'

'That wasn't what Rob said.'

Your words punch into me.

'When did you see Rob?' I ask.

'I didn't. He texted me.'

'Texted you?'

'Because he was worried about you.'

You wave and smile at the waitress, who starts to weave towards our table.

We order fresh coffee for you, and chocolate cake and cappuccino for me. The waitress presses our order into a small handheld machine and disappears to the next table.

'Why is Rob so worried about me?'

'He said you weren't yourself on holiday. You didn't seem to enjoy spending time with the children, apparently.'

'Well, did you when you were on holiday?'

Your toffee brown eyes widen as you look at me.

'Yes.'

Yes?

Jenni. You sanctimonious, husband-stealing bitch.

When I arrive home, chicken nuggets and chips are beginning to sizzle in the oven as my mother listens to Pippa read. The boys are making strange shapes with Play Doh. From the moment I open the door I feel superfluous. A feeling I do not like. A feeling I frequently have to live with these days.

'Hello, Mummy,' the boys say without turning from their Play Doh shapes.

'Good day?' Heather asks me, without lifting her eyes from Pippa's reading book. Pippa continues reading in a strange monotone, high-pitched and proud. Two monkeys are stuck in a tree. Who is going to help them down? The monkeys' mother, apparently. Uninterested in the antics of the monkeys, I go upstairs to my bedroom to change. As I unbutton my nurse's uniform to throw it in the laundry basket (which is full again), my mobile phone rings. I pick up.

'Hi Carly. It's Craig.'

Craig. Jenni's husband. Craig. Handsome. Too handsome. The sort of good looks that I have difficulty trusting. He can have whatever he wants too easily, with too many of the opposite sex. Or so it seems to me. But you don't think like that, do you, Jenni? You love him. You trust him. I mustn't judge him by his looks. Just because he can, doesn't mean he does. Or does it?

'I'm planning a surprise birthday party at the pub for Jenni on Friday night. Can you and Rob make it?' Craig asks.

'That sounds great.'

Dancing to please Jenni. Great, Craig, great. We all dance to please bitch-whore Jenni.

Friday night. Walking to the pub, arm in arm with Rob, carrying the lilies I bought for Jenni. A chilly summer evening, the pavement still wet from earlier rain, making my world look grey – grey upon grey. The lilies make me think of my father's funeral, of the curved petals crawling across his casket – soon to be destroyed by the heat of the furnace. My mother standing next to the casket, trying not to cry. Mother, still so bereft without my father, seven years since his death just before Pippa was born. Seven years of centring her life on us.

As soon as I enter the pub, I push death away. We are wrapped in noise and warmth. Jenni moves towards me, smiling. So pleased to see me. Trying to make me feel warm. Trying to make me feel special.

I hand her the lilies, and the card I have chosen, and she shrieks with delight. A small shriek from the back of her throat. Jenni. They are only lilies.

A few minutes later we can't get near Jenni and Craig; so many well-wishers have turned up. I sit at a small rickety table by the log fire, which the landlord has lit even though it's summer, while Rob heads for the bar. Jenni is surrounded by people, her head is thrown back. She's laughing. I stare at her: Jenni looking so good, chestnut hair falling in waves across her shoulders, a simple dress extenuating her slimness, her fragility. The fragility which makes people want to protect her.

'I thought it was just Craig and me, coming for a quick drink,' I overhear her explaining to yet another person I don't recognise.

Rob returns from the bar with a glass of red wine and a pint of Doombar.

'She knows so many people,' Rob says, his eyes following mine as I watch.

'It's the choir thing.'

'It's the church thing.'

'Maybe it's because she's nice,' Rob says.

'Nice is such an ordinary word.'

'There is nothing ordinary about Jenni.'

'Don't start that again.'

'I didn't start it in the first place.'

Saturday morning. I'm in the car with John and Matt. Pippa is out for the day at a friend's house, doubtless being drowned in pink. Pink-walled bedroom, pink ballet dresses, a selection of dolls all dressed in pink. Suffocation by candyfloss.

'Where are we going, Mummy?' Matt asks.

'Snakes and Ladders.'

'Why isn't Daddy coming with us?'

'His turn for a lie-in.'

'What about Jenni and the other Gospels?' John suggests hopefully.

Wincing at the use of the word Gospels, the cheesy nickname Jenni has coined for our children – Matthew, Mark, Luke and John, the conjoined products of our NCT friendship.

'I thought we could enjoy some time on our own,' I reply.

'Please, Mummy. Phone Jenni. You can talk to her while we all play on the slides,' Matt begs.

Jenni. Holding my hand and laughing. Jenni. Before she started making cow eyes at Rob. I push the memory away.

'You'll have to make do with Mummy,' I snap.

I signal to pull off the main road, and turn into the car park of the state-of-the-art climbing facility. Brightly coloured plastic slides and climbing nets, all hidden from parental sight by giant yellow plastic walls. It's simple, and expensive. You pay for your children to go in. They take their shoes off, leave them with you and disappear. You sit and drink coffee. You read a book or a newspaper. They reappear several hours later, hot, sweaty and requiring drinks, but too tired to give you any more trouble for the rest of the day. A perfect way to keep children amused on a Saturday morning. Maximum expense. Minimum effort. My favourite treat for them.

After I have flashed my credit card, my sons disappear through the yellow and blue plastic doorway that leads to the gargantuan play frame. I buy a large cup of coffee and a shortbread biscuit from the café and set myself up at a table. I plug my earplugs in (small foam ones that I bought at Boots yesterday), spread my newspaper out on the table, and home in on the magazine supplement.

I must have fallen asleep because the next thing I know, I open my eyes to find John shaking my arm. He is red-faced, blond curls plastered to his head with sweat.

'Can I get you a drink?' I say dutifully.

'When we've found Matt.'

'Found him? I thought he was with you.'

'He was, Mummy, but when I went down the wiggly slide, I thought he was behind me but he never arrived.'

'He's probably just in another part of the slide complex. Let's go and ask the staff.'

Holding John's hand, I venture through a yellow and blue doorway, into a world where toddlers tumble and twist through nets and tubes, thundering towards me at frightening velocities. But it's only me that is intimidated, not the toddlers. They are laughing and smiling as their chubby bodies slide and bounce. At the bottom of every tube or net there is a substantial amount of blue matting and a Snakes and Ladders guard; a young adult wearing a canary yellow sweat shirt. I approach the nearest guard, clinging tightly to John's hand to keep him with me.

'Excuse me,' I say to him, a boy of about sixteen. A boy with a pulpy face, a rash of spots on his right cheek. 'I can't find my other son.'

'What's he wearing? I'll look out for him.'

I hesitate.

'Black jeans and a T-shirt,' John replies before I can remember.

'And his name?'

'Matthew Burton. Matt for short,' I reply.

'Tell me a bit more about what he looks like.'

'He looks about five – but he's only three and a half. And his hair is blond, like his brother's.'

'That's me,' John proudly informs the pimply youth.

'Wait in the café, I'll go looking for him and bring him to you as soon as possible,' he replies, a little sharply. He is looking at me critically, but I ignore him.

By the time he has finished his sentence John has freed himself from my hand and is climbing up a purple net. Before

I have returned through the plastic door to the café for another cup of coffee, John is already halfway up the giant play frame.

Half an hour later, a man wearing a suit and an earpiece is standing in front of me holding John's hand. Attached to his shirt is a plastic badge telling me that he is the manager of Snakes and Ladders. Only his badge and his earpiece prevent him from looking like a funeral director, so low are his eyes, so dark his grimace.

'I'm sorry to say we can't find your son Matt on the main play frame,' he announces.

My stomach tightens in annoyance.

'He went in. He must be there,' I reply.

'We've checked every camera for twenty-five minutes.' There is a pause. 'Is it possible he ran past you and went outside?'

'I wouldn't have thought he would have done that.'

'Is it possible?'

'I fell asleep. So it's possible. Unlikely, but possible.'

'We have another play complex outside. Maybe he went there.'

'Why would he do that without telling anyone? He's never been there before.'

John starts to cry. 'I want my baby brother.'

I lift him into my arms.

'We'll find him. He can't have gone far,' I tell him.

We follow the manager out of the Snakes and Ladders indoor arena, across the car park towards a large wooden climbing frame built in the shape of a fortress with boardwalk walls. The castle teems with children racing around the walls. I stand next to the manager, clinging on to John who is still crying, and a fist of panic suddenly squeezes me inside. Where is my son? Where has he gone? What's happened to him? Then almost as soon as I start to panic, in the edge of my vision, like a speck

15

of dust irritating me, something makes me turn to the corner of the climbing frame, and for a split second I think I see a boy of about Matt's size, with blond curly hair.

'What is it?' the manager asks. 'Did you see something?'

'I thought I saw him.' I shake my head. 'But maybe I didn't.'

And then I see him again. Matt. Matt's hair. Matt's red face. Matt's black jeans and new flashing trainers running down the steps of the castle towards me. I manage to keep calm in front of the manager – who no longer looks funereal – the swarming children, and their over-vigilant parents who are hovering anxiously by the play frame. But as soon as I strap him into his car seat to drive him home I smack him, hard on his cheek. He cries. John starts to cry in sympathy. I drive home with two crying boys who are howling and bellowing, wishing I knew where I'd put my earplugs. As soon as I have pulled the car into the drive and switched off the engine, I lean into the back of the car and smack Matt again. Hard, on the opposite cheek.

~ Jenni ~

'Why have you invited them midweek?' Craig asks as he loads the dishwasher. 'It's my early shift. I'll be exhausted.'

'I'm worried about Carly. I need to talk to her.'

'Because?'

'She's always been edgy – in a fun sort of way. But the balance has tipped. Now she's just edgy.'

'Well, it must be hard work being married to the local GP who works every hour that God sends, working herself, and bringing up three small children. So I do sympathise but' – he shrugs his shoulders – 'can't you talk to her by yourself?'

'I wanted to show her some hospitality. Hospitality at home. A deeper sort of friendship. You know how much she means to me. I can make dinner.'

I kiss him and he pulls me towards him, wrapping me in his arms and holding me against him.

'Can't you put it off until next week? Give us a bit of time on our own when the children are in bed?'

'I told you, next week I'm going to see my mother.'

'Not again,' he complains gently.

I shrug my shoulders.

'I don't have a choice. You know that.'

Our dinner-party menu. Beetroot salad, followed by spinach and ricotta lasagne – which took too long to make as I had to cut all the stalks off the spinach. The kitchen looks as if it has exploded; there are pans and cutlery across every surface, as I didn't have time to wash up before Carly and Rob arrived. I'm not sure why I've bothered to go to all this effort as so far I've had no meaningful conversation with Carly. She is behaving in a way I've never seen before, spending her time weighing up Craig, her eyes all over him when she hasn't noticed me watching. Carly. Wearing a low-cut top and too much make-up. She has gone for the smoky-eyes look. Carly. Laughing too loud at Craig's blokey jokes, and every time she does so Rob looks embarrassed. Rob, clean-cut and sensible in his stone-washed jeans and carefully ironed shirt. Even Craig looks surprised at the depth of Carly's laughter.

I excuse myself and leave the room, walking back to our small galley kitchen to fetch dessert and put the kettle on for coffee. As I wait for it to boil, I look around at the culinary debris and sit on the low windowsill looking at the mess. Craig was right, entertaining like this is too much in the week. And he has to be up at five o'clock in the morning to start his shift at the fire station. He was recently promoted to leading fireman. I am so pleased for him. Craig, the only man I have ever loved. Unlike Carly, I haven't had much experience with men. Craig is the only man I have slept with. I know that seems strange in this day and age of openness and overt sexuality, but it's because of my religious convictions. My relationship with God. A relationship I am proud of. I don't feel constrained or repressed because of it. God opens my life out.

Craig and I met late, and so the time we have had together

was almost immediately shared with the children, which is why we have to guard our relationship so preciously. It can be such a struggle to try and find each other between sleepless nights and children's tantrums. So far at least, I think we are managing.

But things are going to become more difficult.

My mother has been diagnosed with ovarian cancer. Too late. As is all too frequently the case. When the consultant told her last week, I was there, holding her hand, looking into my father's eyes.

The kettle boils and I pour water on top of the freshly ground coffee beans waiting in the cafetière. I reach for the Eton mess I messed up earlier, and return to the party – followed by the fear of suffering and loneliness. Followed by my father's eyes.

Carly's cheeks are slightly red and the tip of her nose is glowing.

'Craig tells me you have to go on hospital duty next week without the kids. Can I be of any help?' she asks as I serve her a generous portion of dessert. Perhaps a bit more food will sober her up.

Rob stirs in his seat uncomfortably.

'Have you run that by your mother, Carly?' he says.

She turns to him, eyes glazed.

'Whatever do you mean?'

'Nothing. Let's talk about it later.'

'I have other things in mind for later,' Carly says, giggling and stabbing her fork towards a strawberry. She misses and bangs her fork onto her plate. Metal scrapes against china.

Rob looks across at me, his eyes speaking to me – *see what I have to put up with*. I do not reply with mine, because after all, no one ever sees inside someone else's relationship.

~ Rob ~

The children are in bed. It took me an age to settle them. Carly, you are sitting in the easy chair in the kitchen, watching me cook a stir-fry with your piercing eyes of china blue. With your Marilyn Monroe looks and your volatile personality. Carly. So colourful. So challenging. You have put on a little too much make-up, as you always do just before I come home. Tonight it has smudged around your eyes.

'Have you been crying, Carly?' I ask.

'No,' you reply, taking a large slug of wine and crossing your legs, forcing me to admire a pair of shiny high heels I haven't seen before.

I stir the sweet and sour noodles.

'Are you sure?'

A flicker of the lines around your mouth.

'Why?'

I take the stir-fry off the heat.

'Well, your make-up's smudged.'

'Are you criticising me again?' you ask with a smile. An over-egged smile that doesn't quite work. Carly, sometimes your smile frightens me.

I serve the food into large china bowls and we sit opposite each other at the table, a lighted candle and the cruet between us. Without tasting my endeavours you take the salt and pepper and lash it across your food. I want to reprimand you. But I cannot. You are like an awkward teenager and I need to address one issue at a time. And tonight I have a more important mission. I take a forkful of food.

'Carly, why did you slap Matt on the way back from Snakes and Ladders?'

'He deserved it,' you say violently. A pause. 'Are you going to call the police?'

'Of course not.'

I lean across the table and put my hand on your arm. 'I just want to talk about it.'

'I'm not one of your patients, Rob. Leave me alone.'

I remove my arm. We sit and eat in silence for a while. I can't resist saying more.

'Are you still cross with me about Jenni?' I ask softly.

'It shocked me that you want to fuck her.' You emphasise the word fuck almost jubilantly; its guttural ending spitting out of your mouth.

'Fuck her? When did I say that?'

'That's what you meant, isn't it?'

'You twisted my words. You pushed me.' I pause. 'Please, Carly, stop this. I love you.'

~ Carly~

Rob is in bed before me; he always is. I slide in next to him and he moves towards me across our silken sheets.

My luck is in.

I know he wants sex.

Last night he was too tired, and as soon as I got into bed he told me, by rolling over into his sleeping position: on his side, elbow out. The position he always uses when he isn't interested. But not so tonight.

He is hot.

I can smell it.

He moves towards me, erect. He pushes my hands behind my back with one hand, puts a pillow under my rear with his other and goes down on me. I love this. Every flick of his tongue is exquisite. Perfect. Delicious. Whipping me into a frenzy of lust so perfect that as soon as he enters me I am ready to climax. But I hold off because I want more – I want this to last forever. Wrapping my legs around him, I push him further into me, pressing my feet against his bum. Thrashing. Gyrating. Moaning uncontrollably. I reach for his balls and squeeze them, climaxing hard. This is beautiful. This is what I need.

Rob is a gentleman. A real gentleman. My joy is his aphro-disiac. Now I have finished he lets himself go; jerking, grunting in my ear and juddering. We fall apart exhausted, exhilarated. I am still so charged it will be a while before I sleep. He closes his eyes and I can sense the moment he slips into dreams. I wait until I am sure he is sleeping, then I get out of bed and head for the bathroom. I sit on the toilet in our compact en-suite, but my nervous system is still so charged that I cannot urinate. Instead, I play with my clitoris. Legs apart on the lava-tory is a good position. I climax again.

This time I am thinking of Craig.

~ Jenni ~

I am living within my own personal nightmare, the sort we all have to wade through at some point in our lives. Nothing seems real. Nothing tangible. One day I will wake up to find that this is not really happening – that my sixty-six-year-old mother will carry on mothering me forever.

Craig has tried to comfort me. He held me in bed while I cried. He listened to me when I vented my anger – listened with his ears and with his eyes.

Rob came round to see me a few afternoons ago, when I was still at home on my own with the children. He fitted me in in the middle of his home visits. I made him a cup of tea and he stayed for an hour, making me feel guilty for taking up his time. When he left, he pressed his card with his mobile number on it into my hand in case I needed any advice – day or night. He told me the dire statistics for my mother's stage of ovarian cancer and lectured me on pain relief. I asked how Carly was because I hadn't seen her since our dinner party. He didn't reply as he was too busy fussing over my mother.

Carly. I think of her blue eyes, the deep blue of the sea. I didn't manage to pop and see her before I left, but I know from Craig that she is helping me, by helping him with the children while I stay with my father in Chessingfold, over an hour away. My mother is incarcerated in St Richard's Hospital, laid low by her chemo, so I'm chauffeuring him between their bungalow and the ward. And Craig, my rock, my brick, is looking after the kids on his break between shifts. Even though I miss him and the children dreadfully, I don't want the little ones here at the moment. They must not see my mother like this.

My parents' bungalow is packed with family treasures and memories; photographs, ornaments, tarnished silver cutlery. A conch shell I found on the beach when I was three. When I hold it to my ear I can still hear the sea. I spend too much time looking into the past, not knowing who worries me more; Mum or Dad. They met at school when they were fourteen. A lifetime together. I don't suppose they can remember a life apart. Dad hardly leaves my mother's side. He sits with her while she has her chemo, watching its poison drip into her body. He sits with her as she sleeps.

~ Carly ~

Two days after Jenni has left to be with her mother, the object
of my now regular late night masturbation is standing on my
doorstep. In my fantasy, he is a cross between Jude Law and
David Beckham. In reality, he is a slightly overweight thirty-
eight-year-old man with a dimple, wearing jeans with holes
in and a Canadian-style woodcutter shirt. Rob has been called
out to an emergency; a suspected severe stroke in one of his
elderly patients. Craig steps into the dull light of my hallway
and towers above me. He is a big man. Much bigger than
Rob.

'Thanks for having the children,' he says.

'My pleasure. Did my usual. Another trip to Snakes and
Ladders.' I smile at him. 'How's Jenni getting on? I haven't had
a chance to ring her.'

'No news is good news. Her mother's holding on at the
moment.'

I put my hand on his arm. 'It must be awful for her.'

He follows me into the sitting room, which is superficially
tidy, the usual litter of plastic toys thrown into the cupboard at
high speed.

'They're all asleep,' I continue. 'Exhausted. You can leave them here tonight if you like. I'll run them back in the morning.'

'Are you sure?'

'Sure I'm sure. It's not a problem.' I smile. 'But before you go, do sit down and relax for a bit. Would you like a glass of red wine?'

He sits on the sofa. The wine is already open on the mantelpiece and I pour us a glass each. As I hand Craig his glass, our fingers touch. I leave my fingers resting on his for as long as I can before he moves them away. I sit next to him on the sofa, pushing my leg against his. Again he moves away.

What is it, Craig? Are you frightened of me?

The door key rattles as it turns. Rob is home. His footsteps pad across the hallway. The sitting room door opens and he is standing in front of us, dripping with familiarity. I know from the shadows of sadness beneath his eyes that it hasn't gone well for his elderly patient.

Craig jumps up from the sofa.

'Thanks so much for looking after the boys. Great to see you both, but I must go. I'll leave you in peace.'

'You're welcome to stay, mate,' Rob tries to insist, but Craig is almost at the sitting room door.

'No thanks. Stuff to do. Got to make the best of my opportunity while Carly has the children. It's been rather hard work lately.'

'Carly has the children?'

'Yes. After a day out. Fast asleep upstairs.'

'Wonders never cease.'

I give him my look. My 'stop teasing me' look.

'I'll drop them round after breakfast,' I say, following Craig to the front door, leaving my husband to pour himself a glass of wine and sprawl across the sofa.

In the hall, Craig kisses my cheek. A dry, pastry-brush kiss.

'Thanks again.'

I open the front door and he walks slowly down the front path. Halfway towards the gate he turns to look back. I give him my best smile, the one I practise in the mirror sometimes. My Scarlett Johansson look.

When I return to the sitting room, Rob is lying on the sofa, feet up on the arm, shoes tossed off in front of him. He moves his legs so that I can join him.

'What was all that about?' he asks.

'Me being helpful with the children? Haven't you noticed? I'm turning over a new leaf.'

'Of course I haven't noticed. I don't notice anything except for my patients.' He laughs as he waves the remote at the television. 'If there really are five children upstairs let's hope they stay asleep.'

~ Jenni ~

I hold her frail hand and comfort her. I lift water to her lips to ease her dry mouth. I keep to a routine: food supplements, anti-depressants, pain relief. Days and nights are dominated by medicine; morphine in higher and higher doses. Outside, beyond these four walls, other people's lives continue. People rush past late for work, or laugh into their mobiles. The postman drops letters we no longer care about. Strangers stagger past the end of the road, late at night, after an evening at the pub. They are ignorant of the thin existence we cling to in here. The edges of their jovial conversations pull me towards happier times, but we each have one turn at life and I must accept hers is almost over. I have prayed and prayed to the Lord, and still she isn't getting better. It must be her time.

Sometimes when she has enough energy, Mother still worries about small details, irrelevancies to me, given the state of her health. Whether the bins will be put out at the front on Wednesday. Whether the dishwasher has been emptied. Maybe the routine of minor details helps her hold on to life. But for the most now all she does is sleep.

I fear that I will lose my father almost immediately after she dies. He is not coping; when he isn't staring at my mum, he stares into space, leaving me to run the household. He does not eat. I don't know whether he sleeps. From time to time he clings to me and cries and cries.

I miss my family so much, stuck here in this prison of death. My husband, the musky sweet smell of him. The kindness in his eyes. My boys. The softness of their skin as I hold them at bedtime, cheek to cheek. Their energy. Their laughter. I hope everything will be all right when I'm back home with Craig. Lately, as I spend so much time sitting here, watching my mum sleeping, the rise and fall of her body beneath the counterpane, I feel my family moving away from me. Craig is coping so well without me. Better than I expected. Carly is being so helpful, which is unusual. She seems to have risen to the challenge of five children, coping better than she does with just her own. She has the constant support of her own mother, Heather – I hope it is not Heather who is bearing the brunt. A few months ago, I was worried about Carly; not enjoying her summer holiday, not enjoying her husband or her children. I was sad for her. But now, the tables are turned, Carly is on top of everything, and it is me who is sinking into quicksand.

Mum is calling me. A weak cry on the edge of the wind.

~ Carly ~

The boys are restrained in their car seats; tightly, as if they are convicts, and Pippa is sitting – back straight – on her booster seat. Everyone is making too much noise, Pippa being Little Miss Cheery, Little Miss Too Helpful, as usual.

'Quiet boys,' she thunders, making more noise than they are. The percussion already beating around my temples explodes. I pray for the ibuprofen I took twenty minutes ago to start working, and press a button on the steering wheel. Classic FM glides silkily into the Volvo. I turn the volume up to drown out the sound of the children. 'Fingal's Cave' by Mendelssohn takes me away from here. I could be swimming in a Scottish ocean. Watching waves crash through sea-hollowed rocks. Anywhere but here.

A horn beeps discordantly through the music. The car behind is telling me the lights have changed. I press the accelerator and the car jerks forwards across the road junction in the middle of town. Next left and we are outside Craig and Jenni's house – a few more minutes and I'll only have my own three to put up with. Half an hour and Rob will be home. Rob. Always so helpful. Always doing something useful.

Working at the surgery. Looking after the children. Doing DIY at home.

Please, Rob, will you just grab a glass of wine and sit and talk to me? Even if the children are running wild upstairs. Even if the dishwasher needs unloading. We had a world together before we had the children. A world of quiet conversation on the sofa. Gentle nights out sharing a Chinese, a curry. Trips to the theatre. Trips to the cinema. Holidays that were holidays, not child-care assault courses. And now? The children are drowning me, stopping me from being the person I used to be. No longer Carly, but 'Mummy', a stereotypical shadow of what is inside me. *Mummy. Mummy. Mummy.* The word is beginning to disgust me. As I attempt to park the car, the rear beeper chirruping like a maniac, my stomach tightens as I think of last night. Rob hovering over me as I loaded the dishwasher.

'Don't stack the bowls that way. They don't fit properly.'

He took them out. He put them back in again in a row on the upper shelf.

'There you are.' A pause. 'See.'

And then he turned to me and gave me his concerned, patriarchal look – the look that makes me want to shout; staring at me too intensely, knitting his brows together.

'Carly,' he said, 'I know you're finding this stage difficult.'

'Don't you?' I asked, standing with my hands on my hips, my arms and legs wide apart. 'Don't you find it difficult, Rob?'

'Demanding. Not difficult.'

'What's the difference? You're getting pedantic enough to become a lawyer.'

'Maybe. In another life.'

He snapped the dishwasher shut and it started churning water. He challenged me with his eyes.

'What would you do, in another life?' he asked.

'I don't even know what I want to do in this one.'

'Nihilistic,' he muttered.

I looked at him standing in front of me, face laced with a frown, forehead a river bed of wrinkles, and missed him. Missed the man who would have laughed and dragged me to the pub, words like nihilistic never even thought of, dead on his breath before they became real.

'I'm not perfect enough for you, am I?' I heard myself shout, hard-edged and strident, tears peppering my eyes. I blinked to push them back. He took me in his arms.

'Carly, none of us are perfect. You're as perfect as it gets.'

My body stiffened against his. 'I know that's not what you think.'

'Come on, Carly, leave it, I was only trying to help.'

'And how exactly do you think criticising me helps?'

My stomach knots as I remember. Rob's face contorts in my mind and becomes Craig's. Craig's face with its slightly suppressed aura of irresponsibility. Perhaps that's why I am pulled towards him right now. Responsibility is killing me.

I sit in the car, noise sliding around me, and close my eyes. I am undressing Craig, moving my hands across his torso, down, down towards his jeans. I squeeze my thighs together.

How long have I wanted to have sex with him? For as long as I can remember? Or for as long as Rob has wanted Jenni?

I am back thinking of the first time I saw his almost naked body. In a swimming pool at Center Parcs. A child-centred weekend, several years ago. He was wearing white Aussiebum swimming shorts.

'Mummy, are you all right?' Pippa squeals, shaking me by the shoulders. I open my eyes. 'Are you going to take the boys out of the car, or do you want me to?'

She is leaning through the gap between the front seats and unbuckling them for me. I watch her and wonder what it is like to be her age. Loving life without sex, drugs or alcohol.

Getting high on sweets, fizzy drinks and simplicity. If only I could go back to a time when strawberry laces would have satisfied me.

Craig answers the door, bare chested, a damp towel draped around his midriff. His body is not as toned as it used to be; fat nestles self-indulgently on his belly. But then, I'd like to try some self-indulgence right now. His boys run into their house, past his legs, through the hallway into the sitting room.

'Sorry. Had to clean up after a shout.'

Fireman's speak for being called out. Craig the hero. I raise my eyes from his torso and hold his gaze.

It's been so long since I flirted with anyone. Bitch-whore Jenni, is this how it's done?

~ Craig ~

I pad to the front door, still wet, water puddling around my feet, tracing my passage across Amtico flooring. I open the door and Carly is standing in front of me. My boys run past me into the house. Always running, hurtling towards the next thing; this evening it's a Spiderman cartoon. They disappear into the sitting room.

By Jenni's standards, Carly is wearing too much make-up, but I like it. It suits her. She is bright.

Carly Burton bright. Stage bright, with her red shoes, red lipstick and lemon-bleached fifties hairstyle. She smiles, a Hollywood smile so wide she might swallow me. I step back a little and look down at her well-toned legs, her pointed knees. The sort of knees they use on Jimmy Choo photoshoots. And then I blush. I look up, away from her pussy pelmet skirt to find her saucer-like blue eyes watching me.

'Thanks, Carly,' I say. 'Thank you so much. I owe you big time. One day I'll make it up to you. I'll pay you back.'

She puts her hand on my shoulder. It burns into me. I smell her breath as she leans towards me. Mint and vanilla. Strong enough to get high on.

'Sooner rather than later, please,' she says, tracing her index finger across my right cheek.

I catch her hand in mine.

'What are you playing at, Carly?' I ask as quietly as possible; I do not want the children to hear this.

~ Carly ~

Rob is away. Jenni is away. The children are all at my house for a blast – as much fun as it is possible for young people to have. I have taken them to Snakes and Ladders again. I hope they don't get fed up of it. I can't cope with looking after so many children if I have to do anything more strenuous. I've taken them to McDonalds, too. I have let them choose a bag of sweets each at the sweet shop on Church Street, the old-fashioned one with a bow window, black and white floor tiles and rows of jars containing everything from aniseed balls to toffee bon-bons. Now they are wide-eyed with exhaustion, ready for bed, sitting in a row on our sofa watching a weird cartoon, a cross between *Pokémon* and *Frozen*. If Jenni knew about the sugar they've eaten I know she wouldn't approve. Her nose would wriggle in that strange way I used to think was cute. I am sick of the bitch-whore's tricks – wriggling her nose like Samantha in *Bewitched*.

I open a bottle of wine while the children watch the end of the cartoon. Just one glass before Craig arrives. It slips down so quickly; I can't have poured as much as I thought, so I top it up. Melon and blackcurrant. Perhaps a hint of raspberry. As soon as the cartoon is over, I snap off the TV. I stand up and try and look jovial, smiling like one of those inane CBeebies presenters.

'Race time. Upstairs and into bed. The winner gets a surprise tomorrow.'

And so they hurtle past me, squealing and shoving. I have to intervene as Luke is almost pushed down the stairs. Pippa is the winner. Matt and John whinge. Mark and Luke don't complain; they have been well trained by Jenni. They clean their teeth and snuggle into bed like a pair of little angels. As soon as I've got them all settled, the doorbell rings.

Craig.

He is here. Stepping into my hallway, handing me a bottle of Merlot and a bunch of pink carnations. He plants a kiss on each of my cheeks, irradiating me with the scent of his after-shave. I thank him and he follows me into our compact, candlelit kitchen where the table is laid for supper. I retrieve the opened wine from the sitting room, surprised to see that only half of the bottle is left, and pour us two large glasses. He watches me serve up the oysters I nipped off to buy while the children were choosing sweets. I've never liked them, they taste of seawater, but Jenni once told me they were Craig's favourite. So tonight, oysters it is.

We sit at the table, slurping them from their shells and wiping our plates with ciabatta bread. I wince inside every time I swallow one. We drink too much wine, finishing my bottle, his bottle and opening another one. We look at one another in the candlelight, playing with one another's eyes. He seems smaller in the candlelight, the shadows softening his bulk.

'How's Jenni getting on?' I ask topping up his glass.

His eyes harden. 'Her mother's dying, so how do you think?'

'I can't think about death, it terrifies me. I have a head in the sand approach to it. Maybe if you're religious it's easier.'

I'm aware that I'm having to concentrate not to slur my words; deliberately clipping my consonants and shortening my vowels.

'Maybe everything's easier if you're religious,' Craig says, leaning forward intensely.

'Jenni and Rob, our God Squad,' I say and laugh.

I am sober enough to see his hard eyes piercing towards me.

'God Squad – sounds like an army. It's not as intense as that.'

'I know, I know,' I slur quickly, 'I was only joking.'

Bitch-whore Jenni, when I've seduced your husband the joke will be on you.

'Well, it can't be that bad if you can joke about it.'

'Craig, I never said it was bad. Come on, time for the next course.'

I stand up and start to clatter runny French cheese and Waitrose sunflower seed biscuits onto the table. We pick at the cheese and finish the wine. We devour lemon tart from the local bakery and open a bottle of Tokai. As I reach for the coffee machine, the room starts swaying gently. Time for coffee and San Pellegrino.

I balance my way from the kitchen into the sitting room, concentrating hard not to drop the tray loaded with water and coffee. Craig follows me; we slump next to one another on the sofa. I hand him a glass of water and a cup of espresso, aware that my hand is trembling.

'You can stay the night if you want.'

His face blurs in front of me. Even though I can hardly see them, I try to focus on his eyes and give him my come to bed look. Through the fug of my mind, I hear him say,

'Carly, you must know I can't do that.'

~ Craig ~

'Carly, you must know I can't do that.' I say the words, but they cost me.

My cock is pulsating in my pants, so much so that it hurts. I close my eyes and will it to stop. Since I married Jenni, I have made such an effort to be faithful. Because I love her. I love Jenni so much. I hold her hand in my mind and pull her towards me. She smells of roses and patchouli oil. She is my angel.

Carly, you must know I can't do that.

But the pulsating rage of my cock is increasing. I stand up. Carly stands up too. I am stepping towards eyes of china blue. My arms are pulling her towards me. Plump. Warm. Welcoming. Hungry lips kiss mine. An animal about to devour me, smelling of musk, incense and desire. I can't contain myself. We fight to remove each other's clothing; ripping, pulling, a disorganised frenzy. She is stroking my cock, and I feel for her. She is ready for me. Within seconds I am inside her, pumping into her as she falls backwards onto the sofa. I close my eyes as I pump. She moans like a feral animal as I explode inside her.

~ Jenni ~

I'm FaceTiming you, Craig, because I'm missing you. I'm missing your comfortable arms around me. Missing the feel of you. The heat of you. I am not FaceTiming Luke and Mark because seeing me may unsettle them when they seem to be doing so well with you.

Your smiling face appears in front of me – a 'beam me up, Scotty' moment – a miracle too futuristic to be real. But it is real. You are smiling up at me from my iPad as if you were in the room. For a second I think I can smell the hard-edged scent of your favourite aftershave. It's there for a second and then gone.

'How's it going?' you ask, your face crumpling in concern.

'She had a good day today,' I say, trying to sound bright, trying to smile, wanting to let you know I'm not going to drag you down. That I can cope.

What I've told you is true; she has had a better day. But better is a comparative term. Still she has slept almost incessantly, like a small baby bird, bony and vulnerable, her Egyptian cotton bed sheets her nest. Still she hasn't eaten, even though I tried to force a gel pack of sugary nutrients between her teeth. Still her chest wheezes like wind in the trees. But today, at least, morphine has contained her pain.

'How are the boys?' I ask.

'Fine.' You pause, watching me watching you. 'Honestly,' you add as if I might think you were lying.

~ Carly ~

I arrive first. I always arrive first. The receptionist at the Travelodge recognises me as soon as I enter, a red baseball cap covering my short golden hair – for I use the same disguise every week.

I perform my usual ritual, once I've checked into the room. The ritual I have honed over the last few weeks, ever since my first night with Craig. Closing the curtains. Lighting a joss stick. Stripping to my stockings and black lace body. I am wet and throbbing just thinking about him; he is the best lover I have ever had. Sex with Craig has improved sex with Rob. Craig has taught me new tricks and Rob enjoys them, not knowing who to thank.

Sitting on the bed, legs apart, right hand inside my silken panties, I play with myself idly, just as a warm up, feeling the erect springy bud of my clitoris like a taut piece of guitar wire.

He's here. I am pressed against him as soon as he's inside the room, the door closed safely behind him. His lips find mine, his tongue penetrates my mouth. I remove his jacket. My hands tremble as I unbutton his shirt. We are on the bed now, ripping one another's clothes off, my large breasts wide and firm, topped by their perfect jutting nipples. The large breasts that I am so proud of. I sit next to him on the bed, laughing with happiness. Moments like this are the best moments of my life. I know how to sit, legs to one side, indenting my waist to show my perfect breasts to advantage. He nuzzles towards them, but I move away. Not today. There are other plans today.

I pull away from him to admire him. He has pale skin and dark hair; he is beautiful. Lucky Jenni. But at least I can have a piece of him. Rob wants a piece of Jenni. I want a piece of Craig.

I take him into my mouth and my body is racked with desire. I love his taste, his smell. I play with him at the back of my throat. He pulsates inside my mouth in waves. And now he goes down on me, teasing me. But he doesn't let me come. Not yet. We scramble apart and together in knots of passion. I am not sure how or where our limbs begin. We are off the bed and I am crouching in front of him on all fours. He is behind me and I am neck-stretched ecstatic at the feel of him inside me, at the touch of his fingers on my breasts and the bud of my greedy clitoris. I put my head back and moan with pleasure. We climax and climax, together. A waterfall that feels as if it will never stop.

~ Jenni ~

My mother is breathing her last. Rapid gasps, as I expected. A birdlike rise and fall of the chest. I open my mouth and shout for Dad. I hold her hand and squeeze it, to let her know I am here. She squeezes back. Dad is here, on the other side of the bed, holding her hand and kissing her forehead. She turns her head and looks at me with cloudless blue eyes, the soft blue of hyacinths. As delicate as a breath of air, this transition from life to death, this gentle stiffness. We sit awhile looking at her. At her cold pallor; she who was always so warm, so full of energy.

I leave the room, letting my father say his final goodbye to her in private. I pace around the bungalow like a caged animal – three steps across the sitting room, three steps back to the hallway and the small kitchen, trying to ring Craig, but he is not answering the home phone or his mobile. I'll wait ten minutes or so and try again. I look out of the window and see two children walking past on their way to school, their whole lives ambling in front of them, and I envy them. I return to the bedroom to find my father still sitting holding my mother's hand; staring blankly in front of him, as he has been doing for so many weeks, as if she has not passed yet. When will reality hit him? How can I look after him? What can I do to make things right for him?

Nothing will ever be right for him again.

I collapse into my parents' Draylon sofa and once again am filled with an overwhelming desire to speak to Craig. The only man I have ever been close to. I felt so embarrassed when he first asked me for my phone number, my cheeks were hot and I knew that I was blushing. Blushing, a habit most people grow out of at school. It is still a bit like that between us. He pays me more attention than I deserve and sometimes I still feel overwhelmed by it. I first set eyes on him when he joined our church choir. I noticed him long before he noticed me; Craig, a man out of my league. I watched him surreptitiously for months before I plucked up the courage to talk to him at tea break.

Before I married him, I prayed and prayed to the Lord. How do you know when you love someone? For in the eyes of the Lord we should love everyone. And the Lord answered my prayers and blessed my relationship. I asked my mother how you know when love is special. She said you just do. After all, she just loved my father. Always. My father and mother made a loving relationship look simple. Simpler than it is. My mind clenches in pain. I'm thinking of their relationship in the past tense. Please God, that cannot be right. Love has too much energy to cease to exist. Love lasts forever, doesn't it? Otherwise there would be no God. The words start to muddle in my head.

I try Craig again. Still no reply. I have no choice but to try and reach him at the fire station. This is an emergency. Surely no one will mind? They confirm what I already knew – that he is not on duty. Maybe he's taken the children swimming or something. But surely he would have told me if he was doing that? Surely he will be home soon? Please God. Please God may he not have had an accident. The dreaded sound of an ambulance siren pushes through my mind. I tremble inside. I am bursting to speak to him, to know he is all right. To impart my terrible news. I know I will feel a little better when I have spoken to the man I love. I try again. I cannot reach him. No reply from home. His mobile goes straight to voicemail. If I can't speak to my husband I need to speak to someone else. Tears of frustration build in my eyes. I ring Carly's mobile. No reply. I ring the surgery and ask for Rob. Apart from Dad and I, Rob is the first to know that my mother has died.

~ Craig ~

Jenni, even when I'm with Carly I think about you. I always think about you. I know I should finish it with Carly, that what I'm doing is wrong. And last night I very nearly managed to. I was going to. I walked to the Travelodge, psyching myself up; practising what I was about to say in my head.

'It's been fun but I don't want to hurt my wife.'

'Carly, this isn't fair on our partners: on Jenni, on Rob.'

'Carly, I promised to be faithful in church. To keep myself only unto her.'

But as soon as I reached the Travelodge something inside me contorted. The fact I shouldn't be there turned me on.

Carly had some MDMA with her – brownish powder in a plastic bag. She showed it to me as soon as I arrived. Then she left it on the side by the kettle.

'Where did you get it?' I asked, shocked.

'From Bob, behind the disused cinema.'

'How did you know about him?'

'Practically everyone in Stansfield knows about Bob.'

I was so taken aback that I think I must have been standing

with my mouth open. She moved towards me and stroked my face.

'You're a very naughty girl,' I said as I started to pull her clothes off; her thin skimpy nurse's uniform, her lacy bra, her black G-string. 'In fact I think you're the worst behaved nurse in the world.'

'I know I am,' she said, standing in the dingy room in the Travelodge naked, ready for sex.

Carly always looks ready for sex. It is part of her charm, her allure. 'And I've got some medicine to give you,' she said as she walked across the bedroom, proud breasts jutting and erect. She shook the powder from the bag into one of the white china coffee mugs, rubbed some on her right forefinger, and walked towards me again. 'I'll show you how it's done.'

I could feel myself straining against my underpants, against my trousers. I removed them to relieve the pressure and started to peel off my shirt.

She was in front of me. She was kissing me. Rubbing MDMA on my gums.

You are a bad girl, Carly. I'm a man who doesn't take drugs.

'You're a bad girl, Carly,' I almost hummed.

'I know I am,' she whispered as she kissed me.

I buried my head in her generous breasts. We clamped together, on the floor, on the bed and my orgasm came slowly. It was tumultuous. Was it the MDMA? Or was it the way she played with me?

Jenni, I love you but I just can't help it. Carly is so naughty, and you are so good.

~ Rob ~

I'm sitting in my surgery, at my battered wooden desk, the desk that I have owned since I was a student, inputting the data from my previous patient. I am surrounded by familiarity and thanks. Thanks is one of the things, even after so many years of practice, that I most appreciate about being a doctor. People are grateful for my help. The telephone on my desk starts to buzz, making me jump a little. I pick up. One of the receptionists' voices comes through.

'Jenni Rossiter on the line. I tried to stall her but she says it's urgent.'

'You'd better put her through, then.'

A voice blistered with tears cuts towards me.

'Is everything all right?' I ask, knowing that it isn't.

'She's gone. Half an hour ago.'

Jenni's mother. My heart sinks. What she has dreaded for so long has finally happened. And now that telling me is over, I hear her tears flow wholeheartedly, no holding back, every sob searing into me as I listen.

'Does Craig know yet?'

The sobs increase. 'I can't get hold of him.'

'Do you want me to try?'

'No. No. I've tried everything. I'm sure he'll ring me back soon.'

The crying continues. It sounds as if someone is rubbing sandpaper across the mouthpiece of the phone.

'Jenni, do you want me to come over?'

'It's too far. I'm at their house in Chessingfold.'

'Do you want to tell me what happened?'

'Dad and I were both with her, holding her hands. We're here at home. She's upstairs in bed.' Silence. She blows her nose. 'Rob, I keep thinking that if I go back into her bedroom she'll just wake up and smile at me and it'll all have been a bad dream.'

'It's natural to not really accept what's happened at first, it's part of the initial coping strategy.' My voice sounds so trite. So inadequate. Computerised words tripping off an automated tongue. I change tactic. 'Tell you what, Jenni. Forget that. I'll go down to the church and pray. Would that help?'

'Yes, yes. Oh, thank you, Rob. Thank you so much.'

What would Carly say if she heard us? Carly and I have had so many arguments lately. Ever since we met, we have always had arguments. Discussions. It's one of the many things I have always enjoyed about our relationship. But recently Carly becomes very agitated when I don't agree with her. Her agitation is tinged with a voice so harsh it almost sounds like hatred. Religion is one of our major flashpoints. She knew I was religious when I married her, so why does she react like this now? I asked her that last night when we were getting ready for bed, and she replied,

'Because you care too much about it.'

I was puzzled. 'Surely caring is good? How can you care too much?' I asked as I was getting undressed.

'If you care too much about one thing, you ignore all the other things that matter around you,' Carly replied, pulling her

51

blue baby doll nightie over her head. The one she always looks so cute in.

'And is that what you think I'm doing, just because I believe in God?' I asked, defensively.

'You need to keep it under control.'

Her eyes were tight, metallic.

'OK. OK. I promise.'

Her eyes loosened a little. She stared at me, childlike and innocent, mouth slightly open. A Botticelli angel, mouth so small and round and perfect. But then her mouth stretched unpleasantly, and our discussion began again.

'If there is a kindly God, why is he so unkind?' she asked me.

'Don't be ridiculous, Carly. God isn't unkind.'

Irritated by Carly's attitude, I stepped into our en-suite. As I brushed my teeth, Carly's shallow words punched into my head on repeat. *If there is a kindly God, why is he so unkind? If there is a kindly God, why is he so unkind?* Irritated, I brushed my teeth too vigorously, and my gums started to bleed. When I returned to the bedroom Carly had settled on her side of the bed, snuggled beneath the duvet. I sidled in next to her and cuddled up next to the back of her baby doll body. She stiffened at my touch. She untangled herself from me, and propped herself up on one arm to stare at me.

'If God isn't unkind, why do so many bad things happen, then?' she asked.

'The bad things that happen are not God's fault,' I replied.

She sighed. A stage sigh, long and contrived. She raised her eyes to the ceiling.

'Whose fault are they, then? If God's all powerful they must be.'

I was tired of this battle now, I wanted to go to sleep.

'Most problems are caused by man,' I said.

'Volcanic eruptions? Caused by men dancing in the middle

of mountains and pushing lava out? Earthquakes? Caused by men dancing underground?'

Once upon a time, I would have laughed at this, and pulled her towards me for a hug. But last night I couldn't manage it. I lay in bed, turning away from her and switching off the light. The words to convey how I felt did not come to me. Perhaps they were never there, for my love of the Lord is deep-rooted and private. Not a showcase to be explained.

Sitting in my consulting room, even remembering our conversation makes me feel bad tempered. I hate it when Carly denigrates the Lord. I switch off my computer and leave, feet slapping across the surgery's pine floorboards. My last few patients look up wearily as they listen to me telling the receptionists that I'm off to an emergency.

Along Stansfield high street, I move past banks, charity shops and nail bars. Past Costa Coffee, Iceland and the estate agents. Into Church Street, our one traffic-free street, past Carly's favourite 'bribery for the kids' sweetshop, towards St Mary's church to pray.

As soon as I enter St Mary's hallowed hall, the Lord presses down on me. I kneel on the front row, in my usual place near the door to the vestry. It feels so different when no one else is here. I have the Lord to myself, his intensity towards me strengthens. I pray for you, Jenni, as I promised, and for your mother. I see your mother running towards you and embracing you. Can you feel it, Jenni? Can you feel it like I do?

And now I pray for Carly. My wife. My beautiful wife with her curvy figure and bell-like laughter. Two Carlys are stepping towards me. One has her head back laughing, the other is crying. Carly is crying inside. I've been so worried about her lately, slapping Matt, her constant mood swings. When I get home from work, she often looks as if she's been crying. The thoughts crowding in on me start to piece themselves together. Dear Lord, if my wife is starting with depression, please help me to cope.

~ Jenni ~

Once again, I'm ringing Craig on my mobile, determined to get through to him this time. I don't want to FaceTime him because I don't want him to see my eyes, puffy from crying. I don't want him to see my hair that needs washing. I don't want him to see my face. In an instant he will realise the depth of my displeasure. My thoughts are spiralling.

'Where were you when my mother died, Craig?'

'Where are you now?'

'What's going on, Craig?'

~ Craig ~

She always arrives at the Travelodge before me. She always wears her nurse's uniform with something not very matronly beneath it. A body. A G-string. Something made of rubber, or satin, or bold-coloured lace. As soon as I see her I get a hard-on. Carly steps towards me and her piercing blue eyes become yours, Jenni. I remove her clothes and she pulls me languorously towards the bed, treating me to her vamped-up smile. Her smile frightens me sometimes. She pulls my clothes away greedily. She moans as I enter her. She is making too much noise. What is she doing? Does she think she's starring in a porn film? But she feels as good as ever and I am off, thrusting and thrashing uncontrollably. When I have finished I pull out of her, and lie on my back on the bed holding her hand, exhausted. Knowing I need to get home. Knowing I keep missing your calls, Jenni.

~ Jenni ~

I try Craig's mobile again. At least I've managed to tell him Mother has died. At least he'll be here soon with the boys, for the funeral. But he's been very busy. Very hard to get hold of lately. I try twenty times. Repeatedly. Twenty times I go straight through to his voicemail. I will ring for as long as it takes. I am pacing up and down my parents' kitchen. Parents. I stiffen as I think of that word; for now it is only my father's kitchen. His kitchen heavy with the aroma of the fish pie I am baking for him; his favourite. I wanted to give him a treat. But even he isn't here right now, he has popped out to see one of his neighbours, something to do with the funeral details. Leaving me alone, longing to see my husband, longing to see my children. Longing for Craig, just to speak to him.

At last. He calls. His voice bursts towards me through my iPhone.

'Jenni.'

Just hearing his voice helps the chaos in my head begin to subside.

'Craig.'

I hear him breathing heavily as if he is walking quickly. I hear the sea-like hiss of traffic.

'Where are you?'

'Just leaving the fire station.' Breathing, breathing, quickly, quickly. A rise in the volume of the traffic.

'Sounds quite noisy.'

'A lot of traffic here tonight. There must be a jam on the bypass.'

My eyes settle on the wall clock by the back door.

'Weird time to be leaving the fire station. What happened?'

He hesitates.

'I just went in to do some extra paperwork.'

'Where are the children?' I ask anxiously.

'Rob's got them.'

'What about Carly? I thought she was helping?'

'Carly's out tonight.'

'Well, she's been so helpful I expect she needs a break.' I pause. 'I'm missing you so much, Craig. And the boys. When are you all arriving?'

'The day after tomorrow. I'm missing you too, Jenni. I love you to pieces.'

The love in his voice is reassuring me. Pushing my fears away.

~ Jenni ~

The funeral. Lilies and roses and sadness, in my parents' local
church. A church with a spire, on the green near the duck
pond in Chessingfold, the South Downs village they retired to.
I tried to persuade Dad to bring her body back to Stansfield,
but Dad was adamant; their life had moved on. I sit next to
him, holding his hand, which trembles in mine. Rob has given
me an emergency Valium from his brown leather doctor's bag
and it has filled me with an artificial sea of calmness which
I'm not sure I like. Carly says she loves Valium, and that she
takes it from his bag sometimes when she knows she's going
to binge on alcohol. She says it gives her an extra buzz. Carly
is always wanting to shock me. To shock everyone. Today she
won. I don't think she should deliberately mix alcohol and
Valium, and I told her that. So she put her head back and
laughed at me, telling me I was a prude, mocking me. Whatever
she says, I still don't think I should drink today. I want to be
calm. I do not want a Carly-type buzz.

My father has coped quite well so far. Better than I expected.
But then Rob says the bereaved often cope well to begin with,
as they're numb to the situation. He says the grief and pain

will come later. He makes it sound as if grief follows a pattern, which surprises me, as I would have thought grief was individual. After all, we are all individuals in the eyes of the Lord.

As for me, I feel pain already. My body aches as if my mother has been cut away from me with a knife. How will I feel when this pain increases?

After the funeral, Dad is coming to stay with us for a short while, so I will be with him when his pain hits, and I will do everything I can to help. But will everything be enough? I turn to look at him. Pain upon pain. Whatever Rob says.

Today in church, it's myself, Dad, Luke, Craig and Mark in the front row, as you would expect. Craig has one boy either side of him; he's clutching their hands, his shiny black hair freshly cut, shorter than ever. My fine-looking man who stands out in a crowd. The boys are already bored and wriggling. I wasn't sure whether they should come. They're too young for funerals but who could I leave them with? And anyway, my father wanted them here. Carly, Rob and Heather are here to support me, sitting on the row behind. Behind them in abundant numbers are the expected army of mourning relatives. Relatives treasured. Relatives tolerated. Relatives we try to ignore. The main one I hope to avoid afterwards is my mother's sister, Rosie. The black sheep of the family. In her case our bugbear is her behaviour with men. Carly laughed when I told her.

'There's always one, isn't there,' she said.

I suppose it's hardly surprising that I'm not looking forward to the post-funeral small talk. I don't suppose anyone ever does. Perhaps it won't be as bad as I expect. People say the funeral is cathartic, so maybe that means that in the end I will enjoy my relatives' company. One of the things I can't understand is how so many people have found time to come to her funeral, to show their respect, when they never seemed to have time to visit her in her lifetime. Sometimes I think respect is a little out of line these days.

Craig looks across at me and smiles. A smile of love. A smile of encouragement. Despite my dark, grief-fuelled suspicion as to why I couldn't get hold of him, he has been marvellous since Mum passed. He took a whole week off work to come and stay in my parents' bungalow with the children and help organise the final funeral arrangements. No one realises just how many minor details have to be attended to until they go through something like this themselves. Craig can't wait to have me back home. He keeps putting his arms around me and telling me how much he's missed me. I feel so safe in his arms, so special, so cherished. How could I have doubted him?

Having the children in the house in the run-up to the funeral seemed to do my father good. It distracted him. Every night he bathed them and put them to bed as I cooked supper. Shrills of laughter and the thunder of tumultuous splashing moved towards me from the bathroom, making my heart sing a little. After bath time, leaving the bathroom floor so wet we could have been flooded, Dad spent so long reading to them that by the time he emerged to eat, my carefully prepared food was almost dried out. But I didn't have the heart to reprimand him. In the scheme of things, what does a bit of overcooked food matter?

Even though Craig had the week off, something big must have been going on at the fire station because he spent a lot of time on the pavement outside the bungalow, speaking on his mobile. Whenever I glanced at him he looked agitated and busy, serious-faced and official. His job is such hard work. Leading firemen are given so much extra responsibility these days.

The organ. We stand and its rich, sweet sound emanates from the balcony above, clawing at my heart. Already I have to work against the tears that are tightening my throat. I clasp the handkerchief in my pocket with my sweaty grip. In my other palm the shake in my father's hand increases. I turn to look at him again. He stands next to me, expressionless now, straight-backed and straight-lipped. The pallbearers walk slowly up the aisle, struggling beneath the weight of my mother's oak casket. One of them stumbles a little, but almost immediately regains his balance.

The casket is placed.

My mother is in front of the altar, wedged between the choir stalls, encased in oak and covered in lilies and roses, her favourite flowers. Where is she now? Can she see us, is she already floating in ethereal soup, looking down? And what has happened to the body she has left behind? I feel sick just thinking about that.

'Nana's inside there,' I hear Luke whisper to Mark. He points. Mark follows his finger, wide eyed. I wanted her to watch my offspring grow.

'We are here to celebrate the life of Lesley Jane Tunnicliffe,' the vicar starts with his exaggerated biblical lilt, vowels all over the place.

The atmosphere in the church stiffens. Everyone is listening. Does celebrating a life make death more bearable? I close my mind and push the vicar's words away.

~ Carly ~

The Travelodge again. Lying in Craig's arms, replete. I can't get hold of any more MDMA. Bob has disappeared. Maybe he is lying low. Maybe the police have got him. I don't think that Craig liked it. He said it made him feel wiped out, half dead, after the initial euphoria. But I found the euphoria fantastic. Euphoria, euphoria, euphoria. Bob, please be there next time. Please give me some more.

Craig is asleep, his breath rising and falling across my cheek. We have not had as much time as usual today as he was fifteen minutes late, and when you only have an hour, fifteen minutes makes a big difference. He stirs and sits up. He edges off the bed, steps towards the doorway to collect his scattered clothes. My stomach lurches with desire to take him in my mouth again as I did after the funeral, bringing him off in the bathroom in Jenni's parents' bungalow, no one knowing we were in there. On a high like badly behaved teenagers. That is what he makes me feel like. A teenager again, on a voyage of discovery. I get off the bed and step towards him.

'What are you doing?' he asks. 'No, Carly. I have to go.'

He pulls away from me and starts to dress, quickly covering himself up with grey Gap underpants. I'll get him something smarter for his birthday. Something more figure enhancing.

I go back and lie on the bed, watching him dress.

'Why are you in such a hurry?' I ask.

He puts his fingers to his lips.

'No discussion. Something to do with my family.'

This is how we have agreed to cope with our deceit, by pretending we don't have families.

'Family. I didn't even know you had a family,' I say and smile.

He smiles back. Fully dressed, he comes and sits on the edge of the bed next to me. He leans across and kisses me gently on the lips.

'Today was great. Thank you,' he says.

'Next week, I've booked a treat.'

'Are you going to tell me or is it a secret?'

'I have to tell you, or you won't know where to go.'

He frowns.

'Where to go?'

'I've booked a hotel a few miles away for us for the whole night; we can have dinner in our room.'

The smile that was still playing at the edge of his lips disappears.

'Carly. I meant it when we said nothing personal. No attachment. A sex-only partnership. Fuck buddies.' He sighs. 'I thought you agreed. Otherwise I would never have started this.' There is a pause. 'How can you expect me to do that?'

'Was our bathroom blowjob nothing personal?'

'It was ten minutes. Like a wank.'

'Is that what I am, a sophisticated wank?'

He looks uncomfortable.

'Surely sex this good must mean something?' I ask.

He doesn't reply. He looks agitated.
'Do you have sex this good with Jenni?'
He stands up to leave, eyes flashing.
'Leave Jenni out of this.'

~ Craig ~

Breakfast in our modern townhouse, sitting at our kitchen table. Eating Weetabix. Sipping Nescafé. The boys are plastering crumbs from croissants on the floor, on the table, and on their faces instead of eating them. Jenni is sitting next to me. I smell her scent; patchouli oil. I think Jenni is becoming very suspicious of my comings and goings. Her eyes have started to swivel too often as she checks my movements. Last time I came back from seeing Carly she made a very pointed comment about how often I was showering. Yesterday morning when I came out of the bathroom she was scrolling through my iPhone. When I asked her what she was doing she said it had buzzed and she was just checking whether anything important had come in. I checked my phone later and I know she was lying. No incoming messages of any kind.

Now as I slurp the end of my Weetabix, her toffee eyes dart towards mine.

'Craig, would you mind picking up Dad's repeat prescription from the surgery? You'll be walking past on the way to the fire station, won't you?'

My father-in-law is living with us at the moment. Or rather

co-existing. He is so bereft without Jenni's mother that to say he is living would be an exaggeration. He is sitting in the living room area of our open plan room in front of the TV, nibbling a piece of toast. I turn my head to look across at him. I don't think he's watching the news. His eyes are hollow and empty. I guess the news is just moving across the screen in front of him.

I stand up and smile at Jenni. 'Of course I'll pop to the surgery. That's fine.'

Ten minutes later, I arrive at the surgery, head down, hoping to avoid Carly. The situation between us is becoming dangerous. I sidle in and mumble to the first receptionist who is free, a mousy woman with thick glasses and iron grey shoulder-length woolly hair. For a second she makes me think about sheep.

'I've come to collect a repeat prescription for my father-in-law.'

'What's his name?'

'Stuart Tunnicliffe.'

She flicks through the pile of prescriptions in the box in front of her, and soon hands me Jenni's father's.

'The doctor's given him three months' supply. Then he needs to come in and have his blood pressure checked again.'

She hands me the prescription and gives me a half smile in dismissal. Before I can turn around and slip out quickly, Carly is standing in front of me looking Carly Burton Bright, Carly Burton Delicious. Her short blonde hair shines in the autumn sunshine that pushes towards us through the window. Her blue nurse's uniform looks as if it has been painted onto her perfect figure.

'Craig Rossiter, isn't it?' she asks.

'Yes.'

'I was about to telephone you. Please come to my consulting room. We need to discuss your blood test result.'

She leads the way. Despite my best intentions, I follow her. Through the waiting room, into her domain. Once we are inside she closes the door, turns a key, and locks it. She closes the venetian blinds.

'I need to give you an urgent check-up,' she says as she slides her hand down my trousers.

I push my tongue into her mouth and tell myself once again, *this has to stop.*

~ Jenni ~

Craig is out at the fire station and I am checking the bank statements. Our balance isn't adding up and I need to double-check it. Debits to the local Travelodge? And then I get it, sudden, sharp, and clear as daylight. Slicing through my mind like a knife. Random facts, facts I hardly noticed, snap together like a jigsaw. Changes in his hours. Copious showers. The phone calls. And I am numb inside like the day my mother died. As if this isn't happening to me. As if I am floating above myself watching someone else.

A key in the lock. Footsteps across the hallway into the living room. Craig is here, standing in front of me; lovable and familiar, bending to kiss me. We kiss and he steps back to look at me.

'What's the occasion?' he asks. 'Is everything all right? You don't usually wait up when I'm on a late shift.'

I flop down onto the sofa. He sits next to me and takes my hand.

'Is everything all right?' he asks gently.

'I hope so,' I say, and then I start to cry.

He puts his arm around me and I wince inside.

'Tell me, Craig,' I hear myself say. 'Are you having an affair?'

'Of course not. Whatever makes you think that?'

I push back my tears, pull away from him and grab the bank statements from the dining table, holding them so tightly that they're crushed between my fingers.

'These,' I say, waving them in his face. 'What have you been doing at Stansfield Travelodge? Why would you need to stay there?'

'I can explain,' he says calmly, standing up and attempting to take them from me. But I will not let them go. I clasp my fingers more tightly around them, crumpling them in my palm.

'Jenni, I can explain,' he repeats.

'Can you, Judas?' I hiss.

I sit at the dining table, still clutching the bank statements, and he sits opposite me, face like a waxwork from Tussaud's.

'Go on then. Explain.'

'I got behind at work – I've been going to the Travelodge to write up my notes.'

'Oh please.'

A silence that stifles. A waxwork face, melting and crumbling.

'It meant nothing, Jenni. I'll end it immediately.'

'If it meant nothing,' I ask, my voice breaking, 'then why?'

He reaches for my hands across the table but I pull away.

'Jenni,' he says, 'I love you more than anything. This woman,' he pauses for emphasis, 'she means nothing to me.'

'But who is she, Craig? Tell me, please.'

~ Carly ~

My mobile rings. I pick up.

'It's over. She found out.'

Shock ricochets through me.

'How does she know? We were so careful.'

'Careful?' Craig hisses. 'Always ringing me. Suggesting weekends away. A shag in the surgery! Do you call that careful?'

'You make it sound as if I forced you.'

'Carly. I need to be brief. I'm not ringing for a chat.' There is a pause. 'She found out from debits to the Travelodge on our bank statements.'

'Why did you pay like that? That was stupid. Was your relationship with me a cry for her attention?'

'Cut the psycho-babble,' he hisses. 'I just didn't think, that's all. I'm paying for it now.'

'Does she know it's me?'

'Thankfully no. And Carly, she must never find out.'

TWO

~ Jenni ~

I have waded through the day, feeling as if I am pushing through mercury or lead. Every movement has been difficult; my limbs have become metallic, the air laced with dread. There were brief, tiny moments when I forgot what had happened. As I held Luke and Mark's hands and we ambled to the play park. As we queued by the ice-cream van, an autumn breeze moving from the river to caress our faces. For a few seconds I forgot.

When the children were at school I went to church – the church where we married, by the river in Stansfield. Wren architecture. Ancient yew trees. My mind rushed back to our wedding day. I was back walking down the aisle arm in arm with my father, the organ deep throated and resonant, pumping from the balcony, the tremble of my bouquet of lilies magnifying the trembling in my fingers. What haunted me most was the memory of the vicar wrapping a cloth around our hands and saying,

'Those who God hath joined together, let no man put asunder.'

Do you remember, Craig?

Home from your shift at the fire station, you stand too close to me as I lay the table. You start to help me. The air around you has an aura. I don't want to be near you. You smell of sex with someone else. Your behaviour has sullied you. The stench of your betrayal will never leave me. You lay the cutlery, I lay the place mats, and when we come close I lean my head away.

We sit around the kitchen table together to eat lasagne; the children's favourite. I push it around my plate with my fork, watching the fat from the cheese coagulate on my plate. No one is talking. I cannot watch you lift your fork to your mouth and swallow without thinking about where your mouth has been.

When the meal is over I snuggle Luke and Mark in front of a film and start to clear the table. As I am loading the dishwasher you come up behind me, kissing me softly on the side of my neck.

'I'm so sorry, Jenni,' you whisper.

Somehow we steer through the evening. We put the children to bed. We sit next to each other on the sofa with a glass of wine each. You are too close to me again, your leg against mine, burning into me. Making me feel hot. Making me feel sick.

'Please forgive me,' you beg.

Is forgiveness to be the crux of our relationship now?

You take my right hand in yours. I allow it to rest limply in your sweaty palm and we sit listening to the sounds of the evening. Next door's television reverberating through the party wall. An aeroplane. A police siren. People laughing on their way to the pub. I place my wine glass on the coffee table and stand up.

'I'm going to bed. You'll have to sleep in the spare room for a bit.'

By morning Rob's receptionist has to allocate his late morning emergency appointment to me because I have told her I'm in meltdown; I can't cope. I lay awake all night in our marital bed, the faint scent of your hair still on the pillow next to me, unable to sleep without you, missing the warmth of your body and the soothing resonance of your breath. I had no sleep all night, and the groundless feeling of panic that I have been trying to suppress since the loss of my mother has risen to a perpetual internal scream that I can't pull away from.

So I am Rob's priority patient, his cheery voice announcing my name over the internal speaker system as I walk towards his consulting room, trying not to trip over Lego from the children's box in the corner of the waiting room. I knock on his door and receive the cursory, 'Come in.'

His small room looks as if it has seen better days, complete with its chipped desk and obligatory couch with a paper towel spread across it. When invited I sit on a small leather chair opposite his desk and find myself distracted by a photograph of him with Carly, Pippa and John, presumably before Matt was born. They must have been walking in the Lake District or Wales; they're standing in front of a rocky peak, dressed in waterproof jackets. Carly is wearing no make-up and looks very relaxed and happy. Far more relaxed than I have seen her for a while.

'How are you?' Rob asks.

My mouth opens and no words appear; tears stream down my face, their salt biting into my skin.

'What's happened, Jenni?' he asks gently.

'It's Craig. He's been having an affair.'

He exhales. 'Stupid bastard.'

Rob's words resonate inside me, and for the first time since I found out, I laugh. A nervous laugh, not a real laugh.

'Exactly,' I say, pretending to be confident.

'Jenni, keep calm. There's so much that can be done to help with relationship difficulties.'

'That's just it,' I say, fighting for breath between sobs. 'Until yesterday evening I didn't think we had any relationship difficulties.'

I sit wrapped in his eyes. Something about his green-grey irises flecked with peppery dots suffocates my tears. But the scream inside my head continues. The scream inside my head that I think will never stop.

~ Carly ~

Saturday lunchtime. Jenni, you are sitting opposite me in the wine bar, your large cowpat eyes trying to drown me. We have ordered a bottle of Pinot Grigio and a plate of tapas. But you're not drinking. You're not eating. You're sitting still, hands clasped together on your lap as if you are praying.

Jenni Rossiter. Praying mantis.

'You've got too much to lose if you break up this relationship,' I tell you, finishing my third glass of wine and helping myself to some more tapas. 'It can't be much fun for children being shunted between different homes at weekends – particularly when they get older. And what about the finances? One home is far less expensive to maintain.'

You don't reply; you sit in front of me, bereft and sanctimonious. Eventually, you speak.

'You talk of practicalities. Don't trust and faith mean anything these days?' you ask.

'Surely it shows trust in the strength of a relationship to let someone go and then welcome them back?'

'I didn't let him go. He just went.' There is a pause. 'The thing is, I can't imagine what this woman must be like. She picked him up at the Travelodge apparently. Asked him if he would help her park her car and then invited him to bed. I can't understand why he went.'

'Is that really what happened?' I ask, surprised at the contortion Craig has given you.

I try to top up your glass, but you put your hand firmly across the top of it.

'What sort of woman would do this?' you ask, eyes spitting towards me.

How can I explain that I was trying to chase away the shadow that is burying me? The shadow that, however hard I try, I cannot push away.

~ Jenni ~

'What sort of a woman would do this?' I ask as we sit opposite each other in the dimly lit wine bar, surrounded by Saturday lunchtime chatter.

You pour yourself another glass of wine. Your fourth glass, Carly, and it is only 12:30 p.m. I don't know how your liver and your skin cope. I'm worried about your drinking. I think I need to talk to Rob about it. You lean back in your chair, a half smile on your face, as if you are about to relish answering me. I don't really want an answer, Carly. I just want you to listen like you used to. I want you to empathise. Remember, I haven't got my husband. I haven't got my mother. Carly, push back time a little. Give me your friend-ship.

'To some people sex is as basic and necessary as going to the toilet,' you say.

Louder and more bombastic than you have ever been.

'I hope the woman who did this drowns in her own excre-ment,' I reply too quickly, realising almost immediately how childish this sounds. How feral and unpleasant.

You respond, stiffening, as if I have electrocuted you.
Carly.
That is when I first smelt you on him, and him on you.

~ Carly ~

I am back home from my rendezvous with Jenni. I ring the front doorbell to warn my mother I am home, turning my key in the lock at the same time to increase my speed of entry. I meet her rushing towards the door across the hallway, looking tired.

'How's Jenni?' she asks, as she slows down.

'Unhinged,' I reply.

'Wouldn't you be?'

I don't reply.

I follow my mother through the hallway of our detached thirties house towards our kitchen/breakfast room, past a table on which Rob and I have been incarcerated in a silver frame, smiling benignly on our tenth wedding anniversary. We felt so proud of ourselves, so celebratory, downing a whole bottle of champagne and having sex in our bedroom before dinner. My mother opens the door and my children unfold before me. They are sat eating chicken nuggets and chips, basking in the late October sunshine that rises across our garden towards me, bouncing off a carpet of twisted golden leaves, which need clearing. Another chore for my list. The children, wide-eyed with greed, continue shovelling fried food and too much ketchup down their throats as if they haven't seen me. They don't even look up.

'Can I get you anything, dear?' my mother asks.

'No, thanks. I've had tapas.'

When they have all finished guzzling, my mother clears the children's plates and presides over the serving of jelly and ice cream.

'Jelly on a plate. Jelly on the table. Wibble wobble. Wibble wobble. Jelly on a plate,' she says repeatedly, and everyone laughs.

Hilarious, obviously.

Food and hilarity over, faces wiped and dishes cleared, the children disappear upstairs to Matt's bedroom where my mother has helped them set up the Scalextric set this morning. Its buzzing fly drone drills into my temples, threatening to give me a headache.

'Poor Jenny Wren,' my mother says.

My headache begins.

'Jenny Wren?' I ask, not trying very hard to keep the edge out of my voice. Her affectionate nickname for Jenni irritates me.

'She always seems so vulnerable.'

'Not as vulnerable as she is right now.'

'I think I'll pop and see her this evening – see if there is anything I can do to help.'

Mother. Always fussing over Jenni. They formed a bond over childcare when I went back to work in the surgery. Visiting play parks together. Taking the children swimming. Healthy country walks collecting leaves and berries. Today the closeness of their nature-table relationship is really pissing me off.

'You might bump into Rob. He said he might go round too,' I say. The edge in my voice is definitely not fading.

'He's only trying to be helpful, Carly. Surely you know that?'

'Yes. Yes. I do. Course I do,' I reply a little too quickly.

My mother sits looking at me across the pine dining table. 'You have a perfect relationship,' she says. 'Don't spoil it.'

'No one has a perfect relationship,' I snap.

There is a silence between us. I look away from her, then back. 'Look, Mother, please could you just stay a bit longer and keep an eye on the children? Perhaps I'll feel better if I have a shower. Freshen myself up.'

'Of course. My pleasure. I promised Matt one last race.'

'Thanks.' I reach across the table and touch her hand. 'I don't know what I'd do without you.'

'You'd be fine, Carly.' There is a pause. 'You'll always be fine.'

'I don't feel fine at the moment.'

'Gwandma. Gwandma. Your turn,' Matt yells down the stairs.

The sound of his voice is an automatic trigger for my mother to rise and do her duty. With Rob and my mother it is always the same – the children are above everything in their pecking order. I drag myself upstairs, heavy with too much lunchtime alcohol, heavy with the weight of my own insignificance, to douse myself in the power shower. Perhaps the shower will energise me, make me feel ready to cope with the rest of the day. I undress and put on my new shorty bathrobe, pottering around our bedroom, tidying up a little, before I freshen up. I hear car tyres scratch across gravel, a key scraping into the front door lock, and Rob is home, earlier than usual, after his monthly turn at Saturday surgery. I hear a fragment of conversation with my mother. Laughter. Feet padding up the staircase. Then he is here, opening the door to our bedroom, putting his doctor's bag in its special place in the corner and smiling at me benignly, as benignly as in the photograph in the hallway. A smile without mischief. A smile reserved for difficult patients. And for me.

His first question.

'How's Jenni?'

I stiffen.

Jenni. Jenni. Jenni.

'Much as to be expected,' I snap.

He sits next to me on the bed and silence falls heavily between us. I look out of the bedroom window and see the ungainly lines of the row of houses across the road. Our house is not what you'd call a gem of British architecture, but we've done our best with it. Oak floors, toffee leather sofas, pale green paintwork. Very John Lewis. Very Dorset Cereal. Despite its ample size we have cluttered it with plastic toys and paperwork. Cluttered it with the debris of our lives. I look over the road at a mirror image of our house and ask myself if I lived there, in another life, would it be any better? Probably not. But it would be fun to try.

Rob's voice cuts across the weight of our silence.

'Even if she is just as to be expected, perhaps you could describe it for me?'

'Ranting and unpleasant. Wanting to bury Craig's lover in excrement.'

'Well. Can you blame her?'

'Her vocalisation was rather visceral.'

'At this stage in the process I wouldn't dwell on her every word.'

'OK. I won't.'

He pulls me towards him and kisses me, pushing me back on the bed and undoing my bathrobe. I start to undress him, pushing my breasts into his face. Our usual moves. In their exact order. No variation. What we do always works.

It's over. I really need that shower now. He is collecting his clothes from around the bedroom where I have thrown them, grinning from ear to ear, and whistling. Rob always whistles when he is happy. He turns to me.

'Maybe Jenni should try revenge sex,' he says, erect at his own suggestion.

I look away without bringing myself to reply.

~ Jenni ~

From the moment I enter the church, its silence presses down on me, filling me with the presence of God. Light pushes through the stained glass window behind the altar, dust dancing in its pathway, illuminating baby Jesus. He sits on a stern-faced Mary's knee, pointing his index finger at me. Pointing, through a fog of dust and incense – making me feel his love.

I pray. Or try to. Closing my eyes tight and pushing the world away. Turning my mind in on itself and concentrating on my husband, on every detail of his body, from the freckle to the side of his ear to the long slender line of his feet. His laugh, his smile, his face when he told me he had been unfaithful. I look up at the stained window, at the fine-coloured beauty of Madonna and child staring down at me. As I continue to stare, transfixed by the beauty of the Madonna, Mary is becoming Carly. Soft dark hair thickened by peroxide, face fattening and starting to laugh. She is pointing at me, mocking me. Her laugh, gentle at first, becomes harsher and harsher. A mechanical, piped laugh. And then the laughing fades, and behind the laughing I hear choral music. Through the beauty of the music, Carly holds her arms out to me.

'Forgive me,' she begs.

Forgive you? Not ever. Or at least not yet.

~ Carly ~

My mother tries to suppress the frown that is trying to furrow her forehead. She stands up and starts to clear the dishes. I sit and watch her bustling about my kitchen in the Jamie Oliver apron that Rob bought her. She is squeezing out too much washing-up liquid in her usual way; banging the pans together. My headache reaches a crescendo. I put my head in my hands, rubbing my temples to try to ease it. My mother looks across and sees me watching her.

'Are you all right?' she asks.

She walks towards me, smelling of soap suds.

I try to form the right words. 'It's just that everything seems so heavy. So difficult. Some days I just feel as if I can hardly move.'

'What do you mean?' she asks.

Silence suppurates because try as I do, I cannot explain the vacuum I am living in. I cannot break through the loneliness of it. The fug in the room tightens around me. I am looking at my mother from inside a plastic bubble. A plastic bubble I cannot reach through.

~ Rob ~

Another week gone by. Saturday morning again. Getting up at 6 a.m. to look after the children so that Carly can have a lie-in. Carly, so exhausted recently. Thank goodness for CBeebies, even if its name sounds like baby dribble. I sit dozing on the sofa for hours, curled up with my offspring. Enjoying the warmth of them, the scent of them, as they watch TV. When Carly eventually staggers downstairs in her pink fluffy dressing gown I extricate myself and step into the kitchen to make her a cup of tea. She follows me. We sit at our antique pine table sipping Earl Grey.

'Did you sleep OK?' I ask.

'No.'

She is sitting, head in her hands, tears pricking at the edges of her eyes.

'I've been awake since four.'

'Carly, you need help.' I pause.

'Because I can't sleep?'

'Because you're depressed. You need to go and see a psychiatrist.'

'Of course I don't need a psychiatrist.'

89

'You could just go for an assessment.'

'Why should I?' There is a pause. 'Why do I need a psychiatrist when I've got you?'

'I'm a GP. I only know a little about depression.'

'Why do you think I'm depressed?'

I reach across the table to hold her hand. 'Because the light has gone out of you.'

Tears begin to stream down her cheeks. She squeezes my hand so tight I fear she might break it.

'Please, Rob. Promise me you won't send me to someone. Can't you see that it will destroy me?'

'Why will getting help destroy you?'

'Because . . . because . . .' she stammers. 'I need to cope on my own.'

I see a flash of determination in her eyes. The determination that I fear will be her downfall.

~ Rob ~

I press the buzzer of Jenni and Craig's now Craig-less mock-Georgian townhouse. Craig has moved round the corner, back into his parents' house where his old bedroom is still intact; a mausoleum waiting for him, walls still covered with school team photos and a poster of Pamela Anderson after her first boob job, so old now that it's curling at the edges. The door opens and Matt and John are standing in the hallway.

'Uncle Rob,' they say almost in unison, clinging to my legs. 'We thought you were Daddy. Daddy's coming round now.'

And then Craig is there behind me, and the boys have relinquished my legs and are climbing up their father's body. He hoists them up, one in each arm. They wrap their legs around his waist and for a second my heart lurches in agreement with Carly, who insists Jenni is being selfish, splitting up the family. But when I see Jenni standing in front of me, thin as a rake, her large eyes circled by the black tell-tale rings denoting lack of sleep, my heart lurches again.

'Hello, Craig,' she says, voice clipped, managing a tight smile in his direction.

Her hands are trembling. I want to take her in my arms and protect her. As Craig leaves with his sons, he whispers in my ear.

'Thanks, mate. Thanks for coming to stick up for me.'

Jenni and I are alone in her hallway. She bursts into tears and moves towards me. She clings on to me so tightly and cries so hard that I fear she will never stop. Her body pushed against mine feels bony, so different to Carly's soft curves. I cannot help myself, I lean down and kiss the top of her head, putting my nose into her soft shiny brown hair. She smells and tastes of patchouli oil and honey. She doesn't seem to notice my indiscretion, her body continuing to heave against mine. Her sobs increase. I reach in my pocket for my handkerchief and hand it to her.

After what seems like an hour, but may only be ten or twenty minutes – I don't know because my arms are holding her so tight I can't see my watch – Jenni's sobs eventually begin to quieten and she pulls away from me.

'Thank you,' she whispers. 'Come in.'

I follow her through the rest of her tiny hallway, through the dining area of her open plan living room, into the seating area where she collapses into a small floral sofa. Feeling guilty about our physical contact which I fear Carly would not understand, I clear a few toys off the sofa opposite and sit down, as far away from her as possible. The room is in disarray; littered with Duplo and jigsaw pieces, soft toys and scattered dressing-up clothes. The glass coffee tables (not sensible with toddlers) are covered in crumbs and finger marks, empty plastic beakers and coffee cups. The curtains are unopened. I spring up and open them. Jenni blinks her red-rimmed doe eyes as the sunlight hits them.

When I am sitting down again, arms and legs crossed to signal my formality, Jenni sniffs and then says, 'Rob, why are you here again?'

Almost a reprimand. But not, because of those soft brown chocolate-drop eyes. Fudge brownie, mixed with vanilla.

I uncross my legs, lean forward and say, 'Craig asked me to come. He wanted me to tell you, on his behalf, just how sorry he is, how much he loves you, and that he will never ever do it again.' I pause. 'He wanted me to ask you to give him a break.'

~ Jenni ~

I sit at the front of the Eucharist service, with my father who is staying with me, praying for the strength to forgive Craig. My father has advised me that I need to move past this, because life is short and we must appreciate people while we have them. Bereft of my mother, he would say that. But what would he have said if she had been unfaithful? Mother or Father, unfaithful? That wouldn't have happened, would it? If only my mother were here, so that I could talk to her. Why do you have to take people away so completely, Lord? Why can't they at least just talk to us from Heaven, even if we can't see them and hold them any more?

I have taken to having imaginary conversations with my mother as I go about my chores; as I clean the bathroom or drive to the supermarket. And every morning, lunchtime and bedtime I pray to you, Lord. But so far the peace of forgiveness has not settled on me. Memories of happier times dance on the periphery of my mind. Craig and I bringing our first child home, swathed in the shawl my mother had knitted for him. Wrapped together in love, slow dancing at a Christmas party. Walking in the park; feet crunching across burnished leaves.

But Carly is walking across my memories, destroying them. I am trying to stop her but I cannot. I must pray harder. I know, Lord, that you reward those whose prayers are genuine. I must make my prayers work. Carly and Craig. I picture them lying together, dying together, slowly, in pain.

Retribution, not forgiveness. Oh how my prayers have failed, Lord.

~ Craig ~

I miss Jenni so much. The warmth of her body beside me at night. The steady rise and fall of her breath. Her slim frame curved around mine. I miss the quirky things she used to tell me about her day, about the children. Without her I can't even concentrate on my favourite TV programme. I save up things to tell her, like I used to, until I remember she does not want to listen any more.

And the children. I cannot bear to think about the children. Seeing them every other weekend is difficult. They treat me with distant politeness, as though I am a stranger.

So this week on Tuesday morning, when Jenni interrupted my breakfast by texting me about Relate, it was a no-brainer. And now on Friday evening, an hour before I need to leave for our first appointment, I am ready to go, wearing my interview suit, grey silk tie and a pink shirt, shoes so highly polished I can see my reflection in them. Mum said I had put too much aftershave on so I have doused it off with a sponge, and now I am pacing about my childhood bedroom. The bedroom in which so much has happened. I had my first girl in here, one heady weekend of my youth when my parents were away. It was where I used to sing, too. Sixteen years old with a second-hand karaoke machine, singing my heart out, psyching myself up for band auditions that never happened. I used to really care about it. These days, I don't feel like singing any more.

I look at my watch. Fifty-nine minutes before I need to leave. I might as well go and sit in the lounge and watch TV with my parents. That seems to be all my elderly parents do these days. Prepare meals and tidy up, drink tea and fall asleep in front of the TV. I have so little to do at the moment; half the time when I'm not on shift, I join them. Today, as usual, I find them semi-comatose in front of the early evening news. The lounge is too hot; stifling, and as soon I am sitting down with them, I join them in sleep. When my iPhone alarm goes off I pull myself into wakefulness. At last it is time to leave.

Jenni is waiting for me outside a primary school, in the centre of town. A primary school between the police station and the post office, the place Relate use for their evening sessions. Jenni, mouth in a line. Jenni, wearing her best suede boots and the coat I bought her last Christmas.

'Thanks for coming,' she says, without curving her lips.

'That's OK,' I say.

We walk in silence, side by side, into the red brick Victorian building, which needs a lick of paint. This red brick building is impersonal, uncomfortable, draughty and cold. Everywhere we walk our footsteps echo. Not quite sure where to go, we hover in the entrance hall. I pass time by reading the notice board. I try to admire the children's paintings Blu-tacked to the walls. But surrounded by clumsy brush strokes, the cardboard smell of poster paint, and the endlessly wounded look on Jenni's face, I am not appreciating them very much. Eventually, when we're wondering whether to give up and go back to our respective homes, a woman puts her head round a door at the end of the entrance hall and calls us into her office. She is about fifty with a cosy, 'come and sit with me in the front parlour' sort of smile. We follow her into her office and close the door behind us.

'Welcome to Stansfield's Relate,' she says as we all sit down together in a triangle of grey plastic chairs. 'My name is Edna. Edna Caldwell.'

Edna has done what she can to make the environment more hospitable. She has a lavender scent diffuser and a photograph of her children on the desk. At least I presume they are her children.

Jenni crosses her legs and folds her arms across her chest.

'What exactly are you hoping to achieve from this, Jenni?' Edna asks.

'I want to learn to forgive him,' she almost whispers, brown eyes moist, about to explode with tears.

'What do you need to forgive him for?'

'I'm sure you know. You must have read the notes. His sordid and illicit affair.'

Edna turns to me. Her face hasn't moved. As if whatever we say can't shock her. She is totally used to this; immune to our suffering.

'And you, what are you expecting from couples' counselling, Craig?' She simpers a little too long on my Christian name, over-warm and over-friendly.

I inhale.

'I deeply regret what I have done. No one is more important to me than my wife. I hope our counselling will help me to demonstrate that.'

'Then why did you do it in the first place?' Jenni hisses.

I turn to her. She is crying and so am I. I am crying inside.

'I can't answer you. It was just sex. Meaningless sex.'

'How can sex ever be meaningless?'

'It can. It was.'

'If sex is meaningless I never want to have sex with you again.'

We sit in silence, Jenni staring blankly in front of her, eyes unfocused. After a while she stands up.

'Sorry, Craig. I can't do this. This isn't going to work.'

I stand up and move towards her.

'Please, Jenni. Please try,' I beg. 'I'm so sorry. I miss you so very much.'

'Missing you is only the beginning of the hurt you have caused me,' Jenni says bitterly and walks out. Leaving me alone in this soulless room with Edna, the rest of my life stretching in front of me, to dwell upon her words.

~ Carly ~

My life is shit.

Jenni, all this business with you and Craig isn't helping at all. Rob is so distracted that instead of helping me with the children at weekends like he used to, he spends half of his time bolstering you up as you lurch from one emotional crisis to another.

My sex life is shit too.

I have tried to contact Craig a few times to request that we rekindle our relationship, but no sooner do I dial his number than I am cut off. He's come round to our house a couple of times to see Rob, but despite my extravagant attempts to catch his attention with my eyes, or by brushing my hands across his, he has studiously ignored me. Once when we were alone in the kitchen for a few seconds he just rasped under his breath: 'Leave me alone, Carly. It's over.'

And so, reluctantly, this is something I have been forced to accept.

I repeat – my sex life is shit; it has become very tame; perfunctory. To make it less shit I would like to take another lover, but working as a nurse/receptionist in my husband's

100

medical practice and spending the rest of my time at home with small children is not the environment to discover a plethora of lovers. A plethora of lovers is what I need to make up for not having Craig.

Worst of all, Jenni, my ex-best friend, you are a sanctimonious bitch. Oh me. Oh my. My husband's been unfaithful. Cow eyes. Tears. That's all we ever get from you these days. The more time I spend with you the less I like you. How did we become so friendly in the first place? How could you ruin your marriage over one apparently meaningless affair? I suspect even the vicar despairs of you.

My mother says I should be more sympathetic. Any sadness leading to family breakdown is intolerable, so I am trying, and next weekend we are helping you move out of the lovely three-bedroom townhouse that you shared with Craig into a flat above a shop; it's what you say you want. Rob will drive the hire-van. Rob and Craig will move the furniture. I will provide help with any last-minute packing, and moral support, while the older generation will look after the children.

The fateful day arrives. Our alarm clock shrills into the bedroom. Rob rolls across the bed towards it and thumps it off with the palm of his hand. He buries himself back into the bed and nuzzles towards me.

'It's a first for the alarm to go off before we hear the children,' he says.

'Mmm. It's nice to catch up on our sleep for a change.'

'Sleep? Is that what we need to catch up on?' he asks, running his hands over my naked breasts, caressing my stomach and moving down. I am ready, waiting for him to put me out of the frustrated misery I have sunk into, but just as he reaches the bud of my clitoris, sending pulses of electricity down my spine, there is a knock at the door and Pippa is there, standing in the middle of our bedroom in her pink velvet dressing gown.

'Come on, you two,' Pippa chirrups, 'Nana's here with Jenni's boys, and breakfast's ready. Scrambled eggs and croissants, remember, Mummy? Nana's treat.' There is a pause. She stands at the end of our bed, head on one side. Seven going on twenty-seven. An advantage to be on the right side of.

'Nana asked me to remind you, Daddy,' she continues, 'the van is booked for 9 a.m. and it's 8:20 now.'

Rob groans, reaches for his dressing gown from the floor beside the bed, wraps it around himself and heads for the bathroom.

'Thank you, Pippa, we'll be down in about five minutes,' I say, hoping she'll go away. With a toss of her straw-coloured hair, she obliges. Thank God.

By the time we enter the kitchen, the children have disappeared to watch TV or play computer games in another part of the house. My mother is washing the last few dishes. We skip breakfast and grab coffee before Rob leaves to get the van, whistling along the pathway as he goes. Rob always whistles when he's happy. Why is he so happy, Jenni, that you're moving house?

Craig and Jenni's father, Stuart, arrive at the same time. They move along our garden path together, making polite conversation. Nodding their heads. Sharing clipped grins. Stuart, so fine-featured and thin, Craig broad and enormous beside him. Although Stuart is trying to be polite, his immobile eyes shout of disapproval. They come into the kitchen, and Craig stands there by the counter, avoiding eye contact with me, avoiding eye contact with anybody; an eagle of a man, proud and taut, attractive to look at and difficult to read. Today he is wearing builder's overalls to demonstrate his readiness to help – thunderous, ponderous, stone-faced. The atmosphere hangs heavily. I am relieved when Rob returns with the ubiquitous white van he's hired, and it's finally time to go.

Rob and Craig take the van. Stuart and Mother take the kids. I walk to Jenni's house on this dull damp morning, cold nipping at my exposed skin, damp seeping into my bones. Everything looks grey. Grey upon grey. The grey of Stansfield with its rain and mist and steely sky, rain spotting into metallic puddles, grey-faced people scuttling past, shoulders down, ducking from the wind. The council building, the library, Costa Coffee. The Travelodge. Everything is grey. The Travelodge. My stomach tightens. How much do I miss my visits? More than I can ever explain.

I arrive at your house, Jenni – a row of mock-Georgian townhouses up a side street near the fishmongers – before Rob and Craig get here with the van. As I walk up your front steps, which rise above your garage to your ground floor entrance, I see your face fleetingly at the window, hovering like a ghost's – pale skin, eyes dominating it like saucers. You don't smile. You don't wave. Your face dissolves and you reappear at the front door to open it.

'Thank you for coming,' you mutter, eyes down. 'Everything's packed.'

I follow you into your living room where your life surrounds you in boxes, coffee tables on their side ready to be carried out, sofa and chairs pushed together.

'The things with red dots on are mine and the ones with blue dots are for Craig,' you say. There is a pause. 'I thought we could load Craig's stuff into the van last so that it can be the first out.'

You sniff and cough a little and then you are crying. You are in my arms, your head against my chest, gulping for breath, sobbing and wailing. I stroke your back gently to try and soothe you.

'Rob and Craig will be here in a minute with the van,' I warn you. 'Are you sure you want to go through with this?'

'You know I do,' you whisper. 'I have to.'

I see the van arrive, over your shoulder, through the hall window. Craig gets out of the passenger seat and walks up the steps to the front door, watching us through the window. He sees you crying in my arms and his body crumples. He turns, says something to Rob and walks off round the corner. He can't cope. He still loves you. Even after everything you are putting him through. Everyone loves you, Jenni. What have you done to deserve that?

The doorbell rings. You detach yourself from me and move towards the doorway to answer it. By the time I reach the doorway you are clinging on to Rob, just as a few minutes ago you were clinging on to me. I stand behind you in the hallway, watching you clenched together, feeling superfluous again. Sanctimonious bitch. Do you want to move or what? And what makes it worse is the sight of Rob simpering into your ear.

'I know this is difficult. But I think you're doing the right thing. The brave thing.' His voice is soft, coaxing.

I look at Rob holding you in his arms talking shit, and I want to damage him. Or you. Or both of you. Perhaps I'll just settle for you.

'Come on,' he says, still holding you in his arms but leaning back so that he can look at you as if you are precious. 'Are you ready? Shall we get going?'

You bite your lip and nod.

'OK then?'

You nod again.

Rob pulls his phone out of his pocket.

'OK. I'll phone Craig and tell him to come back.'

After a while, Craig returns looking stoical, and we pack the van. You are coping now, Jenni. Except for the occasional sniff and long-ish visits to the toilet, you are fine. As requested, we clear each floor of red dots first then return for the blue. The whole process takes several hours. Working hard has softened the atmosphere, diverted our attention from each other.

We have almost finished. Jenni, you and I are on the top floor in the large bedroom your boys always shared. The men are downstairs making a cup of tea. This room is cluttered with boxes, more boxes than any other room has produced; boxes and boxes of toys. It is a light room at the back of the house, with two large windows looking out onto the neat row of gardens behind. It has always been my favourite room in this house. Jenni, you spent so much time decorating it for the kids, and interior design has always been one of your strong points. I stand looking at the remnants of the boys' bedroom – not much left now, just the blue wallpaper with miniature rabbits on. The pale blue curtains and the beanbags are packed. The children's beds with white, wooden, painted bed frames are in pieces, waiting to be removed. I look at what is left and I feel sad. Sadder than sad. What are you doing to your family, Jenni?

You try to guess what I'm thinking.

'I can do it again somewhere else,' you tell me wistfully.

'I'm sure you can,' I reply, trying to placate you, not wanting a cascade of hot tears to fall again.

In the far corner, to the right of one of the windows, one of the boxes has fallen over, spewing its contents across the floor. Duplo. The pieces have scattered everywhere. You move across the room, pick up the box and on bended knees start to scoop the Duplo back inside. Instead of helping you, I stand watching, wondering yet again why you are doing this – how you think it will make things better? Your shiny chestnut hair falls across your face. Your lean pale fingers with their perfectly manicured unpainted nails pick up the last few pieces of Duplo. You stand. You pick up the box. You turn and walk towards the door with it, weaving around dismantled furniture and other packing boxes. You are coming towards me; I am hovering between you and the doorway. You look distant, as if you aren't concentrating. I move my body from your pathway but I leave my leg sticking out. By mistake.

You hit my leg with both of yours. It's my right leg, and it seems to whack into your limbs, hitting you just below the knees. I see you tumble in slow motion. Bad things always happen in slow motion. You are falling forwards, rolling headfirst. The box is flying through the air. I cannot move. I cannot stop you. The box lands first and Duplo explodes across the room. You put your arms out in front of you to break your fall. You land heavily on your right arm and slide across the carpet. And now the paralysis that came over me has gone, and I can breathe and move freely again. So I move towards you and sit on the floor next to you.

'Are you all right?' I ask.

You wince as you sit up, rubbing your right elbow with your left hand to soothe it.

'I'm sorry,' I mutter. 'I'm not sure what happened.'

You sit looking at me through your painful saucer eyes.

'I wasn't concentrating. It's just carpet burn. I'm sure I'll be fine.'

And Rob is arriving with a cheerful smile and a tray of tea, Craig glowering behind him. We sit and drink the tea, in a line, backs leaning against the wall, and when we have finished our tea, Rob inspects your arm. The way he touches you so tenderly makes me feel sick.

'No harm done. I've got some antiseptic cream in my bag – I'll put some on your arm when we go down.'

But there has been some harm done, I can tell from the

way you keep looking at me, Jenni. And it was a complete accident.

Jenni Rossiter, how many times do I need to say this? You are such a sanctimonious bitch.

~ Jenni ~

Craig and Rob are waiting in the van, and Carly is waiting in her Volvo while I say goodbye to the house. I have lit some joss sticks I bought at TK Maxx and am sitting cross-legged in the middle of the sitting room, praying peace into the house. For this house needs peace after all that it has suffered. When I arrive at my new home I will pray for peace there too. I close my eyes and raise the palm of my hands to the ceiling. But the person I need to pray for most is Carly. Carly, who Rob has told me is severely depressed now. Carly, whose plan to ruin my life has seriously misfired.

~ Craig ~

At the end of a difficult day, Rob and I are having a pint in the White Swan. Oak beams. Warm beer. But the atmosphere is stilted. Rob's disapproval of my treatment of Jenni emanates from every pore. Fortunately, despite the difficulties now percolating between us, we have managed to work really hard together to help Jenni move into her flat. She has been left there, as she wished, with all her furniture in approximately the right place. Carly has gone to help her mother put the children to bed. Our children are staying with her and Rob for a few days, until Jenni sorts herself out.

Will Jenni ever sort herself out?

It was almost more than I could stand seeing her leave the house we worked so hard to afford; the house we spent so much time and energy planning and decorating. It was our safe place. Our sanctuary. But Jenni said that after what I'd done it was no longer safe. She needed to start again. When I arrived this morning to find her weeping in Carly's arms, I nearly collapsed with pain. I had to leave and walk along the river for a while to allow my body to quieten. By the time Rob rang me to tell me Jenni was ready, I knew I had to pull myself together and go back. And so I tried to suppress my mental anguish. To psychologically anaesthetise myself, so that I could help the wife I betrayed.

Despite my brave attempt it was almost too much for me to see the damp, cramped flat above the bakery that she has moved into, where our sons will soon join her. The flat is dark. The flat is cold. The only view from the front is of traffic pushing along the high street, and from the back, the bin storage area for the row of shops behind the flat.

After her rather tearful start, as the day progressed nothing seemed to perturb Jenni. She appeared calm and determined. Shortly after she arrived in her new home she sat cross-legged in the middle of the flat burning joss sticks, praying the peace of the Lord into the house. Does she really think this will help? I always was surprised about how religious Jenni was but her faith is becoming stronger and this joss sticks, mumbo jumbo thing is worrying.

The other worrying person is Carly. Carly has become like the bad fairy in a pantomime, bringing darkness and shadows across the stage. I am never relaxed when she is near. Is it because I'm frightened that she'll spill the beans? No. I don't think so. After all, she has more to lose than me now if she does. Carly represents the loss of my marriage and so for this reason I resent her. The other reason I want to pull away from her is because I no longer desire her, but she still desires me. It makes me feel unbalanced and uncomfortable. The desire I can no longer assuage drips off her in buckets. Has Rob really not noticed? Or is he too busy making eyes at Jenni? *Is* he making eyes at Jenni? Or is it just a loving friendship? I have been told loving friendships exist. And Rob is such an affable bloke, except now, sometimes, with me.

'At least it's over, mate,' Rob is saying. He is smiling at me, pretending to be laddish over his pint.

Don't try too hard Rob. I know you don't mean it.

'Yes. Yes,' I reply. 'Now I can live in peace and go internet dating.'

'Would you dare?' he asks, eyes on stalks.

'Only joking. I've got to show Jenni I'm a one-woman man from now on. Even if it takes years.'

'So not even the slightest online flirting?'

'Definitely not.' There is a pause. 'What do you take me for? An idiot with my brains in my cock?'

'Do you really want me to answer that?'

~ Jenni ~

Cross-legged in the middle of my new home, burning incense-scented joss sticks in the corners of my living room, praying peace into my home, into my life, I sit in the lotus position, arms raised above my head in the shape of an Egyptian urn. My prayers sing across my mind; into the bones and carcass of my home, into every crack and crevice. I am cleansing it. I am cleansing myself.

~ Craig ~

Sitting on a bench at the play park watching my boys as they balance on metal tubes painted bright red and blue, as they swing like monkeys on plastic ropes, as they climb and jump like a pair of wild animals. Sitting on a bench on my own on a Saturday morning looking like a real plonker, waiting for DIVORCED to be branded on my forehead. It is only a matter of time, now, and then I will become a round-bellied scourge of society, red-faced from consolatory drinking, burdened with bad temper and disappointment. An internet-dating liability.

Jenni is the only woman I have ever loved, apart from my mother, of course. Jenni is completely different from all the other women I have ever chased. They have always been more brash, more like Carly. At the thought of Carly, my fist clenches and my jaw tightens. How could I have been so foolish as to get involved with a whore like her? When I had someone so gentle and sweet and kind as Jenni.

Jenni. I first met Jenni when she was working at St Jude's Hospital. She gave up nursing when we had the children; balancing both sets of shifts was too difficult. I think she vaguely knew Carly when she was training, but they weren't friends, just acquaintances. Their friendship came later, here in Stansfield.

I close my eyes and try and push the thought of sex with Carly from my mind, the memories of coming between her generous breasts, the blowjobs. No better or more interesting than my sex life with Jenni. Just different. Every woman tastes and feels different. Believe me, I've had enough of them.

I met Jenni singing at St Mary's church, where the rehearsals for our local choral society were held. I was on temporary secondment to an office job, and they were advertising for new members. This was my opportunity to sing in a group. Something I had wanted to do for years. As a teenager I had wanted to be the lead singer in a band. Doesn't every young lad? I went to a few auditions but no one ever wanted me. I resorted to hours of karaoke in my bedroom, but as the years passed I decided that to join a choir was probably the best option. People say that singing in a group is uplifting, cathartic. For me it was the singing, for Jenni it was an extension of her religion. Singing for the Lord. Singing for the Holy Trinity. Jenni was still working shifts and didn't make all the rehearsals. I had been attending for a while before I saw her.

She was an angel with eyes like hot chocolate, singing in the choir stall opposite me. Shiny brown hair. Oval chorister mouth. Cherry red lips. It was months before I managed to talk to her. It finally happened over lukewarm tea at a break during the rehearsal for the Christmas concert; an over-ambitious production of Faure's Requiem in D Minor.

'Do you think we're strangling it or enhancing it?' I asked.

She blushed. She laughed.

'An interesting combination of both,' she replied, drawing me towards her with her eyes. Jenni, your eyes are to die for. Jenni, as soon as I saw you I was lost.

But our first date was not a great success. She seemed so wary, later telling me that I seemed like the type to pounce on the first date, and that frightened her. I suppose I usually did. But it didn't seem right with Jenni. It was that voice, that educated voice, which made me think maybe I should behave differently, and those eyes.

Eyes to take me to heaven.

I ended up spending more money than usual, trying to impress her. I made the wrong call, taking her to a fussy restaurant with food that mostly involved offal or cruelty to animals, or both, and soon found out that she was a vegetarian. A glance at the menu. A request for a cheese omelette. I ordered a bottle of wine and Jenni didn't touch it, so I drank the whole bottle myself. I don't think that impressed her either.

The second date was more relaxed. It needed to be or I don't think our relationship would have progressed. And for all the stiffness between us on that first date, I wanted it to progress. I hadn't felt like this before. Whether a date worked out was a matter of indifference. I went out with so many different women in those days. None of them ever moved me.

Jenni cooked a meal at her flat. Stuffed mushrooms and couscous. She was renting a studio flat on the high street in Stansfield, on the corner above the benefits office. Cheap and damp and badly furnished. The traffic noise inside sounded like the swish of the ocean – swirling and repetitive. I've never liked traffic noise. The flat needed double glazing. The flat needed total refurbishment. But Jenni was innovative and she had done everything she could to try and improve it. Large fronded plants, painted floorboards and scatter cushions. Scented candles to mask the smell of damp. Low lights and mood music.

We sat opposite each other on a pair of brown cushions and ate our healthy supper. Jenni was wearing a bright red jumpsuit, which clung to her slender figure. She had tied her long dark hair back in a ponytail and enhanced her eyes with black kohl. She looked neat and crisp and oriental, except for her silver

115

gypsy loop earrings. We didn't speak as we ate, we just sat cross-legged, looking into each other's eyes, the music swirling around us – something electronic and experimental. We didn't drink. Jenni served sparkling mineral water, but even so I was beginning to feel as if I was on a high. When we'd finished eating I asked her my first question.

'How long have you lived in Stansfield?'

'All my life.' There was a pause. 'Except when I was starting my nursing training – I had a few years in a students' hall of residence in London.'

'What was that like?'

'Well, I was glad to get back here.'

'I've lived here forever too,' I had said. 'I still live with my parents. Why haven't we ever met before?'

'Stansfield's not that small, and I guess I'm quite a lot younger than you.'

She cleared away the dishes and offered me fruit and yoghurt. I refused. Then she came back and sat next to me on my scatter cushion. I could feel her breath on my cheek. I could smell her. Honey and patchouli oil; that heady scent. I put my arm around her and we fell backwards on the cushion so that we were both lying looking at the ceiling. She had painted the ceiling magenta and stuck plastic glow stars on it, stars which shone a little in the dim light. I thought it looked seriously weird but I didn't comment. She seemed like a frightened rabbit and I didn't want to upset her.

'You're so lucky to have your parents around,' she said, a high-pitched whimper in her tone. 'I used to live with mine until a year ago.'

'What happened?' I asked softly.

'When they retired they moved away, to Chessingfold, a village near Midhurst.'

'That's only about an hour away.'

116

'I know. I shouldn't have minded so much. It's a two-hour round trip though and I was used to seeing them every day.'

'Could you have gone with them?'

'Not really, it would have been too far to commute to my job. And I couldn't have left St Mary's – all my friends in bible study, my friends in prayer group.'

I looked into those sable brown eyes; they were beginning to shine with tears.

'It took me a while to forgive them. I figured that they moved away because they didn't love me, so I grieved their loss.'

I was perplexed by this. By this level of insecurity. By this level of sensitivity. But I continued to look into those eyes and tried to look sympathetic. I watched her wipe her face with her fingers, smudging her heavy eyeliner slightly. She continued.

'I've come through it now. My mum said one day I would understand and now I do. Chessingfold, where they've moved to, is a peaceful area, so perfect for retirement, for leisure. The air smells fresh there. Stansfield is so busy and bustling with so many facilities for working people and families. They just grew out of Stansfield and needed to get away.'

She smiled at me, a half smile, tentative and shy.

'They do actually seem to still love me.'

'I'm sure they do,' I said and kissed her.

Oh, those soft cherry blossom lips.

I melted into her and kissed her and kissed her as if I would never stop. She seemed to be enjoying it, kissing me back, exploring my mouth with her tongue. I caressed her back and started to undo the zip of her jumpsuit. She pulled away as if I had burnt her. She sat up and looked at me, lips parted in indignation.

'What are you doing?' she asked.

'Well, er, um. Well, I'm sorry,' I mumbled, not at all sure what to say. Wasn't it obvious what I was doing?

'Craig. I would have thought you realised. I'm a Christian. I don't believe in sex before marriage.' There is a pause. 'So it isn't at all appropriate to try and undress me on a second date.'

She said this still looking at me in a come to bed way, a way that let me know she was tempted.

I didn't find this emotional repression easy. It wasn't what I was used to. But there was something about her denial, her unobtainability; it fascinated me and instead of pushing me away it pulled me towards her. Despite the sexual barrier between us, our relationship quickly grew. Obviously I took sexual solace elsewhere, what else could I do? I tried to water my infidelity down with as much masturbation as possible. But inevitably, the sexual tension between us became unbearable and hastened our trip to the altar, where I promised to be faithful.

Faithful.

A big issue for me. And I succeeded for a long time, as Jenni, although inexperienced, was quick to learn and responsive to my touch. I loved her more than anything. Her confidence seemed to grow and grow as she was wrapped in my love. The timid doe-like creature she once was blossomed into a much more outgoing, forthright young woman. Jenni. I miss you. I still love you so much. I would do anything to get you back. Anything, Jenni. Do you hear me?

I push my memories of you away, Jenni, and find myself on my own in the play park, still watching my boys frolicking. A woman arrives with three children and sits on the bench next to me. Her children join my boys at the slide. Everyone is climbing up it instead of sliding down it. The woman is the sort of woman who looks as if she thinks she's attractive. Over-bleached hair. Too much red lipstick and gold jewellery. Enough perfume to give anyone who comes into contact with her asthma. The sort of woman who probably doesn't look very good without make-up.

'Look at them doing everything the wrong way round.' She laughs at her own observation. 'How old are yours?' she asks.

I do not reply. I pretend I have not heard and stand up to pace around the perimeter of the play area. She shrugs almost imperceptibly and starts to fiddle with her phone. My phone throbs in my trouser pocket. I fish it out. Carly.

I press ignore. The button I should have pressed in the first place – the button I will always press from now on. Any other woman. Ignore. Ignore. Ignore.

~ Jenni ~

Rain on the day of the church fete. Water ricochets off the church roof. Off the gravestones. Off the cheap canopies from B&Q that the committee have erected at the last minute, after listening to the weather forecast. The graveyard is transformed. A cake stall beneath the yew tree. A 'guess the weight of an oversized bible' by the church wall. Tombola. Lucky dip. White elephant. Bric-a-brac. Balloons streaked with raindrop tears. Sodden bunting.

I smell bacon sandwiches. I follow their salty, earthy aroma, which I find so unpleasant and take up my post buttering bread. Six of us, shoulder to shoulder behind a trestle table. So many of us because of Health and Safety, each doing a separate chore, hands wrapped in thin plastic gloves. The rain penetrates the sodden canopy above us, drips of water starting to land on my hair. One slithers down the back of my neck. I watch the rain falling in bullets from the metallic sky, low tumbling clouds cascading towards us. So few people have come to the fete, we've hardly sold any bacon sandwiches. One to the vicar who proclaimed, in his ecclesiastical way, that it was delicious. One to the organist. Two to people dashing through the churchyard on their way to the shops. Sarah Donnelly, who is in charge of our stall, invites us to buy a bacon sandwich each to boost our depleted profits. I cannot oblige as I am vegetarian. I pay half price for two slices of margarine-covered bread. The cheap margarine tastes soapy and unpleasant. It coats my teeth. I try and wash it down with a slug of coffee, or rather a slug of a brown hot drink from a Styrofoam cup, which I inadvertently take a bite out of. I am hardly eating anything since Craig left. The coffee and the soapy margarine, and the smell of the bacon, is too much for me and makes me feel sick, suddenly and dangerously sick. I need to go to the toilet.

'You'll have to excuse me a moment,' I say to Sarah Donnelly, 'I need to go to the lavatory.'

'Can't you wait until the end of the shift?'

A teacher. Well-meaning but bossy.

''Fraid not,' I say. 'I'm desperate.'

'OK. OK. Jane will have to double up; cooking bacon and buttering.'

'See you in a bit.'

I reach for my umbrella and escape to the toilets, past the crèche that has been set up in the vestry. I see my children, sitting in the crèche, playing with the church's toys, so old the plastic has faded, drinking cheap orange squash that looks like urine. I ignore them. I don't want to distract them. They're quite happy at the moment not knowing where I am, but as soon as they see me they will want me.

In the toilet I am violently sick, the smell of the bacon fat still surrounding me. The vomiting expunges me; I feel better. I clean myself up as best as I can and run into the vicar on the way out. The vicar. The last person I'm in the mood for. Artificial ecclesiastical joviality is not helping me at the moment. The truth is, nothing is helping me at the moment except Rob. Rob seems to always know the right line to take with me to help me feel positive. I suppose it's his GP training. The vicar is a young man without a partner, a young man who doesn't seem to understand the pain I'm going through. He is wearing skinny jeans, a North Face jacket and his dog collar; head crowned in an Australian leather bush hat to protect him from the rain. He looks jaunty and alternative – at least for a vicar. He grins at me. I try to grin back, hoping I don't smell of sick, but my face has forgotten how to smile these days.

'Just the person I wanted to see,' he says. 'I want to talk to you about Craig.'

Not now please.

'I hear you've sold the family home.'

I do not want to talk to him about this. Or anything.

'Who told you?' I almost snap.

'I have my sources.'

'That makes you sound like a detective.'

'A vicar sometimes needs to be.'

His eyes are twinkling into mine from beneath his bush hat, as if he is judging me.

'So the bible readings and guided prayer didn't help, then?'

'They did in a way,' I stammer. 'They helped me find the direction I was happy to go in. The path in the way of the Lord that was right for me.'

A platitudinous nod of the head.

'I just couldn't live with infidelity. Love should never fail.' I continue. 'From Corinthians. Wedding special.'

He shuffles his weight from foot to foot for a few seconds, biding his time, considering what to say.

'Well, that's one way to interpret it. I'm glad the Lord helped you reach your decision.' There is a pause. 'Any time you need to talk again, come and see me at the vicarage. Ring first, just to check that I'm there.' There is a pause. 'But remember, Jenni, those who God has joined together let no man put asunder.'

His words stab into me and make me want to cry. To cry out and tell the world about Carly. But I can't. I can't because I mustn't hurt Rob.

Stepping outside again, I find the rain has subsided to a grizzly drizzle. By the time I return to my bacon sandwich duties, a well-ordered queue is dispersing nicely and my services are superfluous. Released to wander about beneath my umbrella, I buy a sponge cake with pink icing on, and win a bottle of sweet sherry on the tombola. I look at my watch. Time to help Rob. As I scuttle towards the coconut shy, the drizzle fades and the sun begins to soften through blurred cloud. By the time I arrive, Rob has already set everything up – three coconuts are balancing on cupped sticks, a table and chair have been carefully placed for taking the money.

'Good day,' he says.

He steps towards me and places both his hands on my arms, bending towards me to whisper in my right ear.

'Are you all right? You look pale. Really pale.'

'I'm fine. I just had a reaction to the smell of the bacon sandwiches.'

'I'll avoid that stall then,' he says, kissing me on both cheeks.

His lips sear my skin and I feel flushed and know that I am blushing. As he steps back I hope he hasn't noticed.

'How's life at the surgery?' I ask to try and distract him from my colour.

He shrugs his shoulders.

'All right but we're stretched at the seams, desperate for another receptionist. I can't seem to find the right person. I don't suppose you know anyone suitable you could push our way do you?'

'I'm so stay-at-home these days, Rob. I don't know anyone like that.'

'Pity,' he says and flashes his cracked smile at me. 'Well then, what do you want to do? Money or coconuts?' he asks.

'Money,' I volunteer, moving away from him to sit at the plastic table. A queue has already formed so I start dealing with it. As I hand a young lad his change I look up to see Rob showing our first customer how to throw; a young boy of about four in a blue raincoat. Rob's slender frame is riddled with kindness and my heart jumps a little. How could Carly misuse him so? And he doesn't even know. If he was mine I would treasure him and look after him. Always.

'Not bad, is he?'

I turn my head and find myself looking up at Carly herself. Standing in front of me wearing a garish raincoat with matching plastic boots and a hat. Glowering at me, eyebrows pushed together. She almost intimidates me, but I'm getting used to her mood swings now.

'Would you like a turn?' I ask.

'I like to think I can have a turn whenever I want one.'

'I'm sure you can.'

She laughs.

'Whatever. I was just passing through. As I'm sure you know, church isn't my thing. Religion is counter-productive indoc-trination. John Lennon's "Imagine" sums it up. The world would be better off without all religions.'

She stands, legs apart, crossed arms, still glowering. Glowering makes her face look like a gargoyle. A handsome gargoyle. Carly has such strong-boned features that even when she's cross she looks good. No wonder Craig was tempted. My stomach feels as if it's being squeezed by a fist, and for a second I think I need to vomit once more. I look up at Carly, her face still puckered into a heavy frown, and am suddenly reminded of something my mother used to say when I had a bad look on my face. *Take that look off your face, or if the wind changes direction it'll stay like that.*

My mother's love is coming to me, breathing across the years. My sickness is subsiding. Remember, she is telling me, Carly is ill. It's sad what is happening to her. Carly is really ill. She never used to behave like this.

'Richard Dawkins has looked at the average IQs of those who are religious and those who are not. Do you know what he found?' Carly is saying, a twisted grin on her face.

'Let me guess. Those who aren't religious are far more intelligent?' I say, making sure I sound light. As if her insults don't matter. Because that is what they are, insults – not the prophetic comments she supposes.

'Correct,' she says, blowing Rob a kiss across the graveyard. But her efforts are wasted. He hasn't seen her.

She turns and weaves away, unsteady on her feet. If it wasn't so early I would suspect she had been drinking. Maybe it's just her boots, slipping in the mud. Relief sears across me as I watch her slide away.

~ Carly ~

The bitch-whore is flirting with Rob at the coconut shy. I caught her red-handed. Little-girl-lost look, hair tied back in a ponytail, trying to catch him with her Julia Roberts smile.

~ Carly ~

I lie in bed fully dressed, pulling the covers over me, not even bothering to take off my shoes. My mother has taken the children to school even though it's one of my days off, because I need to catch up on my chores. Chores and jobs. So much to do that it's overwhelming. The kitchen is grimy. The garden a jungle. The washing basket exploding. Everything Rob possesses needs ironing. A volcano of bills erupting through the letterbox. Cooking. Cleaning. Shopping.

The voices in my head keep whispering, telling me all the things I should be doing, but I cannot move. The ache between my shoulder blades is overwhelming me. I stay wrapped in my bed covers, shrouded in my clothing, like a sweaty hamster buried in a nest. I cannot sleep. I cannot get up. I lie in bed, thinking about the way I felt when I first met Rob.

The smell of my first hospital comes back to me, antiseptic tinged with lemon aftershave. We are standing next to each other looking at the notice board, back then, before I even knew who he was. He smiles at me and my insides collapse. Then he walks away.

I see him again a few days later, in the canteen, having lunch at a table near the window. I notice an empty seat opposite him, take my opportunity, and join him. Watching him eat. It is midsummer and sharp sunlight sculpts his craggy features; his prominent nose, his long, balanced face, his ridged cheekbones. But it is his eyes that interest me most. Green cat's eyes speckled with kindness. He looks across at my plate of chips.

'You'll have to ditch the saturated fats if you want to keep a figure like that,' he says.

'Who are you to tell me what to eat?'

'A young man who wants to be a GP.'

Green eyes hold mine.

'Or rather a young man who would like to buy you a drink when we come off shift.'

'I'd like that. Yes, please.'

I remember the rest of my shift passing in a blur. Meeting at the back of the hospital. He took my hand as we walked across the road to go to the pub. I knew from that moment I would fall in love with him. A pulse of excitement rising in the pit of my stomach. But where has that feeling gone? What has happened now?

I cannot sleep. I sit up, stretch and yawn in a final attempt not to waste the day, but the mess of our bedroom overwhelms me. His sweaty jogging clothes in the corner where he's dropped them. My make-up and costume jewellery cluttering my dressing table. Empty mugs, books and unopened post bury our bedside tables. Shoes carpet the floor. A pile of unread newspapers climbs the wall by the door.

Such a mess, so overwhelming. I can't deal with it. So I close my eyes and play with myself. Gently to begin with. Round and round with the bud of my clitoris, pushing hard and fast. I come slowly, tumultuously. And then I feel a little better. Climaxing is the only thing that helps clear the darkness. I miss all the extras I had with Craig. Masturbating helps, but it is so predictable. On your own, the orgasm is never quite the same.

Still heavy, mind operating through a fug, I pull myself out of bed. At least I don't need to get dressed as I'm already wearing an old tracksuit. Acceptable daywear. I look at my watch. Time for a glass of wine before my mother and the children are home. Alcohol will soften me, lighten the fug, make cooking fish fingers for tea more tolerable.

~ Rob ~

I ring the doorbell and hear footsteps rushing to answer it, thundering down the bare staircase at the side of the shop. A blur of colour through frosted glass and Jenni is here, opening the door and smiling. She has begged me to come, and even though the situation with Carly is worryingly precarious, to appease Jenni I decided to make an exception. One last visit on my own. Jenni needs my support, my friendship. For one last time.

The air around her is scented with jasmine. She wears a red silk dress that clings to her and silver earrings in the shape of the Christian fish symbol. They catch in the light as she moves her head.

'What's the occasion?' I ask.

'Celebrating my life in my new home.'

Her new home, a flat above a shop. So claustrophobic after her modern mock-Georgian townhouse. But she's lived in a flat off the high street before, apparently, and so this is what she wanted. Carly and I tried everything to encourage her to stick at it, to try a little harder with Craig. But she pleaded with her eyes and told us that she could not. I walk behind her, every footfall on the stairs exploding into the air like a drumbeat as the stairs are bare wood. Carpet-less. We stand together on the top step while Jenni pushes the door to her flat open.

We enter a different world; a world that pushes the rest of existence away. She has painted the hallway magenta, vibrant and bold, to brighten it up. And she has found the money to put in the thickest shag pile carpet I have ever seen, so extravagant a rodent could hide in it. Through the hallway we emerge into the sitting room. At first sight it appears oriental but when I look closely it is pretty makeshift. Low-slung sofas covered in cheap throws, which are bright red and shiny, embossed with blossom trees and women in kimonos. The lighting is very low. I suspect it needs to be to maintain the effect.

'What do you think of what I've done to it?' Jenni asks. 'Quite different from when you helped me move in.'

'It's wonderful,' I reply, politely.

The boys are snuggled up together, rucking up one of the throws, watching the large TV in the corner. They are engrossed in a cartoon, a show in which a man is being chased across the desert by a camel with exaggerated hooves. They don't see me at first. I stand close to them, watching them. Jenni stands next to me. Luke is almost four now, the same age as my Matt, and Mark two years older, the same school year as John. The Gospels. Jenni's lame joke about their names. Or at least Carly says it's lame. But then Carly thinks everything is lame at the moment – and still she resists my help. Her condition is tearing me in two. What kind of a doctor am I that I can't help my own wife?

The cartoon ends and Jenni switches off the TV.

'Uncle Rob,' Luke says. 'Have you come to help put us to bed?'

I look across at Jenni. She looks back as if to say 'please'.

'Yes.'

'Are Matt and John in bed now?'

'I expect so, yes.'

Heather is at home looking after them; she hardly ever seems to leave our home these days, Carly is having so many issues.

Luke and Mark extricate themselves from the sofa, hug Jenni and pad across the living room towards their shared bedroom. I follow them. Their bedroom is no longer a bedroom but a land of adventure, twin beds side by side framed by sheets pinned to the floor and ceiling, hung in the shape of a tent. They snuggle beneath rainbow-coloured duvets and ask me to choose a story from the bookshelf by the door. Because of the makeshift tent, once I have chosen I have to crawl onto the bed and lie down between them to read. Luke is sucking his thumb, already almost asleep. I read *Aladdin*, and when I have finished he has gone. Soft limbed. Open mouthed. Clinging to a baby lamb. But Mark is wide awake, wriggling beneath the duvet. He sits up, face bursting with excitement.

'I want to tell you a secret.' There is a pause. 'Mummy doesn't know I know.'

Fingers across pursed lips. A loud expulsion of 'Sssshhhh' followed by a giggle.

'Mummy is getting us a puppy. For Luke's birthday next week. For both of us, really.'

'That's fantastic. Really fantastic. How exciting.'

'I can't wait. I heard her on the phone talking to Granddad. That's how I know.'

'What sort are you getting?'

'I don't know that.'

'So it'll still be a surprise, then.'

He nods his head, grin so wide, his teeth splitting his face in two like a pearly zip.

'With all this news, young man, how am I supposed to settle you for sleep?'

'I'll just lay back and count puppies.'

'That's very clever. How far can you count?'

'I can count to fifty – I'm trying for one hundred but I get a bit mixed up after fifty.'

'Well, best drop off quickly then.'

'If I can't count the puppies, I'll just watch them in my head.'

He giggles again as he lies down, burrowing into his bed, pulling his duvet around him.

I smooth his sheets and kiss him on the forehead.

'Good night. Thank you for telling me,' I whisper.

When I amble back into the sitting room, Jenni is struggling to open a bottle of Prosecco.

'What's the occasion?' I ask as I move across the sitting room to help her.

'To celebrate my move.'

I take the bottle from her.

'Let me.'

The cork pops out with a vigorous thud and I pour us a generous glass for each of us; Jenni's solid wine glasses from Ikea take a lot of filling. We sit on opposing throw-strewn sofas and raise them.

'Congratulations,' I say, smiling at her uncertainly, not sure whether living here like this, away from Craig, is really something that merits celebrating. But then sometimes even if things are not better, pretending to celebrate them marks their passage, the transition. Reminds us that, however much we might not want it to, life continually moves on.

Jenni is sitting across from me, trying her best to be cheerful. Sweet but depleted. As if part of her is missing. I want to put my arms around her and protect her, but I know that I cannot.

'I know I shouldn't keep you, I'm sorry. I just wanted some company,' she says as she sips her wine. 'Selfish of me.'

'It's good to be here,' I tell her. 'I wanted to know you were OK.'

We sit in silence, sipping our wine, the sounds of Stansfield moving past outside. The hiss of traffic. A police siren. Raised voices of a group of youths. On the way to the station? On the way to the pub?

'Rob, I'm fine. I'm doing my best. The best I can do for the time being.' She stirs on her sofa, awkwardly. 'But I have to warn you about something.'

'Warn me?'

'Yes. The receptionist's job that you mentioned, I'm thinking of applying for it. I know I'm a nurse but I haven't worked since the children were born. Working as a receptionist in your surgery would help get me back in the flow of things – help boost my confidence.'

Her brown eyes flow into mine.

'I just wanted to know what you think? Whether you'd consider my application?'

'Jenni, you'd be perfect. You know how much we need someone good.'

I stand up and walk towards her. I kiss her on both cheeks. Then my lips become distracted. One little platonic pucker hovers briefly and almost touches her mouth.

~ Carly ~

Eyes on fire, I stand in front of him naked, my voluptuous body creamy and delicious, large brown nipples sticking out like toffee treasure, begging him to suck them.

'Please get dressed, Carly. You know we arranged to meet because I want to talk,' Craig says with as much authority as he can muster because I can see through his trousers that his erection is so out of control it must be painful.

I dress like a stripper in reverse, tantalising him as I raise my black lace panties across my hairless crotch. Leaning forwards to cup my generous breasts in fingers of leather. And finally the pièce de résistance – my new black fishnet catsuit.

'You can't go home looking like that. Where are your proper clothes?'

I walk to my bag in the corner and pull out a bottle of red wine, fill the water glass provided by the Travelodge and take a huge slug.

'I thought we came here because you wanted me.'

'I came here to tell you how much I love Jenni.' There is a pause. 'I'm devastated about my relationship ending, and I will do anything to try and get her back. Anything. I want you to know that I regret what happened between us.'

He stands in front of me, near the door, panda rings beneath his eyes and I know he hasn't been sleeping.

'Please, Carly. It's over. Please stop ringing me,' he begs.

~ Craig ~

It's a nippy May day, nippy and overwhelmingly wet, rain falling in a sheet so dense that I can hardly see through it. Not very good for one of my special days with the children. I sigh inside as I ring the bell of the flat where my family now live. The door opens, Jenni hovering behind it, to reveal my sons trussed up to protect them from the weather, in cheap waterproofs so baggy they make them look fat, so baggy they may have difficulty even walking to McDonalds.

I hold gloved hands and we walk in silence, or rather I walk and they wobble, past estate agents and charity shops, past Iceland and Natwest Bank until we reach McDonalds. We leave a trail of puddles as we leak across the floor towards the counter. Neon lights and plastic padded walls surround us and warm us up a little. McDonalds. McDonalds. I am so sick of McDonalds. So bored of quarter pounders with cheese, and chips that taste of cardboard. But when you are separated from your wife in Stansfield, and you need to entertain your children, there aren't many places to go. I cannot take them to my parents' house. At the moment my mother has a flu-like illness, as Jenni calls them, and she doesn't want the children to catch it. But even when she is well she doesn't find having them in her home easy. She has poor eyesight and they fiddle with everything. The settings on the TV, the DVD player, they make things difficult for her when they leave. What about the library? I could try going there but how would I sell that to them? Sometimes I think that Stansfield is a constraining dump. Children are not welcome in the pub. Children are not encouraged in any of the fancy restaurants on Church Street. So it's McDonalds. McDonalds. McDonalds. The plastic palace forming the centre point of our high street, and of my family life.

We eat burgers, and chips laced with ketchup. We gulp drinks laden with additives, as we slowly dry off. During the course of our quality time together, Luke laughs once, and smiles half a smile twice. The worst is that when I ask Mark what school is like, he says: 'The head teacher pisses me off.'

I am shocked.

'Why?' I ask.

He doesn't reply.

Another sentence would be too much information. Where has he learnt language like that? Certainly not from Jenni. Carly uses language like that. Maybe he's spending too much time with her boys. I look at my watch. Time's up. I need to take my sons back. I wrap them up as carefully as I can in their drenched clothing and hold their hands as we retrace our steps.

For the second time today I ring the doorbell of my family's new home, the claustrophobic place that Jenni has insisted on owning. This time she opens the door without hiding behind it. She looks like an angel. Sleek hair. Soulful eyes. Eyes to take me to heaven. The boys run away from me, past their mother, straight towards the stairs without saying thank you. I don't really blame them. It wasn't much fun. I look up. Struggling down the stairs towards the boys is a loose-limbed powder white puppy with floppy paws and floppy ears. Luke picks the puppy up and cradles it in his arms like a baby.

'You didn't tell me you'd got a dog.'

My voice sounds critical, accusatory. Hurt and exclusion hang in the air around us. I always wanted a dog and Jenni refused to have one. Luke turns around with the puppy, who lies perfectly relaxed in his arms. He walks towards me.

'Here, Dad,' he says. 'Give him a cuddle.'

The puppy is wriggling now as I take him in my arms. I bend and kiss his head, his fur soft against my lips. He smells of Jenni's perfume. She must have been cuddling him while we were out. I nuzzle my face against his and bite my lip so hard that I almost draw blood.

Pain to prevent tears.

~ Rob ~

Friday evening. When I get home, Carly is lying across our sofa, drinking a large glass of red wine.

'Your turn to settle the children,' she says. 'They're upstairs, playing hide and seek.'

I plod upstairs to do my duty, hearing the children thumping about in the attic.

'Coming, ready or not,' I shout to floods of giggles and skidding feet.

I clump up to the attic, my feet a warning.

'Fee Fi Fo Fum, I smell the blood of an Englishman.'

More giggles. More scraping feet. The wardrobe door closing. Surprise, surprise – when I open the door to our large attic playroom, it appears to be empty.

'Fee Fi Fo Fum. Where has everybody gone?'

I open all the cupboards. I open the wardrobe, where I hear breathing and see child-sized lumps sticking out of one of Carly's evening dresses.

'No one here,' I announce, closing the door again. As I thud across the bedroom, obviously defeated by their cunning, the wardrobe door bursts open and my offspring run towards me, screeching with laughter. They catch me by the legs and chorus, 'Silly Daddy.'

I shouldn't have got them so worked up, it takes me ages to settle them. I read and read to them, in the end falling asleep whilst Pippa is still awake. My week in the surgery has been long and hard, made worse by my last two home visits to terminal cancer patients, one whom is only a child. I open my eyes to find my daughter watching me.

'Daddy,' she says, 'I love you too much.'

'And I love you twice as much as that.'

Half asleep and very hungry, I finally make it back into the sitting room where I suspect Carly will already be slushy from the quantity of wine she has been drinking as she watches *EastEnders*, her favourite soap, on catch up.

'You took your time,' she says.

'I got them too excited by playing hide and seek.'

'If I've told you once I've told you a million times, the best thing to do with children is ignore them.'

'Thank you for that practical advice.'

'Pleasure.' There is a pause. 'And help yourself, there's some cheese in the fridge.'

'Cheese?'

'What's wrong with cheese? You like cheese.' There is a pause. 'Or you always used to. I'm not so sure what you like any more.'

I was right about the amount she has been drinking. Her voice has an edge to it; a wine-tainted edge. I pad to the kitchen and fetch myself a plate of cheese and biscuits, then sit on the armchair by the TV scoffing them down. When I've finished I place the plate on the floor and sit back to watch the show with her. On screen, a man with black hair and large eyes is shouting at his family, the tone of his voice exceedingly unpleasant. Before I have remembered who he's supposed to be, Carly snaps the TV off with the remote. Her face is fixed. Brittle.

'Carly, whatever is the matter?' I ask.

'I found something out today that you should have told me.'

'Oh?'

'You've offered the receptionist's job to Jenni.'

My heart sinks. Jenni. Again.

'When were you planning to tell me?' she spits.

I shrug, 'Tonight, I suppose.'

'Tonight's not good enough. You should have talked to me as soon as she applied.'

Her voice is raised. Her face red and flushed.

'Wow, Carly. I didn't mean to upset you. I should have told you but I've been so busy at the surgery; I've hardly seen you.'

'That's no excuse. You must have known that if you'd asked my opinion I would have advised against it.'

I raise my eyebrows, surprised.

'Why?'

'She's not got the right qualifications. She's a trained nurse.'

'She hasn't worked as a nurse for a while; she's happy to do the receptionist job and she needs the money.' I pause. 'You know how badly we need an extra receptionist. Everyone's been having to work overtime for months.'

Carly sits on the sofa, shoulders up. A cat with heckles raised, curvy and dangerous.

'You should have run it past me.'

I sit in silence for a while. When Carly gets like this I'm never quite sure of the best way to cope with her. She's always been a bit prickly, a bit difficult from time to time. I never used to mind. It was occasional and I used to accept it as interesting; challenging. But her behaviour is so erratic these days that despite my medical training it really throws me.

'You've never been interested in staff demographics before,' I comment gently.

At first she doesn't reply. She sits looking thunderous. After a while she leans forwards and twists her mouth to say,

'I want you to retract the offer.'

The ecstatic look on Jenni's face when I told her she had the job is seared deep in my unconscious. It rises to the surface.

'I can't.'

Carly's voice slices towards me.

'Legally binding, is it?' she asks.

'I can't – on a personal level.'

'On a personal level?' She pauses. 'What's that supposed to mean?'

'Come on, Carly. She's your friend. That's how we know her in the first place.'

I sit looking at Carly, at the look on her face, and want to know what happened to the good fun, kindly girl I married. She puts her head back and laughs.

'Your precious Jenni's gone off the boil a bit since she left Craig.'

'Wouldn't you in those circumstances?'

Carly doesn't answer that. She's too busy weaving across the sitting room to the drinks cupboard. One bottle down. One to go. I walk across the room and put my hand on her arm.

'Carly,' I say. 'Don't you think you've had enough?'

She turns her head towards me. Sharp blue eyes hiss into mine.

'Believe me, I've hardly even started. Leave me alone, Rob.'

For a second I wish I could. But then I think of Pippa and the boys, and my heart explodes with love.

'I can't leave you alone. You're my wife. My responsibility. You've had enough, I'm telling you. Please don't drink any more tonight.'

Her acidic breath pushes against my cheek. She shakes my hand from her arm. Her arm moves back. Her fingers widen. I see her hand move, slowly, slowly, towards me. She slaps me hard on the cheek. My eyes water. Pain burns across my face. I step back as she fumbles for another bottle of wine, struggles to open it. I don't offer to help as she breaks the cork in half and has to push the bottle opener in again. She eventually fills her glass and returns to her favourite position on the sofa. I retreat to the armchair, face still smarting.

'You need help, Carly.'

'Stop spending time with your bitch-whore and give me some, then.'

~ Rob ~

Back home from a big day out. Chessington World of Adventures is exhausting, I'm not sure I can face going there again on my own with our offspring. Three children to one adult is one too many to supervise properly; after all, I only have two hands. If it wasn't for the fact that Pippa is so sensible I'm not sure I would have coped.

The children, high on sugar and roller coasters, bounce around on the front path while I rummage through my pockets for the front door key. I have rung the bell twice but Carly hasn't heard. At last the keys are in my hands and the lock is turning. At last we are bumbling through the doorway, keen to tell Carly about our day. But Carly still hasn't heard us; she must be upstairs.

'Carly,' I shout.

No reply.

'Mummy,' Pippa shouts.

Still no reply.

'Perhaps she's gone out or she's having a shower. I'll go upstairs and look. Pippa, can you get the boys a drink, and pop them in front of the TV?'

'Sure.'

Pippa takes her brothers to the kitchen and I dash up the stairs two at a time, winding myself, for I am worried now. I open the bedroom door and she is there, fast asleep in bed.

I walk over to look at her. Her face is bloated with sleep. She lies on her back, mouth open, air catching in her chest as she inhales and exhales. With a start I see that my medical bag is upended and open on the far side of the bed, pills spewed around it. I shake her shoulders to rouse her, trying to bury my panic.

'Carly! Are you all right? What happened?'

She opens her eyes and looks at me.

'Hello, Rob,' she whispers.

'What is it, Carly? What have you taken?'

'Zopiclone,' she mutters. Her eyes are closing.

I shake her shoulders again, harder this time.

'How many?'

No reply.

'How many?' My voice rises to a shout.

With her eyes still closed, she lifts her right hand towards me, two fingers extended and bunched together.

'Two? Is that all? Are you sure?'

She nods her head.

'Sure I'm sure,' she whispers.

'Anything else?'

'Wine. Wine. Wine.'

An empty bottle of red wine by the bedside table. It looks as if she didn't even bother with a glass.

'Anything else?'

I shake her shoulders, trying not to panic. Panic never helps.

No reply.

'Anything else?' I pause. 'Carly. I really need to know what you have taken. If you've taken anything else, please tell me now.'

146

'Wine and two zopiclone,' she mutters. 'I couldn't get any E.'

E. Please God, don't let her start messing with recreational drugs as well.

Her head turns to the side and she slips back to sleep. I gather the scatterings of my medical bag. Two zopiclone are indeed the only things missing. Everything else can be accounted for. And no remnants of anything dubious like MDMA lying around, nothing unmarked, suspiciously frondy, or homemade powder-ish. Relieved, I sigh inside. After inspecting our bathroom cabinet to check that everything is in order in there too, I sit on the bed, watching her chest rise and fall, staring at her pale face surrounded by golden curls. In sleep she looks so innocent. So vulnerable. I have been a doctor for so long that I'm usually numb to situations like this. Immune. But this is different. This is my wife. If she was a patient I would call an ambulance. To be sure. To cover myself. But this is my *wife*. The person I have vowed to look after in sickness and in health. Please God. Let me look after her myself.

I lift her and prop her back up with pillows. She stirs a little and opens her eyes. Holding her head back, I push a dose of emetic through her lips with a spoon. She winces at its taste. In twenty minutes or so she will vomit to clear her stomach contents – a bit old fashioned but it works. I sit in our bedroom armchair by the window, watching her drift in and out of sleep. Every so often she opens her eyes and smiles at me. Aware that I am here.

The vomit finally comes. She rushes towards the bathroom, holding her stomach. She leans over the toilet bowl and spews ruby red liquid. When she has purged herself, I settle her back into bed. I leave her to sleep.

Downstairs Pippa is in charge. Pippa, nearly eight years old now and innovative. She has made a picnic with bags of crisps and biscuits; I can tell from the debris. And she's found some coke from the treats cupboard. After a day at Chessington World of Adventures I'm not sure anyone needed any more coke. Now as if in compensation she is trying to make the boys eat fruit. She has her head on one side, and is lecturing them about five-a-day. They are looking at her wide-eyed. As soon as she sees me she runs towards me and hugs my legs.

'Daddy, Daddy, is Mummy all right?'

'She's fine. Just sleeping.'

'Can I go and see her?'

'No. Not yet. You might wake her. You can tell her all about your day out in the morning. Come on. Let's get you all to bed.'

The normality of putting the children to bed is a release. Pretending everything is all right for a while. But it isn't all right, is it? Sometimes it feels as if it will never be all right again.

~ Jenni ~

My first day as a receptionist at Stansfield's Riverside Surgery. I arrive at 8:15 a.m., not feeling very confident. It has been four and a half years since I've been in any sort of paid employment, and I've been worrying about everything. Worry, tunnelling through society, leaving our foundations weak. Worry, weaving warren–like passageways through our minds, allowing us to silently destroy ourselves. I am always worrying. About my dad looking after the boys and the puppy, even though he seemed quite excited about it; the flame he had in his eyes when my mother was alive beginning to flicker back. Worrying about what to wear today. In the end I chose a white blouse and a brown A-line skirt. Just the sort of thing to blend into the background. For that's what I find easiest at the moment. To blend into the background. What do I mean, at the moment? I've always been a bit like that.

Four doctors, one of whom is Rob, are already here, in their consulting rooms getting ready for surgery. Sharon, the eagle-eyed practice manager, a portly middle-aged woman with shoulder-length grey hair and a northern accent, is taking me under her wing. Showing me how to answer the phone. How to allocate appointments on the computer system. Giving me a long lecture on which patients should be given priority and why. Nearly everyone seems to be given priority in this surgery. Kindness lives here; nestled comfortably between the telephones and the filing cabinets. Sharon is the woman who Carly always used to describe as her mentor, helping her to settle in when she first came to work as a nurse in the surgery. Sharon. Carly's second mother apparently.

So far today no sign of Carly.

Sharon hovers over me as I take my first phone call – a man so elderly that his voice has become scratchy, suffering from piles. He seems to enjoy describing them to me. Carly finally arrives, wearing her garish raincoat, the one she was wearing at the church fete. Red plastic. Matching hat, wellington boots and perfectly applied lip gloss. A fifties screen goddess. Over the top. As she dashes past I expect her to stop, open her raincoat to display a sequined leotard and tap dance across the waiting room. But no, she has gone past, without even looking at me, no acknowledgement, not even half a smile, leaving me to make the scratchy old man's appointment. I look out of the window. It isn't even raining.

As the morning progresses I begin to feel more relaxed. So far the patients have been at ease talking to me, happy with the appointments I have arranged for them. Twice I've checked with Sharon to make sure I've logged everything correctly. Both times I had. And so, by lunchtime as I leave the surgery to go and buy a sandwich, I am hopeful that I will be able to do this job.

The sandwich bar across the road from the surgery is over-crowded, hissing with steam from the cappuccino machine. I queue for ages for coffee and an egg and cress sandwich, and then can't find a place to sit. I walk up and down the narrow aisle between the tables, looking for someone to share with. A red raincoat on the back of a chair.

Carly.

'Do you mind if I join you?' I ask.

'Feel free,' she says, without looking up from the newspaper she is reading.

I sit opposite her, undo my fawn raincoat, and start to eat my sandwich. The bread is soggy. I will bring a packed lunch tomorrow. I take a sip of coffee and scald my tongue. Carly looks up. She fixes her powder blue eyes on me.

'Oh. It's you.'

'Yes. It's me. Hello. I started at the surgery this morning,' I say. 'I wasn't sure whether you'd seen me.'

'I always notice you, Jenni.'

Another bite of my soggy sandwich. Another sip of my coffee. It is still too hot.

'Is it going all right?' Carly asks with acid eyes.

'Sharon has been very helpful. I've answered a few phone calls.'

Acid eyes darken.

'I'm sure you'll do very well, as long as you stay off my territory.'

Do you really want to get territorial about this? Carly, I know what you did.

'What territory do you mean?' I ask.

She leans forwards and whispers the words.

'My husband. Stop trying to play with him.'

'I'm not.'

'I don't believe you.'

'What can I do to prove it?'

'Don't work at the surgery.'

'But, Carly, I need this job. With Craig and I living separately, I need more money.'

'I warned you that you would.' She shrugs her shoulders. 'Find another job. You're exploiting your friendship with us.'

'Is friendship exploitation?'

'Don't play with words, Jenni. You know what I mean. We were friends until you tried to steal Rob.'

The Lord is inside me, helping my confidence to grow.

I stand up to let her know I am going. I lean forwards to make sure that she can hear me, catching her eyes in mine.

'I'll stay to get the experience I need. And I'll leave as soon as I've built my CV up. That's the best offer you're getting, Carly.'

'If I were you, I wouldn't stick around too long,' she replies, but her voice is weak, and her watery blue eyes are dissolving in the strength of mine.

You do not scare me, Carly. You've become a bully. Bullies will have their comeuppance in the eyes of the Lord.

~ Carly ~

My dream world is clearer than my real world. It is in my dream world that I can see. Really see. Watching Jenni as she sits in her flat, praying in the lotus position. A bag of bones dressed in red, wearing Christian fish earrings. Planning to steal Rob and my children. Laying her final plans. She has written them down and hidden them in a journal she bought at Paperchase. A journal she keeps in her handbag, wrapped in wide red plastic bands. She takes the journal with her everywhere so that no one can steal it. She consolidates her plans when the children are in bed, puppy at her feet, listening to Enya and burning joss sticks. For everybody knows, Jenni is seriously weird.

Jenni is intending to live with Rob, and all our children, Pippa and the Gospels, in a house near the church. Her flat is too small for them all and she is looking for somewhere bigger at the moment. I know she is.

In the clarity of my dream world, the faces are so sharp they look as if they have been chiselled with a knife. Fluffy white clouds look like metallic pan-scrubs. In my dream world, Rob is arriving at Jenni's flat. It must be Saturday because he is wearing jeans and his old college rugby shirt. She welcomes him into her living room with a smile and closes the door behind him. He moves towards her in a slow motion montage, arms stretched, mouth opening. The volume of the music ever increasing. They meet and clamp together. Enya is chanting. They are smooching. Smooching and kissing, lips bound together. They move towards the sofa and collapse onto it. She is tearing his clothes off. He is sitting on the sofa naked and she is bending her head over his crotch to give him a blowjob, chestnut hair splayed across his thighs. I cannot take my eyes away from his face. His head lolls back and he closes his eyes. His pleasure builds. His face becomes contorted with ecstasy. When she has finished she sits next to him on the sofa, holding his hand and admiring him; doe-eyed.

The more I watch, the more I scream and scream silently. I scream and scream until the scream becomes a sound. I wake hearing my own scream. In Rob's arms. In my own bed. Wet with sweat, dampness pooling behind my knees, in the small of my back. His voice comes into focus.

'Carly, Carly, are you all right? You were having a terrible nightmare.'

I breathe out. 'I'm all right now that you're here.'

'I've been here all the time.'

~ Jenni ~

I am returning from lunch when I bump into Carly leaving the surgery, our paths crossing in the car park.

Carly. Lemon delicious.

Golden hair shining in sharp winter sunlight, her yellow figure-hugging dress and black jacket clinging to her like sugar coating. Over the top for popping into the surgery. And her perfume. Well, I think she must have spilt it.

'Feeling better?' I ask.

'Much. Thanks. I've just been in to check a few things.'

'Rob said you were taking the day off.'

'Did he?' There is a pause. 'When did you speak to him?'

'First thing. When he was on the way in.'

'And what did my husband say about my medical condition?'

'That you were unwell and taking the day off.'

'Next time you have a tête-à-tête, perhaps you could update him on the improvement in my symptoms.'

'He was just informing the office. I didn't speak to him personally.'

'Thank you for clearing that up.'

A lemon sugar smile.

She walks away.

Not understanding what she's doing here when she's supposed to be resting, I push my way back into the surgery, negotiating the elaborate press button door system for wheelchair users. There's a locum standing in for her, she has no need to come in. I'm grateful that she's on her way home. Grateful to be away from her. The smell of her vanilla perfume is everywhere. As I move towards my desk in reception, Sharon looks up from her filing and says,

'Carly popped in to leave you a message. Left it by your computer.'

'That's funny. I just met her in the car park and she didn't say anything.'

Sharon shrugs.

'Well, you know Carly. Mind of her own. That's what we all love about her.'

I look across at Sharon to see if she is joking, but her eyes and mouth are flatlining.

There is no message by my computer. I try to click it back on with my mouse, but it won't come on. So I have to switch off and restart. When I finally get back into my area of the computer system, my data input from this morning is missing; all of it. I try and try to retrieve it but I can't. Deleted by an intruder. Thank you, Carly.

Message received loud and clear.

~ Carly ~

You're so bad at your job, bitch-whore, I can't wait for Rob to sack you. Yesterday I was off work with a migraine. When I returned this morning all the patient records were in chaos. You had deleted half of our patient notes from the computer by pressing the wrong button. The rest of the records are alphabetically jumbled, so we can't retrieve them either. A formatting error, so to speak. Congratulations, bitch-whore, I don't know why Rob employed you in the first place. You've never been trained as a receptionist.

After making my discovery I switch my computer off and march along the surgery corridor towards Rob's consulting room. As senior partner, he must be informed of serious matters immediately. I knock on the door and stand outside impatiently. No reply. I open the door and step right in. No time to be wasted as we move to your dismissal, Jenni. We can't risk any more mistakes. My husband is leaning forwards listening intently to an elderly male patient who I recognise as Benedict Tootle. Rob looks up, surprised. As soon as he sees it is me his eyes cloud with worry.

'Carly, is everything all right?'

'I need to talk to you urgently.'

He frowns in concern.

'I'll come and find you as soon as I've finished this consultation.'

It was always like this; Rob has always put his patients first. I knew this when I married him. It seemed to matter less in those days. Back then he always had time for me as well.

'Thank you,' I say without meaning it.

I slam the door as I leave.

Back in my consulting room I buzz Sharon on the internal telephone.

'Please put my patients on hold.'

I can't cope with my patients until I've dealt with you, bitch-whore. I can't be expected to palpate sagging breasts, dispense holiday disease advice, and take copious amounts of blood from people who mostly have nothing wrong with them, when the patient records are in chaos. If I can't concentrate properly I might hurt people as I withdraw blood.

I pace up and down waiting for Rob. He is taking so long – what on earth can be wrong with Benedict Tootle? Does he have Munchausen Syndrome? Is Rob writing a letter to the BMJ about him? About twenty minutes later Rob finally arrives.

'What's the matter, love? What's happened?' he asks as he walks towards me, face riddled with concern.

'Sit down, Rob. We need to talk.'

'I've got another ten patients waiting; if it's just talking, can we talk tonight?'

Just talking. Just talking. How dare he say that? Something explodes inside me but I manage to contain it.

'Talking's important,' I manage to say as I fix him with a look he usually takes notice of.

He looks back at me and sighs.

'OK then. If it's that bad.'

Slowly, slowly, he walks towards one of the laboratory stools dotted at the edge of my room, in front of the counter space. I sit next to him. He leans towards me.

'I'm all ears. How can I help?'

All ears. A second ago he was sidling back to his patients, without even waiting to know what I wanted to talk about.

'You can help by trying not to sound like a slime bag. I'm your wife, not one of your over-adoring patients.'

'I know – I've noticed,' he says with a feeble grin.

'There's someone else you've been noticing too much. Someone who is incompetent at their job.'

His eyes stiffen, as if he knows what's coming.

'Who, Carly?' he asks in a jaded voice.

'Bitch-whore Jenni.'

He stands up.

'Carly, I am fed up of this childish language. Surely you know that speaking like this is both offensive and inappropriate?'

He's walking towards the door

'I know far more than you think, and you must let Jenni go.'

He is looking at me in the patronising way he does when he thinks I'm pissed.

Put that look away, Rob Burton, I'm not pissed today.

I stand up and put myself between him and the door. I push my eyes into his. His eyes are green, watery and insincere.

'Jenni has messed up our computer records; she did it yesterday when I wasn't here to help her. It's serious, Rob. I need to send out reminders to people who need smear tests, without the correct data back-up I can't do my job.'

His eyes widen.

'Are you sure? She's always seemed so capable on the computer.'

159

I tense my neck muscles, giving him my most piercing stare. 'Yes, I'm sure.'

'Well then,' he says, eyes avoiding mine. 'We'd better do something constructive about this.' He pauses. 'Let's send her on a computer course.'

'Get real, Rob. We need to sack the bitch, not send her on a training course,' I shout. The shout rises up through my voice box, resonant and loud.

He steps back from me. He shakes his head.

'How can you talk about a friend like that?'

'Because everybody needs to know she's incompetent,' I snap. Someone is knocking on the door.

'Carly. I need to get back to my patients. And you must get back to yours. We'll deal with it tonight.' He pauses. 'Is that all right?' he asks.

I say 'Yes,' but I mean no.

Of course it's not all right.

~ Jenni ~

The atmosphere in the surgery has cracked – something's wrong. The noise level is different; the patients are more chattery as they wait. Discontent is hovering instead of kindness, which is why the patients seem so loud. It's Friday morning. We're not usually this busy on Fridays. Monday is normally the worst, after all the stored-up weekend illness. Sharon is the front receptionist today, signing in patients as they arrive. A long queue has formed. I'm sitting next to her, answering the phones, which are ringing every few minutes so I can't abandon them to help her. For the first time since I joined the surgery I feel overwhelmed by the sea of patients seething towards us. The waiting room is clogged. An elderly lady, Mrs Frobisher, who comes every Friday to have her blood pressure checked, can't even find a seat. I see her from the corner of the receptionists' window, looking around uncertainly, rubbing her back because she's in permanent pain. I know about her pain because she often mentions it to me. I put the phones on hold for a few minutes and go to help her. I ask a mother to put her toddler on her knee. Soon Mrs Frobisher is sitting down, looking relieved.

As I return to reception I overhear someone complaining to Sharon in a very loud voice.

'I've been waiting over an hour for my blood test. I'm hungry. I'm thirsty and, as I said, I need to get to work.'

As I get closer I realise it's Mrs Robertson, a single woman in her early forties who I know from church.

As soon as she sees me Sharon commands, 'Jenni, I'll deal with the phones. Go and see what's happening. Rob hasn't called for his next patient yet and Mr Tootle left twenty-five minutes ago. No one has seen a nurse. Perhaps Carly hasn't arrived yet. Maybe I'm going mad but I thought she was here.'

Sharon is trying to placate Mrs Robertson as I sidle out of the sanctuary of our receptionists' enclave. I step through the heaving waiting room, along the corridor to Rob's consulting room, and knock on his door. No reply. I open the door and step inside to check he's all right. He isn't here. He's left his computer on. His old computer that hums to itself. I keep telling him to upgrade it, but he says he's frightened of technology. I keep telling him I can help, but he takes no notice.

Where is Rob? Do you have a problem, Carly, and he has gone to see you? A difficult case that you need to discuss before you start your list? I retrace my steps back along the corridor, towards your domain. Once again, I knock. No reply. But I hear voices. Raised voices. Carly and Rob arguing. I knock again, louder this time. Still no reply. Then I shout, 'Is everything all right?' through the closed door.

Footsteps move towards the door. It opens. Rob is standing in front of me, pretending to smile. I know that smile. His mouth moves but the rest of his face does not. But, Carly, you do not smile. You are pretending you don't know I'm watching you. Pretending to check your phlebotomy equipment.

'I'm sorry,' Rob says. 'Tell Sharon I'll buzz for my next patient

in a few minutes. I'll stay late; as long as necessary to catch up.'
He moves towards me. I can almost taste his breath. Peppermint
and sandalwood, clear cut and fresh.

'Are you OK?' I ask.

'I'm fine,' he says. 'Everything's fine.'

I know he isn't, but I will talk to him later. For now, I step
aside to let him past. He walks away from me towards his
consulting room. I start towards reception. Carly, I hear your
heels banging along the corridor behind me. You tap me on
the shoulder. I turn around to find you fixing me with angry
eyes.

'Jenni. We need to talk, in my consulting room.'

You punch your words towards me like a threat.

I sigh inside. I follow you into your lair. You insist I sit in
your prickly horse-hair chair, and are staring down at me from
one of your plastic bar stools. I've never seen you look so
thunderous. You are making me sweat.

'I've spoken to Rob and have recommended that he sacks
you,' you tell me, in a voice that sounds like a newscaster
announcing a mass shooting.

I knew you were angry with me but I wasn't expecting this.
I feel winded. My breath has been pushed out of me.

'Whatever for?' I ask.

'Incompetence.'

Even though I'm sitting down, I fear I will faint. I sit bent
over, head in my lap, while I compose myself. The strength of
the Lord moves towards me and makes me feel a little better.
I look up.

'You've messed up all the patient notes,' you continue. 'Half
of them are jumbled so I can't retrieve them. Half went missing.'
There is a pause. 'On my day off – yesterday.'

You're smiling at me now, Carly, aren't you, because you
think you've hit the jugular? Well think again. The battle between

is only just beginning. And Jesus is on my side. I remember your unexpected visit to the surgery. I push back.

'You did it. You're setting me up.'

'Prove it,' you taunt, putting your head on one side. If you are trying to look sweet, Carly, it doesn't work.

'Sharon knows what happened,' I retort.

'Jenni, you're pathetic if you think my mentor is your best shot to lie your way out of this one.'

'Carly,' I ask, 'what's happened to us? We used to be friends.'

~ Carly ~

The bitch-whore was so upset after our meaningful little chat that she had to go home early. But when she got to the surgery car park someone had let her front tyre down. Who would do something as unkind as that to the stupid little stick-insect? She went home, a little tearful, on the bus.

~ Jenni ~

I am sitting with Rob in his consulting room. The door is safely locked so that no one, especially Carly, can disturb us. Rob and I are buried in each other's eyes; buried with concern for her.

~ Carly ~

I have retreated to bed again; it's my safe place. When I am in bed nothing bad will happen to me. I empty the contents of my handbag across my duvet, scattering pills over it like confetti. A stash of tranquillisers, anti-psychotics and anti-depressants, raided from the surgery and from Rob's emergency bag. Oh and I managed to get some MDMA. Whoopee. What to do? What to do? Mix them up like a lucky dip of sweeties and take them at random? What about that? A medical lucky dip. Washed down with plenty of alcohol. I cannot manage without alcohol.

Good.

I laugh aloud, scoop up my first handful and swallow them. A swig of wine straight from the bottle. Jenni still has a picture of Craig in her wallet. I saw her looking at it in the café last week. She still wants him. I lie on my bed, smelling and feeling Craig. I reach for my mobile and text him. He doesn't text back. I ring his mobile. Ten times.

Everything is blurred, the bedroom is a sea of colour. Some people in uniform are scooping up my drugs. Sometimes I think I can hear Rob's voice, but then it fades again. I am being lifted onto a stretcher, tucked into a blanket, carried downstairs at an angle. I try to speak but I cannot. Outside now, I hear the hum of passing traffic and feel cooler air pass across my skin. Someone speaks in my ear. I smell cigarettes on their breath. My eyelids are heavy and I cannot keep my eyes open. Someone is leaning over me, hands on my shoulders, shaking me gently.

'Stay with us, Carly; stay with us.'

On the edges of my mind there is an ambulance, an ambulance that is moving. It's the siren that gives it away. A repetitive wailing, pulling me towards my destiny, crying to the world of my distress. A siren that wraps itself around me and engulfs me. I cannot move away from it. I cannot see. I cannot think. All I can do is listen to the avalanche of noise surrounding me. Rob is here. I can't see him but I can feel him. A judder and the siren finishes. Silence. A release. A metallic clatter pushes through the quiet and the ambulance door opens. My eyes are beginning to focus. Now I can see Rob. He is holding my hand. His green eyes are watching me. He's with me as I am stretchered through the casualty waiting area. As I am lifted onto a bed. He is with me as a nurse with sharp eyes and elephantine legs is stripping me and putting me in one of those hospital robes that never fit – an army of nurses behind her, moving towards me. I cannot stay awake any longer. I cannot hold on. Oblivion is whispering to me, telling me that she is sweet. I step towards her and allow her to swallow me up.

When I wake, I'm in a different hospital bed, a bed near a window looking out onto the hospital car park. The cars are fuzzy at first but their metallic shells sharpen in front of me. I know Rob is here. I sense him. I smell him. I turn my head to find him with my eyes. He is sitting in a chair next to the bed, watching me. He stands up and walks towards me. He leans across and kisses me on the forehead. I try to hold him and that is when I realise I can hardly move because I'm attached to so many medical tubes and wires.

~ Rob ~

I kiss her on the cheek and walk away, but she is oblivious to me again. Asleep, golden curls spilt across the pillow like honeysuckle, face paler than pale. Why, Carly? Why? Why couldn't you cope with our life? What should I have done to make sure you could? Please God. I know I can't press rewind – but give me a second chance. Please God, if you can.

Approaching the nurses' station. Moving towards the staff nurse who is sitting at her desk by the ward telephone, filling out paperwork. Praying to God. She looks up as I pass.

'Rob, may I have a word?'

'Of course,' I say.

I pull myself away from my prayers and begin to see her. Her rounded features. Her ample bosom. Tired eyes looking at me over her paperwork.

'Has the doctor spoken to you?'

'No. Not yet.'

'We've confiscated your wife's personal belongings including her phone, just until her condition is clearer. Would you mind taking them home?'

'Of course not.'

The nurse bends and fumbles beneath her desk, producing a clear plastic bag, Carly's possessions visible. She hands it to me. If only Carly's mind-set was so easy to see.

I drive home on automatic pilot, suburbia moving past me like a ghost town. A world I do not recognise, a world I do not see. Blurred houses sliding past my periphery, their brick-work indistinct and grey, followed by the green interruption of the park.

Rewind. Rewind.

That's all I can think about.

If I could press that button, where would it stop? At what moment did her life pivot? Rewind to when? To what? Pippa's birth? The Gospels? Is this Jenni bitch-whore stuff just a red herring? Did Carly start being difficult long before then?

Always difficult?

Always challenging and fun?

Which is it?

I press into my box of memories, determined to pull the good ones out. For bad memories will overtake and destroy me. I prefer to leave them boxed. Good times stretch their fingers towards me, brushing across my mind. I bend my head towards them, allowing myself a sensation of the past – yellow stone and golden fields, memories drenched in sunshine. Golden Carly memories. Carly, my good-time girl. And then again the brush stroke of my memory starts to darken, making me frown, making me want to turn on the light.

Light.

Lights.

Left at the traffic lights, second right by the greengrocer. Copthall Gardens. The car pulls into the drive. Ignition off. Home.

As soon as I open the front door Heather is there, standing in front of me, pushing her worry towards me. Before I have closed it. Before I have taken my coat off. Before I have put Carly's plastic bag on the hallway table.

'How is she?' she asks.

'Fine. She's going to be fine.'

Heather's face is sucked in, in a way I have never seen it before. Tight, as if she's being held together by cling film.

'Do you call recovering from an overdose *fine*?' she asks.

'I know. Sorry. I mean fine under the circumstances.'

We stand in the hallway, eyeball to eyeball, conjoined in a deep drowning sadness; a sadness we need to swim through or walk away from.

'We failed her, didn't we?'

'Come on, Heather, it's not that simple.'

I'm too tired for this, but Heather will not leave me alone. She will not drop it.

'It is that simple,' she replies. 'We should have sent her to a psychiatrist a year ago.'

Heather. Is she a mental health expert now? My temples tighten as if I'm about to have a migraine.

'Everything's always easier in retrospect. She begged me not to send her to a psychiatrist. She was hysterical when I mentioned it,' I reply.

'Hysterical? Hysterical is serious. That's when we should have made her go.'

Possibly for the first time ever, I feel like shouting at Heather. I have to breathe deeply in and out to control myself. I do not want to upset Heather, she's always been so good to us.

'Made her?' I manage to ask softly enough, so I allow myself to continue. 'How were we supposed to do that?' I pause. 'In all my years as a doctor I've learnt how difficult it is to section someone. How much they resent it, at the time and in later years.' I shake my head, eyes almost filling with tears. 'I just couldn't do it to her.'

171

Please, Heather, go away, I need to be alone, I think to myself but don't say. Instead, 'Can I give you a lift home or would you like to stay over?' slips out politely.

When Heather has, much to my relief, plodded upstairs to the guest room, I pour myself a nightcap. After a few sips I remember Carly's bag of possessions and make myself go and check them, before I forget. As I pull her phone out of the bag I see she has been texting Craig. Voyeuristic, I read not just the outgoing text, but the whole chain.

THREE

~ Rob ~

The crunch of bones and his face crumples beneath my fist, blood coagulating on my knuckles. Blood spurting. Blood being absorbed by his paisley silk dressing gown. His paisley silk dressing gown, dated but dapper. Craig staggers backwards, holding his nose.

'What the fuck do you think you're doing?' he asks.

Blood seeps out of his mouth through his teeth, moving towards me in spittle.

'To you she was just another in your long line of whores. To me she is special.'

'I'm sorry, mate. Really I am.' There is a pause. 'She said you had an open marriage.'

'An open marriage?'

Her lie twists inside me like a knife.

Craig is cleaning himself up with his handkerchief. How could she lie about something as sacred as this?

'I'm sorry, mate. I didn't really believe her. I didn't want you to find out. This whole business has ruined my life. Are you going to let a bit of sex destroy all that you have?'

My fist tightens. It takes all my strength and belief in the Lord to stop myself hitting him again.

~ Rob ~

I have parked my car and am marching towards Carly's ward, body pounding through the hospital, thumping through every doorway. Just as I pass the nurses' station, one of them stops me.

'The doctor's with your wife at the moment. Please could you just wait in the holding area over there until he's finished? And then he wants to see you.' She waves her hand towards a small sofa opposite the nursing station.

I hover hesitantly. 'Can I get you a coffee or anything?' the nurse asks.

'No, thanks.'

Sitting in the waiting area. Nothing to do but watch the nurses. Paperwork. Nurses always doing paperwork. And I am just sitting here. No television, no magazines, no newspapers. Nothing to do but watch two nurses filling in forms. Sitting in the waiting room, my anger towards Carly rising like a volcanic eruption inside me. I get up. I start pacing up and down, trying to contain it, taking fifty paces south, fifty paces north, repeatedly, like a caged polar bear. I hear footsteps in the corridor. I look towards the sound. A man with a beer belly and pointed shoes is walking towards me. As he gets closer I see that his pointy shoes are not shoes but brown shiny boots made of crocodile skin. Crocodile skin is illegal, isn't it? Now I realise the man with the cowboy boots is Carly's consultant. Almost as soon as I've worked out who he is, he is standing in front of me, looking at me anxiously. I watch him swallow slowly before he speaks.

'Dr Burton, I have carried out a preliminary assessment of Carly this morning and I am going to admit her to the assessment area of the psychiatric unit.' I nod my head in nervous acceptance. Dr Willis continues. 'But before we admit her fully to the unit, she needs a series of further tests and as such I would rather you didn't visit her today.'

I stiffen inside. Carly is my wife. I have always been beside her to look after her.

'Why ever not?' I ask sharply.

'We need her to be as calm as possible.'

Calm as possible. His words cut into me.

'Are you saying she's not calm when she's with me?' I ask, white-hot anger burning inside me.

'Family visits do tend to excite patients with severe mental health issues.'

Severe mental health issues. Severe. The worst news. I feel overwhelmed. Devastated.

'So you think it's severe?' I whisper, as if I can't bear to hear the word.

'Yes. Undoubtedly,' Dr Willis punches back.

I feel faint. I want to sit down. I want to be anywhere but here. My discovery of yesterday seems almost irrelevant now, but then I remember the sordid pornography I read in those texts.

'Can I ask you something?' I say. I cough in embarrassment. 'Do you think overt sexual behaviour may be part of her illness?'

'Yes. Definitely.' There is a pause as he readjusts his comb-over. 'But I think aspects as sensitive as that need to be addressed at a much later stage. At the moment we are just treading water.'

Treading water myself, I walk slowly away.

~ Carly ~

My body is trapped in a hospital bed, with linen so clean that it cuts against my cheek. I am living in a world of white and grey that smells of antiseptic, wired up to so many machines that I cannot move. Watching and waiting. Watching. The patient next door and the patient across from me are both sitting up in bed to eat their breakfast. The patient opposite is banging the top of a boiled egg so hard that I imagine it is a head and she is trying to kill it. A tray of food hangs across my bed, but I can't free my hands to eat it. Waiting. To see Rob. To see my family. I close my eyes and the sweet gentle fingers of sleep push towards me.

Pinprick brown eyes pierce through a face of leather – a face of leather that is too close to me, asking me questions. Words ejaculate from my mouth. Words about Craig. About the size of his penis and the way he made me come. About the Travelodge. Time has gone into freefall.

The drugs trolley rattles down the ward. We are all panting for it. The lights are out and everybody is talking loudly. Morning bustle. Curtains opened by a starchy nurse with a smile like vinegar. Lunch. Afternoon tea weak as water served in green pottery cups. Rich Tea biscuits.

Visitors. Pippa staring at me, wide-eyed. My mother holding my hand, face permed with a frown. And Rob. Always Rob. Holding my hand. Kissing me on the cheek. Smelling of home.

~ Rob ~

Jenni is sitting opposite me at her kitchen table, engulfing me with her candy-store eyes; fudge brownie mixed with vanilla.

'You made quite a mess of Craig's face,' she says, her voice matter-of-fact, not critical.

'I know,' I say, remembering the feel of his nose crushing beneath my fist. 'And what worries me most is that I'm not even sorry.'

Her eyes darken for a second.

'He came here for a clean-up. And to tell me the truth before I heard it from you. He might as well not have bothered. I already knew.'

Her words run through me like an electric current.

'Already knew?'

'Yes. I sensed it ages ago from the look on Carly's face when she spoke to me about Craig's affair.' Jenni's face is laced with sadness. 'I didn't tell you because I didn't want you and your family to be hurt as well.' She pauses, tears welling in her eyes. 'I'm sorry, Rob. Really I am. I just didn't want you to go through the hell I've been through.'

If Jenni knew, how could I have not noticed? What else have

I missed? Is it because of my lack of empathy that Carly became so ill? Should my preoccupation with the surgery no longer be a matter of pride, but a source of regret?

Jenny leans across the table and takes my hands in hers.

'For me it was the worst pain,' she says. 'Worse than anything. Worse than losing my mother.' There is a pause. 'I can't forgive Craig.'

She starts to cry, as if my pain has opened her wounds again. Her tears sear into me.

'Can you forgive Carly?' she asks.

'Oh, Jenni, I hope so,' I reply. 'If I can't, it will be the end of me.'

~ Carly ~

I am dressed. Nowadays that passes for progress. Dressed and walking in the patients' garden, surrounded on all sides by the four wings of the hospital; buildings so tall that the gardens don't get enough sunlight. Benches and grass. Fleshy-leaved bushes. Willow trees. Several patients sitting outside in their hospital dressing gowns, sitting alone at separate benches, staring at the air in front of them. Air that smells fresh and sweet. It has been raining and a thrush pecks at the grass, hunting for worms. I look up. A plane scrapes through the sky miles above me, leaving a chalky trail in its wake. I envy the people in the plane their freedom to go where they want. The captive freedom of being in transit. I sigh inside. I ask myself, how long have I been here?

Weeks.

Weeks that feel like years.

I look at my watch. Almost visiting time. Time to go inside and wait. Along a magnolia corridor with no windows, shoes clicking across plastic tiling, all the way back to my room. My room is too small to put many clothes in; it contains a wooden plank disguised as a bed, and a chair that looks like a hand-me-down from an old people's home. Plus the flowers that Rob bought me last week.

I sit in my chair by the window, stomach tightening in anticipation, trying to read a self-help book on depression. But I can't concentrate. The self-help book tells me that lack of concentration is a symptom of depression. But how can depression self-help books be of any use if patients can't concentrate enough to read them? I close the book, distracted by every sound that passes in the corridor. Every scuffle of feet, every word, every whisper could be my family.

The door is opening and they are finally here. I stand up and Rob is taking me in his arms, smelling of antiseptic and aftershave, wrapping his arms around me and comforting me. Making the world go away. My mother is waiting behind him for her turn.

'Mummy, Mummy, I've made a tank for you,' Matt says, holding out two cardboard boxes stuck together, one painted red, one blue, powder paint flaking off in scabs.

I disentangle myself from Rob to accept my present.

'Thank you,' I say, placing it on my bedside cabinet.

'Mine's a Dalek,' John says holding his model out.

Silver foil and pipe cleaners. I put it on the bed as there is no room on the bedside cabinet.

'Fantastic.'

Two more ornaments for the ward's TV lounge.

Pippa stands in front of me, blonde hair falling in ringlets on her shoulders, hands on hips.

'I've been too busy looking after everyone to make models,' Pippa says with a shrug. I almost cry. Everybody else laughs.

~ Rob ~

Bone-achingly exhausted, I fall asleep at the start of the Sunday church service as I am praying, nodding off in the kneeling position, my forehead resting on the pew in front of me. The movement of the congregation standing for the first hymn wakes me and I open my eyes to find that the children have gone to Sunday school, leaving me at the front of the church without them, inhaling the scent of incense and hymn books.

By the time we reach the sermon it washes over me, the vicar's words running together, floating above me. The congregation blurs. Kindly mid-life faces. Tired, bent, elderly people. Never enough youngsters, not even now with our trendy new vicar to attract them. Madonna and child look down from the high window behind the altar. The vicar's voice continues. Because I have missed the thread of what he is saying, for once I am bored. I am not usually bored, you know that, Lord, don't you? Usually the vicar's words push towards me with relevance and energy. But not today. I reach for the bible on the shelf in front of me. It falls open at a well-thumbed page: Corinthians 13. Wedding special. Jenni's favourite. Everybody's favourite.

Love does not delight in evil but rejoices with the truth. It always protects, always trusts, always hopes, always perseveres. Love never fails.

Love never fails.

I look up. The vicar, dressed in one of his finest vestments, a robe of white silk embroidered with gold, is beginning the Eucharistic prayer. Refreshed from my catnap, and my reading, I pay attention now as he moves towards communion. My love for the Lord, for his sacrifice, is burning inside me with a deep-rooted energy, sustaining and emboldening me. I am longing to eat and drink the body and blood of Christ. To imbibe my share of eternity.

When my turn to take communion finally comes, an usher standing at the end of my pew, inviting me to come forwards, I find myself moving into the aisle behind Jenni, who turns to me and smiles.

Too friendly, Jenni. Too friendly.

I lower my eyes and walk behind her to the altar – step by step towards communion. Behind hair of polished chestnut, behind slender shoulders, step by step between the choir stalls, the choir singing a psalm and watching us.

When we finally reach the altar, Jenni kneels to my left. I kneel next to her. Hands knotted together and clasped to my chest, I close my eyes and pray. Thank you, Lord, for allowing me to take the sacrament. I feel you, Jenni, praying next to me. I feel your love for the Lord and the pulse of your breathing in time with my own. I open my eyes and turn my head to look at you, kneeling next to me, accepting a wafer in your palms and slowly, slowly, reverently, reverently, lifting it to your mouth. Your red cherry mouth.

At the end of the service, weaving out through the tardy congregation who are laughing and chatting, enjoying their weekly greetings, trying to move towards my children who will be waiting at the church exit, Jenni, you sidle up to me from nowhere.

'How's Carly?' you ask.

'Not too bad, thank you.'

'That doesn't sound very positive.'

'Well, I need to be patient.'

'How's that going?'

'That depends which way you look at it.'

'What's that supposed to mean, Rob?'

You put your hand on my arm, and lean towards me. Put those eyes away, Jenni. The children find us. Pippa and the Gospels, bouncing around our feet, demanding to go to each other's houses.

Put those eyes away, Jenni. And those cherry red lips.

~ Carly ~

I am up and dressed, sitting in my chair, feeling so much better, so much better than I ever imagined possible. Although my consultant, Dr Willis, counsels me to go slowly.

'Slowly. Slowly,' he says to me, dragging the word to make his point.

My family's visits are like liquid gold. Pippa continues to amuse everyone by pretending to be in charge of the household while I am gone. Maybe it is more than pretending. Pippa Burton, aged eight now, calls herself the housemistress, Rob laughs as he tells me. One evening when he returned from the surgery she had collected all the dolls, soft toys and figures she could find from around the house and placed them in rows on her bedroom floor. She was standing in front of them, waving her index finger and lecturing them on sharing chores and time-management.

'What do you think she'll be when she grows up? A monster or a management consultant?'

'What's the difference?' I ask, and laugh as he takes me in his arms and kisses me.

'Carly, I can't wait to have you back. I miss you.'

There is a split second when I know from the look in his eyes that he means it, just a small moment before my doubts move towards me again.

'Pippa will add me to her collection, put me in her room and lecture me,' I say, continuing the joke to distract me from the darkness that still hovers over me.

'Pippa lectures everyone. She's even been to advise her head-mistress lately.'

'What did she say to her?'

Rob's face furrows a little as he pushes to remember, then, 'She told her to tighten up school security,' he said.

'Why did she need to do that?'

'She thinks if the school gate is left open too long at pick-up and drop-off, the reception class who don't know any better could run away if they wanted.'

'What's made her worry about that? Do you think she's been thinking about trying to escape?'

'She's just a busybody.'

'Don't say "like her mother".'

'I wasn't going to!'

A pretty busybody with her blonde curls and a heart-shaped face. Last time I saw her she said to me, 'If you're not home in time for my birthday, Mummy, I will sue the consultant.'

Sue the consultant? Where has she learnt to speak like that? From school? From the television? The boys are terrified of her.

Every time I see the boys, tottering towards me down the ward, carrying chocolates and flowers, paintings from school, full of news, full of Luke and Mark's puppy, my heart breaks in two. They sit either side of me on my bed and snuggle up. I pull them towards me and place their cheeks against mine. I inhale the feel of young skin. The scent of new life.

'When you come home, can we have a puppy too?'

189

'Sorry, boys. I'm allergic to dogs.'

'Is that why you're in hospital?'

'Of course not.'

'Then why are you here?' Matt asks.

'You have an illness, like flu, only it's in the head,' John informs me. 'That's what Daddy says.'

'Daddy should know, he's a doctor,' Pippa says. 'He's right, isn't he, Mummy?'

'Daddy's always right.'

Pippa stands in her command position, hands on hips, head on one side.

'Don't exaggerate. Tell the truth or you'll never get better, Mummy.'

My stomach tightens. So many truths. So many issues. So many private sessions with my consultant in his room at the end of the corridor.

White noise. Vanilla scent. Dr Willis sitting opposite me. Listening. Listening. Listening. When I stop talking, he questions me again. About Rob. About Craig. About Jenni. A barbed wire contortion of problems, knotted together like a fist. Sex addiction. Alcohol addiction. Confidence issues. Issues about Rob and Jenni. Bitch-whore Jenni.

Jenni. Jenni. Jenni. Deep breath. Say her name again. Jenni. You need to let her go. That is what Dr Willis and I practise most. Letting Jenni go. I lie on the couch in his consulting room and inhale and exhale. Every time I exhale I let her go. I have her picture in my wallet taken on a day out together a few years ago. I look at it every night and every morning. Dr Willis, I am doing well.

One day soon, I promise, I will let Jenni go.

~ Jenni ~

Everyone is here for Sunday lunch, filling my small flat-above-a-shop with chattering and laughter. Everyone except Craig.

Craig is not on the guest list.

Heather and my father sit at one end of my makeshift dining table, MDF on top of breeze-blocks, and Rob and I sit at the other, Pippa and the Gospels filling the space between us. Our puppy, Charlie, is sitting beneath the table licking the hand of whoever gives him the largest titbits. I am pretending not to notice. I have painted my face with my best make-up and Rob swallows me with his eyes, watching me wherever I go.

Turkey breast rolled in bacon. Gratin dauphinoise. Roast potatoes and parsnips. Red cabbage. Ratatouille. Wine jus, not gravy. Yorkshire pudding perfectly risen, baked to a crust. And for me, the resident vegetarian, ricotta soufflé.

The table looks fantastic. A white linen tablecloth with a red chiffon table runner – candles, napkins, and flowers. Christmas, but not Christmas. The whole hog. The whole nine yards.

I serve up with the help of Heather and Pippa. Rob carves. When the plates are piled high with steaming food, I raise a toast.

'To Pippa and the Gospels.'

The children raise their Ribena goblets, the adults raise their claret, and a rush of warmth fills my heart. We sit and eat and silence falls. Rob is stabbing his fork into some red cabbage. He looks up at me and our smiles meet. It is like that with Rob and I; our smiles often meet.

Pippa leaves her food and comes to sit on my knee. She strokes my cheek.

'If our mummy doesn't come home, will you be our mum instead so that we can have a puppy?'

Rob's face freezes. Heather and Rob lock eyes for a second.

'Of course Mummy's coming home,' he says violently.

I just smile, and continue to stroke Pippa's hair.

~ Carly ~

When I have let Jenni go, they will let me come home. But it is Jenni who I still dwell on, in spite of everything. What do I mean, in spite of everything? It all happened because of Jenni.

I am up and dressed, sitting in my chair, dwelling on her long brown hair and muddy eyes. On her thin snapping bones. On her kindness. On her laugh. She is my friend, not my enemy. My friend. That is all she ever has been. Nothing more. Nothing less. Not even to Rob. Rob and Jenni. A concept that doesn't exist. That never existed. Dr Willis is helping me reprogramme my brain to accept this. With breathing exercises, and talking therapy. With self-help books and a double dose of Prozac.

Sitting in my chair in my hospital room, with its lack of colour and minimal comfort, an image forms in front of me. Rob arriving for his morning surgery, wearing his pale grey suit, the one I helped him choose in the sales. Striding past reception, past Jenni who is answering the phone. She waves her right hand as he passes. He nods. And that is all. No deep-throat eye contact. No pouting lips. No lingering glances. Just a man on his way to work, and his receptionist. Jenni and Rob. Friends. Nothing more. Nothing less.

The image keeps rolling in front of me. Jenni finishes her telephone call and gets up from her chair. She smooths her skirt and runs her fingers through her hair. She grabs her handbag and saunters out of reception to the staff toilet, where she adjusts her make-up. Kohl eye pencil and teenage lip gloss. Jenni, you are too old for that look. She brushes her hair until it shines like a conker. Then she sprays perfume at all of her pulse points, and shakes her hair as she looks in the mirror, like a model in a shampoo advert. What are you doing, Jenni? Bitch-whore Jenni?

'Watch me, Carly, watch me, I'll show you. Like you and Craig showed me.'

She enters Rob's consulting room and locks the door behind her. His face lights up as soon as he sees her. They are making out, eating each other, mouths wide like hungry lions, removing each other's clothing in a frenzy. They look as if they are high on drugs. Rob tears Jenni's blouse. Jenni pushes him backwards into his consulting chair and goes down on him, chestnut hair spilling over his thighs. A blowjob. Always a blowjob? Jenni, can't you think of anything else? He strokes her head as he comes. His tenderness makes me feel sick. Really sick.

I close my eyes so tight that I am pressing my eyeballs against my skull. I need to push their image away. I must. I must make it go. It is an image. It isn't real. It isn't what's happening. Even though it's so clear, I know it isn't happening.

I stand up and open my eyes. Jenni and Rob have gone. The silence of my hospital room presses against me. Silence washes through my mind and soothes me. I reach for my handbag and pad towards the bathroom. Once inside, I lock the door and sit on the toilet seat wrapped in bruised yellow light, fumbling in my handbag to find my purse. With trembling fingers I find Jenni's photograph, carefully stored in the side pocket. I sit looking at the photograph and I am back on the day it was taken, when we were both heavily pregnant with our first boys; the first half of the Gospels. A day out with Pippa, to the beach, swinging her along between us; every time we raised her feet from the sand, she put her head back and roared like a lion. Pippa always liked you, Jenni.

Do you remember?

Jenni, I am not going to let the ogre you have become inside me keep haunting me. The tremor in my hands increases as I rummage through my bag to find the matches I found in the TV lounge last week. I light one and set fire to the corner of your photo. The flame catches but struggles to survive. A curling orange edge slowly chews your face away.

A face that is no longer a face, but a carcass of ash.

~ Rob ~

Jenni and I sit in church together on the front row, the vicar energising us from the pulpit. I want to hold her hand but I mustn't. I think about Carly with her pale stretched face, and my fist clenches. Thou shall not commit adultery. Thou shall not commit adultery.

Carly committed it first.

After church we walk along the river, Jenni and I, Pippa and the Gospels. A soft September day, the river a kaleidoscope of silver and grey. Pushing past willow and beech trees whose sun-toasted leaves are turning crisp and golden, twisting and falling thick as the first snow. The children are well ahead. Bikes and scooters. Shouting and laughter. On the way to the tea-shop by the bridge. This time I cannot stop myself. I take Jenni's hand in mine and pull her towards me. Red cherry lips stick to mine.

~ Rob ~

Dr Willis has asked to see me. To see him at a time that suits him I've had to pay a locum to cover me at the surgery, which is why I'm irritated that he's late. I guess it's also personal pride that is niggling me; his time apparently more important than mine.

He's finally condescended to arrive and I am being escorted to his NHS hospital consulting room by a nurse in a stripy uniform. She knocks on the door on my behalf. A muffled, 'Come in,' reaches us.

She opens the door but only I step through the doorway. She retraces her steps along the corridor, leaving the faintest whiff of her perfume on the air.

'I'm so sorry I kept you waiting,' he says with a tired smile as soon as he sees me.

'No problem,' I reply, charmingly. Sometimes my hypocrisy worries me. It certainly used to bug Carly.

Carly. The person we are here to talk about. My stomach knots.

'Do sit down,' Dr Willis instructs, gesticulating towards a 1960s Scandinavian chair that has seen better days, waiting for me in front of his desk.

I sink into it.

What does he want to see me about? What is he going to say?

He is sitting watching me with tight brown eyes, so tight they look like hazelnuts. He is a leathery man, a bit like Paul Hogan's Dundee, always wearing his strange crocodile-skin boots like a trophy. He has a tanned face, cracked with wrinkles, and a most unfortunate comb-over. He leans back in his chair and folds his arms.

I hear the distant roar of an aeroplane. An ambulance siren. Someone whistling in the corridor. Dr Willis swallows. I watch his Adam's apple move up and down in his throat. He straightens his back.

'As you know, your wife's illness is very complicated,' he begins. 'Her depression, her low self-esteem, her alcoholism,' he pauses for breath, 'mixed with paranoia and sex addiction.'

His words push towards me and make me feel desperate. I know what he is telling me is true. But still, it upsets me to hear it wrapped together so clinically. There is no room in this description for the woman I fell in love with. No room for the fun, for the life, for the love.

He leans forwards, fixing his squirrel eyes on mine.

'It's the sex addiction that I want to talk about. How much of it have you observed?'

'I found it very difficult when I realised she'd been sleeping with an old friend of ours.'

He nods. 'Ah. I expect having an extra-marital affair was a manifestation of her illness, Rob. I'd advise you not to confront her about it. I fear it would damage her recovery process. Your approval of her is paramount. Paramount.'

I sit staring at him.

He is looking at me, beady eyed, like a bossy teacher. Trying to make me feel as if I'm at school again. I lean back in my chair to pull away from him. 'Thank you for all your help. I can't wait to get her home.'

As soon as I've thanked him, his chest puffs out like a prize peacock.

Carly, how come this arrogant bastard has helped you so much when I couldn't? What has he got that I've not?'

~ Carly ~

My drug regimen is stable and my consultant wants me to return to my normal life now – completely, and as soon as possible – despite the debacle when I set the hospital smoke alarm off. In six months' time he wants me off all medicine completely.

Getting to this point has not been easy. I have been in a dark place. A place I thought I would never escape. They say everyone who recovers has experienced a lowest moment – a point from which they know they have to pull away. How can I describe to anyone the abyss, the fear I was living in? The swimming through a never-ending tunnel of darkness, and then, after months of both drug and talking therapy, the light starting to shine in front of me, pulling me forwards, bathing me in a veneer of normality; occasionally able to laugh with Rob, to talk to my mother and care about what she was saying. To enjoy myself.

Beginning to forgive Jenni. Not that she had done anything. I had nothing to forgive. I was being paranoid about her. Catastrophising, the consultant calls it, catastrophising about her effect on Rob. And now I have moved away from the darkness that was engulfing me, I am her friend again, wanting to help her, wanting to protect her, just like I always did. Just like everyone else does.

Jenni has been coming to visit me here every week, as part of my recovery process. It has been good of her to spare time for me. But then I would have done the same for her, wouldn't I? We sit together in the TV room at the side of the ward overlooking the car park, and a nurse brings us lukewarm cups of weak tea in blue NHS cups. The first time she came, we just sat drinking tea and smiling at each other periodically. Her fringe had been cut in a layered, rounded edged, pudding basin way. The rest of her hair had grown long and jaunty, flicking up slightly at the end – a cross between Sandy Shaw in her heyday and an Egyptian princess. Wearing plum nail varnish, which shone in the striped light dappling through the venetian blinds, and no make-up. Her skin is so smooth, she doesn't need it. My breath resonated through my chest as I looked at her and exhaled. I wasn't up to saying much. As she left she squeezed my hand and told me it had been good to see me.

She continued to visit. Slowly, gradually, over the weeks we began to chat. I laughed once again when she referred to the boys as the Gospels. My stomach began to ache when she told me how lonely her father was. One day I reached across and stroked her pretty hair. Chocolate silk infused with the scent of honey. My friend is back where I guess she always was. Loving me, supporting me.

And now I am sitting in my room next to my stripped bed and packed suitcase, listening to the distinctive sound of Dr Willis walking down the ward towards me, boots clicking on tiled flooring. Even the tap of his feet sounds confident. Dr Willis wears a bow tie; people who wear bow ties always seem to brim with confidence and make me feel rather tired. He pulls up another chair from the next room and sits next to me, leaning close. An enthusiastic smile. Alligator teeth.

'Well Carly, this is it. Are you ready?'

'I hope so.'

'That's not very positive.'

He leans back in his chair, folding his arms and stretching his legs in front of him.

'I'm a bit scared actually. I'm scared of slipping into a bad place again.'

'You won't.'

'How can you be so sure?'

'We've been through this so many times. Now you've experienced a crisis, you and Rob will be far more aware of the warning signs. You can still see me when you need to, to chew over any problems.'

He leans across to the end of my bed, whips my chart from its clip, and scratches his signature to confirm my release.

FOUR

~ Carly ~

In the car with Rob on the way home, the outside world moving past like a cinema screen, every detail sharpened and enhanced. Rain slicing into the puddles on the street. The exhaust from the car in front rising like a cloud painted on canvas. Stansfield moves past me, the high street with its clumsy red brick architecture, functional rather than pretty. The block of flats. The fish shop. The squashed-in surgery, with no more room for development.

I look across at Rob, sitting with one hand on the wheel, the other resting on his leg as we wait at the lights. He seems so distant. I don't know what to say to him. I don't know what to ask him. So we sit in silence as we turn left and then right, and park in our drive.

We manage to get inside before being overwhelmed by a welcome party. Our house seems so luxurious and comfortable after the hospital. Today I will forgive 1930s architects anything, as I enter our sitting room to become a princess in a palace, a palace decorated with balloons and bunting. Balloons and bunting of pink and green. Matt hugs and hugs me, clinging to my legs so that I cannot move. John joins in too. Two sons with untidy blond curls. Two sons sweet enough to eat. My mother, eyes soft with tears, leans across the boys and clings to my chest. They can hug me and kiss me for as long as they like. I can never have too much of it.

Pippa looking taller and prettier than ever enters the living room holding a cake with *Welcome home Mummy* piped in icing on it, in colours to match the room. The cake is so big she is having difficulty carrying it, arms stretched, biting her lip as she concentrates, walking, slowly, slowly towards the coffee table. She places it down with a bang.

'Look what Daddy and I made, Mummy. You weren't home in time for my birthday, so I decided we should have cake today.'

Alone together in our bedroom, anticipation hangs heavily in the air between us. Rob steps towards me.

'Are you feeling tired?' he asks.

I shake my head and start to get undressed. He helps me, undoing my bra and kissing me. A shy kiss, testing me, as if he has forgotten what I taste like. I melt towards him and now he is hungry, he is greedy, pulling my clothes off, pushing me towards the bed, opening my legs with his knee, penetrating my mouth with his tongue. We are both naked. His lips are on my breasts, his fingers playing with the bud of my clitoris. A slipstream of sensation overwhelms me. His tongue is strumming me. His fingers are everywhere and nowhere. I do not know where. And now he is inside me and I am climaxing. A climax so intense it hurts, and before I have reached my final crescendo, he is joining me, thrusting and moaning.

We finish and lie tangled together, sticky with the scent of sex.

'Thank you,' I whisper, and drift into a restless sleep.

The night is long and refreshing. Every time I wake up I

relish Rob's arms around me. The comfort of my own bed. The wetness between my legs. Shapes shrouded with familiarity moving towards me in semi-darkness; my dressing table, my wardrobe. My family alive and breathing all around me.

At last morning slices around the curtain edges, and I throw the covers off and get out of bed. So much to do. No time to waste. On a neon high. Everything around me electric. The shower cuts into me as I wash. When I look out of the bedroom window I see the sun sharpening across the bushes in the garden. My bedroom is bright and beautiful, every photograph on my dressing table poignant, every ornament priceless. What are you on, woman? What are you on?

My mother cooks breakfast for me: scrambled eggs on toast. Gourmet, obviously. Michelin-star material. And as I am tucking in watching Pippa, Matt and John wolfing down their Frosties, I want to scoop them in my arms and hold them there forever. What happened to me? Why had I stopped appreciating this?

~ Carly ~

My mother takes the children to school and I walk around the corner to the surgery, holding Rob's hand. He doesn't want me to start work yet. He wants me to readjust slowly. But I have insisted. After two weeks at home, despite my post-hospital high, I am frightened I will stagnate. His palm feels hot in mine as we move, past the charity shops, past the pharmacy, past the Chinese restaurant until the surgery unfolds in front of us. Riverside Surgery, looking better maintained than I remember. Even the bricks look cleaner. The plants in the small garden at the front look more exotic. Into the reception, where he drops my hand. As soon as Sharon sees me she hugs me, wrapping me in the reassurance of her kindness and her plumpness. Wrapping me in her scent of violets and lavender.

After greetings and good wishes are over, I walk along the corridor to my consulting room. It is just as I left it, except for the new bouquet of flowers to welcome me back, standing in a cut glass vase by the autoclave. The chair by the window where the patients sit to receive their injections still needs re-covering. The fridge still hums as if it is about to break down. My shelf of medical journals and books still needs tidying.

A knock at the door. The handle is turning and, Jenni, you are here, thin and wiry like a greyhound, filling my room with your eyes.

'Welcome back,' you say.

'Thanks,' I mutter. 'Thanks. I made it. Got through it.'

My words hang in the air between us. I hesitate, then I continue.

'I just want to apologise, Jenni. For the way I behaved about you working here.'

Your plum nail-varnished fingers stroke my arm. Your cow eyes soften as you step towards me.

'I know you didn't mean it. You weren't well.'

I smell your scent of honey and patchouli oil. I smell your fragility. Your vulnerability.

'It must have been very difficult for you, Jenni.'

You shake your head and your glossy hair ripples like the surface of the sea in a soft summer breeze.

'What was difficult was worrying about you,' you say slowly. Very deep and resonant.

I exhale slowly and completely.

'And thanks so much, Jenni.' My breathing goes wrong. I am not sure whether I am inhaling or exhaling, or receiving oxygen by osmosis. 'For everything you've done while I've been in hospital,' I gush, words tripping over one another in their rush to escape.

You are twirling a silver skull ring around on your finger, looking at me with those eyes.

'It's been my pleasure,' you say, deeper this time.

Inhale, open that ribcage. Exhale, push, push, push. I put my arm around skeletal shoulders and say, 'What about a sandwich together across the road at lunchtime?'

Weaving through the day. Patient after patient. Getting used to listening again. I had forgotten how much patience it takes. No coffee break. Longing for lunchtime, just like I used to.

Jenni, you are waiting for me in the foyer in your favourite suede coat that Craig bought you last year. Stepping out of the surgery, linking arms with me, laughing with me like you used to. Shoulders clenched to make room for the couple who are sitting next to us, surrounded by the hiss of the cappuccino machine. I order smoked salmon on rye. You order egg mayo on brown.

'How's Craig?' I ask.

After so long, still your face clouds, still your chocolate brown eyes darken. You don't reply.

I survive an afternoon of baby clinic. Chubby dimpled babies with skin like silk. Long-limbed scraggy ones. Over-anxious mothers asking me complicated questions about metabolism, about the weight and height centile charts.

When my shift is over I lock the nurses' station and make my way to the car park. I am relieving my mother of school pick-up. She's been so busy for so long, she needs a break.

I park my Volvo with difficulty in the cramped parking area of the C of E school my children attend, and walk, head high, heels clicking towards the school gate. School-gate pick-up. Inane conversation and small talk. Jostling for position. Boasting. I've always left it to my mother, never wanting to work that hard. But she is tired and the children are my responsibility. You can do this, Carly. You can do this. My mother says they are all very nice. She talks about them incessantly. But to me they are still the school-gate mafia. Women who haven't succeeded at their careers, proving themselves to society by entering the realms of perfect motherhood. Star charts, and home-cooked suppers. Every single conversation, every song they sing, every game they play with their children, educational, competitive. Legoland mothers. Thorpe Park and Chessington

World of Adventures don't get a look in. I hear their braying voices everywhere in Stansfield; in the surgery waiting room, in the supermarket. Women for women like me to keep away from.

A group of them are standing to the right of me. I ignore them and watch the headmistress through the classroom window, reading everyone a story before they go home. The children sit cross-legged in a semi-circle in front of her, wide eyed and listening, except for two boys at the back who are having a fist fight and giggling. The yummy mummies' voices are undulating past me. I expect they're talking about their children, about the results of their last spelling test or their advanced reading age or something. But no. The hot topic is internet dating, and whether they'd prefer a blind date with Matt Damon, Hugh Jackman or Matthew McConaughey.

'What about Harry Stiles?' one of them giggles.

'Jeremy Paxman?'

'Boris Johnson?'

They all burst out laughing like a bunch of hormonal teenagers.

Perhaps I should edge across and suggest Benedict Cumberbatch or Martin Freeman.

Carly. You can do this. You can do this.

~ Jenni ~

Carly, you are back. Back home from hospital. Back at work. Subdued and a lot thinner, your once creamy breasts shrunk to the size of mine. Back and well enough to come to the annual surgery shindig, a disco boat party on the river that runs through Stansfield. I asked why they have it in the winter when it's cold. It's cheaper, apparently, so that everyone from the surgery can be invited. An annual ritual. No-shows unacceptable.

I'm standing in the saloon of the boat, which smells damp and musty, sipping cheap champagne and feeling chilly. The champagne is so sweet that it coats my teeth, ready to damage them. Two sips and I abandon it. Across the shoulders of one of our new GPs, who is eulogising about a recent computer upgrade he is suggesting for our surgery, I watch you, Carly, I watch you with Rob. The young doctor's words merge together, faraway and irrelevant, as Rob leans across to whisper something in your ear. You giggle, teeth together. Girlish. Pretty. Rob is seemingly engrossed with you, but from time to time he glances across at me.

The boat's engine increases in volume as we are steered towards the middle of the river, water rippling and swirling beneath the bow thruster. It is already dark, with only a slither of moon. As I look through the boat saloon's large picture window I see the streetlights along the bank piercing through shrouded shades of black. The river forms the darkest part of the landscape, but here and there it is studded by reflections, from the fairy lights decked around the windows of the boat, from the streetlights, and the diminutive moon – here and there it is jewelled.

I make my excuses to move away from the talk of ram and megabytes and move closer to the window. The sound of the water lapping at the bow of the boat as the engine thrusts us forwards is more relaxing than the strident voice of the over-confident new surgery member. The disco begins, bass thumping out and drowning everything. The sound of the water. The sound of the over-earnest doctor. Dominated by the pump and grind of the music, I head for the bar.

The queue for a drink is building. A sea of my surgery colleagues pushing and chatting around me. The barman, a young lad with a nose ring and an elaborate tattoo on his neck, has difficulty coping on his own. The beer pumps are stiff and slow.

A tap on my shoulder. Hot breath in my ear.

'I'll tell you what, let us get this. You go and get a table.'

Rob. I'd know his voice anywhere. I turn around to see him hand in hand with you, Carly, grinning at me with his eyes.

'What would you like?' he asks.

'Sparkling mineral water, please.'

'On the heavy stuff then?' he says and laughs.

Rob can laugh all he likes. At least I'm not like his wife. I go and find a table at the edge of the dance floor and sit and watch a few people start to dance. After twenty minutes or so, laden with a round, you both join me. The music too loud to make conversation easy, we sit awhile, sipping our drinks, watching more and more people joining in the dancing. Abba. The Jackson Five. Stevie Wonder. The O'Jays. I watch you, Carly. Necking your red wine. Abba starts up again. 'Dancing Queen'. Your favourite. You stand up.

'Come on, Rob.'

You walk to the dance floor hand in hand; you are sylph-like after your illness, gyrating your hips as you walk. As soon as you arrive at an empty space on the dance floor, the music changes to a slow number. He puts his arms around you and pulls you towards him. You are moulded together, gently swaying until the music changes to the Freak, when you both leave the dance floor and weave your way back to the table. As soon as you arrive you reach for your glass and drain it, without sitting down.

'I'll get another round. Same again, Jenni?' you ask.

'It's my turn.'

'No, I insist. You've been so helpful while I've been away.'

A light, nonchalant statement – as if you've been on holiday.

'Well, thank you, then. A small white wine this time, please,' I reply.

'Rob?' you ask.

'No, thanks.'

You frown in annoyance.

'What kind of a doctor doesn't want to drink at his office party?' you ask, fixing your head on one side and widening your eyes.

So you don't want to get pissed alone. That never used to bother you. Does this mean that your behaviour is improving?

'A doctor with a lot to do tomorrow,' Rob replies firmly to your question.

You walk towards him, lean down and kiss him. A slow languorous kiss that I do not enjoy watching. Is this how you used to kiss Craig? When you have released him you turn around slowly to smile at me. A ghost of a smile. Then you scoop up our glasses, and sashay to the bar.

Alone at last. Rob switches chairs and comes to sit next to me. He leans his head towards mine, so close I can almost taste his breath.

'How's it going?' I ask.

'Not too bad, but she's very fragile.'

She looks as indelicate as ever to me.

'In what way?' I ask.

He raises his green eyes to the sky.

'Every way you can think of.'

'So a slow dance with me would tip her over the edge?'

He doesn't like that. His body stiffens as if he has been electrocuted. His green eyes darken.

'Obviously. Yes.'

'I was only joking.'

'It's not funny.'

'Another time then?' I say, running my hand through my hair and holding my eyes in his.

And I see an expression I have never seen before. A stony, frozen glimpse of fear. There for a second and gone. There but not there.

He turns his eyes away from mine and fixes them on you, Carly, as you move towards the bar. The earlier rush has died down now and you are soon being served.

The music pounds in my ears and starts to give me a head-ache as I watch you. You walk back, fingers stretched around our drinks. Rob is dashing towards you to help you, relieving you of his pint. Even though you are thin, you still have curves. In your eyes. In your smile. The curves and warmth that men have always liked. I don't like thinking about your attractiveness. I don't like thinking about Craig.

You put a small glass of Chardonnay in front of me.

I smile weakly.

'Thanks.'

You sit down and start to guzzle your own larger glass. Rob sits on the other side of the table now, the other side of you, as far away from me as possible. I sip my wine slowly, looking out of the window, ignoring you both, ignoring the dancing, watching the riverbank slip by through the window. I finish my wine, stand up and stagger forward haltingly, as if I wish to go somewhere, but cannot. I hold my hand to my head. Rob shoots up from his seat.

'What's the matter?' he asks.

'I feel faint.'

'Sit down. Put your head between your legs.'

I do as he says. He is leaning over me, arm on my back. The damp smell of the boat's flooring rises, astringent in my nostrils. The stench is so strong. This boat must have been flooded at some point. Flooded and left to rot.

'I feel sick,' I mumble, 'I need to go to the bathroom.'

Retching as I walk, I hobble towards the bathroom, waving you both away, insisting you do not join me. When I enter I dive into a cubicle and lock the door. I put my fingers down my throat and vomit. I lie on the cubicle floor, arm sticking out beneath the raised door and close my eyes.

Time passes, drifting in and out of sleep, until someone is pulling my arm, someone is rattling the toilet door. You, Carly. And Rob. I hear your intermingled voices.

'Please, Jenni, wake up.'

'You need to get up and open the door.'

'I feel dreadful. I can't move. I can't focus,' I reply.

'Please try, Jenni,' Rob begs.

Slowly, slowly, I pull myself to standing. I fumble with the door lock. It opens and I collapse into Rob's arms. Carly, you are standing next to him, eyes sharp with concern.

'Please, Carly, go and find the skipper. Use your charm to get him to speed the boat up a bit. We need to get Jenni ashore as quickly as possible,' Rob says.

You dash out of the bathroom to do as Rob has asked – you will be gone a while, finding the crew and talking to them. I cling on to Rob as if I will never let go. He guides me up the stairs to the deck. It is cold and I haven't got my coat with me. Rob covers my shoulders with his jacket and holds me tightly against him to keep me warm. We stand clamped together for a while, the breeze from the river whipping across our faces. He is constantly squinting into the distance looking for you, Carly, but you still haven't found your way back to us. When he sees you he will take his arms away from me as quickly as if I am scalding him. But for the time being you aren't here, and I have your man to myself.

'Hopefully the fresh air up here will do you good,' he says.

I giggle. 'That's the sort of thing my mother used to say.' I pause. 'And she was right. I do feel a bit better already.'

'Whatever happened, Jenni?' Rob asks. There is a pause. 'It's not like you to have too much to drink.'

'Carly must have spiked my drink. Don't you remember, I only had the glass of wine she bought me?'

I turn my face to his and watch his green eyes cloud with fear for the second time today.

~ Carly ~

It is my day off and I am following you, to find out what you're up to, Jenni, you who have taken the day off sick because apparently I spiked your drink. What am I supposed to have spiked it with? You're so thin that you can't take much alcohol. It's obvious you were pissed.

You take the children to nursery school, parking the car in St Agnes road and walking them around the corner, holding their hands, laughing and chatting, looking like a perfect mother – but I know the truth. You're a liar, aren't you, Jenni? You chat awhile to the other mothers after you have dropped the children, stretching your neck back as you laugh.

You drive to St Mary's church. The river is high today. Grey choppy water nuzzles the church wall. You park well away from the river and the church. I park even further away, tailing you from a distance. You open the gate to the churchyard and meander up its stone path, past yew, cedar and beech. Trees wide-girthed with years. You pull on the heavy church door and it creaks towards you. You sit on the front row of pews, head in your hands. You're praying. You do not see me for I stand in the shadows by the font, silently choking on stale incense. The heady air within the church presses down from the rafters and stifles me, leaving me fighting for air. I imagine your prayers; self-interested and sycophantic. Prayers for your family, your children, not prayers for the world. At last you stand up, bow to the altar and cross yourself. You walk slowly down the aisle, heels clicking across granite. When you are gone, I step out from the shadows behind the font into the main body of the church. Down the aisle, through an avenue of half-light, into daylight, which hurts my eyes and makes me blink.

You pick the children up from nursery school, less chatting and laughing this time, all the mothers in a hurry to take pasty-faced, pale-eyed children home for lunch, except for you, you are too lazy to cook lunch. You go to that weird café by the bridge; all haloumi cheese, chickpeas and falafel – making your children eat food that kids never like.

Then at the play park – the one by the railway with a helter-skelter slide, you do not watch the children properly. Sitting on the bench by the exit you stretch your long neck back and raise your head to the sun as Luke falls over and cries and Mark comforts him.

Back home now, I am outside, parked at the end of the side street over the road, watching you, Jenni. Watching you for as long as it takes. I am almost asleep, eyelids and shoulders drooping, mind withdrawing into my body, falling into the delicious sweetness of oblivion when I see movement. Your front door opens. You place your rubbish on the street, ready for the bin men tomorrow, pressing two bin bags against the wall on the pavement at the side of your front door. You see me and wave.

~ Jenni ~

As I put my rubbish out for the bin men tomorrow, I see a car, a brown Volvo estate parked on the side street across the road, a woman in the driver's seat with an abundance of blonde curls. Is that you, Carly? Have you been following me? I saw someone in the distance that looked a bit like you near the church. And at the Moon Spinner Café. I smile in your general direction and wave, just in case it is you – but I do not wait to see whether you wave back. You do not frighten me, Carly. I don't really care whether you are following me or not.

Ten minutes later, Rob is here, standing on the doorstep. I step outside and snog him, a real snog like teenagers do, putting my tongue in his mouth. I run my hands across his back and pull him more tightly against me, feeling his erection through my jeans. Overwhelmed by desire, I want him, right here, right now, but I manage to contain myself until we are inside, pulling him into the hallway, still snogging him, as I remove his jacket and tie.

'I've glued the children to a Muppets film,' I whisper in his ear as I close the door.

We tiptoe up the wooden staircase, mouths conjoined. We

force ourselves to separate and creep across the sitting room, past the children who are snuggled together on the sofa wrapped in Luke's comfort blanket, engrossed. We go to my bedroom, and I lock the door.

~ Rob ~

She steps outside and tries to kiss me, a real snog like teenagers do, putting her tongue in my mouth. The scent of patchouli oil engulfs me. She runs her hands across my back and pulls me tightly against her, pushing her leg against the crotch of my jeans. For a second I am overcome with surprise and respond a little, enjoying the feel of her, enjoying her desire for me. But this is wrong and I know it, and even though I have been tempted for so long, I stiffen, close my mouth and step back from her. Toffee brown eyes attempt to draw me in.

'Come inside,' Jenni whispers in my ear, pulling me into the hallway by my tie, still trying to kiss me as I continue to close my mouth and resist her. She leaves the door wide open and attempts to remove my jacket and tie, whispering, 'I've glued the children to a Muppets film.'

I close the door and stand firmly in the hallway.

'What are you doing?' I ask. 'You rang the surgery and asked me to come round quickly because you were feeling rotten.' I pause. 'You've obviously made a full recovery.'

I put my arms on her shoulders.

'Jenni, please, Jenni, stop it. I need you to leave me alone. I'm not the unfaithful type.'

'Not like your wife.'

I still can't bear to think about Carly and Craig.

'Leave it, Jenni. I need to move on.'

~ Carly ~

He's leaving, kissing her again. If I had a gun I would shoot him in the side of his head by his temple. If I had cyanide I would make him swallow it. If I had a knife I would slice it through his jugular.

Getting into his car, the bitch-whore standing on the pavement next to him. My mobile buzzes. He's texted me.

On the way home with a takeaway.

On the way home with a takeaway, his car pulls out and he passes through the traffic lights, out of sight, leaving his bitch-whore to return to her brothel. His bitch-whore in her skinny jeans that emphasise her fragility. A woman with no breasts. A woman with anorexic, pre-pubescent attractiveness. How unhealthy is that?

I drive home like an automaton, pushing through the traffic; if anything requires a higher thought process there will be a fatality. Fortunately no one steps onto the zebra crossing in front of me, no cyclist overtakes me on the inside across my blind spot, and I arrive home without causing any damage to find children's car seats, sports bags stuffed with clothing, and a box of toys, and books, waiting by the doorway. The children are in the kitchen jumping up and down with excitement, raiding the treats cupboard. Of course. Off to Nana's caravan for the half-term holiday. In my anger I had forgotten.

'You look pale, Mummy, are you all right?' Pippa says, her long blonde hair wound around her head in plaits.

'I'm fine,' I say, holding on to the kitchen counter to stop myself from fainting.

My mother enters the kitchen, car keys in hand.

'Do you want to come with us?' she asks.

'No. No, thanks. It would have been nice but I need to stay here. I need time with Rob.'

I step forward to hug her, and as I do I feel a gushing sensation at the base of my neck, blood leaving my brain, forcing me to cling on to her, hoping I'm not going to faint. I feel hot. I feel sick. But I hold on to my mother, with her rolling-pin arms and solid breasts, and slowly, slowly, everything comes into tighter focus. But she has felt me falling against her.

'Are you all right?' she asks, voice scratched with worry.

I straighten up.

'Course I am, yes.' I pause, letting go of her and stepping back in the hallway. She stands in front of me, eyes burning with concern.

'Are you sure?'

'Of course I'm sure,' I say, trying to reassure her with a bombastic raising of my voice.

'All right then, I'll phone you later,' she says. 'But remember, if you need me at all, just call.' A pause for a final concerned stare and then she lets go. 'Come on, children,' she says, opening the front door.

We load the car. We fix the children into their seats. Sitting in the driver's seat ready to leave, my mother winds the window down and blows me kisses. They all blow me kisses.

When they're gone I lie on the sofa and try to relax. I'm

finding breathing difficult, my chest struggling as if there was a weight on it, so that every breath I take is deep and over-considered. My left arm is going numb and I know I'm having a panic attack. I find the paper bag they gave me at the hospital, and walk around upstairs on the landing trying to breathe into it, trying to increase or decrease my carbon dioxide levels – I'm supposed to know which but I can't remember now. Anyway, it's beginning to work, the pains in my arm are subsiding and my breathing is easier. Breathe, breathe, breathe without thinking. Breathe, breathe, breathe.

Rob is here. His car pulls into the driveway. He is whistling. Doesn't he even feel guilty? His key turns in the front door lock, and his footsteps resonate across the hallway. The smell of an Indian takeaway. Footsteps in the kitchen. Then I am behind him, punching him all over, throwing the takeaway on the floor, at the ceiling. Screaming. Like a wild animal in pain. There is curry everywhere, like blood at a crime scene.

He is holding me, trying to calm me, but the more he tries to calm me the more I hit out. In the end I stop screaming, I no longer have the energy to continue hitting him, although I want to. Oh yes, I want to. I pull away from him and we stand in the midst of our curry-splattered kitchen, staring at each other.

'I was there. I saw you,' I shriek. 'You can't deny it now, can you?'

'Carly, let's sit down and talk.'

I sit down, right there on the kitchen floor in a pool of chicken tikka masala. I don't care about anything. I don't care about my clothes. He sits too, cross-legged opposite me. His biscuit-coloured Gant chinos will be ruined, but I don't care about that either.

At first we do not speak. We sit, eyes locked. Rob's eyes are usually an indeterminate colour somewhere between blue and green, pale and not particularly reminiscent of the sea. In certain lights I even wonder if they are hazel. Today, maybe the last day I ever speak to him, they look grey and speckled with worry. His usually easy-going face is tinged with a hardness that I have never noticed before.

'I was waiting outside her house.'

'Why?'

'I was following her and I saw you together.'

'She made a pass at me. I pushed her away.'

I feel as if I am moving through a dream scene that is not really happening, but somehow through the watery air I can speak.

'I knew. I always knew. I told you, but you wouldn't admit it.'

'It wasn't like that. I love you so much, Carly. She's been coming onto me since we found out that you had been having an affair. Since I found out about you and Craig.'

Found out about you and Craig. Found out about Craig and me. His words echo in my head. Is my world about to stop turning, just when I was managing to hold on to it?

'You found out about Craig?' I pause. 'And didn't tell me? How? When?' My heart has gone into overdrive.

'The messages on your phone – just after you were taken into hospital,' he says.

I feel shaky.

'But . . .' I splutter. 'I slept with Craig when I was ill.'

I die inside. This will be the beginning of the end of our relationship.

'Whether you were ill or not, it took some getting over it. I wouldn't want to do the same to you. Carly, we are two of a kind, meant to be together. Please, let's forget about Craig and Jenni. I love you. I can't bear to lose you. Especially now, when you've fought so hard to get better. When you have been so brave.'

Rob takes me in his arms and holds me against him.

'Does Jenni know?' I ask.

He is stroking my back. I can't see his face.

'I've not said anything.'

I rest in his arms and my body begins to calm.

~ Carly ~

I'm at an emergency consultation in Dr Willis's private room in Harley Street. Harley Street with its elegant Georgian houses, faded brick and arched doorways. Dr Willis didn't want me going back to hospital, because he didn't want me to feel trapped. So I came here, coped instead with the silence of the waiting room, a silence so heavy that even turning magazine pages felt conspicuous. And now I have been summoned and am sitting in his traditional room, with its wood panelling and leather-topped desk, winged chairs and thick pile carpet. I am sweating. The oil painting behind Dr Willis's desk is over-whelming me, swirls of colour masquerading as clouds moving closer and closer.

'Carly, how's it going?' he asks.

I retract my eyes from his painting, lower them and fix them on his face. As impassive and hard to read as ever. Eyes that are cold but not unkind. Rob calls them his squirrel nut eyes. Rob. Thinking of Rob makes the knots in my stomach spasm more tightly. I put my hand on my stomach, wince in pain and bend forward a little in the hope it will ease.

'Are you all right?' Dr Willis asks frowning with concern.

'I told you. I should have stayed in hospital,' I reply, straightening up because the pain is easing a little.

'Why?'

'It happened.'

'What happened?'

'My catastrophising came true. I saw them together. He denies it. He says he was just checking on her but I saw them kissing.' I pause. 'Kissing,' I repeat, almost shouting now. Dr Willis stares at me, head tilted to one side. His frown is deepening.

'When?'

'Last night. I was following her.' I am watching his hands, his fingernails resting on his Harley Street desk. I see his fingers rise in exasperation.

'Why were you doing that?' he asks, his face now almost overwhelmed by his frown.

'Because I don't trust her. That's why I need to be re-hospitalised,' I tell him slowly.

'You've been hospitalised for three months. You're not ill enough to spend the rest of your life in an institution, Carly.' His voice is stern. Funereal.

We sit looking at one another. His frown has stabilised. Perhaps it is even reducing a little. His marble eyes rest on mine. He is using silence to force me to speak.

'I'm going to see Jenni tonight. She's asked to talk to me,' I tell him.

He taps his pen. 'Well, surely that's a good thing?'

Dr Willis's face is moving away from me, instead I see Jenni and Rob locked in an embrace. Embracing right in front of me.

'I don't think so. Talking won't help.'

'Talking always helps,' Dr Willis says, his voice piercing through the image in front of me.

I laugh. 'You're a therapist. You have to say that.'

Now, Jenni and Rob are really ramping it up, fucking on the floor beneath Dr Willis's desk as he makes notes on a pad in front of him. He looks up.

'Tell me, Carly, if talking won't help, what will?' he asks.

'Never seeing her again.'

He shakes his head.

'You can't just erase people that annoy you. Jenni's your friend. Your husband's friend. You know that. This is your first hiccup since you came out. I'm sure you can deal with it.'

'Hiccup? My husband kissing her?'

'Carly, calm down. You know you suffer from paranoia. It could have been a greeting kiss, or a kiss of friendship?' He pauses.

The image of Rob and Jenni fucking in front of me bursts, like a balloon, it just pops and goes. Dr Willis continues speaking, his words push towards me.

'You've had couples' therapy with Rob. He has reassured you that he loves you.'

Dr Willis's words are spiralling in my mind.

'He loves you. Rob loves you, Carly. Be strong, be confident. He loves you, believe it and you will move away from the circle of suffering you are trapped in.'

Dr Willis's words set off in my mind like fireworks. They mean something this time.

~ Carly ~

I'm sitting on the sofa at your flat, bitch-whore Jenni. We're sharing a bottle of wine, surrounded by candles and incense; something incendiary on every surface. Tibetan monks are chanting through the sound system. You look rather weird in your red kimono embroidered with gold thread, hair clipped up in a bun with a wide ivory hairgrip, eye-liner painted on in a thick slant. Your dog and your children are nowhere to be seen, all tucked up in their bedroom asleep. The chanting of the monks is growing louder. You smile at me, stretching your bright red lipstick towards me, from the sofa opposite.

'So,' you say, sipping your wine. 'Did Rob tell you he's in love with me?'

Of course he fucking didn't, bitch-whore, because it's not true. I've finally found the strength to stand up to you, Jenni. To push away my fantasies about you and my husband. I'm having my husband. Not you.

'No. Quite the opposite,' I say calmly.

'He's not telling you the truth then.' There is a pause. 'I've held him off for as long as possible. But you need to know, Carly, we're in love.'

I am laughing inside, Jenni, because you are so ridiculous.

I take a slug of wine. You continue.

'We need to be friends, Carly. We always used to be. Our children will be spending so much time together.'

I believe Rob. I believe Rob. Bitch-whore, I am just playing along with you. Friends? Now I really know that you're mad.

'Do you mean you're going to live with him?' I ask, ice-calm.

You nod your head.

'How dare you?' A little outrage to floor you, to make you think I believe you. By the way, your cowpat eyes look like shit.

'I could have said the same to you about Craig,' you almost spit in reply.

I hold your eyes in mine.

'You knew about me and Craig?'

You don't reply.

'That's the first time you've had the honesty to come clean about it,' I say. I take another sip of the wine. It tastes bitter. 'I never intended to take him, just borrow him for a bit.' I neck a large gulp of the wine, to help me relax. 'I wasn't well at the time.'

'You use your mental health as an excuse for everything. I just want you to know, no one "borrows" Craig for a bit,' you reply.

Your cowpat eyes are becoming larger and larger. Your words are spinning around me.

I need to go to the toilet. I stand up. The room starts to spin, like the words. Your face has become a blur of red. Is it the drink? Is it the diazepam? I head to the bathroom, or try to. But walking is difficult. I can't co-ordinate my movements. The room spins so fast. Faster and faster. I am falling. Falling and falling. Tumbling off a precipice, still spinning. Falling and spinning, into black upon black.

~ Jenni ~

Another sip of wine and then you stand and ask me where the bathroom is. I gesticulate towards the right of the sitting room, past my tiny kitchen. Two steps and you fall, sideways in slow motion.

I turn to stone. Paralysed. I cannot move towards you to help you. You land and it looks as if you have stopped breathing. The paralysis has gone and I am free to move again. I turn you into the recovery position and administer resuscitation, pressing on your nose and breathing into your mouth. I pump your chest and work up a rhythm. Suddenly you gulp for air and now you are breathing. I cannot rouse you but your chest is moving and air is passing between your lips. I abandon you to dial 999.

Four minutes seem like four years before three paramedics, two men and one woman, are clumping up my stairs in heavy black boots, the sort of boots that mean they can kick a door in if they have to. They check your pulse, your vital signs. They attach you to a machine. They give you oxygen. The men lift you onto a stretcher, and carry you downstairs. The woman hangs back.

'Can you tell me exactly what happened?' she asks.

'We were drinking wine. We'd had about a glass each when she stood up to go to the toilet and collapsed.'

Through the window I see you disappear into the ambulance. The doors are closed. Lights flash.

'Could she have taken something else?' the paramedic asks.

My insides jump as if I've been electrocuted.

'What makes you think that?'

'The rigor in her body. Her pupils.'

Oh, Carly, what has happened? What have you done to yourself now?

'She has a history of overdosing.'

'On what?'

'Her prescribed medicine – diazepam, anti-depressants, sleeping tablets. She's just come out of hospital after a major breakdown.'

The paramedic's eyes sharpen with concern.

'I'd better go,' she tells me. 'I've got her phone, so I'll ring her husband. You stay here. I want the police to check the scene.'

'Why?' I splutter. 'What on earth are you thinking?'

'We need to be as certain as we can about what she might have taken.' There is a pause. 'About what has happened to her.'

I taste salt in my mouth and realise I am crying. The paramedic leaves my flat and the ambulance drives off, siren wailing. Sobbing softly, I tidy up the room. Everything back in its usual place, I change out of my red kimono, into my jeans and a white embroidered shirt. I sit on the sofa and wait, bracing myself for a call from the hospital to tell me that you are dead. Bracing myself for the police. Waiting for my father to arrive to look after the children. I wait and wait and wait. Around me everything has stopped, as if I am sitting in the middle of a photograph or a painting, in the middle of a motionless stage set. The children do not wake or cry. I can't concentrate on television, or listening to the radio. I cannot think. I cannot read. My eyes focus on anything or nothing. A cushion on the sofa. A scuff mark on the wall. Even sound has stopped. I cannot hear the passing traffic. Or the voices from the shop beneath. All I can hear and see is you falling, Carly. All I can think about is whether you're still breathing.

Eternity is interrupted. I open the door to a female police officer with strawberry blonde sculptured hair who smiles at me and shows me her badge.

'Sergeant Anita Berry,' she says. 'The ambulance service sent me. Can I come in?'

'Yes, of course,' I say, my voice fragmented by tears.

She follows me up my noisy stairs, and I thank the Lord that I have been blessed with children who seem to sleep through anything, and a puppy who has responded well to cage training. All together in the back bedroom, fast asleep.

'Do sit down.'

She sits on my sofa, and as she does she crumples the throw. She tries to smooth it.

'Don't worry. It always does that. Can I get you anything? Tea? Coffee?' I ask.

'No, thanks.'

I hover in front of her, still standing. There is a pause.

'Have you heard how your friend is?' Anita Berry asks.

'No. But I'm hoping no news is good news and that at least she's stable.'

'Look, Ms Rossiter, this isn't a crime scene. Nothing has happened. I think the paramedic was just being edgy. Just to keep her happy, do you mind if I have a look around?'

'Not at all. Of course not.'

Anita Berry stands up.

'Just one thing though,' I add. 'We were drinking wine. I

washed the bottle and put it in the recycling, and I'm afraid I washed the glasses. I just didn't think. An automatic reaction. Do you want to take them with you anyway?'

'No, thanks. I'm just here to see if she dropped any pills or anything.'

'I didn't see her do that.'

Anita Berry stands up with a shake of her layered hairstyle. 'If you don't mind I'll just have a quick look around.'

'It won't take long. It's a very small flat,' I tell her.

I follow her as she inspects. A little look under the sofas. A re-arrangement of the throws. A quick inspection of the kitchen cupboards. Into the bathroom. A hearty rummage through the bathroom cabinet. Into my bedroom. A lot of interest in my dressing table, particularly my second drawer where I keep my mini-pills. And then a march towards the children's bedroom.

'The children and the puppy are asleep in there.'

Anita Berry stops in her tracks.

'I won't disturb them then. Everything seems in order.' There is a pause as she smiles at me. 'Thanks for letting me look round. I'll leave you in peace now.'

I see her back down our noisy staircase to the doorway. As she leaves she puts her hand on my arm, eyes brimming with sympathy.

'I hope your friend will be OK.'

'So do I,' I reply, biting my tears away.

By the time my father has arrived to look after the children, Carly, and I have managed to reach the hospital, you have been admitted to the Critical Care Unit, the same unit you started in last time. I walk through endless empty corridors to find you lying unconscious, wired up to so many machines that with my rusty nurse's training I find it hard to decipher which

237

machine is which. You're breathing steadily and artificially, your skin like pale fabric against the pillow. Heather and Rob are sitting on chairs one on either side of you. Heather looks at me, nods, and turns her attention straight back to you. Rob stands up and kisses me politely on each cheek. He is Rob – but not Rob. A diminished version.

'Have you any idea what happened?' he asks.

'She wanted to see me, to talk to me. She begged me to let her come round, so I agreed.'

His eyes dart towards Heather.

'Let's just step away for a few minutes,' he says.

He takes my arm and leads me out of the ward, towards a seating area by the toilets. We sit down together. It is quiet here, away from the nurses' station. It's so late at night now, there is hardly any movement; not many staff, no visitors. The thin electric light in the corridor is turning everything grey.

'What did she say?' Rob asks in a whisper.

'We'd only had a glass of wine each. We didn't have time for much of a conversation. She just stood up to go to the bathroom and collapsed.' I pause, my eyes filling with tears. 'It was awful, Rob. I resuscitated her and called an ambulance.' Another pause, longer this time. 'I did everything I could.'

~ Craig ~

It was Jenni who blasted Carly's news down my mobile as I stood in my parents' hallway. In case I didn't know. In case? How should I know? I stood by the umbrella bin and the coat stand, finding it difficult to know what to say to Jenni. If I sounded too upset she would be cross, if I didn't sound upset enough I would be accused of not being empathetic. So I took a fine line between the two, sorry, but not too sorry. After which Jenni said,

'Well, however sorry you are, you've got to take it on the chin, your ex might not make it.'

'She's hardly my ex.'

'What is she then?'

Silence down the line.

Shortly after we terminated our conversation, the news of Carly's situation had started to sink in. It is hard to imagine her downfall. The more I think about it the more I can't believe what has happened to her. A strong, bold, poster-paint woman like Carly.

Later on, I pick up my boys for the evening. We go to McDonalds, as usual. Sitting surrounded by air conditioning and plastic, again, eating a Big Mac and chips with a supersized coffee whilst the boys chomp through a mountain of nuggets and guzzle a sea of ketchup. When they have finished eating, Luke looks up at me.

'After tea, Mummy said I should ask you to come home and help bath us.'

'Why?'

He shrugs his shoulders.

'We wanted you to. She said you could.'

My heart pounds. Can I bear this? Sudden inclusion that she may denounce at any time? We tidy up our rubbish and meander back to my family's new home.

When Jenni answers the door, her hair is tied back in a ponytail and she isn't wearing any make-up. She looks about twelve; dappled with innocence.

'Mummy, Mummy, Daddy's come, like you asked.'

She steps away from the door and leads us upstairs, where the vacuum cleaner is standing in the middle of the living room next to a plastic box overflowing with cloths, gels and polish. The room smells of artificial orange blossom, which burns through my nostrils and infiltrates my chest, making me cough.

'Sorry,' Jenni says and opens the window.

Charlie is unleashed from somewhere, lolloping towards us. A wagging fur ball, gyrating with energy, pushing against me. Putting his snout under my arm, demanding my attention, forcing me to stroke him. I pet him behind the ears and he feels so smooth and silky that I cannot stop. Stroking him is addictive. I stroke him and stroke him, his hips, his flank, placing the side of my face on the side of his head to feel his fur against my cheek. The puppy is grunting. The back of his throat almost purring with pleasure. I look up. Jenni's brown eyes are fastened on me.

'Daddy, Daddy,' the boys chant repeatedly, jumping with excitement.

Charlie has abandoned me. He is chasing the boys and barking. Everyone is laughing.

'Come on,' Jenni says, 'I've run the bath already. Into the bathroom, everybody.'

The bath is overfull, exploding with bubbles, filling the room with the scent of honey and lemon. Naked already, the boys jump into it, pushing a tidal wave of water across the bathroom floor. Jenni scolds them lightly, so lightly they don't notice. They sit in the bath, fighting with snowball bubbles. The puppy sits by the bath watching them. Jenni and I sit together on the floor behind the puppy. For a second I forget we are no longer a family.

'Can Daddy stay and read our story?' Luke asks.

'That's the plan,' Jenni says.

The plan? What plan? I look across at her, surprised. If she has a plan this is the first I've heard about it.

Put those eyes away, Jenni. Don't hurt me again.

The boys climb out of the bath. Jenni pulls the plug out as I swaddle them in towels. The water from the bath roars down the plughole, terrifying the puppy who tries to hide beneath Mark's towel. We all stroke his head and laugh. Next it is Batman pyjamas, story and milk. At story time Jenni disappears. We put the puppy in the cage in the corner of their bedroom. He seems to be happy in there, close to them, surrounded by his puppy toys, one eye open, one eye closed, almost asleep. I read them *The Tiger Who Came to Tea*. They have always loved that. I read it again and again. At first they join in, chanting the words, laughing and giggling. Gradually they quieten and eventually they fall asleep. Luke is lying on his back, mouth open, arms above his head, face still flushed from the heat of the bathwater. Mark has curled in a ball, fist clenched. I kiss each of them on the forehead and creep out of the bedroom, closing the door, slowly, slowly, so as not to wake them, so as not to wake the puppy.

I head into the living room.

'Would you like to stay for a drink?' she asks.

A no-brainer of a question.

'Yes please.'

I sink into one of the sofas. She has already opened a bottle of wine; it is waiting on the dresser with two glasses. She pours us a glass each, hands one to me and sits directly opposite me on the mirror image sofa. I sit sipping wine, trying not to listen to the Gregorian chant music she so likes. It has never been my favourite.

'Last time I was drinking wine like this, Carly was here.'

Carly. I wish she hadn't mentioned her.

'It must have been dreadful for you,' I say carefully. I feel as though I am walking on ice.

'It was. It was awful. She must have taken so many tablets before she arrived to be so ill. I mean, she's still in a coma.' There is a pause. Her brown eyes darken. 'It really makes you think, someone almost losing their life like that.'

'What has it made you think, Jenni?'

She shakes her head a little, almost imperceptibly, and shrugs her shoulders.

'That life is too short. We must make the best of it.'

Her chocolate eyes are sparkling and dangerous.

'I don't feel I'm doing a very good job of that at the moment. Losing my wife, losing my family,' I tell her, trying to stop the tears I feel welling up in my eyes.

I swallow in an attempt to push them back. She is looking at me anxiously, looking as if she wants to say something.

'I think we should try again,' she tells me.

I think we should try again. Did I hear that properly? After

242

so many problems? After selling our house? Am I fantasising? Am I dreaming?

'Did you hear me, Craig?' She puts her wine glass down, pulls up from her sofa, and walks towards me. She is standing in front of me with her hands on her hips. A vision from heaven. Eyes to drown in. Cherry red lips waiting to be kissed.

'I think we should try again,' she says. 'But I want you to understand, Craig, if you ever stray again, I'll kill you, and I'll kill your lover.'

I am drowning in those eyes. I am kissing those lips.

~ Jenni ~

Rob calls my name and I walk down the corridor to his consulting room, past the nurses' room, which used to be Carly's territory, past the children's toy corner and the store cupboard. I knock on the door and enter as soon as he invites me. He swings his chair around.

'Jenni, are you all right? You don't need to book an appointment like this. I would see you anytime. Surely you know that?'

I sit in the patients' chair opposite him.

'I just wanted to keep things formal.'

'Formal?'

A frown shadows his face. I hand him a letter. He opens it and reads it, then looks back up at me. His face is shocked.

'But why are you handing in your notice?'

'I'm moving away – with Craig.'

'With Craig?' he stammers. 'But I thought . . .' He hesitates. 'You said you'd never go back to him.'

'He's still my husband. The father of my children. After everything we've all gone through, I've realised I believe in the sanctity of marriage.'

'But,' he exclaims. 'You always said the opposite. You believed in fidelity, and he'd breached it.'

We sit looking at each other, silence pressing against us. After what seems like forever, he opens his mouth again.

'It's since Carly's collapse, isn't it?' he says.

I do not reply.

'Has Carly's illness been your retribution?' he tries again, tapping his fingers on his desk, not far from her picture. 'Is that what this has all been about, retribution?'

'Rob, I knew you'd be upset. That's why I wanted to keep things formal. I don't think any of us can cope with more emotion. Craig and I move away next week.' I put my hand on his arm. 'But we've been through so much together, let's make sure we keep in touch.'

FIVE

~ Rob ~

You lie on your back, mouth open, intubated – the breathing dead; paler than pale. Heather and I are sitting together, watching your chest rise and fall. As I watch you, Carly, the past feathers my mind. We are tumbling together across bed covers, laughing. I am running my fingers through hair that feels like silk and smells of cinnamon, burying myself in your breasts, in your warmth, in your life. I reach for your hand and hold it, but it lies limply in my palm. Your eyes open for a second. A trick of the light, of the shadows that surround you. I lean across to watch you more closely. A cruel, cruel trick of the light.

Back to the surgery for the afternoon clinic, pushing you from my mind as much as possible. Somehow at the surgery I override the memories and continue. I walk through the waiting area, nodding at the receptionists as I pass. Moving past row after row of elderly people with grey hair and grey clothing, past young mums with out-of-control toddlers they are trying to placate, worried middle-aged patients with frowns and spreading bellies. One of my patients smiles at me and I nod my head politely as I scuttle through the waiting room, trying to ignore the sound of coughing and sniffing, the undercurrent of bored chatter. Hating myself for keeping the sick waiting.

I open the door of my consulting room and Sharon is there, placing a cup of tea and a biscuit on my desk. A crumbly shortbread in a plastic package.

'I thought you might need it,' she says, turning to me. 'How is she?'

'The same.'

'Do you think I'd better stop asking?'

'If there's any news I'll tell you. How about that?'

Sharon's hazel eyes are filled with pity, which makes me feel uncomfortable. I never envisaged a life that would make me eligible for it. She bustles out. I sigh inside and press the buzzer for my first patient.

My first patient is suffering from anxiety. However hard I try to help her, she can't contain it and so I have to refer her on. Most of my elderly have arthritis or heart problems, or both. And one, a particular favourite of mine, a square-faced octogenarian lady with a feisty laugh and sparkling eyes, has a severe bout of bronchitis, which she is susceptible to from time to time. I treat a young woman for a UTI. And then anxiety again. So I prescribe diazepam, anti-depressants, paracetamol, beta-blockers, amoxicillin, trimethoprim, simvastatin, keeping my computer notes up to date between patients. Their problems are turning my attention away from my own.

At lunchtime, Sharon brings me a sandwich from the shop over the road; soggy ham and tomato on brown, with another cup of tea. Her eyes are still heavy with sympathy, still making me feel uncomfortable. Then it's time for home visits. The day draws on as I drive around Stansfield, visiting people who are dying of cancer. The last one is a middle-aged spinster with colon cancer who has chosen to stop taking chemotherapy and let her end come naturally.

She opens her eyes as I enter her bedroom. Against all the

odds, despite the ravages of cancer, she still looks pretty. Her hair has grown back, and although no longer shiny, it curls around her piercing eyes and high cheekbones. She is propped up on a frilly pillow surrounded by a floral duvet and the scent of stocks. She loves the scent of stocks; I brought her some last week.

Just as I am about to check her heartbeat with my stethoscope, she says to me: 'I didn't expect it to be this bad. I feel as if I'm rolling off a cliff.'

'So do I.'

'You'd better hold on tight, then. For Carly's sake.'

'You know about Carly?' I ask.

'Bad news even reaches a mausoleum like this.' There is a pause. 'What are her chances?'

'Slim.'

'Better than falling off a cliff, then. Hold on to her, Rob,' she whispers. 'Hold on to her and she won't fall off like me.'

'I promise you I will hold on tight. Tighter than tight.'

I place my stethoscope on her chest. She winces at the coldness of the metal. I listen to the beat of a heart that will not beat for much longer. Just a matter of time before it stops. At the moment it's a bit fast, almost fibrillating, but not too bad. As I remove the stethoscope, she reaches for my hand. I take her hand and sit on the edge of her bed holding it. She smiles, a half smile, and closes her eyes. She looks so still. I bend across and kiss her on the forehead. A gentle kiss to wish her safe passage.

Back home. Heather has fed the children, supervised reading and bath time, and has them sitting in a line on the sofa, good as gold. They are shiny and clean, watching *Fantasia*. There is always a film addiction, something they want to keep watching and watching, making my life a little easier.

'Daddy, Daddy, please can we stay up to watch the end of this?'

'Yes, you can.'

I flop on the sofa to cuddle them. Matt and John wriggle onto my knees, one on each leg, wrapping themselves around my torso like ivy. Pippa snuggles up by my side and I put my arm around her. I inhale baby shampoo. I inhale Badedas. Heather, relieved of responsibility, puts her head back, closes her eyes and falls asleep. Her once clear skin is now dappled brown like potato peel. Her hair, once streaked with brown and grey, is now a garish ghostly white. For a second, in my mind's eye, I think I see Carly sitting next to her, kicking off a pair of killer heels, flopping back in the sofa to guzzle a large glass of wine. Heather turning to look at her daughter fondly. I tear my eyes away from them, used to many such mirages when I am at home, and try to concentrate on 'The Sorcerer's Apprentice' from *Fantasia*. The music is evocative. Too evocative to be accompanied by Mickey Mouse, who steals the Sorcerer's hat, imbuing him with magical powers. In his dreams he can control the world, the stars, the tides, the seas. When he wakes, his world is flooding. He tries to control it, but he cannot. The water rises and rises. The more he waves his wand, and the more he tries to clear it up with his broom, the more it rises. The graphics are so clear, so intense, the water looks as if it will burst into the sitting room and drown us. At last the sorcerer reappears, and puts everything right in an instant. How I pray for that. Dear Lord Jesus, how hard I pray for that.

~ Jenni ~

A fresh start with my husband, Craig.

Those who the Lord has joined together, let no man put asunder.
Do you remember, Craig?

We have moved to Trethynion, an old fishing village in Cornwall, postcard pretty, curling around an old stone harbour. We're in a two-up two-down terraced cottage, with twelve-inch walls and an inglenook fireplace. There are geraniums growing on the porch, and a sea view from the upstairs windows – if you stand on tiptoes. The children walk to school along the beach. As well as Charlie we now have Lucy, a long-haired black and white cat. The two animals sleep curled up together at night. Our cottage is so small that we know what each other is doing most of the time. A situation, after what happened in Stansfield, which I like.

When my father visits he has to stay at the local pub, which is attached to the side of our cottage in a row that weaves down to the seafront. He doesn't seem to mind. He has formed quite a rapport with the landlord, a middle-aged man with a beer belly and a robust laugh. On Saturday nights, long after last orders, when other customers have gone home, the landlord has a lock-in with his favourites, and always includes Dad, if Dad is around. A late night pint and a laugh. A change of environment has given my father a new lease of life.

Craig has joined the local fire brigade, but it is so remote where we live that firemen don't have full rotas at the fire station. On the rare occasions they are required, the fire brigade control pages them to come in from their homes. As Craig is so much less busy than he used to be, he's become a bit of a house husband. He keeps telling me he's bored. Bored of being associated, or hardly associated, as he puts it, with a fire station that doesn't get any shouts. He loves the children, and seems to enjoy the time he has with them. But he doesn't like cleaning. He doesn't like washing. He doesn't like ironing. He has told me he hates cooking, especially the sort of food I like; recipes with too many ingredients that take too long to chop up. He's fed up of listening to pompous drivel on Radio 4, which he only puts on because he doesn't have anyone real to talk to.

But then, even in Utopia not everything is perfect. I have to drive an hour each way for my job at the local teaching hospital where I am training to upgrade my nursing qualifications, and the cottage is a bit damp, but we're working on it.

I've joined a new church. You can drive along the A road that passes the top of the village to get there, but I prefer the footpath that runs from the centre of the village, along the harbour wall and up the cliff path, beyond the beach. I love to climb the hill path serenaded by the peal of church bells and the whisper of the sea.

This morning, I have taken the hill path and am slightly winded after the climb. I cross myself at the church entrance and bow my head as I move through the arched doorway of the porch. Past the notice board and the umbrella stand, through medieval doors heavy with years, into a church with white painted walls and arched windows. No stained glass, no colour here, just oak pews darkened by time and an altar of brass. A stone pulpit of white, with no choir stalls.

The congregation comprises six people. A man of about fifty with rounded glasses and a long pointy face, who usually wears walking boots, a purple North Face jacket, and a green woolly hat with a bobble on top. Three old ladies with fingers like gnarled tree trunks, who sit in a line clutching their hymn books. A teenage girl with scarlet lipstick and a nasal piercing. And me. The same six people every week.

We acknowledge each other with half a smile and then sit ignoring each other as we wait for the service to start. We have no organ. No choir. No heating. No hymn sheets. No flowers. The vicar looks as if she should be Sharon from the surgery's sister with woolly hair and eyes like a sheep, wearing a simple cassock with no embroidery. And when we kneel to pray I commune with all my friends at St Mary's. My prayers float up and combine with theirs. My prayers, as always, combine with yours, Rob. I pray for you, and I pray for Craig. I pray for my sons. And Carly, I pray for you too. I pray for you, my old friend, more than anyone else.

~ Carly ~

I'm still here, Jenni. I can't see, but I can think. I began as dead as dust but now I've turned to mist. An ethereal mist, transient and grey. I roll across the land at dawn, or at midnight, pushing my fingers into other people's lives, looking everywhere for you, Jenni, to find out what you've done.

~ Rob ~

It's at church when I miss you most, Jenni, when I'm sitting with Heather, Pippa and my half of the Gospels, listening to the organ announcing the start of the service. I miss you turning to me, smiling at me with your eyes. The shape of the back of your head as you pray. Your sweet vulnerability, the pride I took in protecting you. I see your hair streaming behind you like a banner as you climb the path to your new church. I see you, and know you still think of us, because you tell me on the phone.

This Sunday, Heather and I have somehow managed to tear Pippa and our half of the Gospels away from the TV, give them breakfast, dress them in clean clothes, and arrive here just in time for the early service – rushing in at the back to sit in a row to the far right of the pulpit, behind a severe-looking family with long backs and long noses. In seats where we cannot see the choir. In seats where we cannot see the vicar. The first hymn pounds out and the children filter away to Sunday school; Pippa, garish in a neon pink frock with matching hair bobbles that look like pink cherries, the boys neat in jeans and T-shirts. The hymn rolls around the church, resonating off brass and brick, vibrating against the windows, ending suddenly with an unmelodious judder. The organist stopped three notes too soon, and the choir overcompensated. We all sit down and the tired scratchy voice of a member of the congregation starts to lead today's prayers. She prays for absent friends.

Absent friends. For Carly. For you, Jenni. I see you now as I saw you the first time I came across you both together, on the sofa at the NCT evening, both heavily pregnant, looking like beached whales. Craig and I enticed you to the pub on the way home. That night, the first time I saw you, Jenni, you walked with Carly to the pub, arm in arm, stopping beneath the streetlight at the corner. Do you remember, Jenni? You whispered something in Carly's ear; she put her head back and laughed.

Carly, please open your eyes and laugh like that again. Jenni, you must be content. Be happy with Craig. Carly will come back to me and God will love us both forever. Carly will come back to me and our souls will float in heaven.

~ Carly ~

I am no longer a mist. I am a woman with a body locked in dreams. In my dreams I am falling. You have put something in my wine and it tastes bitter. I am falling. You are laughing, your face contorted. You are trembling with anger and moving towards me as I fall.

'No one borrows Craig and lives,' you say as darkness tightens.

And somewhere through the darkness, Rob is speaking in a voice I cannot hear.

~ Jenni ~

Wind buffets the car as I stamp the accelerator pedal down. I'm on the coast road, pushing through blinding rain towards my nursing exam. Nothing, not even the ravages of nature, will stop me from getting there. I haven't eaten, I haven't slept, but that doesn't matter because I'm running on an adrenalin high. I have worked so hard for this exam that I cannot imagine life beyond it. The exam is a brick wall in front of me, which I am going to smash through and only when it is over will I step back to assess the damage the stress has done to me. But needs must. Craig isn't earning much money. I need to pull myself up.

The journey seems to take forever as the car continues to plough through horizontal sheets of rain. Eventually I arrive at my examination venue, the Town Hall of our local market town. Despite the quaint charm of our fishing village, the market town is disappointing. Mixed architecture and too much traffic; not enough funding to build a bypass. Town and Town Hall are equally disappointing. The Town Hall looks like an ugly Methodist chapel, an unappealing mix of red brick and pebble-dash. I step inside into an entrance hall corridor with peeling plaster on the walls.

High ceilings and echoing feet.

I walk, clutching my pencil case and my examination number, towards reception to find out exactly where I need to get to.

'Right and right again,' the receptionist informs me with a toss of her head.

Right and right again. I'm in a sea of candidates, nursing candidates from all over Cornwall. The faint hum of subdued chatter. The occasional sliver of nervous laughter. Nausea curdling in the base of my stomach, rising as I walk. Surrounded by people who cannot possibly be as worried or as nervous as me. I retch into my mouth and swallow it. A taste like the smell of camembert. I retch again.

Silence as we enter the exam room. The desks are laid out in candidate order. I am in the front row, in the corner by the wall clock, every tick pulsating in my head. Waiting to be allowed to turn the exam paper over. The invigilator stands at the front, wearing a cherry red suit and pink lipstick. Pink and red rotating. My stomach is churning and my temples are thumping. The invigilator makes a show of looking at the clock near me and checking it against her watch. As soon as the long hand reaches the top, she makes her announcement.

'You may turn your papers over.'

Hands trembling, I obey. Words swim in front of me. I blink and they come into focus. I push the world away. I can no longer hear the clock. My head stops thumping. The taste of vomit in my mouth has disappeared. My hand writes seamlessly. At pens down I have just finished the last question. Perfect timing? Please God, I hope so.

~ Craig ~

Where have you gone, Jenni? I never see you. You've been working so hard for your exam, stuck upstairs in our bedroom revising, when you're not on duty at the hospital that is. When you do take a bit of time off you're too tired to talk to me. The rest of the time, I still don't get a look in because you are praying. Church on Sunday. Choir on Wednesday evening. Every morning and just before bed, praying. Your compulsive praying is really irritating me. Sitting on your dressing table stool, head down, hands clasped together, as if you think you are Madonna or an angel. Are you trying to grow wings? I don't like the way you have started adding the phrase 'please God' to one too many sentences. You told Jono from my watch that you were born again. Since then he's stopped inviting me to the pub. Perhaps he thinks I've given up drinking.

Yesterday morning I was brave. I tried to speak to you about the religious war that is about to break out between us. You were sitting in your usual angelic dressing table position. After about twenty minutes of creeping around trying to get dressed without disturbing you, I couldn't stand it any longer. I stood behind you and tapped you on the shoulder. You turned your head towards me and opened your eyes. But your eyes weren't focusing. They were trance like. As if you'd taken something.

'Don't disturb me, Craig, I'm with the Lord,' your lips hissed in a strange monotone.

'Please, Jenni,' I said, 'stop this. Come and sit on the bed with me and talk to me, before you go to work.'

'I can't. I'm talking to God.'

Oh, Jenni, how I wish I was as important as God.

~ Carly ~

In my dreams, we are sitting in your contrived apartment, Jenni, surrounded by deep pile carpet and silken throws. Magenta red is overwhelming me. You are crumbling a tablet between your thumb and forefingers, grinding it into my wine. You hand me the wine in a large silver goblet and now I am drinking it. It tastes bitter, but I am necking it; gulping it back. And once again you are laughing at me, telling me that Rob is in love with you. It is funny how much he is in love with you when most of the time I feel him here with me. I can hear his voice but I cannot speak to him. I know he is near me. I feel his hand in mine.

~ Jenni ~

As soon as I arrive home from work, Craig says, 'We need some quality time together. We're going out for dinner.' He almost glowers at me. 'To talk.'

I wince inside. I hate talking when I'm tired. I hate the expression quality time. Time is just time. Before I can open my mouth to explain that I'm exhausted, our babysitter arrives. She is here standing in our hallway, taking her coat off, smiling at Craig. She looks like a younger version of Gaby Roslin. She has smooth skin and an elfin smile. I met her at church. A friend, of a friend, of the vicar's daughter. Craig is annoying me by spending too much time looking at her legs. We say goodbye to her – Craig, I fear, reluctantly. He is grumbling at me at the moment for praying so much, but prayer is comforting me as I try to rebuild trust. Trust. He has broken my trust and it will take the rest of my life for that to heal, if it ever does. At the moment I'm just trying to plaster over the cracks.

We walk towards his favourite restaurant, holding hands in silence. A restaurant in an old boathouse at the edge of the village. It is midweek and there are not many people about. An old man on the way to the pub. Two teenagers smoking on the harbour wall. The night smells of sea and silence.

The old boathouse is now a red-carpeted stone-walled restaurant dripping with fishing nets full of glass balls and dried starfish. A scented red candle burns in the centre of every table. It's midweek; we are the only people here. The waitress is a young girl with bleached white hair cut short like Annie Lennox. She leads us to a table in the far corner, next to one of the fishing nets. For the second time tonight I notice Craig looking at a younger woman's legs.

Look but don't touch, and I would prefer it if you didn't even look, I warn him with my eyes.

We sit down and she hands us a menu and a wine list, making a vague attempt to pull down her pussy pelmet; which is exactly that; it really only just covers her private area. If she moves too quickly it might slip up over her bottom and end up as a belt.

'Can I get you anything to drink?' she asks.

'Two gin and tonics, please,' Craig says without consulting me.

Annie Lennox saunters off and Craig turns his eyes to me.

I pick up the menu and read it. Very 1970s. Pâté, prawn cocktail. Too much steak. No goat's cheese. No pulses. Oh to be at home eating something healthy. I silently salivate at the thought of the carrot and lentil soup I bought at a health food shop yesterday, waiting for me in the fridge.

Before too long, certainly before I've decided what to risk eating, Annie Lennox returns with the gin and tonics. She places them in front of us. They are overfull. She spills a little off the top. A minuscule pad and paper appear from somewhere, I'm not sure where – I didn't think that skirt had room for a pocket. She is standing with her weight on one hip, pen poised.

'Have you decided yet?' she asks.

'No,' I say.

'Yes,' says Craig. Our voices collide.

Annie Lennox's eyes dart between us.

'Should I give you a minute?'

'Yes, please.'

Annie Lennox leaves.

'Can't you see anything you fancy?' Craig asks, brow frowning in concern.

'Just spoilt for choice,' I say, forcing a smile. A few minutes later, 'I tell you what, I'll have a salad to start and an omelette for the main course,' I manage.

'And what about wine?' he asks, his eyes dancing enthusiastically.

'You choose.'

Now we are ready to order, as is often the case, the waitress has disappeared. We sit and wait, sipping our gin. We sit and wait, looking at each other. When I look at Craig these days, I no longer see him from a distance, as others see him. Everyone else always tells me how handsome he is. After the way he's behaved I hate it when people admire his looks. Do they think I'm not attractive enough for him? Do they think he's too handsome for his own good? But I do not see his exceptional looks any more. All I see is a slightly overweight middle-aged man, whose jowls are beginning to drop, beginning to incubate a paunch. It doesn't really matter what he looks like anyway. I don't need to see him from a distance. He is just part of me. Part of my life.

Annie Lennox arrives with her notepad and a flourish. Craig orders for both of us. He has chosen pâté and steak. Too much protein, Craig. Annie Lennox saunters off and this time Craig refrains from glancing at her legs.

'How was your day?' he asks.

'Fine,' I reply.

'Fine?' his voice sounds stretched. 'Perhaps you'll pay more attention to me, Jenni, if I speak as if I am asking you an exam question. Please expand and explain?'

'I mean, it's not that interesting to talk about.' I shrug a little. 'That's all.'

He reaches across the table to take my left hand in his. His eyes are brittle and tight. He leans forwards.

'OK, your choice then. You start. What do you find interesting to talk about these days?'

I take a deep breath.

'I want to know when you're going to start coming to church with me. And the children. They've stopped coming to church since we left Stansfield. I want us to go together as a family.'

Brittle eyes become tighter.

'Jenni, you know I'm not a Christian. We discussed it before our wedding.'

'But things are different now. We have the kids, they're getting older.' I feel tears welling. 'They need a Christian upbringing.'

He exhales sharply. He shakes his head.

Annie Lennox is here. She stands by the table, elbows wide, as she screws the bottle opener into the cork. It takes her an age to bed it in, and then it sticks as she tries to retract it.

Please, God. Make Annie Lennox go away.

Eventually she manages to ease the cork out. Then she pours the wine out from a great height.

My prayers are answered. Annie Lennox finally retreats.

I lean across the table towards Craig.

'The children need a strong Christian influence.'

His jaw is tense like his eyes.

'They've got that in you.'

'Seriously, Craig. They need a clear message. From both of us.'

He takes a large gulp of his wine, eyes holding mine.

'I just can't do it, Jenni,' he says. 'I'm not a Christian. You know that.'

~ Carly ~

'Carly, Carly, can you hear me?' a voice asks.

I do not reply. I lie wrapped in stiff cotton sheets, watching a woman wearing a blue cotton nurse's uniform pressing a buzzer at the side of my bed. She leans over me, eyes searing into me.

'If you can hear me, blink,' she says.

I blink.

Her eyes widen and she leans over and presses the buzzer again. I struggle to sit up in bed, fighting against the drip line that is tangling against me, but I can't manage. I just lie still, eyes open, watching her watching me. Beyond the nurse, the room begins to come into focus – white upon white, shiny and hygienic. I move my head to the side. I see a picture of Rob and the children in a wooden frame balanced on the white cabinet next to my bed. Pippa has her fingers bent to look like claws and is pretending to roar. Then the world becomes fuzzy as I drift back to sleep.

~ Rob ~

'I have to go. It's an emergency.'

I move through the surgery, past the waiting patients, past the receptionists into the car park, so distracted that I'm not sure I'm safe to drive. But I'm too impatient to wait for a taxi. I skid my car into reverse, almost hitting the silver Mercedes parked behind me. The traffic on the main road traps me in the car park. Every light is against me. At the hospital, the car park is so busy that I have no choice but to park on a grass bank and hope I won't get ticketed.

Through the double doors of A and E, through the trauma unit, straight to Critical Care, bursting into your room with the staff nurse following me. You are fast asleep, just as you were when I left you this morning. Fast, fast asleep. I am drowning in disappointment, tears pricking my lower lids. The staff nurse puts her arm on my shoulder.

'She was awake for about half an hour. She's only just gone back to sleep.'

I sit down next to you and take your hand.

You're asleep but your sleep is different, you're moving a little, your eyelids flickering. I sit watching your thin stretched

271

face, your lips jerking at the edges, longing to take you in my arms, longing to speak to you. Every minute that you stay asleep feels like a year. I play games in my mind, telling Pippa, telling Heather that you have woken, and that you are sitting up asking to see them. That I am holding your hand across the table at a candlelit dinner. I squeeze your fingers in mine. For a second I think you squeeze back.

~ Carly ~

In my dreams I fall again and you are laughing, Jenni, face contorted, long dark hair tangled and matted. I land heavily on a hospital bed and open my eyes. Rob is sitting next to me, blurred, as if separated from me by a mist. He smiles and moves his face closer to me but still I cannot see him properly.

'I can hear you but I can't see you very well,' I say, but he doesn't reply.

I close my eyes to dream again.

~ Carly ~

I wake up in a hospital bed in a room that looks blurred, as if it has been made of fuzzy felt. Rob is here, holding my hand. I strain towards him. I want to feel his lips on mine. He moves towards me. Our lips meet.

Electricity. Sweet electricity.

I press my lips against his, firmer, tighter. But then I remember what I have to tell him. I pull my lips away. I try and tell him about you, bitch-whore Jenni, but I'm not sure any words come out. He has not heard me. His expression does not change.

~ Rob ~

Yesterday you told me that you can hear me but that you can't see me. A start, Carly, a start. And I think you can see me a little. Today you smiled when I entered the room. When I stroked your back. When I made a clumsy attempt to hug you by dodging your lines. I sit and watch you lying there, breathing shallowly, paler than pale.

Then after a while, the miracle that I have prayed for for months happens; your eyes open for me – tentatively, heavy lidded, but properly. They open and they remain open. I lean across towards you, into your line of sight and smile. You stir in the bed and pull yourself up to a sitting position. Blue eyes sharp like copper crystal. Eyes locked into mine. Carly, I have waited for this moment for so long, practised what I will say to you so often, but now it is here I cannot find the words to explain my emotions. So I take your hand and wait for you to speak first. After a while you are straining to whisper. I move the bedside chair closer.

'Rob, I need to tell you something.' I lean forward, desperate for your words. You pause and squeeze my hand tightly. 'Your little bitch-whore tried to kill me.'

~ Craig ~

Bored as I wait for the teachers to release my children, I stand pretending to be interested in the school notice board. A woman comes and stands next to me, leaning forwards as if she is straining to see. I can smell her perfume. Even though I make a point of no longer looking at other women, I allow myself to turn and glance at her. She is tall, almost as tall as me, and she has shoulder-length glossy blonde hair cut in a bob. She runs her fingers through her hair and shakes her head as she reads. My glance is turning into a stare but I seem incapable of turning my head away. She has brown eyes, much smaller than Jenni's, and pouting lips. Even more pouty than Carly's. A few drops of perspiration have formed on her upper lip and I watch her wipe them away with her index finger. She smiles at me warmly. Why is she smiling like that? Is she lonely?

'Are you going to the homemade cake sale?' she asks.

'Social event of the century. Of course I'm going.'

She laughs politely. 'I am too. It's in the hall now. Come with me if you want to know the way.'

I walk across the playground with her, towards the school hall, which smells of sweaty trainers and overripe cheese.

Come on, Craig, you know the rules, any other woman but Jenni – ignore. Ignore. Ignore.

That night in bed, being near to Jenni makes me feel breathless, as if the air doesn't contain enough oxygen. I breathe quickly, my erection pulsating. I put my arms around her and pull her towards me. I caress her breasts but they feel soft and spongy. Flat. Without desire. I reach for her clitoris and she widens her legs. She goads me with her eyes. I know what she's thinking: *Get it over with so that I can go to sleep.*

I try to excite her, but nothing works. She turns away from me and opens her bedside drawer, pulling out the lubricant she seems to need these days. She wipes it on herself and on me as well and then she turns over languorously and allows me to enter her from behind. Her nipples are semi-erect now, I tease them as I pump. She is no longer Jenni, but Rupert's mother – blonde and busty, creamy and delicious, breasts as ripe as cherries. I try pressing my usual button: any other woman – ignore. Ignore. Ignore. But I cannot. It doesn't work. I cannot stop fantasising about Rupert's mother.

'What's Rupert like?' I ask Mark the next day as we are having breakfast.

'He's a bit of a wimp.'

'So you don't want to ask him for tea or anything?'

'No, thanks, Dad.'

In the end I get to know her through work. It's eleven o'clock at night, and I'm drinking hot chocolate and watching a bit of TV with Jenni before we go to bed. My phone rings: I'm called to the fire station. A flurry of activity, flinging on my uniform and running to the station, which is just around the corner, still doing my jacket up. Good job Jono and I volunteered to check all the breathing apparatus earlier. We haven't had a shout for weeks. We're very charged up. Exhilarated. Except for Jono, our driver, who is calmer than calm. He wouldn't be allowed to drive if he wasn't. The engine pushes into darkness, lights flashing, siren howling, twisting along narrow country lanes. Turning into a crescent drive, towards a detached Georgian house, almost a manor house but not quite; perfectly balanced architecture and a Downing Street front door. The door opens and Rupert's mother is standing there with wet hair, wearing only a pink bath towel. Our eyes are out on stalks.

'I'm so sorry you've been disturbed. I was in the bath when the fire alarm went off.' As if we haven't noticed. She continues. 'Nothing's on fire, I can assure you. I think the links to you must be faulty. Maybe a spider has got inside the detector or something.'

I step forwards from the men.

'Don't worry. We don't mind coming out. It's our job. Better to be safe than sorry,' I say, taking over from the Station Officer, hoping he won't have a go at me later. 'But do you mind if we just check inside?'

'No. Of course not. Thank you. My son, Rupert, despite all the noise, is still asleep in his bedroom.' There is a pause. 'And my husband's away.'

She steps back from the doorway. We put plastic covers on our boots and step inside. She hovers in the hallway as we check everything out. A quick glance in the kitchen. A quick look at the boiler and the fireplaces. It only takes about five minutes to see that everything's fine.

As we leave she says, 'Craig.'

So she knows my name.

'We've seen each other at the school gate, haven't we?' She holds her hand out to me to introduce herself. 'I'm Ana. Anastasia Donaldson.'

278

I stand looking at her. She pauses.

'Do you think you could come back tomorrow and help me check my alarm? The company we use haven't been very reliable.'

That's a no-brainer.

'Of course.'

The next day I am here at ten-thirty on the dot as requested. This time she is dressed; wearing jeans, and a figure-hugging polo neck jumper. Don't look, Craig.

'Thank you so much for coming,' she says as I step into the hallway. 'It was very nice of you.'

We stand in the hallway, beaming ridiculously at one another like a pair of awkward teenagers, as if neither of us knows what to say or what to do. Pulling myself together, I snap off the grin.

'How many detectors are there?' I ask.

'One in every room. Two in the larger ones.' She pauses. 'And the control panel is in the basement.' She smiles at me again. 'Should I take you there first?'

'Yes, please.'

I follow her as her heels click across black and white marble, past sultry paintings of mountains and forests, past tangled golden wall lights, through a doorway at the back of the hall. Down a scarlet-carpeted staircase, down, down into a vaulted stone basement, where she flicks a switch to illuminate row after row of wine bottles, and a line of control panels. I stand in front of the control panels. There are so many that for a few seconds I feel confused.

'The smoke alarm control panel is the first one on the right,' she says pointing to it.

'Thanks.'

'I tell you what, I'll leave you in peace to get on. Give me a shout from the hallway when you've finished.'

And she disappears somewhere into the vastness of her home. I start at the control panel that indicates which smoke detectors require checking, and then I go through them room by room. The house is so large it takes me hours. Seven bedrooms. Seven bathrooms. Kitchen. Kitchen dining area. Kitchen sitting room. Formal dining room. Three drawing rooms. Conservatory. Breakfast room. Two studies. When I am finally ready to leave I stand in the hallway and shout: 'Anastasia!'

Within seconds she appears from one of the smaller drawing rooms and gives me a friendly smile. 'Thank you so much. It's taken so much of your time. Have you any time left to have a coffee before you go?'

I know I should say no.

But I hear myself say, 'Yes.'

Anastasia must like proper coffee because a metal machine that looks as if it should be in Starbucks sprawls across the left-hand side of her restaurant-sized kitchen. She twists handles and turns knobs and eventually produces two small white china cups steaming aromatically. We sit opposite one another at her glass kitchen table and I take a sip. It's so strong that I cough.

'It's so good of you to help me. My husband isn't around.' There is a pause. Her face becomes pinched and strained. 'I expect you heard on the grapevine that my husband and I are getting divorced.'

'I hadn't, no. My wife, Jenni, and I only moved here fairly recently. We're not part of the local mafia yet.' I pause. 'I'm very sorry to hear that.'

'I'm not,' she replies, a little too boldly to sound genuine. She is biting her lower lip a little with her teeth. I know that trick. Hurting yourself to distract yourself from crying. I pull my eyes away from her face and look at the floor, just to give her a moment.

'So it was your decision, was it?' I ask after a few moments.

'Yes.'

'I suppose that makes things easier.'

'It hasn't been easy.'

Her fingers are tightening so sharply around the handle of her coffee mug that I fear she may break it.

'It's never easy.'

'You sound like you know.'

'Almost.' I pause. 'And almost's bad enough.'

'Almost? What happened?'

I sigh. I really don't know why I do this when I've hardly met her and I'm so ashamed about what happened between Carly and I, but I tell Anastasia the truth.

'I had a brief affair.' I pause. 'My wife and I are still recovering from the aftermath. Still working things out.'

'Well then,' she says with an awkward smile, 'I'm sorry to hear that too.'

We sit in silence for a while, and then I can't help myself.

'What happened with you then?' I ask.

Her eyes are filling with tears now; not even biting her lip can prevent them. 'I just can't talk about it yet.'

~ Carly ~

I'm tired. So tired. Lying here, drifting in and out of sleep.
People come and go. Rob. Mother. Pippa. John. Matt. Rob,
here again, holding my hand, reassuring me, kindness in his
green freckled eyes. Somewhere through this fug of rest, and
sleep, and love, I remember what happened. I know I must find
the words to tell someone. But every time I try I'm not sure
my words come out. But my strength is returning. I warn you,
Jenni, you've not got long. Do you hear me? Not long before
everyone knows what you have done.

~ Craig ~

Anastasia Donaldson infatuates me with her amazon limbs and her Emilia Fox cuteness. Blonde hair. Brown eyes. A perfect combination. Her educated accent tumbles like sugar candy from her caramel throat. My eyes follow her at school drop-off and pick-up. The children used to walk to school along the beach, but now I take them in the car, and park as close as I can to her shiny new Range Rover, almost as big as the school mini-bus. We joke about that with her.

~ Carly ~

Today my body is Herculean – I'm riding on air. I wake up and hold my hand down to press my buzzer and call the nurse. I hold it down for a few seconds and when she doesn't appear I hold it down again. After a while a nurse comes scuttling down the ward. She arrives at my bed with a half scowl, half smile.

'Are you all right, Carly?' she asks.

'I need to see Dr Willis. It's important. I need to tell him something.'

'Is it anything I can help you with?'

'No. I need him. It's something he's been helping me with for years.'

She checks my machines, and my lines briskly, with a sense of nurse-like urgency; quick and efficient, but slow enough to be sure not to make a mistake. I watch her with a sense of regret. That's what I used to be like. When she seems satisfied everything is fine, she steps away from my bed to page Dr Willis.

She comes back. 'He's on the next ward,' she tells me. 'He'll be over as soon as he can.' She looks at me consideringly. 'Would you like some water?' she asks.

'Yes, please.'

She fills my glass from a jug on my bedside cabinet, and places it on the tray that swings across my bed, careful to make sure it's in a position I can reach.

Miss Calm-Efficiency then puts her head on one side as she looks at me.

'If you need me for anything at all, just buzz.'

Miss Calm-Efficiency leaves.

I sit in bed sipping water, waiting for Dr Willis, looking at my bland surroundings, trying to find something interesting to rest my eyes upon. But the only colour in the room is the photograph Rob brought from home. The one of our family trapped in time on that Breton campsite. Pippa pretending to be a lion, showing us all her claws. Today I know I need to show mine.

Dr Willis is coming, I hear the familiar sound of his cowboy boots stomping noisily down the corridor. He is here, standing next to my bed, leaning forwards face furrowed with concern.

'How are you feeling, Carly?' he asks.

'I'd like to say never better, but that wouldn't be quite true.'

He laughs. I try to laugh with him, but no laughter comes. He pulls up a chair and sits next to my bed. As he crosses his legs his trousers rise up his legs a little, displaying his crocodile boots.

'The nurse says you asked to see me.'

I pull my eyes from his boots.

'Yes.' I pause. 'Now I've come round properly, and I'm gaining my strength, I want to tell you that I'm certain Jenni Rossiter tried to poison me.'

The frown in his eyes tells me that he doesn't believe me.

'How?' he asks.

'She put something in the wine I drank just before I collapsed.'

'Did you see her do this?' he asked, leaning back in the thin plastic hospital chair.

'No.'

'Then how do you know?'

His lips are thin and tight, as if he is trying to stop himself from treating me to a critical smirk. I feel like treating him to a punch in the nose to make him see sense.

'How do you know this?' he repeats.

'I just do.'

He raises his eyes to the sky, not bothering to disguise his exasperation now.

'That won't go very far with the police.'

A headache is starting to splinter through my head, but nothing is going to stop me from dealing with this properly. So I ignore the pain, and say,

'Dr Willis, no one has ever believed me about Jenni, and after everything that has happened you still won't believe me now. But regardless of what you think of my medical condition, I have a right to speak to the police.' I pause. Then I raise the volume of my voice a little. 'I am demanding to see the police. I want you to get them to visit me.'

I clench my fist and bang it onto the insubstantial swinging tray in front of me. My water glass falls over and spills onto my bedclothes, Dr Willis grabs some tissues from my bedside table and dries it up as much as he can. Then he steps away from the bed and looks down at me, eyes hard with concern.

'I will call the police to come and see you. But this is what I think, Carly. We took a blood test when you came in and you were pumped up with your usual problems: Valium and alcohol. I think you took it before you went to see Jenni.' He pauses for breath. 'And you know paranoia has always been a large part of your problem. You can't blame Jenni for that.'

I shake my head. Tears of exasperation are pricking in the

corner of my eyes. My cracking headache is getting worse. But still I push through, through pain and exasperation, and say in a loud strident tone,

'Just because I've suffered mental illness doesn't mean I have no rational judgement. It doesn't mean that everything I say should be minimised.'

'Carly, I'm not trying to minimise you.'

I eyeball him as hard as my exploding headache will allow. 'You may not be *trying* to – but you are.'

~ Craig ~

Anastasia and I are going for a quick coffee after school drop-off and my stomach is full of butterflies. A feeling I rather like. I have never felt so young and innocent in all my life, even when I was. I feel fresh, untainted. As if my life is just starting. All because I've met Anastasia Donaldson.

She mentioned coffee casually as we walked across the car park. I almost dropped Luke's hand. Afterwards on the way home I started worrying about whether he'd heard us. I don't want him mentioning it to Jenni. Anastasia and I are only friends. There is nothing for Jenni to know. So later on in the evening I was wily. At bath time (it's always bath time now before Jenni gets home), I played a silly game – guess what Daddy's doing tomorrow. Thankfully Luke hadn't cottoned on.

After the children have been dutifully deposited, Anastasia and I drive to a hotel she likes called The Old Coastie. It is perched on the coastal path, on the outskirts of Trethynion, away from prying eyes. It's not that we're getting up to anything, we're not even flirting, but the school-gate mums are such gossips, so good at misinterpreting. She drives ahead in her Range Rover. I follow her in my car. We wind down country lanes for a few miles until we pull off to the left, into the long driveway of the hotel. Here the vegetation changes. The lane is lined with rhododendrons, so old they are as big as trees. It's February now; they are bulging with heavy buds, waiting to burst into flower in the spring.

We arrive. We park our cars next to each other beneath a gnarled old oak tree that stands in the corner of the car park. As we walk together towards the hotel my hand touches hers by mistake.

The Old Coastie is very sophisticated. Far more sophisticated than the sort of places I usually go to with Jenni. Jenni likes vegetarian cafés with small wooden rackety tables that serve chopped-up salads full of ingredients I do not recognise. If it is my turn to choose we visit a chain that serves pizza or good value steak. Or the Old Boathouse. It leaves a bitter taste in my mouth remembering my last conversation with Jenni there.

Anastasia and I step into The Old Coastie holding hands. Holding hands feels comfortable. The first thing I notice is how peaceful it is. It's only 9:30 in the morning and not many people are here, just an elderly couple on a sofa by the open fire, and a young woman drinking a latte and reading the newspaper. At this time in the morning I would expect it to be quiet, but there is something settled about the room, about the cracked leather chairs, the long polished table laden with newspapers and glossy magazines, something that tells me this is always a place of peace.

We sit on a sofa by a large bay window that looks out across manicured gardens leading to the sea. A chilly February day, the sea looks icy pale, uninviting and distant. We order coffee and American-style cookies. Anastasia insists on the cookies. She says they are mouth-watering here. We still seem to be holding hands.

'Thanks for coming, Craig,' she says, 'I need someone to talk to. It's very kind of you.'

Her brown eyes are so much smaller than Jenni's. So much brighter. So much less plaintive.

'You've had problems and overcome them,' she continues. 'So many people don't understand what I'm going through.' There is a pause. 'I just feel so lonely. So abandoned. I really wanted my relationship to work.'

One sweet tear rolls from her eye, down her soft caramel cheek. She catches it with her finger and pushes it away.

'That's how I felt when Jenni left me,' I say.

'Jenni left you? For how long? How did you get her to come back?'

'I really don't know. Happenstance perhaps. Anyway,' I shrug, 'it's your turn. I want you to go first. Tell me what happened. Get if off your chest.'

I feel your body brace itself; your leg is pressing against mine.

The coffee arrives with its plate of accompanying cookies. We stop holding hands, as if we suddenly realise we are, and know that we shouldn't. The waitress pours the coffee. We thank her. She walks away.

'Come on, Anastasia, tell me what happened with your husband. I've been to hell and back. You don't need to feel embarrassed talking to me.'

'I know I don't need to, but I do.'

She puts her coffee cup down on the table and turns to look at me. She may be heartbroken but she has determination in her eyes.

'Ok then, here goes.' She takes a deep breath, and then, 'Ted's a bond dealer in London. Works all hours. But he set us up to live here. He bought a pied-à-terre in London and we hardly ever saw him. It wasn't supposed to be like that. He was going to work three days a week from here. But he couldn't do it. It was impossible, or so I thought. I wanted to sell the house here and move back to London – but he wouldn't hear of it.' She pauses. 'I expect you can guess the rest?'

'Another woman in London?'

'Well, yes. But worse.'

'Worse?'

'I found out yesterday that he's having a baby with her.'

'Pea-brained idiot.'

'Exactly. That's what I thought.'

Our eyes meet and for some strange reason we both laugh. When the laughing has subsided we both eat a cookie to cheer ourselves up. They are addictive. As soon as I've finished the first, I reach for the next.

'The thing is,' Anastasia says, 'if I'm honest with myself, I had felt for a long time that I didn't know him any more.'

'What was it like when you did know him?'

'It feels so very long ago that I don't remember clearly.'

I sit looking into her eyes, trying to be sympathetic, but I am not sure it is working. As Jenni often reminds me, empathy is not my strong point.

'Actually,' Anastasia says, 'maybe he was right to find someone else. We weren't good together. Ted was very critical, very controlling. I want someone better. Someone who accepts me for what I am, someone I can have fun with.'

'That's what I want as well.'

'I thought you said you were happy with your wife?'

'I said we're still working things out after my affair.'

She stiffens slightly.

'You mentioned that before.' There is a pause. 'Why were you unfaithful?'

'I don't know.' I shrug my shoulders a little. 'Maybe I was already bored of Jenni but I hadn't really realised it.' I pause as I think about it. 'So maybe it was a cry for help.'

291

'Help?'

'Yes. To get our relationship back on track. Or a catalyst for escape.'

She sits finishing off her now cold coffee, contemplating me.

'So you really think an affair is a cry for help?' she asks.

'I don't know — but it's a good excuse.'

'Is it indeed,' she says and starts to giggle. 'I never thought of it like that.'

I've never met a woman like this before, who shrugs off my bad behaviour and laughs.

~ Carly ~

The police are here. When I was younger, we used to call them the pigs. There are three of them. Two men, one woman. Surrounding me. Standing around my bed. A nurse is here, fussing around the pigs. Helping them. Pulling chairs up for them to sit on. Offering to fetch them cups of tea. It's a good job I've got my own room, otherwise all the other patients would be craning their necks. The female pig has beautifully cut hair. She must go to a really expensive hairdresser. In my normal life I would want to find out where. The police have introduced themselves, and shown me their badges, but I've already forgotten their names. I think the woman's name begins with A. They are sitting too close to me, crowding me, making me feel claustrophobic. The darkness of their uniforms shrouds them in seriousness – crime and death hover around them like vultures. Why did we ever call them pigs?

'You wanted to talk to us about what happened to you,' the female officer says, leaning towards me.

Jenni, I told her everything. Do you hear me? Everything that you did.

~ Rob ~

Carly, when I arrive to visit you, you are sitting in your armchair, dressed in the new wrap-around dress that Heather brought in for you yesterday; cornflower blue to match your eyes. Freshly washed curls feather your oval face. You always were a looker, Carly, weren't you? Adding colour to wherever you went. You still do that now. Despite everything. Despite your illness.

Your face lights up as soon as you see me. You stand up and move towards me. You cling on to me so tightly I can only just breathe. I wrap my arms around you, and stroke your back to comfort you.

'Carly, you're doing so well,' I tell you. 'Dr Willis is very pleased with you. He thinks seeing the police has been cathartic. You've moved on in leaps and bounds in recent weeks.'

'It's been so hard, so hard,' you are whispering. 'I can't wait to come home.'

~ Craig ~

Anastasia and I are friends, and I don't mean on Facebook. Since we became friends, I keep finding myself singing a song in my head. An old, old song that I once knew by heart many years ago. A song my grandmother used to like, trumpeted out by Fats Waller. A silly song no one ever sings these days. 'Let's sing again, let music in your heart . . .' It's just stuck in my head and it's so long since I felt like singing anything. I sing it at odd times. On the way to the school drop-off. On the way to the supermarket. Yesterday I found myself humming it in bed.

~ Carly ~

'Come on, Carly, please lie on the couch. Relax. In whatever position suits you best.'

I kick off my shoes and lie flat on my back as usual, arms by my side, staring at the ceiling, at the off-white gloss paint. I close my eyes. The first chords of 'Fingal's Cave' cut into the room. I try to lose myself in it, try to let it wrap around me.

'Breathe in deeply,' Dr Willis instructs. 'Hold it. Hold it. And now let it out. Slowly, slowly, keep pushing, push the anger out.'

I breathe in and out slowly, slowly. In. Out. Slowly, slowly, until I am almost asleep. But the second Dr Willis turns the music off, I sit up.

'I need to talk to you,' I say.

He frowns a gentle frown; a ripple across his forehead.

'Again? But, Carly, I need you to relax.'

'I thought talking was good.'

He suppresses a sigh.

'We're making good progress, Carly. I spoke to Rob about it. About the way you've come on since the police visit.'

'That's what I want to talk about. You told me they found nothing. No evidence. I want to know more detail.'

'OK, OK Carly, I should have explained it a bit more thoroughly, but I didn't want to confuse you until you were feeling well enough to cope.' He pauses. 'Are you sure you're up to this today?'

I'm sitting up on the couch, back straight, arms folded. I fix my eyes into his.

'More than,' I insist.

He takes a deep breath.

'Well, it was a three-point investigation. First, they re-interviewed Sergeant Anita Berry, the police officer who visited Jenni's flat the night you were brought into hospital. Second, they ran a background check on Jenni.' He pauses. 'Finally, they had their forensic team re-run a test on your blood, the night you came in to us. And . . .'

Raising my hands and eyes to the ceiling, I finish his sentence for him.

'They found no evidence to suggest Jenni poisoned me,' my voice is tense, stretched.

'That's right.'

I sit looking at him. At his confidence. His slimy comb-over. At his bow tie. My anger is solid. Contained and immovable. No one believes me while I'm incarcerated in here. He leans towards me. I know what he is going to say.

'Your treatment won't really move forward until you fully accept what has happened.' There is a pause. 'The sooner you accept you attempted suicide for the second time, the sooner we will be able to confront your issues and the sooner you will be able to go home. You want that, don't you?'

My anger is my power, my energy.

'You know I want that, yes,' I tell him.

'Come on, Carly, let's try again. Another relaxation therapy.'

He puts the music back on. I lie back and prepare myself to tolerate it. My anger is my power, my energy. I will keep it buried deep inside me, and use it to escape.

~ Craig ~

I shouldn't be fucking Anastasia. I promised myself, I promised Jenni that I would never be unfaithful again. But when I am with Anastasia the rest of the world disintegrates; I see nothing but her.

It is not just that I'm fucking her, I'm fucking in love with her. I know I should stop but I cannot. I need more time. I will sort my life out so that I can be with her properly. I will let Jenni down gently. Everything will work out. Everything will be all right. One day. I will take control of my life. One day I will do everything right.

~ Jenni ~

Rob asked me to return to Stansfield, Carly, to visit you. It's a long way to come, a big ask for me these days, taking a day off work, getting up early to catch the fast train, making sure Craig is organised to look after the children. He has seemed so distracted lately. Less argumentative towards me about my love of the Lord. Less critical of my vegetarian diet. A bit scatter-brained. I hope he isn't about to be ill. I had to be very clear with him about the children's routine while I was away. But despite how much trouble it has been to get here, I'm glad I've come, Carly. Rob says that because of your paranoia towards me, it's very important you see me before you are released from hospital.

Your eyes are smiling at me like they used to, before you were ill. I hold your hands. They feel warm in mine.

'I needed you to come,' you tell me, 'because I wanted to show you that I'm better. Really better this time. I know I've been delusional, and my delusions being about you must have been very difficult for you. But . . .' You pause, and press your blue eyes into mine. 'I really am through it now.'

Your candyfloss hair shimmers in the dead electric light of

the hospital. For a second it makes you look ephemeral, like a ghost. Whatever you say about how much better you are, you've been so ill for so long, I can't help but be suspicious that you're being overly positive.

'What's made such a difference?' I ask, trying to suppress the concern in my voice.

'My drugs have been more carefully balanced. Aeons of CBT with the man who practically invented it. So you can't get better than that. And I just feel right.' You smile and raise your forearms in the air. 'My illness is no longer part of me. I have stepped away from it. It's as if a switch has suddenly been pressed in my mind and I'm free. Everything is back to how it was before my depression ever began. As if my depression never happened.'

'I've read that people who are cured often say this,' I reply.

'Yes, well, that's what's happened. I mean, I'm still on a cocktail of drugs, including Prozac, and probably will be for the rest of my life. But what's wrong with that? They're simply balancing my brain biochemistry. My serotonin. The world seems a different colour to me now, Jenni.'

'What colour was it in the first place?' I ask tentatively.

'Black. Blacker than black. '

Blacker than black. I shudder inside. Please God, I pray. Please God, make sure she makes a full recovery this time. If not, it's too much for all of us. Too much for me. Too much for Rob. Dear God, please do not put us through this again.

~ Carly ~

Last time Rob drove me home from hospital I was on a neon high, the outside world moving past me like a cinema screen, every detail sharpened and enhanced. I remember rain slicing into puddles. Today as Rob is driving me home, the world is soft and normal. Today I am really going home.

~ Rob ~

My heart sings with praise for the Lord. I have my Carly back. The real Carly. The one I met in hospital so many years ago. Last time she came home she was over-exhilarated; like a distended balloon, her drinking still out of control. One gentle pinprick and she might have popped. But now she smiles like she used to smile, her lips move in tune with her eyes. She laughs at things that used to make her laugh. She cries at things that used to make her cry. She is in balance with the tempo and rhythm of the universe. She has the balance necessary to survive.

~ Carly ~

Easter weekend and we are escaping Stansfield – all five of us piled into our Volvo estate. Even though we haven't left yet I am beginning to smell the sea, astringent in my nostrils, making my heart jump at the memory of family holidays. We always used to have a family tradition, the first person to see the sea had to shout 'Neptune!' As we approach the coast I'll get our children to do the same. Our children are laughing and joking, quipping about the Gospels. Excited about seeing Jenni. They always liked her so much. We hardly ever see her now. That thought causes me to ache inside. An ache of regret for my aggressive behaviour. No wonder she moved away to make a fresh start. But I should feel positive. My life has been going so well since I came out of hospital. I am Carly Burton again. The person I was when I married Rob. Carly Burton *Bright*.

That's what my friends used to call me. That's how I feel now. Shiny. Happy. Bright.

Travelling to the southern tip of Cornwall is an almost endless journey. Or at least that is how it seems to me; for many, many hours we see nothing but a grey expanse of motorway. We listen to Stephen Fry reading *Harry Potter*. We play I Spy. Everyone, except Rob who is driving, has inter-mittent sleep. Eventually the scenery becomes more interesting as we leave the M5 and take the A38 towards Dartmoor. At one point I wake from a doze and see Daphne du Maurier's Jamaica Inn.

At last, minds and limbs stiff from travelling, we arrive at Trethynion, the fishing village near Penzance that Jenni and Craig have run away to. Their village is chocolate box pretty. Tooth-like cottages glued together in a horseshoe around a small harbour dotted with fishing boats. The village has a pub, a newsagents and a disused lifeboat station, nothing much else, and I suspect that most of the cottages are let out to holiday-makers. So is it real? Does it have life? Jenni says so when I talk to her on the phone. Turquoise sea and white-washed cottages. Gulls calling above us, telling tales of the ocean. People from the past: pirates, smugglers, fishermen, whispering to me.

Craig and Jenni step out of their cottage, hug and kiss us and guide us to where we can park, in a bend in the road opposite the lifeboat station. When the car is parked Jenni and I hug again. Her arms feel like sticks in mine. She is thinner than ever. Craig towers over her and smiles at me distantly without making eye contact. Craig, you don't need to ignore me. I am safe now. Can't you see that?

We check in to the pub where we're staying because Jenni and Craig don't have enough room to put us up, and then we all meet up in the bar. The children are so pleased to see each other they can't keep still. None of them can, not even Pippa who is doing her best to be sensible, trying to get the boys to play cards. She stands in front of me, hands on her hips.

'Mummy, if they don't start to behave soon I'll take them for a walk.'

Not sure I want to be worrying about my offspring walking on the harbour wall in the dark, I try to distract them by giving them some money for the jukebox. As Metallica grunts from the shimmering contraption in the corner I regret my idea. Why don't children come with an off button? Fortunately, before too long they are occupied, building houses with beer mats, necking fizzy drinks and crunching crisps. Jenni and I are sitting next to each other, sharing a bottle of Rioja. Craig and Rob are nursing their pints across the table from us, in this pub with its beams and brass, nooks and crannies. The ceiling is covered in pottery beer mugs hanging on hooks. The patterned carpet and velvet curtains look as if they have been there about fifty years. Jenni looks at me with her chocolate-drop eyes.

'Congrats on doing so well in your exam. Nurse Practitioner. Such a step up,' I say.

'My confidence is improving. There was a time when I first went back to work that I never would have thought I could do this.'

'I'm sorry. I'm so sorry. It can't have helped how I treated you when you first came to our surgery.'

She puts her hand on my arm.

'Please, Carly, stop apologising. You didn't mean it. It's all water under the bridge now.'

'Thankfully.'

I turn to look at Craig. He seems distracted, ignoring Rob, looking out of the window. He suddenly gets up.

'Excuse me a moment. Just had a text from a fireman from another watch, he's just outside in the car park. The guvnor wants me to ask him a favour, since I know him, and I might as well talk to him in person since he's outside. It'll save a phone call later if I go and speak to him now. Do you mind?'

'Of course not,' Jenni says.

He leans down and kisses her before marching out of the pub. I want to know what he is up to. To see what his work colleague is like. To see a slice of his life. So I stand up and tell

Jenni and Rob that I need the loo. But when I reach the entrance to the pub, instead of turning left to go to the ladies cloakroom, I turn right and step outside through the pub's arched front door. But I do not see Craig in the car park. I see a large figure that must be him further away on the harbour wall. He is rushing towards a tall blonde woman who is standing looking out to sea. He walks in front of her and she turns towards him. He puts his hands on her waist, he pulls her towards him and kisses her. Tender as tender can be. Craig, how can you do this? You are disgusting. How dare you double-cross Jenni again? My heart thumps in anger as I march back to the pub. You are lucky she hasn't found out yet. Kissing someone else in public. So far, so good for you – Jenni is still talking to Rob.

Craig, what are you doing with a giant of a woman almost as tall as yourself?

Why do you want someone else except Jenni, when you didn't want me?

Tell me, Craig. Please.

~ Craig ~

I am lying in Anastasia's bed, nestled between sheets of Egyptian cotton, holding her in my arms.

'Anastasia, she knows.'

'Jenni?'

'No, Carly. Jenni's friend from when we lived in Stansfield. She saw us on the harbour wall when she was in the pub.'

'How do you know?'

'When we were canoodling, I turned around briefly. I thought I saw her standing by the doorway of the pub, frowning towards us.' I pause. 'I wasn't sure. But she had such a horrid look on her face when I went back into the pub.'

'Did she say anything?'

'Only with her eyes. I think the woman's dangerous. She's a bitch. I know her. It's only a matter of time before she tells Jenni.'

'Carly, is she the woman you told me about? The one that was infatuated with you and caused all the trouble?'

'Yes.'

Anastasia clings on to me more tightly.

'Craig, I love you. The last thing I want to do is to make

your life difficult. Do you think we should hold off for a while?'

'We should.' I pull her towards me and kiss her caramel lips. 'But I can't, Anastasia, I can't manage without you. We'll have to take the risk.'

~ Jenni ~

I feel you moving further away from me again, Craig. Further than our usual differences. An extra feeling of distance. It started several weeks ago as a nebulous feeling, like a mist of rain hanging in the air, brushing against my skin and making it feel wet when it isn't even raining. But it's becoming more solid. After how you behaved with Carly I will not be made a cuckold of again. This time I'm on it. Checking your phone messages when you're asleep. Infiltrating your email. Frisking every pocket, every place you put your fingers. So far all I've found are arrangements to meet firemen at the pub, a dry cleaning receipt and two toffee wrappers. But wherever you go, whatever you do, Craig, I'm warning you – you need to be vigilant. And because I haven't caught you yet, I'm upping the surveillance.

I book a day off work without telling you, get dressed, take the children to school because it is my turn and pretend to leave for the hospital. But I double back on myself, park my car in the space reserved for guests by the lifeboat station and wait. Half an hour later your car slithers past.

At home doing paperwork today? Where are you going, Craig?

I follow you, like a heroine in a TV crime series. On TV the heroine always makes it look easy, back relaxed into her seat, perfectly made-up eyes seeing easily into the distance. But I am leaning forward, neck stretched, eyes bulging, trying to keep your little grey Polo in sight, trying to keep at least one car between us so that you don't see me.

You're leaving our fishing village and pulling onto the A road towards Penzance. You turn off into the next village and with so little traffic, I am forced to hover further back. Winding lanes and tumultuous hedgerows. So many bends I feel sick. You pull into a crescent drive. I park my car behind the hedge. I watch from behind an oak tree. You have slung our Polo clumsily across a Georgian doorway with an air of easy familiarity. You are smoothing your jacket and ringing the doorbell. The Palladian house stretches either side of you, a house with the symmetry of beauty. Perfection. Perfection surrounding it; manicured hedges, gently sloping lawns of felt. Perfection steps from perfection, tosses her head and kisses you.

Judas, Judas, Craig.

~ Craig ~

Everywhere I go, Jenni, your eyes follow me. You even comment about the length of time I spend on the lavatory. But surely if you'd found out about Ana you would have come clean about it?

~ Jenni ~

Craig, love of my life, my dear heart, since I bought you that present, that brand new iPhone with a tracker in it, I know where you are at all times. I know where you go, Craig. I know. You go mostly to her house, the one she once shared with her husband. Sometimes you walk along the cliffs. Sometimes you hold hands as you stroll along the beach. Sometimes you swank it up at The Old Coastie. Sometimes you go to the pub. I know where you go. I imagine what you do. It's what you do that torments me. It's what you do that eats me up.

~ Carly ~

Saturday afternoon. I ring your mobile, Jenni, and you pick up immediately. Where are you? The line isn't clear. It sounds muffled, as if it's windy. Are you on the cliff pathway walking towards the church? You took us there when we visited. Do you remember, Jenni? You and Rob went into the church. I waited outside. I don't like churches. They stifle me. Take away my breath.

'Are you all right, Jenni?' I ask.

'Yes,' you say.

You say yes, but I know from the tone of your voice that you mean no.

'What are you up to?' I ask.

'Walking,' you reply.

'To the church?'

'Past the church — along the cliff towards the next village.'

'Sounds windy.'

'It's blowing a few cobwebs away.'

'Where are the children?'

'At a party in the village. I'm picking them up later.'

'What about Craig?'

'Out with a friend.'

Your voice whines in the wind, tight and taut, like an over-strung violin.

Out with a friend? Have you found out about his Amazonian woman? Found out that he's double-crossed you? He hasn't just double-crossed you. He's double-crossed me. Why does he want someone else except you, when he didn't want me?

~ Craig ~

Lying in bed with Ana. Buried in her scent. Buried in her eyes. Wanting this moment to go on forever. Midday sun playing around the curtain edges, reminding me that there is a world outside.

'When are you going to tell her?' Ana asks.

'Give me two weeks. I'll tell her when the boys go to stay with her father for the half-term holiday. It'll be best to deal with it when they're out of the way. She went apoplectic over Carly and I didn't love her. This time she'll be . . .' I pause. 'Well . . . she'll crucify me. Or send me to burn in the fires of hell.'

'Do you really think she's dangerous?'

I laugh.

'No. Of course not.'

'You don't sound very convincing. And what about the other one? Carly. The one that kept pestering you for ages after you broke it off. What about her? Is she dangerous too?'

~ Carly ~

Pippa is helping my mother lay the table. She is nearly nine now, tall for her age, long and leggy, looking absurdly grown-up in her Levi jeans and the Victoria's Secret sweat top that Mother bought her last Christmas. I am cooking pasta, heating up a ready-made sauce, about to call the boys in from the garden, when Rob arrives home from the surgery. He makes his way across the kitchen to kiss me first. He always kisses me first. His kiss tastes of sandalwood and kindness. Rob is so kind. Always will be. Always was. His kindness has helped me survive. After kissing me he turns his attention to my mother and Pippa.

Soon the pasta is steaming on the table, and the boys have been hauled in from the endless game of handball they play together across a net they have strung across the whole width of the garden. Pippa has forced them to wash their hands before they sit down. As I sit at the head of the table, doling out pasta, I tell Rob, 'I rang Jenni today.'

The atmosphere in the room tightens around me.

'How is she?' Rob asks.

'There's something wrong in her life right now.'

Rob's looking at me, eyes blazing with concern. Concern for me? Or concern for Jenni?

'How do you know? What did she say?'

'She didn't say anything. I just know.'

His face is stern.

'If she didn't say anything, how do you know?'

'I just do,' I tell him emphatically.

He is sitting staring at me, pasta going cold in front of him.

'That's what you said when you . . . you know . . .'

He means when I thought she'd poisoned me. He doesn't want to repeat it in front of the children.

'You need to stop this "I just know" business,' he continues, stabbing his fork into his pasta ferociously.

'I'm better now, Rob. Not everything I say and do is wrong.'

~ Jenni ~

Judas. You have returned from a quick pint with your firemen's watch – just in time to babysit. I'm off to a PCC party in the vestry, leaving you to spend the evening flicking the remote at the TV. But there won't be anything on to your taste; I have porno-protected the set.

'I thought I saw Carly today,' I tell you as I reach for my coat from the hooks by the door.

You look up, surprised.

'Really?'

'I followed her from the car park. She was marching purposefully up towards the pub. A lunchtime rendezvous, I imagine. She was moving so quickly I couldn't catch up with her. I yelled, Carly! Carly! Carly! and she turned around. That's when I thought it must be that big woman from school – Ana, I think she's called. She looks a bit like Carly from the distance. I couldn't really see which one of them it was – but Carly wouldn't travel so far for no reason, so it couldn't be her.'

I watch him like a hawk. His face doesn't change.

Judas. Judas, Craig.

'So did you talk to her, then?'

'No. As soon as I decided that I was being stupid and that it couldn't possibly be Carly, I just turned and walked the other way.'

I slip into my coat and step across the room to kiss him goodbye.

'I won't be late. One-pot boeuf bourguignon in the oven. And I've decanted a bottle of Louis Jadot for you. Beaujolais Villages. Your favourite.' I blow you a kiss as I leave. 'Enjoy.'

~ Craig ~

You step out into the night. I hear the door close behind you. Playing games with me, mentioning Carly, mentioning Ana. They're not that alike. Are they alike in your mind? Are you telling me that you know? The truth will be common knowledge soon. I will have to face the truth and so will you. If you know now, I can stand up to you. I can cope with your anger. I was only waiting a little longer to make it easier for the boys. The TV screen flickers in front of me. Unwatched. Irrelevant. I turn my mind in on itself to concentrate on my feelings for you, Jenni. But I cannot feel anything. All I feel is numbness. I used to think I loved you, but actually, I think what I had was a desire to protect you.

You drain me. Ana feeds me.

Ana. Ana. Ana. I wish I had met her ten years ago. The things we could have done together. Ana listens to me. She makes me laugh. Laughter is powerful. She knows I'm not perfect and she doesn't mind. She forgives me. Her life is her own, not crowded out by Jesus.

Jesus.

Jenni, your religious fixations are getting worse. Now you go to church every day. You pray every morning and every evening for an hour, sitting in the lotus position, burning joss sticks, listening to monastic chants, joining in with an eerie whisper. What once seemed lovable and quirky about you, now has become other worldly, as if your life is on hold, waiting to be lived in heaven. Ana is like me, living in the moment. I need to break away from you, Jenni, to allow myself to step into each day properly. I have confused infatuation with love and now I need to pull away. How will I tell you? How will I explain? I begin to imagine it.

'We need to talk.'

A calm voice. Deadpan delivery. A deep breath.

'We need to talk, Jenni. I fear I've made a terrible mistake coming back to you. We've grown apart. The fairest thing to do for both of us is to share custody of the boys and separate.'

'I've been feeling the same, Craig; we both need space.'

Your hand is on my arm. You are smiling sadly.

'We don't need to instruct solicitors, let's sort things out with a mediator.'

Or. A second scenario.

'We need to talk, Jenni. I fear I've made a terrible mistake coming back to you. We've grown apart. The fairest thing to do for both of us is to share custody of the boys and separate.'

'I'll fucking kill you, Craig.' Red faced. Sharp fisted.

I push the image of Jenni's spitting eyes away and become aware of the heady scent of boeuf bourguignon, bouquet garni and bay leaf. Jenni has cooked my favourite meal. As I pour myself a glass of wine a wave of guilt pulses through me. I slump back onto the sofa, sipping the wine, trying to process the TV picture. *Midsomer Murders*. Filmed on a village green lined with thatched cottages. A body discovered in front of a yew hedge, found by an old lady riding past on a bicycle with a basket on the front. The wine I am drinking tastes a bit sharp. A bit lemony.

As if I've just cleaned my teeth. Maybe it's just too cold. Maybe I should put it on the Aga to warm it up. I stand up and the world falls away.

SIX

~ Rob ~

As our car pushes into the night, Carly sits next to me red eyed and tight lipped. Her emotion cuts into me, threatening me. I had come to terms with what happened between Carly and Craig. Its insignificance.

But Craig's death has enhanced its importance.

Death eulogising facts. What is wrong with me tonight? I thought I had moved past this.

'How do you think Jenni is coping?' Carly says between sniffs.

'You know my theory. She'll be numb at the moment.'

Our car batters into the night for hour upon hour. Carly falls asleep. I put the radio on. We arrive at 2 a.m., too late to check in to the pub, but we are armed with futons and sleeping bags and Jenni knows we are coming, so we knock. She comes to the door in her dressing gown, face swollen from weeping.

'Thank God you're here,' she whispers, clinging first to Carly and then to me.

Clinging to me like she used to, as if I am precious. We step inside the cottage, dumping our luggage by the door. Jenni and

Carly slump next to each other on the sofa. Jenni has retrieved a tumbler of whisky from the floor by the sofa.

'Help yourself,' she says, gesticulating towards the decanter and glasses on the dresser behind the sofa.

I pour Carly and me a generous slug each and sink next to Jenni on the sofa.

'What happened?' I ask.

'I told you on the phone. When I came back from the PCC party I found him dead on the floor. Right here.'

She points to the carpet in front of her. She is sobbing now, shoulder-heaving sobs, struggling for breath. Carly and I sit one each side of her, arms around her back, holding her.

~ Jenni ~

Inspector Browning is sitting in the corner of the sofa. In Craig's place. The place he must have stood up from just before he collapsed. I'm sitting in a floral armchair opposite him. Inspector Browning, here yet again, invading my space. His third visit this week. Doesn't he appreciate the anxiety I am wading through? What does he know about trauma? The trauma of finding a husband purple-faced. No longer a husband, but a stiff upon the floor? What does he know about the post-traumatic stress syndrome I am being pulled towards? Forensics crawling all over my cottage doesn't help, and neither does the painfully slow progress of the autopsy. The only person who is helping is Rob. Carly is trying to help, but somehow I get the feeling she is only just coping herself. Her attitude is too ethereal, all wistful sighs and staring out of the window. My mobile rings. I look at the screen.

'I need to take this, Inspector.'

We are in an area of poor reception so my father's voice crackles down the phone line like a Dalek.

'Jenni, are you all right?' he warbles.

'I'm as all right as I can be,' I say.

'Just to let you know the children are OK. A bit quiet, but I've been distracting them. We've been baking.'

'Dad, thanks. Inspector Browning is here so I'll ring you later on. On the landline.'

'Inspector Browning. Again?'

'Again.'

'Chin up. Love you.'

'Love you too.'

I click the phone off and the image of my boys icing fairy cakes falls away, leaving me looking at the beaded pearls of sweat peppered across Inspector Browning's forehead. He frowns.

'This must be very difficult for you,' he says in a crusty northern voice.

'Difficult doesn't quite cover it,' I reply.

'I'm sorry, Mrs Rossiter, but I need to ask you a few more questions.'

'Fire away.'

'Tell me again where you found the suicide note.'

'On the dresser, behind the sofa, behind where he collapsed.'

The inspector is looking at me, eagle-eyed.

'Please take me through it again, why you didn't give it to us immediately?'

I sigh inside. Here we go again, for the fifth time.

'I was devastated when I found the body. It was a while before I realised there was a note on the dresser. After I'd read it I was heart-broken and distracted. Far too upset to think about protocol, you know what with the emergency services arriving and everything – so I just folded it up and put it in my pocket.' I take a deep breath.

The inspector is frowning at me.

'And what eventually triggered you to remember that we might be interested in it?'

'Later on when I was getting ready for bed, after they'd taken

328

Craig's body away, as I took off my jeans, I realised it was there. Remembered about it. Before that I was just thinking about Craig being dead.' I paused. 'And then I telephoned you immediately.'

'Were you shocked by its contents?'

'Of course I was shocked. I had no idea my husband was conflicted between me and Anastasia Donaldson.'

~ Carly ~

Jenni, staying at your cottage at the moment is difficult. Watching you so woebegone, so bereft, your saucer-like eyes more pitiful than ever. Missing my children. At least your children are being spared the funeral plans as you have dispatched them to your father's. I have no privacy here, no time to myself, no time on my own with Rob, as the cottage is crawling with police and funeral arrangements. Hopefully progress towards the funeral will speed up when the inquest is over.

The police have interviewed you about your husband's death. How did that make you feel, Jenni? And now Inspector Browning is interviewing me, in the living room of your compact cottage, droplets of perspiration adorning his forehead. He wipes them away with a large white cotton handkerchief.

'Can I get you a glass of water?' I ask.

'No, thanks, Mrs Burton, this won't take long. I'll get straight to the point,' he says as he puts his handkerchief in his pocket. 'Did you have an affair with Mr Rossiter?'

I feel as if I've been punched in the stomach. I wasn't expecting to be asked about Craig.

'Yes,' I reply, wishing he hadn't started on this. My relation-ship with Craig is ancient history.

'For how long?'

'It didn't last long.' I sigh. 'It was a long time ago now. It was of no significance.'

'How can an affair be of no significance?' he asks, eyes narrowing.

'Because it was just sexual. Have you heard the expression "fuck-buddy", Inspector? It was like that.'

His body stiffens as I utter the words 'fuck-buddy'. Inspector Browning; a man who never fucks – a man who always makes love.

'And did you know about Anastasia?' he asks.

'I thought he was seeing someone because I saw him kissing a leggy blonde when we visited a few months ago, but I didn't know her name.'

'Saw him?' He pauses. 'Where?'

'We were all at the pub together – the one in the middle of Trethynion – their family and mine. We'd come to stay for the weekend. I went to the loo, and then I didn't feel too good. I needed a bit of fresh air so I went to the front door of the pub and stepped outside. That's when I saw him. On the harbour wall with the blonde.'

'And did you tell Jenni about this woman?'

'No. I didn't want to upset her.'

'She never mentioned her to you?'

'No.'

'And then? What happened then? Did you confront Craig about it? Tell Rob?'

'And then – nothing – we've been back home in Stansfield, we hadn't seen Jenni or Craig until we received Jenni's call telling us that Craig was dead.' I pause for breath before I continue. 'It was the most terrible shock.'

I sit looking around the tiny cottage, at the inspector filling the space where Craig used to sit, regret piercing into me. Perhaps the inspector is right.

There is no such thing as an affair that doesn't mean anything.

~ Rob ~

An hour's journey to the coroner's court. Hands on the wheel. Eyes on the road. Too many lorries driving too close together, overtaking each other on hills, slowing us down. Jenni in the front passenger seat, Carly directly behind her. The silence between us is solid. Tangible. Last night we talked and talked and drank and drank, which is why I am having to push through a weary body and a headache to concentrate. I turn the radio on. Classic FM. As the stilted resonance of violin and oboe slices into the car, the atmosphere tightens.

For a second I take my eyes off the road to look across at Jenni. Her eyelids, already closed, seem to clamp shut more tightly, her skin flickering, twitching. Her hands are clasped together as if she is praying. Jenni Rossiter, praying mantis. That's what Carly used to say before her first breakdown. Well, Jenni looks like that today. Today, on this day of conclusions. Of rubber stamping. Of ritual release. This day we need to pass through.

I look in the rearview mirror and Carly's pale blue eyes catch mine. Eyes that tell me she wants to go home. Eyes that are tired of staying in Jenni's small, cramped cottage, sweating with Craig's memory, wanting to go home and recover from the shock of his death in our own environment. Eyes that want to go home to her mother, to her children. Eyes tired of endless visits from funeral directors with tight-lipped sincerity wearing black cashmere coats whatever the weather. People too familiar with death. The stigma of death clinging to them.

Craig. An ordinary bloke whom death has eulogised. Jenni and Carly, both devastated by his death. And what about Anastasia, the mysterious woman he was shagging? Craig has left heartbreak in his wake. If I popped off like this would anyone care, really care like this about me? A stab of unreasonable envy cuts into me. For how can I reasonably envy a man whose decomposing body is soon to be buried? A man whose life has been cut short aged just forty.

At last we pull into the car park of County Hall, a modern concrete and glass monstrosity surrounded by grass. No trees. No flowers. No softness. We get out of the car. Carly and Jenni link arms and walk slowly across the car park like a pair of old ladies; broken and twisted, clinging on to each other with rounded shoulders, looking at the ground instead of the horizon so as not to miss their footing. I walk behind them. Has his loss brought them closer together?

We arrive, moving through rotating glass doors. We are vetted by security. An usher directs us to court four on the second floor. We trip to the lavatory. To the coffee machine. We sit waiting, lifting plastic cups containing tasteless warm liquid to our lips. Looking at the magnolia wall. At the floor. Until, after what seems like hours, it's time to go in.

I take the women's hands in mine. Both of them are trembling, as if they have advanced Parkinson's disease.

Despite the brutalistic modernity of this County Hall, the coroner's court is standard, unremarkable. Like a miniature magistrate's court. We sit at the front, still holding hands. We stand up in respect when the coroner arrives; he is about sixty with a ruddy face and white hair. Like a slim Father Christmas. He sits down. We sit down. He looks straight at us as he speaks.

'I do not need any more time over this. I have read the evidence. I have studied the autopsy report. My conclusion is suicide by drug overdose.'

~ Carly ~

It pours with rain on the day of Craig's funeral, bullets of
metallic liquid exploding on the bonnet of the car as we follow
the funeral cortege along the main road towards the church.
Jenni has insisted on walking there via the cliff path. Alone. We
all offered to accompany her: me, Rob, her father, her children,
several of Craig's colleagues from the fire brigade. But no. Jenni
wanted time to herself. She set off half an hour before us,
decked head to toe in Gore-Tex, striding out in her leather
walking boots, something soft and black to change into in her
backpack.

The car carrying Craig's coffin leads the way. The second
car contains Craig's parents, Jenni's father and the children.
Rob and I have the third to ourselves. Shiny black cars in
convoy, shouting of death. Rob is looking straight ahead, at
the back of the driver's head, a hardness in his face that I
have not seen before. As if he is putting a protective layer
around himself, pretending not to be here. The car smells of
furniture polish and grief. Of suppressed tears. Funerals are
hell on earth. When I die I do not want one. I want a
non-funeral. I heard about them on the radio. Held at the

crematorium. The coffin goes straight into the incinerator. No hymns. No prayers. No vicar. No congregation. No fuss. The family don't even have to be there. Perfect for people like me who aren't religious. When I discussed it with Rob he said,

'Funerals aren't for the deceased. They're for the people left behind.'

'So you think not having a funeral is selfish?'

'Yes. If you can be selfish after you're dead.'

Craig's funeral is to be very unselfish. Hymns, organ music and lilies. A personalised eulogy. Pallbearers. Ushers. An order of service with a picture of Craig on the front. We have spent hours and hours finalising microscopic details. And nobody has done more than Jenni.

The cortege pulls off the main road and begins to snake uphill, along lanes framed with overflowing hedgerows. The hill is steep. The cortege slows and struggles. Rob reaches across to hold my hand.

'Not far now,' he mutters.

When the shiny black cars are parked in a line, we get out and fists of wind and rain punch our faces. Shivering, we bow our heads and rush towards the church. As soon as we enter I see Jenni kneeling in the middle of the front pew, changed from her waterproofs into black silk, a waterfall of white pearls at her neck, hands clasped together, praying. Her family are moving towards her but she doesn't open her eyes. She doesn't stop praying. Her father, Stuart, is holding the boys against his body, one on each side, squashing them against him as if he wants to engulf them. I can only see the backs of their heads. Their shiny hair.

Rob and I sit in the middle of the church. I close my eyes for a second but do not pray. I open them quickly and sit waiting and watching. Watching Craig's elderly parents walk down the aisle slowly, leaning on sticks. So thin. So fragile. Can a parent ever cope with seeing this?

His chums from the fire brigade arrive with their burly shoulders and strong faces. Sad but not too sad. Suppressing the shared jokes that bind them together. Grinning at each other surreptitiously with their eyes. Sharing a bullish, boyish sense of denial. The landlord from the pub is here, sitting behind the fire brigade crowd, holding hands with his wife.

I turn around to see what is happening behind me. I realise with a start that Anastasia Donaldson is entering the church. She is wearing a floral headscarf to try and disguise herself. She sits at the back, head bowed, but she cannot spare me from her sculptured cheekbones and small darting eyes.

Why did he want her, when he didn't want me? I silently will her to go away before Jenni sees her. Jenni, he loved her more than he loved either of us. Does that hurt you as much as it hurts me?

The organ begins to resonate through the church and I pull my eyes away from Anastasia and face the front. The vicar has arrived. The pallbearers are shuffling in with the coffin. Then it comes to me, clear as day: Jenni should move back to Stansfield. We need another nurse practitioner at the surgery. Stansfield is where she grew up. Stansfield is where she belongs. I am better now. I love my friend and want to protect her. If she comes back to Stansfield she will be safe from the humiliation of Craig's relationship with Anastasia Donaldson. Rob and I will protect her.

~ Jenni ~

At Carly's suggestion, after my sad bereavement, I have moved from Cornwall back to Stansfield to be near my old friends. To take the job of Nurse Practitioner at Riverside Surgery. A GP Nurse Practitioner. My dream job. I am sitting in my old flat above the shop in Stansfield, drinking a cup of black coffee before I go to work. Fortunately we didn't sell this flat. We kept it and let it out. But now, the decor looks tired. The oriental throws are less bright. The shaggy carpet less fat. So I'm working hard when I'm not at the surgery, brightening my home with a lick of paint. Being busy right now reduces some of my aching loneliness. The wide, stretching ache that never goes away.

My life is so different without Craig.

I still have my boys. Children are supposed to be such a comfort. But just at the moment all they do is remind me of my husband. I still have my father. I still have my friendship with Rob and Carly. And of course, I still have God. I will always have God. But, after everything that has happened even God seems more distant at the moment.

So I sit on my battered old sofa, stroking the dog while he

softly wags his tail, swigging the end of my black coffee, looking forward to going to work. At least I don't have to worry about the boys today; last night they slept at their friends' house, and another mother is taking them to school. I extricate myself from the dog who watches me wistfully as I put my coffee cup in the sink and reach for my handbag and coat. The sun is blinking in through my living room window as I walk across the flat, making my world a little less grey.

Walking through Stansfield, everything seems almost the same. Except a few of the shops have closed. And the council have improved the pavements. The lap-dancing club across the road from the surgery has become a nail bar. I'm not sure why we ever had a lap-dancing club here in the first place. I wrote to the council complaining about it when we lived here before. So did Rob. Carly told us both off for being provincial. Provincial. What did she mean by that? She was so friendly at first but now she is worried about my return, I know she is. She has been guarding Rob with her eyes; I see her worry building every day. I turn right at the lights on the high street, into the surgery entrance.

'Good morning,' I say to Sharon, who nods her woolly head.

'Good morning,' I say to Carly.

Carly. So curvy. So Marilyn Monroe sexy. No wonder Craig succumbed to her charms. Craig and Carly. Craig and Anastasia. My jaw clenches.

'See you later,' I say and scuttle away.

Through the waiting room and along the corridor to my brand new consulting room with state-of-the-art equipment and lilac painted walls. I close the door and inhale deeply. I move across my room, sit at my desk and switch on my computer to check my day's patient list. My first patient is a widow like me. Except her husband died of natural causes.

Five minutes later, my patient sits in front of me. Ninety

years old. Wearing a long skirt and a green jumper. Fingers gnarled like bent tree trunks. Skin like potato peel. She has tried to brighten herself up with green eye shadow and red lipstick. But her eyesight is going and she obviously can't put her eye shadow on properly. It is above and below her eyes, making her look like a green-eyed panda. Her skin is so threaded with wrinkles that her lipstick has not managed to stay on her lips, but is seeping into the grooves of her face.

She starts to describe her aches and pains. She has had nearly every major joint replaced, both hips, one shoulder, both knees. So only one major joint left. Benign tumour on her ovary. So many aches, so many pains. When she has finished telling me I have to ask her to repeat them.

She starts again. Chest pain: I check her heart with my stethoscope. It sounds fine, but I carry out an ECG, just in case. The ECG is fine.

A pain beneath the left ribcage. I can't make head nor tail of that.

I put my hand on her arm. 'Mrs Wade, we need to refer you to a cardiologist and gynaecologist. I'll talk your case through with Doctor Burton and ring you tomorrow to let you know who will contact you.'

She is looking at me, eyes wide with concern. She looks as if she is about to cry.

I am only just getting used to diagnosis. Reassurance is more difficult.

'Please don't worry,' I try. 'We'll get this sorted.'

She puts her head in her hands. I stand up and bend down next to her. I put my arm around her back.

'I'll tell you what, wait here, I'll go and speak to Dr Burton now.'

I catch Rob between patients. He listens intently and then comes back with me into my consulting room. Mrs Wade's eyes relax when she sees him. Dr Burton, the most popular GP in Stansfield.

'Thank you for coming to see me, Dr Burton,' Mrs Wade purrs.

He kneels down next to her and takes both of her hands in his. She looks into his eyes.

'Meg, I agree with Nurse Rossiter. A cardiologist and a gynae doctor will sort you out. We will make sure you get seen as soon as possible. I'll ring the hospital this afternoon. And in the meantime you must try and stop worrying. This can be sorted out. It is highly treatable.'

'Really, Doctor?'

'Yes. Really.'

'Thank you.'

He stands up, still smiling at her. Showing her his dimple. Her eyes melt into his.

She pulls herself up from the chair.

'Thank you, both,' she says as she walks slowly out of my room, balancing on her stick.

'A tricky customer. Always fearing there's something else wrong with her,' Rob says as soon as she has closed the door behind her. 'It must be so frightening being on your own at her age.'

'It is at any age.'

We stand looking at each other. I drink him in. His little-boy-lost look. His kindness.

'Thanks for coming to help me,' I say. 'It'll take me a while to build my patients' trust.' A pause. Fixing his eyes in mine. 'Could you come for a drink with me after surgery tonight? To talk things through about our patients?'

'Jenni, no. We're not going for drinks on our own.'

'You don't need to look so deadpan.'

'Jenni,' he says. 'This isn't a joke.'

342

~ Rob ~

We stand looking at each other like we used to. Your hair is shorter than it used to be. Dyed a funky copper colour. It makes you look young and edgy.

'Jenni, no. We're not going for drinks on our own,' I say, trying to sound as if I mean it this time.

'You don't need to look so deadpan.'

'Jenni, this isn't a joke. It's good to have you back. I missed you.' A deep breath. 'But Jenni – you know our . . . friendship . . . confused Carly last time.'

'Confused her?' There is a pause. 'Is that how you would describe her feelings when she was shagging Craig? Confused by us? By our relationship?'

'I don't want to talk about the past. About Carly and Craig.'

'It still hurts, does it?' She is pushing me.

'Jenni, please. The past is the past.'

'The past is confusing. I still worry about that night.'

'Which night?'

So many nights to worry about.

'The night Carly took the overdose.' There is a pause. 'Maybe she wasn't trying to kill herself. Maybe she was trying to kill me.'

'What do you mean?'

'My mind keeps stepping back to the second time Carly tried to kill herself. She came to see me, angry about the friendship between you and I. Suppose she put something in my drink?'

I shut my eyes. I don't want this to be happening again. 'Come on, Jenni, what are you talking about?'

She shrugs her thin shoulders. 'Suppose she put something in my drink and the glasses got mixed up?'

'How?'

'By accident?'

'But. But . . .' I splutter. 'We all know what happened. Carly had taken a cocktail of drugs before she ever got to you. Why are you dwelling on it now?'

'I'm just confused. Over-emotional.' She bursts into tears. 'I know I need to stop it. I need to stay calm. But all my fears from the past keep flooding towards me.'

She is in my arms. And I am stroking her back and whispering in her ear.

'Everything will be all right this time.' I am not sure whether I believe it. Has Carly made a terrible mistake asking Jenni to come home? We were managing. We were coping on our own.

~ Jenni ~

Through the lych-gate to the churchyard, walking over lichen-covered stone. Past the gnarled yew trees. Opening the heavy oak door. It's midweek; there are no services, just people like me coming to pray. The lights are on to welcome visitors but even though it is late summer, the church is cold. It is always cold. I shiver a little as I walk down the aisle, the aisle of the church where Craig and I married so long ago. So long ago that I can hardly remember the girl I was then: so besotted, so in love with him. A long way from the woman he forced me to become.

I sit where I always sit, on the front row to the right, close to the pulpit, and look up at the choir stalls. I kneel down, bend my head and close my eyes. I want God to move towards me again. After everything that has happened, please, God – please, God, come back to me. I close my eyes tighter and turn my mind in on itself. I move to standing, arms out, legs splayed. I stand and stand, and wait and wait, surrounded by cold and silence. Please, God, come back to me, I pray. The atmosphere in the church is pressing against me. I feel it. Solid and finite. Silence pounding in my ears, as loudly as if someone was holding a hammer, and I know that in the noise of this silence God is here, walking back to me. Forgiving me for my sins.

~ Rob ~

I have never experienced anything like this before. Whatever I do, wherever I go, she is there, watching me, taunting me with her eyes. Put those eyes away. Please. Jenni. Please. At the end of surgery she comes to see me to discuss her patients.

Today she is standing in front of me in my consulting room, again. She's lost weight, I'm sure of it. Her nurse's uniform hangs off her like a sack. As she slips into my patients' chair, for the first time I notice she has a tattoo – a heart outlined in black, blocked in in red, about the size of a fifty pence piece, on the inside of her right wrist. It must be freshly done because the skin around it is red, still reacting against an invasion of fresh ink. She sees me looking at it and catches my eyes in hers.

'It represents everlasting love.' She stretches her arm out to show me. 'Do you like it?' she asks.

I don't reply. I take her wrist in my right hand and pull it towards me so that I can inspect more closely. The skin around it is very, very red.

'I'd put some anti-itch cream on it tonight. Itchiness will be the next stage.'

347

'I know. I've got some.' There is a pause. 'Do you like it?' she repeats.

'Yes,' I lie. I take my hand from her arm, and give her a tight smile. 'Jenni, I'm right in the middle of my list. What is it? What did you want to see me about?'

'It's Mrs Mulberry. I'm confused by her symptoms. She's got tachycardia, and bradycardia.'

'Stop bulling me, Jenni. You know she doesn't have both.'

She sits in my patients' chair, knees prim, resting her hands on them. She leans towards me, haunting me with her eyes.

'I just wanted to see you. I've really missed seeing you. I've missed having you to myself.'

'Jenni, you've never had me to yourself. We both know that.'

~ Rob ~

When I go and buy my sandwich at lunchtime I turn my head and she is right behind me. Always right behind me, or right in front of me, large brown eyes engulfing me.

~ Jenni ~

Rob is a few minutes ahead of me on the high street. I see his floppy brown hair and his broad shoulders amply filling his linen jacket, bobbing up and down between an elderly couple and a woman with a dog. Rob always wears a jacket for the surgery – whatever the time of year, whatever the weather. I'd say his look is smart-casual. Always a jacket, but never an austere one. Always a collared shirt, with no tie, and the top button undone. Trousers without a crease. M&S boat shoes. Nothing too fashionable. No pointy-toed shoes. No Hugo Boss.

It's a soft September day, imbued with the last of the summer warmth, the first chill in the air beginning to percolate, making it cold the second the sun disappears behind a cloud. He passes the fishmonger, he passes the greengrocers. On the corner by the bakery, he turns left off the high street, into a side street. He crosses the road and enters a new café that's just opened; one the rest of the surgery staff haven't gravitated towards yet. That's why we meet there, isn't it, Rob? I look at my watch. I walk past the café and amble up and down the side street, looking into other people's houses, stepping into their lives in my mind. Exactly five minutes later, I follow him inside.

The new café is boldly decorated. Blue and orange. Colours that are striking at first sight, not restful colours to live with as Carly always likes. I'm quite the opposite of Carly. I decorate in bold colours, but I have a tasteful personality. Carly Burton, so different to me.

Rob is sitting in the far corner of the café, furthest from the window. He has a table for four to himself, plenty of room to spread out the newspaper he's engrossed in. As I walk towards him his face lights up. 'What a lovely surprise, Jenni,' he says, standing up and kissing me on both cheeks.

Tone it down, Rob. You don't need to pretend quite so much.

~ Carly ~

Communication. Communication. Communication. My mother always says that's what you need for a good relationship. Dr Willis agrees with her. So, Jenni, I'm coming to communicate with you, right now. I'm on the way to your consulting room – Sharon is stalling our patients while we sort things out. I know no one is with you, so I don't need to knock.

I burst into your room to find you typing patient data into your computer, leaning far too close to the screen, squinting. What's the matter, Jenni, do you need glasses? What a pity. Glasses will spoil your looks.

As soon as you see me, you lean back from the screen. You put your hands in the air to stretch out your back.

'Carly, how nice to see you. Can I help you?' you ask.

'We need to talk,' I say.

'In the middle of surgery?'

'It won't take long.'

You give me the look I've always hated; sad, saucer-like brown eyes so large they look like those of an alien, pushing into mine.

'Well sit down, then,' you say.

'No, thanks.' I take a deep breath. 'Jenni, I know I've been ill and everyone fears I may still be a bit paranoid, but I want you to know that I'm not. I've been well a long time now.' I pause. 'You're making cow-eyes at Rob. It's upsetting me. It's annoying me. I want you to stop.'

You get up from your chair. You come and stand in front of me. Our body language is a mirror image. Feet apart. Hands on hips.

Your brown eyes fire to amber.

'Carly, I'm not making eyes at Rob.'

'What are you doing then?'

'I like your husband. I respect him. He's a friend. I get on with him. That's it. End of.' A spray of your spittle peppers my face. 'How can you be like this, if I just smile at your husband, after what you did with Craig?'

Your voice whines and undulates. Your eyes are like large muddy pools – quicksand trying to suffocate me. I look in your eyes and my mind steps back to the past. Remembering the day I burnt your photograph in the hospital toilet. The acrid smell of the burning ink. The shrill sound of the fire alarm cutting through the hospital. The despair in my heart. I push the memory away.

I do not want to go there again.

~ Jenni ~

Carly, you have invaded my consulting room with a display of churlish bad temper. You have disrupted my day. I came back to Stansfield because you encouraged me. What's wrong with you? Telling me it's not working out? That I need to go back to Trethynion? Accusing me of flirting with Rob?

Carly, you are so difficult. So impetuous. But, at the height of your ranting and displeasure, you suddenly stopped. Your face became wistful, it softened. You suddenly put your hand on my arm.

'I'm sorry, Jenni,' you said. 'We've all been through so much together. I shouldn't take things out on you.' You started to cry. You clung on to me, and I clung on to you.

'I'm sorry. I'm sorry,' you said. 'It's just I need Rob so much.'

~ Rob ~

Jenni sidles into my surgery in between patients. She sits in my patients' chair, as usual. But this time there is something wrong, really wrong. She is ashen. Marble-faced. Eyes glazed in a way I have never seen before. As if she is here but not here.

'What is it, Jenni?' I ask gently.

She crosses her legs, suntanned legs without tights. Boyish, thigh-less legs. She sits staring straight ahead, not focusing, tapping her fingernails together. Tapered fingernails. Perfectly manicured like her toenails.

'Anastasia,' she almost whispers.

'Anastasia?'

'Yes. Anastasia. Craig's lover.'

More staring at nothing. More tapping fingernails.

'Anastasia is dead.'

More death. More destruction. Her words hurtle towards me like bullets.

Carly, I tell you about the death of your lover's lover as you stand by the microwave, heating up our Friday night takeaway.

'When? What happened?' you splutter.

'I don't know. Jenni told me today but she didn't give me any details. It's too painful for her to talk about it, apparently.'

'Too painful to talk about?'

We sit at the kitchen table to eat our takeaway. Your face is calm and composed. Is that how you feel inside?

'I can't believe there's another death.'

'Perhaps we can find out what happened on the internet. Jenni said it was all over the papers.' Abandoning my food, I fetch my iPad from the kitchen counter.

I tap the keys and find a newspaper article in the *Cornish Gazette*. I perch the iPad on its stand in the middle of the kitchen table, so that we can read it together.

She died of a prescription drug overdose, apparently, at her house in Cornwall. Linked to the death of Craig Rossiter. Suicide pact. Like Craig, she left a note. Her son, Rupert, found the body and called the police.

'An overdose, again, like me, like Craig,' you whisper. 'Suicide, like my apparent suicide attempt.' Stilted words through closed teeth. Blue eyes darkening to black. You continue. 'She did it. He told me she threatened to. She told him she would kill him if he strayed again.'

Her words cut through me.

'How do you know? Were you still in touch?' I splutter.

'Just once.'

You are almost in tears, head in hands, face crumpling.

'I just went to see him once to check that he was all right.'

You are trying to cry, chest heaving, but the tears do not come. Lies, Carly. So many lies.

I watch you inhaling and exhaling deeply as if you are struggling for breath.

'Jenni did it. She used to be my friend, so I was fooled, but now, I see how she's behaving again. And the same thing has happened too many times. I know she's dangerous.' There is a pause. 'Please believe me, Rob.'

~ Carly ~

My sleepless night is like torture, Jenni, endless and painful,
now I know what you've done. My sleeplessness is hell fire.
The sounds of the night burning against my skin. The blood-
curdling cawing of a crow. A dying fox crying like a baby. But
the sounds that are the loudest are my memories. My memories shout. I remember you telling me that Rob is in love with
you, your words drowning in the smell of burning candles and
incense. Watching you put tablets in my drink. I lift that drink
to my lips and it tastes salty and sweet. And now I am falling,
falling but this time, Jenni, you cannot stop me. I am not
blacking out.

I am walking to your cottage, the cottage where you
murdered Craig. Your cottage with its artificial cosiness and
closed-in life. And now I see where you murdered Ana. I see
it as clearly as the picture in the newspaper article. A Georgian
house so balanced and beautiful, full-length windows with
flounces of silk around them. A shiny front door with a brass
lion-head knocker. The soft sand colour of antique brick. I
open the door and walk through a hallway with a black and
white marble floor, Ormolu lights and dark oil paintings. I

turn into the drawing room. A white marble fireplace surrounded by gold upon gold. Swags and tails. Silk and damask. Like a page out of the Christie's catalogue. And in the middle of the largest sofa is Anastasia, her alabaster skin painted in stiffness.

He loved her, you know that, don't you, Jenni? He loved her more than he ever loved either of us.

At last it is morning. Light curls in around the curtain edges, and the sounds of the morning begin to move towards me. A bus rumbling past. The voices of early morning dog walkers. I have not had a wink of sleep. I lie in bed waiting for Rob to stir, watching his eyelids start to flicker as he moves towards lighter sleep. Watching the way his soft brown hair falls across his forehead. Watching the easy way he breathes. I move across the bed and put my arms around him, running my hands up and down his back. He opens his eyes and grins his lazy grin. The one he uses when he is tired.

'Give us a break, Carly, what time is it?' he says, grin transposing into a yawn.

'Six o'clock.'

He groans and pulls the cover over his head.

'I'm going back to sleep.'

'Rob. I've been awake all night. I need to speak to you.'

He doesn't speak. He doesn't move. He hides beneath the covers, pretending not to have heard me.

I yank the covers off him.

'Did you hear me? I need to speak to you.'

He sits up, arms in front of him to protect his eyes from the light.

'OK, OK. What is it?'

'I'm going to the police. I know she did it.'

His arms fall to his side and he blinks.

'Whoa. How do you conclude that?'

'You know that's what I think. I told you last night,' I tell him, voice clipped.

His eyes are critical. Condescending.

'It's one thing to think something, and quite another to report it to the police. To report it you need to be sure of it. Beyond reasonable doubt.'

'Well, I am sure of it,' I snap.

Now he has the audacity to laugh.

'Do you really think Jenni would kill Craig?' he asks.

'He was in love with Anastasia and Jenni was jealous.'

'How do you know that?' There is a pause. 'Did he tell you?'

'No.'

'Then how?'

'It's obvious.' I am shouting now. 'It's the same as what she did to me. Can't you see that the crimes are linked?'

The police station is on the corner of Green Hill Road and Quarry Street; a red brick Victorian building with Portland stone doorways and mantels. Not mind-bogglingly pretty, but of enough historic interest to be listed. I enter through the large navy blue painted doorway and am disappointed to find myself in a long thin corridor with no windows, which smells of antiseptic and sawdust. The corridor leads to a police officer sitting behind a grille. There is a queue; two people are already in front of me. I close my ears to all sounds apart from the voice of the man at the front of the queue who is leaning towards the grille, reporting an incident in a pub in Stansfield last night. He was beaten up; he is explaining every kick, every strike. And sure enough as he turns I see that his face is monstrous and swollen, with slits where his eyes used to be. When he leaves, the man in front of me takes his turn. This man has lost his passport. Stolen at work by a walk-in thief. This report doesn't take as long.

I don't like this arrangement at the police station. I was expecting privacy. When it is finally my turn I step forward and lean towards the policeman. He's an angular man with a sharp nose and a sharp chin. Flat eyes, as if he is bored.

'I need to speak to someone about something that happened to me a long time ago, in private,' I say as quietly as I can through the counter.

His eyes are no longer bored. He flips into co-operation overdrive. Perhaps he thinks I am a rape victim. I suppose that's what I wanted him to think, so that I could have some serious attention. He presses his hand on a yellow buzzer on his desk, and smiles gently at me.

'I'll arrange for someone to visit you at home.'

Sergeant Anita Berry sits in the middle of our window-facing sofa; I sit opposite her. She has a square jaw and a balanced face; too many right angles to be pretty, but she is handsome in a masculine way. The hairstyle she has chosen is layered and sensible. When she moves her head it floats and softens her.

'Shall we start, Carly? What would you like to tell me?'

She sips the Earl Grey tea I made her.

I tell her about Craig, about Anastasia, about what happened to them. About what happened to me. She listens, patiently, head on one side, eyes narrowed in concentration. I finish with a flourish. 'If you don't handle it properly there could be more death. The woman is a serial poisoner.'

Her eyes flicker a little as I say that. I've overdone it. She puts her teacup down on the coffee table in front of her. She crosses her legs.

'You reported your worry to us when you were in hospital. We cold reviewed your allegations then and we found no evidence to substantiate them.'

'Well, you need to look at the situation far more carefully.

At the two recent deaths. I'm telling you, she tried to kill me because I'd had an affair with Craig. Then he strayed again, so she killed him, and then his new girlfriend.' I pause. 'And she's trying to seduce my husband.'

'Is she indeed? You didn't mention that before.' She is leaning forward, looking at me intently.

'Please listen to me,' I beg her.

'I am listening. I'll discuss this with the chief inspector and get back to you.'

My shoulders sag with relief.

'Thanks.'

~ Rob ~

I'm sitting at my desk, finishing off a few patient notes, wanting to input them while they're fresh in my mind. Suddenly, you slip into my consulting room. With a start, I realise how late it is. There are no other cars in the car park now, the sun is low.

'I'm just inputting data,' I say. 'Unless it's quick, Jenni, let's go through it tomorrow.'

'I'll be as quick as I can, but it's important,' you say.

I sigh inside.

'Well, let me just finish what I was thinking about.'

'That's all right, I can wait.'

You walk across my room and stand behind my desk looking out of the window; I guess you're looking at the sunset. Last time I looked out of the window the burnt orange sky was magnificent. I am concentrating on my last home visit; the patient whose notes I'm typing up. It's a confusing case and I'm worried I could be doing more to help. I think I'll discuss it at our surgery meeting tomorrow. Some of the younger doctors might have a different take on it. Because I'm thinking about my patient, I don't notice quite what's happening. You have drawn the blind and now you are handcuffing my arms and legs to my chair. Cold metal is cutting into my flesh.

I struggle to escape, but I cannot move. You are overpowering me. Overpowering me with your eyes, with your scent. Your silky hair brushes across my face as you bend to kiss me, cherry red lips riper than ever.

You pull my trousers down with my underpants, displaying my erection. The tip of my penis is throbbing.

'Viagra in your afternoon tea, was it?'

I am trying to think negative thoughts, trying to diminish it. But it is becoming more insistent, more powerful. And now, already moist, you are impaling yourself on me; the walls of your vagina tightening around me. Sitting on my knee, legs apart, chest against my chest, playing with yourself, moving up and down. There is nothing I can do to stop you. I cannot move my arms. I cannot move my legs. Your breath quickens in my ear. Remember, Jenni, you are forcing me to do this.

I am not the unfaithful type. Jenni, remember this. Please.

~ Carly ~

You've stopped speaking to me, Jenni. Have you guessed I've set the police on you? You ignore me in the surgery. The way you dismiss me doesn't bother me. I'm well now. You do not scare me any more.

You don't even scare me when I see you coming out of Rob's consulting room at odd times, deliberately straightening your skirt as you pass me in the corridor. I know you're winding me up. Why would he want to mess with a skinny runt like you? Let's stick with it. Keep to this 'not acknowledging each other' game. First thing in the morning when we both arrive, when the receptionists are watching us, even then you do not acknowledge me — not even with a glance. When you first came back to the surgery, for a while you waved and smiled, going through the friendly automated ritual of saying good morning.

But ignoring each other is simpler. There's an honesty about it which I like.

~ Jenni ~

Every night at the end of surgery I come to you with my patient notes, just in case anyone asks what we're doing. For we do not want anyone to know about our relationship yet, do we? It is so good that we like to experiment, isn't it Rob? So good we have discovered that you like to be restrained. And we are going to shake it up again next week. Try a different kind of role play.

~ Carly ~

Jenni. You are watching me and I am watching you. Constantly circling like birds of prey. I can take it, it fascinates me, but Rob has had a nightmare that you raped him. Please, Jenni, he wants you to leave him alone. I'm the strong one now. Try what you want with me, but leave him alone.

After another exhausting day at the surgery seeing too many patients, and keeping an eye on you, I'm cooking lasagne for supper. Quite a fiddle after such a long day but I wanted to make something nice. Our family meals together have always been precious. When I have nearly put my masterpiece in the oven and the kitchen counter is littered with the debris of my culinary talent, Mother saunters into the kitchen from the dining room where she has been conducting a mass supervision of the children's homework.

'I'm worried about Rob,' she says. 'I think Jenni's stalking him.' She pauses. 'I used to be so fond of her when the children were younger. But I'm not so sure any more.'

What have you done now, bitch-whore?

'Yesterday lunchtime when I popped to the bank I saw her. I saw both of them. They didn't see me. Or at least they didn't acknowledge me.' There is a pause. 'She was behind him on the high street. Deliberately following him.'

'Deliberately following him?'

'It was obvious. Everywhere he went, she went.' There was a pause. 'Unless they had arranged to meet by accident on purpose, if you see what I mean.'

My insides coagulate.

Rob is home. I hear the key scrape in its lock, the click of the door as it opens. He is here in the kitchen bending towards me, kissing me. Bitch-whore, go away, leave us alone.

We sit around the large pine table in the kitchen for supper. The lasagne was worth the effort. Everyone seems to enjoy it. I don't eat much. Always watching my figure. Conversation rises and falls around me. They're arguing about someone at school that I've never heard of – my mother seems to know who he is. Teasing Pippa about a boy who talks to her at break times. She is blushing from the roots of her hair to the tips of her fingers. Who is this person? Surely Pippa is too young to have a crush?

I look across the table at Rob, who isn't really listening either, just pushing the remnants of his lasagne around his plate with a fork. He drops the fork and reaches for his wine glass. It is empty, so he reaches across the table towards the bottle for a top-up. He looks tired. There are black rings beneath his green eyes. I know he didn't sleep last night, as I lay next to him sensing his restlessness. Our eyes meet and I tell him silently not to worry. He needs to trust me. Everything will be all right. I will protect our family.

~ Rob ~

Jenni, what was it that Carly used to call you? Bitch-whore. I never liked that expression, but now I know it is true. Bitch-whore Jenni. I can't tell anyone about you.

~ Carly ~

I have no patients today, and so I breeze into the reception area in a brand new outfit. Blue and yellow. I know I look chipper but I don't feel it. I need to look chipper to put you off the scent. I have passed you in the corridor already, practically nibbling Rob's ear, pretending to whisper in it. I just beamed at you both and walked on. How much longer do you really think you'll get away with this, Jenni? The whole thing? All of it?

All the receptionists are here, answering the phones, welcoming patients. Sharon is sitting at a table away from the front desk, flicking through the pile of repeat prescriptions. I walk over to her and whisper.

'Have you got a second? I need a bit of help with the computer in the nurses' station. In private.'

Two of us can play that game, Jenni – keeping secrets and whispering.

Sharon's face softens as she looks at me. She has been my mentor here for so many years.

'I'll just put the repeats out and I'll be right down.'

We sit together in the nurses' station. Sharon in the old horse-hair chair and me balancing over her on an uncomfortable stool from the laboratory area, straining the muscles in my back. The room is large and shabby, a little untidy because it's so multi-functional. I have spent half my life working here and its familiarity folds around me and comforts me. Not for me, the new-fangled state-of-the-art consulting room like you have, Jenni. I could have been promoted to your job if I had pushed.

Sharon is nearing retirement, having worked in this surgery for thirty-five years, since before we even came. Our rock ever since we arrived. Whenever she sees Rob her face lights up. There was a time many moons ago when I used to tease him about this, but teasing him about women with a crush on him would seem tasteless these days. Sharon's greying hair is curly and unruly. She is wearing one of her cardigans that don't quite button across her protruding stomach. I owe so much to her. She's been here right from my first day as a junior nurse in the surgery, giving me the rundown on certain doctors' foibles and warning me about difficult patients.

'Is everything all right, Carly?'

I put my hand on Sharon's arm and look into familiar grey eyes.

'Rob's stressed. He needs a holiday. He works so hard. We all need a break together, to have time out as a family.' I pause. 'I need your help.' I watch her grey eyes turn to black. 'Please book two locums, urgently, one for Rob, one for me. I'm going home to book our holiday. Tomorrow we're going away for a few weeks – all of us and my mother.'

'Tomorrow?'

'It's short notice, but I know you can sort it. Please, Sharon. I'll leave our contact details with you. Don't let anyone know where we are. Not under any circumstances. Rob seriously needs a break. He mustn't be disturbed.'

~ Jenni ~

Carly, you're watching me and I'm watching you. We're playing a game, and I can't tell you how much I'm enjoying it. I watch your clinging attempts to hold your husband's attention. But let me tell you, Carly, men are like dogs: they like fresh meat. It doesn't help that you don't look as good as you used to. You've developed a weight problem. Step into my consulting room any time and I'll give you a diet sheet. Not that that will help much. Your husband is besotted with me. He pants out my name as he climaxes. He pants out my name in his sleep.

~ Carly ~

I leave the surgery feeling your eyes burning into me, scalding my back. I know you are watching me from your shiny consulting room, Jenni; I see the blinds twitch.

I walk through Stansfield, back home. Past a girl in a faded red uniform with eyes as sad as yours, Jenni, trying to get my bank account number for charity. The charity workers always lie in wait at the same corner in between Lloyds and NatWest, a different one every day, a different ploy to try to get my attention. There are too many charities to give to. I walk quickly past them, head down.

Back home, my mother is still here clearing up the breakfast things, Radio 4 droning in the background.

'I thought you were out for the day?' she says, snapping the radio off. She continues to load the dishwasher wearing her long floral apron – the one Pippa gave her for Christmas; Laura Ashley, pretty, crushed flowers, ruffles, bursting with sweetness.

'Look, Mother, I need to talk to you. Tomorrow we're all going away on a surprise holiday. A surprise for Rob. And you're coming with us. Sharon's sorting things out at the surgery. I've come home to book it.' She looks surprised. I push on. 'Top secret.' I put my fingers to my lips. 'All you need to do is go home to pack.'

My mother's eyes gleam with excitement.

'Where are we going?' she asks.

'Somewhere hot.' I take the dishes from her hand and place them on the counter. 'Leave the kitchen to me. I'll phone you later to let you know what time we're picking you up to go to the airport.'

She removes her garish apron and hangs it on the hook by the door. The child-like look on her face reminds me that she's probably not had a proper holiday since my father died. I follow her to the hallway where she retrieves her jacket and handbag. I open the front door for her. She kisses me and skims towards her car as if she is dreaming.

I sigh and pad downstairs, back to my kitchen, my shoulders aching because I feel so responsible for everyone. I make myself a coffee and sit in front of the computer screen, hands trembling. I finish my coffee and make another one. I prefer coffee to Valium and alcohol these days. Coffee helps me concentrate. Internet sunshine cascades in front of me, dancing on hotels, dancing on villas. With the help of Avios, Secret Escapes and flexible budgeting, I book an apartment in Barbados and early morning flights from Gatwick. I spend the rest of the day tidying the house and packing.

I hear Rob's key in the door and rush to greet him. We kiss and his lips feel thin. He is a shell of the person he once was. Rob, but not Rob. What has Jenni done to him? He won't talk about it, except when he dreams. He punches and kicks and screams your name, Jenni, as if he was fighting you. He wakes up in cold sweats.

This evening he comes down the hallway and goes upstairs

to shower as usual, joking about scrubbing away the germs of Stansfield.

I am listening to Elbow on the Sonos system and heating up his supper when he enters the kitchen wearing jeans and a T-shirt, his hair still damp from the shower.

'What's the racket?' he asks as I place his food in front of him. Nothing special tonight; pork chop, baked beans and mash, slightly enhanced by my mother's homemade apple sauce – but only slightly. I turn Elbow off with the remote and sit down next to him to watch him push food towards his mouth without any enthusiasm.

'And what's with all the suitcases?' he asks.

~ Rob ~

Palm trees sway in paradise. I know because I am there, sitting on the balcony of our new holiday apartment, engulfed by the hiss of the sea.

Trying to forget about you, Jenni.

Trying not to feel guilty.

Guilt is a pointless emotion that drags you down, wastes your time and your energy.

I stretch my limbs, pull myself away from the balcony and walk towards the white sugar sand beach where a young man brings me a sun lounger and iced drinks. All I need to do today is to rouse myself from crime fiction and sleep, to swim in a sea as warm as bath water – paradise indeed.

Carly rises from the beach, her soft skin tanning to the colour of toffee, and joins me in the ocean. We wade together through water that caresses our skin like velvet. She tires suddenly and stands up, laughing, pushing her watery hair back from her eyes. She is in my arms, slippery and wet and salty, her firm breasts hot against my chest.

'Let's go back to the apartment. Mother's keeping an eye on the children,' she says, pulling away and smiling the smile she gives me when I know she wants sex. The smile that frightens me.

We run through the sea, kicking through lace-crested water, along the beach to our empty apartment. We lie together on Egyptian cotton sheets. I hear the hissing of the sea and the happy voices of children playing on the beach. We melt towards one another, but I pull back. Carly looks at me wide-eyed, and I think for a second she is going to burst into tears. But then she rolls on top of me and whispers, 'Good job we came away. Before the bitch-whore got any worse.'

~ Carly ~

A world away from the red brick police station in Stansfield with its Saturday night drunkards and layers of dust from passing traffic, we sit up in front of Sergeant Anita Berry in our holiday bedroom. This world has floating drapes and a soft sea breeze. Her face is addressing us from the iPad propped up on the dressing table as we sit on chairs filched from the kitchen.

Anita Berry's beamy smile belts across the airwaves. Her sculptured hair rotates a little around her face as she leans forwards to take a sip of water from the glass in front of her. She puts the glass down and straightens her lips, looking squarely at us now. We move our chairs closer together, closer to her, and hold hands.

'I've looked into it very carefully and there isn't enough evidence to start an investigation.'

The sun pushing through the window behind us is making my head ache.

'But there must be – Jenni's dangerous,' I splutter.

'We have no evidence to support that.'

'But what about the similarities between my "accident" and what happened to Craig and his girlfriend?'

My hand is trembling.

'The coroner concluded that it was a suicide pact between them, and we agree with his opinion.'

'But they didn't die at the same time.'

'We all are aware of that, Mrs Burton. But we are sure it was suicide. We found notes in both cases.'

'How carefully have you checked the notes?'

'Please don't insult us, Mrs Burton. We have carefully laid out procedures. We know what we're doing.'

'Please, tell me, was the handwriting checked?'

'The evidence is consistent. That is all I can say.'

'But Craig was cheating on her, Jenni had a clear motive.'

'She wasn't the only one who had motive, Mrs Burton.'

'Whatever do you mean?'

She stirs awkwardly in her chair.

'Do you want to continue this conversation some time in private?'

Rob leans towards the iPad.

'Carly and I have no secrets – but I'm happy to leave the room, and get back to the beach.'

He stands up. His sandals click across the travertine flooring.

As soon as he has gone, she continues. 'You were having an affair with Craig. He dumped you to go back to his wife and then he got a new girlfriend.'

There is a pause.

'You had a motive too,' she says. 'Can you prove you didn't love him?'

'How can anyone prove they don't love someone? How is whether I loved him or not relevant?'

How dare she dig up old emotion? Emotion swept under the bridge?

'You could have been bitter that he went back to Jenni. The new girlfriend could have been the final straw. The sex stuff you've told us about could just be a red herring to put us all off the scent.' There is a pause. 'You both had access to prescription drugs through your jobs.'

I sit, head in my hands, the heat of the sun oppressive now, making me sweat. Liquid pools behind my knees and at the base of my spine.

I raise my eyes to look at her, trying to push back the tears that are pricking at my eyelids.

'Do you really think this?' I ask.

'No. I don't. If I did, we'd be having a much more serious conversation with you. I'm just making the point that it could have been either of you. The coroner firmly believes it was a suicide pact with a delay between actions. We are satisfied with all the evidence. Please accept what I am saying, Mrs Burton.'

'OK. OK. I find that difficult, but thank you, Sergeant Berry.'

'It's our pleasure. It's our job – what we're here for.'

'Goodbye.'

I touch my iPad screen and thankfully she disappears. What's the matter with the woman, harping back to my fling with Craig? Ice calm inside, I determine to continue my battle without police help. I am strong now. I can cope.

~ Rob ~

Walking along the beach hand in hand, sand crunching beneath my toes like crystal. The heady, heavy sun is pressing down on me, making me feel dizzy. Carly. You have been so worked up since Anita Berry called. So aggressive. So full of distrust of Jenni. It breaks my heart after all the good times we all once shared. After all the problems we've managed to walk away from together. But you're my wife. I must respect you.

'When we get back, I'll ask her to leave,' I tell you in the strongest voice I can muster.

You shake your head.

'She won't go. Even if she does she'll keep coming back to haunt us.' My stomach tightens. You pause. 'Rob. We need to take this seriously. Wherever we go, Jenni will follow us.'

'She's not dangerous. She can't be. Otherwise the police would have followed it up.'

'Do you really think that is how these things work?' you ask.

'I suppose I do. Yes.'

'We need to keep her close. Befriend her. If she really understands how we feel she will let us go. She might leave us alone.'

'You're confusing me, Carly. Running away to Barbados? Keeping close. What are you planning?'

You drop my hand. You pick up a pebble from the beach, a round pink pebble and spin it into the sea. It jumps off the surface of the water three times before it falls. You turn to me, blue eyes turned up to their highest wattage.

'I know what I'm doing. Play along with me, please.'

~ Carly ~

I leave you on the bed where you are sleeping, after making love with me in the afternoon heat. In sleep, the lines that age your face are gone. You are the man I fell in love with so many years ago. Your skin is burnished, toasted to hazelnut by the sun. Your lips are red, and slightly parted. I want to wake you and kiss you, and start again. But I need time alone to think, and so I let you sleep.

I pull my negligee over my shoulders, walk to the window and open the curtains a little so that I can see the white sand and the cobalt sea. The palm trees swaying in front of our window. I close my eyes and listen to the sea; it pushes through every crevice of my mind and soothes it.

Down on the beach, Matt and John are playing; throwing a ball to one another in the sea, aping about, laughing as the waves slap against their legs. Pippa is running after them, trying to supervise them. Trying to get them to leave the sea to help her build a sandcastle on the beach.

My mother is lying on a sun lounger reading a novel. She has hardly moved for nearly two weeks. She doesn't even bother to go into the sea. Resting her joints, she says, so that she will still be able to use them when she gets older.

'Never mind your joints – if you don't start exercising your arteries will clog up and you'll have a heart attack,' Pippa told her, pointing her forefinger at her, head on one side.

Being here is giving my mother time to relax fully, something she deserves after working so hard for so many years. She used to help you too, didn't she, Jenni?

Most of all being here is giving me time to think about you, Jenni. The past, our friendship, moments, highlights, all pushing towards me with cinematic clarity.

Our 'friendship' at nursing college was only an acquaintance from a distance; I was on the degree course, you were studying for a diploma. You've pulled yourself up a lot since then, haven't you, Jenni? Back then, degree girls didn't usually associate with diploma girls, but for some reason you ended up living on the same corridor as me, in a rather downbeat hall of residence. Do you remember, Jenni? Bedrooms so small you could stand in the middle and touch both sides. The kitchen that no one cleaned except you. The rubbish that built up outside.

We were so different, you and me. You didn't drink. You didn't screw anyone. No wonder we didn't hook up. Even then you used to haunt me with your eyes, disapproval simmering when I came back to the corridor late at night with a guy to find you in the kitchen, making jam, or praying; or something challenging and exciting like that. You never went out back then – not even on Saturday nights.

The rest, as they say, is history; Stansfield, in the local NCT, where we finally caught up. I was pregnant with John and you were expecting Mark. As soon as you looked at me I recognised your mud brown eyes, but they no longer seemed to be brimming with disapproval – after all, we were both married women now. We were pushed together by the fear of childbirth, passing through a moment in time together. Not friends that transcend time.

Do you remember the hospital maternity classes? Lectures from midwives on giving birth. Lolling about like beached whales on mats on the floor, not sure why we needed to make such an effort to relax. Do you remember being bitchy about the new mothers on the maternity ward, who came to the hospital shop in full view of all the outpatients, hobbling along in slippers and dressing gowns, looking pained and frumpy? In the end, when it was my turn, I wasn't even strong enough to visit the shop.

Do you remember talking to a new mother who told us she had driven herself to hospital alone, whilst in labour? We gasped audibly.

'Don't worry,' she said, 'I drove over the fly-over between contractions, and in case I broke down, I had my bike in the back.'

Do you remember the frightful Gym Play we used to take the children to? Acrylic fumes of wet mould curling up our nostrils to damage the lining of our noses. It was supposed to be good for the children's co-ordination. Whether it was or not, I don't know. I think it was just an easy way for the people running it to make money from pushy parents. It was certainly no fun listening to toddlers yelling as they tumbled over benches and crawled through a variety of plastic tubes and hoops, sere-naded by nursery rhymes pounding from a poor-quality sound system. The only decent part was the break when the children were silenced by drinking squash with too much sugar and overdosing on cheap biscuits. Oh and the Gym Play coach. Do you remember him? A stocky blond-haired man with muscular thighs. But you didn't fancy him, did you, Jenni? You never leered at other men until you fell for Rob.

I remember that delicious feeling of freedom, when it was

over, and we escaped from the smelly hall to stand chatting outside. I would put my hand on your arm and we would laugh together, about all the stupid things we had to do because of the children.

That was all our friendship ever was really, wasn't it? A school-gate friendship. Transient and meaningless. So meaningless it doesn't matter, Jenni, that you have destroyed it. Our friendship has been destroyed. That is just part of it. Now, to protect my family, I promise you, Jenni, I'm going to destroy you.

SEVEN

~ Rob ~

Back home to a world stripped of vibrant colours. To Stansfield's grey upon grey. To piles of advertising and bills so deep we can hardly push the front door open. To endless patient lists and home visits. And Jenni. The chocolate eyes of Jenni. Watching me when I first arrive at the surgery. Watching me kiss Sharon on the cheek and present her with a gift from Barbados: a lace table cloth. Watching me give out bottles of Mount Gay rum to everyone else. Her brown eyes darkening to black when Carly arrives.

The beach bum I was yesterday is turning into Dr Burton again, settling back into his consulting room with its faded leather chair, and scratched desk. Being sympathetic to Lily Appleton, a ninety-year-old who is losing her memory. Being patient with a young man who is trying to get signed off work with a back problem. He will be disappointed. I can't let him get away with it.

Next up is Shelly Barr. Always in a mess with her contraception – four children with four different fathers, and she is only twenty-two. Living in a council house with her latest boyfriend. I decide to get her a few shiny leaflets advising on contraception. *If* she can read, one might help. I saunter along the corridor to fetch one from the cupboard at the back of reception. Past the nursing station. The door is open and I can see Carly and Jenni, sitting at the counter checking the samples together before they are sent off. Chatting. Laughing. Girls together again. Carly and Jenni with their schizophrenic friendship. As I pass them on the way back they are quieter, sitting together working amicably. Carly sees me and waves me into the nurses' station. I step inside. It needs tidying up, as usual. Leaflets, patient notes and directives from the government lie in piles on the lab-style worktops. Pens. Pencils. Pads. Paperweights. A green plastic rhinoceros-shaped dish for paper-clips. Carly's treasures. Carly's mess.

The room smells of her perfume; the one I bought her at the airport on the way home. Gardenias drowning the background smell of dust and antiseptic. She pouts at me from beneath her tumbling Botticelli curls. Jenni fixes her eyes on mine for a second too long.

Be careful, Jenni.

Now they are both looking at me and smiling. Carly's smile is so bold, so certain. Jenni's is tentative, flashing wide for a second and then disappearing.

'Everything all right?' I ask.

'Carly was just telling me about your holiday,' Jenni says. There is a pause. 'And the party.'

'Party?'

'For bonfire night.'

'I'll fill you in when I get home,' Carly says, continuing to tighten the tops of urine samples. I leave them and saunter back to my room to call poor Shelly Barr.

The day continues to progress slowly, burying me in patient notes, referral letters, bad news from oncology departments, budget worries. The local pharmacist phones to question the accuracy of one of my prescriptions. A medical rep is waiting to see me. I ring Sharon.

'Sharon. Get rid of the rep. I'm so stretched today and I'm not interested in another me-too penicillin anyway. But say it nicely.'

At last, not a second too soon, the evening surgery is over. As far as I can tell from the lack of cars in the car park, everybody else has gone home. I close my blind as the light is fading, sit at my desk and wait.

Footsteps in the corridor. The door handle turning slowly. Brown eyes moving towards me.

'I missed you, Rob. You didn't even tell me you were going. You cut yourself away from me and it was painful.'

'I had to, Jenni. For the sake of my family. You must know how difficult it is for me,' I say as I take you in my arms.

'It's always been difficult for both of us,' you whisper before you kiss me. I kiss back, hungrily.

~ Jenni ~

The bonfire party is approaching and I'm looking forward to it. I have bought a new dress for you, Rob, a dress that emphasises my figure. A toffee-coloured woollen dress that matches my eyes. As you know only too well, chocolate and toffee together are delicious. Rob. I am so sorry for you. The way Carly behaves with her raucous laugh and over-exuberant personality. Carly Burton. Curly hair and stupidity. Like an overweight Golden Retriever. You stay with your chubby wife with a questionable intellect because of your religious convictions. Loving me for so long has made your life difficult, so very difficult. I'm sorry, Rob. Really I am.

~ Rob ~

A bonfire is being built in our garden. The biggest bonfire our garden has ever seen. We have fireworks and sparklers. Homemade fudge, treacle toffee and hanging lanterns. We have a large guy, stuffed with newspaper to help start the fire. He has a languishing head that keeps falling off no matter how much time we spend repairing it. Carly has everyone helping. Pippa, Matt and John. Your boys, Jenni, looking like clones of Craig with their strong frames and clumsy features – the very sight of them making my stomach tighten because of what happened to him. In a few days we will have our party and you will be here, Jenni, enjoying Carly's efforts.

Jenni. Because of what is happening between us I visit church every day and pray for redemption. The church where you married Craig. When I visit church, the noise of the world lessens. We were always the religious ones, weren't we, Jenni? Do you think religion helps? I must admit I sometimes wonder. Being true to your religion isn't an easy pathway. Or at least it seems that way right now. Knowing our affair can't continue. Knowing it should never have started in the first place. Praying. Praying for forgiveness. Praying for the strength to finish it.

~ Carly ~

You arrived at the party early, as I asked you to, and we are laughing and chatting in the garden. Rob is in the kitchen watching us. I see his face at the window, by the kitchen sink. I see his fine head of shiny hair, his broad shoulders. Jenni, he belongs to me. You know that really, don't you? You put your hand on my arm and tell me how nice it is to be together again.

'Like old times,' you say.

It is a crisp November evening and darkness has already descended. The lanterns in the tree above us are bathing your eyes in soft, forgiving light, making the laughter lines around them dissolve a little. For we are not getting any younger, Jenni, are we? The scent of dying pine wafts towards us from the unlit pile of logs.

'Let's get the bonfire going before everybody arrives,' I say. 'I tell you what, you light it.' I pass you the matches and the paraffin. 'Slop the paraffin on, it rained so hard yesterday that the wood's very wet.' I pause. 'I'll go and get us a glass of wine. Red or white?'

'Red,' you reply, starting to twist open the lid of the green paraffin container.

'Hold on a minute. Wait until I'm inside to light it. The smell of paraffin exacerbates my asthma.'

'I didn't know you had asthma.'

'There are a lot of things we don't know about each other, Jenni.'

You put your hand on my arm and drown me with your eyes.

'We have the rest of our lives to find out — now that our friendship is strong again. Now that the past is forgotten and forgiven.'

Forgiven but not forgotten. Forgiven. Forgotten. Which is it, Jenni? Is it either? Your words rotate in my mind.

'Remember to really slop on the paraffin,' I shout back to you, as I head towards the house, towards the wine.

~ Rob ~

I'm washing up at the kitchen sink, watching you both standing together laughing, two shadowy figures beneath the hazy light of a paper lantern. Carly hands you the paraffin, Jenni, and the matches, kisses you on both cheeks and turns to walk up the garden. The kitchen door opens and shuts.

'Have you opened the wine?' Carly asks.

'Yes. It's by the—'

The garden explodes. A volcano of flame, Post-it yellow, cascading towards the sky, engulfing you, Jenni. I grab a bath towel from the laundry room and dash outside, running towards you, towards the furnace that is devouring you. The stench of burning flesh mixed with the heady odour of petrol hits me and forces me back; I cannot reach you, Jenni. My face is scalding. My hair is singeing. I feel it, I smell it. The inferno subsides and I see your charcoaled body. Feeling as if I am moving through a vacuum, I walk back to the kitchen and with trembling hands telephone the emergency services.

Collapsing in the leather armchair in the kitchen, on the edges of my mind I wonder where Carly is. But I cannot go and find her. If I move I will vomit.

The police and the fire brigade are here in minutes. I am not sure who arrives first. The light from an ambulance rotates outside. They trample in and out, between the garden and the house. The fire brigade have brought a hose down the side passage and are drowning the bonfire in foam. It is almost out. Your body is surrounded by medics and police. Police are everywhere, searching our house, searching the shed. The vomit that I have been suppressing surges in my stomach. I rush to the downstairs bathroom – just in time. When I have expunged the turmoil inside me, I have a hot flush and splash my face with cold water from the basin. Then I shiver. My shiver becomes a shake, which builds more and more uncontrollably. I stand still in the downstairs cloakroom, waiting for my body to calm.

When I recover enough to return to the kitchen, the house has become a crime scene, tape across the front door, a police-woman guarding it. Pippa is walking towards the house, arm in arm with my boys. Where are your boys, Jenni? They mustn't witness this horror. If they do it will stay with them forever, contort their memory of the real you. They haven't arrived. The police must have stalled them. They must be at Stuart's. At the thought of Stuart without his precious daughter, my stomach cramps begin again. The policewoman is waving my children away. In the recess of my mind, I know Heather must be on her way to get them. Heather, our backbone.

Carly stands next to me now, stinking of the bonfire, her face streaked with tears and charcoal. We move together into the sitting room and collapse onto the sofa. She clings to me, pushing her smoky hair in my face, making me choke. A policeman is here, appearing as if from nowhere, sitting in the easy chair opposite us. A burly man with high shoulders. He has sandy eyes and sandy hair, which give him a gentle look.

'It looks as if Jenni tried to light the fire with petrol instead of paraffin and the can exploded. Poor girl didn't have a chance,' he says.

'I gave her paraffin,' Carly says violently.

'The red can, the one we always use?' I ask.

The policeman leans forward.

'A red can with paraffin in is still in the shed.'

Carly inhales sharply.

'Do you think you gave her the wrong can?'

Carly bursts into tears. She doesn't reply.

They take Carly to the police station to make a statement whilst I stay at home and console myself with a glass of whisky. Police wearing rubber gloves are everywhere. In the shed. In the kitchen. In our bedroom. Somewhere through the darkness I am moving in, the children are back home, walking towards me in the sitting room. I am too choked to talk to them. I hug Pippa. She smells of apple blossom. I hug the boys. We sit together and put the TV on; its coloured shadows flicker in front of me. I don't know what we are watching. It might be a film. It might be the news. I don't know and I don't care. All that I know is that Pippa and the boys are sitting next to me. The fact that they're there comforts me. Pippa is holding my hand.

At some point, I'm not quite sure when, Carly returns to a place which is no longer a home but a crime scene. Your body, Jenni, is interred beneath a tent, waiting for more forensic analysis tomorrow. We have to move out of the crime scene right now.

'Just for a few days,' the sandy policeman says as he watches us gather a few overnight possessions, making a note of what we take.

'What happened at the police station?' I ask Carly as she stands in front of me trembling, moonlight pale.

'I made my statement. Explained that it was a complete accident.' She bursts into tears, pressing her body against me. 'I don't think they believed me.' There is a pause. 'They say there'll have to be an inquest in a case like this.'

'Of course there'll be an inquest. That must be routine.'

Does she really think something as fatally destructive as this could happen without an inquest?

Too unstable to drive, the police order me a minicab. Heather has arrived; at least our children will be all right. That gives me some small sense of relief. Silently we all pile into the minicab and are taken to the local Travelodge, where Heather and the children disappear to a family bedroom. Carly and I take another double room. We are alone together for the first time since I lost you, Jenni. Where are you? Where has God taken you?

In the plastic privacy of the Travelodge, surrounded by cream walls and MDF furniture, I fling my overnight bag onto the bed, pull out my whisky bottle, and pour a generous slug into a water glass from the bathroom. Whisky mixed with an edge of dry toothpaste.

'Would you like some, Carly?' I ask.

She shakes her head, kicks off her shoes, and sits on the bed supporting her back with two pillows. I remove my bag from the bed and sit next to her, necking whisky. She rocks back and forwards, crying, a high-pitched eerie cry, haunting and ghostlike. I try to soothe her, putting my arms around her shoulders, rubbing her back, talking to her, but her wailing will not stop and the rocking intensifies. The stench of burning which surrounds her cuts into my nostrils, sears through my lungs, my gullet, choking me, making me feel sick.

'What happened?' I ask, but Carly remains unable to speak.

I leave her to her rhythmic grief and move away towards the shower. At the doorway I turn to check on her. Her eyes are clamped shut, she does not seem to have noticed that I have gone.

The bathroom, despite the clanking central heating, is damp and cold. Grey tiles that once were white. A clouded mirror. A stained bath. I strip off my smoke-drenched clothes and step into the shower. The water is lukewarm, and the shower gel provided is thin and smells like washing-up liquid. With considerable effort I manage to work it into a lather on my skin and attempt to wash the stench of smoke away. I rub harder and harder but I cannot remove the odour of your burning flesh, Jenni, or the heat of the bonfire, from my mind. I stand in the shower, pummelled by moving water, wishing I could turn back time. I stay in the shower until the water runs cold and my skin is pink and crinkled. I step out and return to the bedroom to put on fresh clothes from my overnight bag. Carly is still rocking and crying, but silently now. She doesn't hear me. She doesn't open her eyes. I dress and then clean my teeth, as obsessively as I have washed, and then I sit with my arms around her and wait. For her to come round. For her to speak to me.

She melts against me, and falls asleep, still choking me with the stench of the fire. I untangle myself from her, rest her sleeping head on a pillow, and pour myself another whisky.

A knock at the door, loud and demanding. I put my whisky glass on the bedside table and move towards the door, expecting it to be one of the children. But no. When I open it two police officers are standing in front of me. A man and a woman. Young and slim and pale faced.

'May we come in?' the woman asks, her voice harsher than her honey looks. The man is expressionless at her side.

Behind me I hear Carly start to wake, start to stir. The police officers walk into the room smelling of cold night air and authority. Their shoulders and uniforms are tight and stiff.

'What's all this about?' I ask. 'You've already questioned her.'
'It was an accident,' Carly says, in a voice cracked with exhaustion.
'We have more evidence.'

She is looking at me, terrified, asking me for protection with her eyes. She gets up from the bed and stands next to me. I put my arm around her. The blonde policewoman steps towards her. She opens her mouth and starts to speak like an automaton. At first I am so shocked that I am not listening properly and then her words come into focus and I begin to realise she is arresting Carly. I'm familiar with these words only from watching too much crime drama on TV. The speech is in the closing stages now:

'. . . it may harm your defence if you do not mention, when questioned, something you later rely on in court. Anything you do or say may be given in evidence.'

'Are you coming voluntarily or do we need to cuff you?' the male police officer asks.

Carly does not reply quickly enough and so he cuffs her, whipping her arms behind her back. He must have been well trained. He is assertive without being rough. My arm is still around her, trying to protect her.

'Step away,' he requests. 'I'm afraid you're not invited to come with us.'

I let go of my wife and step back as requested. The blonde police officer hands me a card.

'Some information for you,' she says.

Flanking Carly, they begin to escort her towards the door.

'Help me, Rob, there must be some mistake,' she pleads in a fragmented voice.

Somewhere deep inside I do not think this is a mistake. The police are too sure of themselves. Too confident. Before I have managed to find something comforting to say, she is gone. Leaving me alone in this shabby Travelodge that needs refurbishing. Leaving me alone, looking at grey walls, feeling empty inside. I move to the window to try and have a last glimpse of her. I am in time to see her stumble as she gets into the police car. I wave, but it's too late. She doesn't see me. The car drives off, lights flashing, bathing the road in repetitive discord. I return to sit on the bed, to numb my mind with whisky. I drink whisky. Whisky resonant on my tongue. Until I cannot see. Until I cannot think. Until I fall asleep, semi-comatose.

~ Carly ~

A remand prisoner, charged with the murder of Jenni Rossiter, sitting in the transport van, in a cubicle on my way to Moormead prison. No one seems to believe me that I made a mistake; not even Rob. It's Rob's attitude that hurts the most.

Rob, looking even more unkempt than me, was allowed to visit me at the police station before I was transferred into this horsebox. How can it be acceptable to treat people like animals? I could only talk to him from behind a barrier of glass, pressing my face against it to get as close to him as possible.

'What's this about fresh evidence?' he asked.

'They have CCTV footage of me filling up a green can with petrol, at the petrol station, the week before the fire.' I shrugged my shoulders. 'Don't you remember, Rob? You were worried about running out in case the leaf blower needed topping up.' I paused. 'You asked me to fill it up, so I did. It doesn't prove anything. I didn't do it on purpose.'

Rob's freckled eyes looked scared for a second, before he masked them.

'They must think it proves something or they wouldn't have charged you.'

'I'm only charged, not convicted. What do you think a trial is for?' I asked.

Rob, how can you be so judgemental, so harsh?

'OK, OK, calm down,' he said. 'Don't snap.' His face had looked distant. 'It's not easy for you, I know, but it's been a terrible shock for me too.'

He'd put his hand to the glass, as if he wanted to get nearer to me.

'When are you coming home?' he asked.

'Bail will be refused, apparently.'

'Why?'

'They think I'm dangerous.'

'To who? Other people or yourself?'

'Both.'

He sat there looking at me. At my collapsed face, at my crumpled clothing, my rounded shoulders and hands now folded together, my bitten nails. And I sat looking at a man with skin as white as rose petals, almost translucent in the electric light above him. A man who needed a shave, a shadow of a man, with a bad hangover.

'Did you deliberately set fire to Jenni?' he asked me.

I whimpered like a dog that had been whipped, stood up and left the cubicle. Is that the thanks I get for being his long-standing wife, the mother of his children? For him not to trust me. For him not to believe that I am innocent. His words were like a knife in my heart. What did he want? Did he wish it was me that had doused the fire with petrol? Me who had died, rather than Jenni?

The prison transport van moves through Stansfield, past all my familiar places. The children's school. Our 1930s semi. The surgery where Jenni tormented me. Along the A70, towards the motorway. I feel sick and my hands are trembling but I am not going to worry – my 'legals', as the police call them, will sort everything out. As soon as I get the opportunity I will telephone Rob, and tell him to instruct the best barrister possible.

It's all a misunderstanding. All of it. Even this business about not allowing me bail. Where has it come from? I know I will move through this to a better place. I don't have religion like Rob, but since I recovered from my depression, I do have a strong sense that my life will always move forwards, whatever happens. Jenni Rossiter, however hard she tries, will not ruin it again. Jenni Rossiter will never ruin anything again now.

The van is moving along the motorway, high banks, grey upon grey. When we reach the winding, twisting roads of the countryside my sickness increases. Eventually, after several hours of feeling wretched, we arrive at Moormead. Almost as soon as the van begins to slow down, my sickness starts to dissipate. Through the limited vision of my cubicle window I see iron gates open automatically. The van pulls into a tarmac square, surrounded by brick walls, topped with razor wire. A grim, grey nightmare.

The door of my cubicle is opened by a prison officer who escorts me through the yard, into a reception area built of concrete mixed with small stones, two-toned grey concrete everywhere; on the floor, on the ceiling, on the walls. I think there are two other prisoners who have come out of the van, but they are blurring on the edge of my vision. My escort is standing next to me, not taking his eyes off me, as if I am about to bolt. I want to put my hand on his arm and assure him that I am not dangerous. To tell him the truth.

'I am Carly Burton,' I want to say. 'I'm a well-respected nurse, wife of the local GP, mother of three children. Please don't be scared of me.'

But I cannot because I am still cuffed, and he will not want to listen to me. A woman in prison-officer uniform standing behind a glass screen asks us to fill in forms and sign them, pushing them with some bendy plastic pens through a slit in the glass screen. Now he has to un-cuff me. I shake my wrists to encourage the blood flow back to my hands. I open my mouth to speak to him but he gestures to me to be silent, and the look on his face is such that I judge it best to obey him. I stand next to him by a counter against the right-hand wall, filling in my form – my name, address, date of birth, height and weight. Nothing complicated. In the corner of my mind I see a woman who arrived with me struggling to read the form, holding the pen awkwardly. I finish and am escorted into a small side room to find two female prison officers waiting for me, standing either side of a small wooden desk. My escort leaves.

I am staring at them and they are staring at me. Their eyes burn into me. They look dark and smart in their black and white uniforms. Dark and smart and full of authority. These women must not be messed with. One removes and audits my handbag. One examines me with a metal loop, attached to a baton, which periodically beeps across my clothes, across my orifices.

'Everything seems in order,' one of them snaps. 'You'll see the doctor next.'

The doctor's consulting room leads off the reception area and has no windows. A woman of about fifty with iron grey eyes and matching hair is waiting for me, sitting behind a metal desk, surrounded by mauve painted brick walls. She's the first person I have seen who isn't wearing a uniform.

'Do you smoke?' she asks.

'No.'

'Drink?'

'Not for many years.'

'Have you had a problem with drink in the past?'

'No. Why would you ask that?'

Her eyes tighten their focus on me.

'Lying won't help you in here.'

405

'Why do you think I'm lying?'

'Just guessing.'

'I don't lie. You need to know that.'

She leans back in her chair and crosses her legs.

'Take any drugs?' she asks.

'No.'

'Not even the contraceptive pill?'

'Well that hardly counts as a drug.'

She taps something into the computer screen in front of her.

'Do you have any history of mental illness?'

'Nothing I haven't recovered from.'

'Well then, since you're so squeaky clean – you can go straight to your cell.'

I'm walking behind the ample buttocks of my jailer, along endless white painted corridors, up flight after flight of green metal stairs, listening to keys jangling at her waist. She stops outside a cell door and unlocks it. She enters and I follow. A cell with mauve painted walls. A cell with a window that looks out onto concrete.

'This is your new roommate,' the officer says, craning her head up to the top bunk.

The officer leaves, metal grinding against metal as she locks the door behind her.

The blanket on the top bunk moves and a head appears. A head of pale ginger hair. A girl with a thin, mean face – if her eyes were further apart and she had a broader nose she would have been pretty.

'Sarah Jane Moore,' she says. 'Attempted bank robbery.' There is a pause. 'You?'

'Carly Burton. Wrongly accused.'

She puts her head back and laughs. A real hyena cackle.

'We all try that one to start with. Everyone is wrongly accused in here.'

~ Rob ~

It is visiting time at Moormead prison and Carly and I are sitting opposite each other, across a grey, grubby plastic table, trying to act naturally – Pippa at the end of the table.

'Are you all right?' I ask, reaching for Carly's hand and then remembering that I hugged her when she arrived. That's my quota. I'm not allowed to touch her again this visit. I place my hand back on my lap, keep it to myself.

Her head drops.

'No. I'm not all right. Not really,' she replies.

'Are you sleeping?'

'No one sleeps well in here. It's so noisy.'

Carly stares into a space in the air behind me, eyes blind and unfocused.

'We're doing everything we can to get you out.'

Her cornflower eyes sharpen.

'Everything?'

'Yes.'

Pippa stands up. She makes me jump. I'd been so concerned

for Carly I had almost forgotten Pippa was here, sitting at the table with us.

'Are you hungry, Mum? Would you like something from the vending machine?' Pippa asks.

'Yes, please. Chocolate.'

She walks across the visiting area, leaving Carly and me alone. She is Carly but not Carly. A woman in crumpled clothing who I hardly recognise. I feel stuck, as though I don't know what to say.

After a while, I speak.

'What do you do all day?' I ask limply.

'You don't want to know.'

'Then why did I ask?'

'You're a GP, trained to be interested. Trained to be polite.'

'Come on, Carly, stop that. Tell me what it's like.'

A half smile.

'You don't want to know. I promise.'

'So it's sex and drugs and rock and roll, is it?'

'Something like that.' She laughs.

I hear Pippa clicking back, her shoes cracking across the concrete flooring. Carly's eyes shine with greed as Pippa passes her a cup of hot chocolate and a large Kit-Kat. Carly devours the Kit-Kat and gulps the hot chocolate.

'When are you coming home, Mummy?' Pippa asks.

Pippa. Lower lip protruding, legs crossed, foot shaking the way it does when she is anxious.

Carly is crushing her empty cup of hot chocolate in her right hand.

'I don't know when all this will be over. They've not even set a trial date yet. My legals are coming to see me sometime in the next few days.'

She leans forwards as if she is about to put her hand on my

arm, but stops herself. She sits there, biting her nails, eyes softening with tears.

'I didn't do anything wrong. Get me out of here, as soon as possible. Please.'

~ Rob ~

The surgery is ticking on. Without Carly. Without you, Jenni. Without the depth of my old enthusiasm. Heather and Sharon both deserve beatification. Heather, even though her spirit seems cracked by what has happened, still supports me, still helps run my home. Sharon continues to run the surgery. I float in and out of both, vaguely pretending to cope.

Lunchtime. A wet, damp day, moisture hanging in the air but it isn't raining, not at the moment. Moving along the high street, head down, not wanting to speak to anyone, stopping at M&S to buy flowers. Clutching a bouquet, I move away from the high street on to Church Street with its cobbles and individual shops with personality. Towards our church.

Towards the church where you lie. Fresh granite resting brutally on the ground above you. The lilies I put there yesterday haven't withered yet. I lay my new bouquet next to them. Roses and lilies. Ephemeral beauty about to fade. Jenni, you are with the Lord now. Your beauty will never fade. I close my mind in on itself and reach you. I feel you. I breathe your scent. You are here in this moment, watching me like you always used to.

Lunchtime is over. I go back down Church Street, back to

the high street. Past the lap-dancing club that was closed down. Everything is so familiar and yet so distant. Back to the surgery. The surgery I have given my life to. Clean and kind and warm, wrapping me in a blanket of security, giving me a sense of purpose. The needs of my patients pulling me forwards, providing me with a routine to hook my life jacket onto, for outside I am drowning. I push the ghosts of Jenni and Carly away. I ignore the passing whiff of their perfume, the distant sound of their arguments, their laughter, as I move through the reception area where a few patients are already gathering for the afternoon surgery, smiling at the receptionist on duty. I go into my consulting room. As soon as I sit at my desk my phone buzzes. I pick up.

'A man from the Met to see you,' Sharon tells me.

My body goes limp.

'Send him in.'

A few minutes later a ruddy-faced man who looks as if he is seven months pregnant enters my consulting room, extending his hand to me. I take it and we shake hands gently.

'Inspector Johnson,' he announces.

His eyes shine at me as he sits in my patients' chair.

'What can I do to help you?' I ask.

'I've just popped in to look at your staff rota for last year. Double-checking Carly's movements.'

Double-checking Carly's movements. I swallow slowly. I feel saliva move down my throat but it doesn't ease its dryness.

'I expect she was either here or at home looking after the children. She never went anywhere else, except out with a few friends in the evening.'

'Yes. I'm sure, but we just need to check that.'

'So what do you want from me?'

'Nothing complicated. To look at your personal diary. I've just checked the surgery's with Sharon. Carly wasn't here on

411

the days in question. Sharon says you keep a private diary, so I want you to go through it with a toothcomb, and get back to me by tomorrow morning if possible, with your record of Carly's whereabouts on the days we're interested in.'

'Which dates and why are you interested in them?'

'The ninth of July and seventeenth of September – both Saturdays, if that's any help. The days Craig and Anastasia died.'

'But surely you don't think . . .?' I splutter. He is staring at me with hard grey eyes. 'Carly never worked on Saturdays,' I continue. My hands are trembling. 'I'll look it up tonight and get back to you.'

He sits back in his chair a little.

'Thanks.'

He continues to stare at me, smelling of the cold air inside the police station. Making me shiver inside as I remember visiting Carly there, the sting of disinfectant in the air mingled with stale vomit. Carly locked up with Saturday night inebriates. Her whimper of pain when I asked her about Jenni.

'Was she in love with Craig?' he asks.

'No. Of course not.'

'But she had an affair with him, didn't she?'

'If you could call it that. More like a sexual fling. A long time ago, when she wasn't well.'

He crosses his legs. He is wearing dark navy socks with little red dots.

'She hated Jenni Rossiter, didn't she?'

'When Carly was ill she was suspicious of her. Paranoia was part of her illness. But they were very friendly around the time of Jenni's death.'

'But she had complained to the police about Jenni, shortly before Jenni died, hadn't she?' he pushes.

'Yes. But the police had reassured us that she was mistaken about Jenni, so Carly had moved past that.'

412

'She must have moved on very quickly. Complaining about her in September. By early November, Jenni was dead.' He pauses. 'And did Carly suspect you were having an affair with Jenni?'

I sigh inside.

'Inspector, Carly had suffered paranoia in the past, but she's recovered now, so no, of course not. Why would she suspect that?'

'Well, if it were true, for example?'

A stone drops in my stomach.

'I find your suggestion deeply offensive. I'm a religious man, Inspector.'

He leans towards me. His eyes are like polished marble.

~ Carly ~

Oh, Jenni, what are you doing to me? I am locked up in here, all because of that stupid accident. I know I told you to slop the fuel on, but I really thought it was paraffin. It wasn't my fault that it was petrol. It was Rob's. He'd asked me to fill up the spare can with petrol the week before the party. I got the colours mixed up, that's all. Why does no one believe me when we've been friends for so long? And why are the police coming to ask me more questions now, about Craig, about Anastasia? Jenni, what have you done? Have you managed to set me up from beyond the grave?

~ Rob ~

The silence of what once was my home pushes against me. Leaden silence. It is no longer a home, it is simply the house where I live. The children have gone to Heather's for the night. I wade through the silence. Towards a tumbler of whisky and a slouch on the sofa. I close my eyes and feel Carly lean towards me. Her early touch. The way she used to touch me when I first met her. Carly's face contorts into Jenni's. Jenni's face with her vanilla-fudge eyes. My girls. Vanilla fudge and coconut ice both leaning towards me, telling me that they love me. I try to embrace them both in my mind but I cannot quite reach them. They are pulling away from me. I open my eyes. I feel so tired, so very tired. I finish my whisky. I groan inside and force myself to stand up, remembering I have promised the inspector that I'll look for my diary. I haven't been filling it in since just before the fire. Where did I leave it? In my bedside drawers? In the kitchen dresser? I am methodical. I don't randomise things like Carly does. It will be in one of my usual places.

My usual places. My bedside table. The bottom right drawer of my chest of drawers. Downstairs on the kitchen dresser. Looking in my usual places doesn't work. So I start at the top of the house and ransack everywhere. Rummaging. I go through drawers of bunched-up underwear, tangled tights and lacy knickers. Cupboards of children's toys. Children's clothing. Through bookshelves and piles of correspondence. Through our overflowing filing cabinet. I even look in the fridge. In the freezer. In the dirty linen.

Carly must have destroyed it. I can't find it anywhere.

~ Carly ~

Visiting time. I'm sitting at a plastic table waiting for my mother, surrounded by screws. Screws staring at me without blinking, waiting for me to make a wrong move. I have made such an effort to look nice today for my mother. If I look unkempt she worries about me even more, and she worries about me too much already. We are allowed so little pocket money that even getting hold of good-quality soap or shampoo is difficult. So, unless you are an extremely natural beauty, looking halfway decent is impossible. But today with a little help from my cellmate, Sarah Jane, who exchanged her fags for some expensive shampoo, I have managed to minimise the damage this place is doing to my appearance. As I turn my head, soft freshly washed curls vibrate against the edge of my face.

Mother is here, moving towards me. She has lost weight; she's still barrel shaped but a thinner barrel. We greet each other with a hug and then, tired, panda-eyed tired, she sits opposite me and reaches for my hand beneath the table. Her hand feels hot in mine. But we are not allowed to keep touching each other, so a quick squeeze, a glance to check whether a guard is looking this way, he is, and our physical contact is over.

'The bitch-whore set me up. Have you heard about it?'

'Of course I have. The house is crawling with police. With forensics.'

'How dare they charge me with Craig and Anastasia's murders? Saying I forged both suicide notes. Fucking CCTV footage. A blonde woman who apparently looks like me in a canary yellow sundress and matching shoes was filmed on the ninth of July walking across the small car park in Trethynion; the one right by Craig and Jenni's cottage. And on the seventeenth of September wearing a bright red raincoat, like mine. The days of their deaths. So it's me, apparently. Ha ha, I bet it's her in that camera with socks in her bra, wearing a blonde wig. And I bet she enjoyed spending hours trying to get her handwriting to look like mine. She must have seen my handwriting in the logbook in the surgery so many times. That fucking bitch-whore, smarter than everybody thought.'

'Calm down, Carly, don't swear.'

'But I'm frightened. The police want to know where I was on those days and I can't remember. She was cleverer than people thought. She wanted me out of the way so that she could have Rob. The fucking bitch-whore was a witch. A fucking witch.'

'Just stop swearing, please.'

'Swearing is the least of this family's problems.'

'I hate it when you swear. Please stop it. It doesn't help.' Ignoring the rules, she puts her hand on my arm. Her touch comforts me. 'I've been thinking hard.' She pauses. 'Those two Saturdays must be two Saturdays when we went shopping together.'

'Shopping?'

'Yes. We were always going shopping together at weekends, weren't we, Carly?'

'What about the children?'

'Can't you remember? The children came with us.'

'Will they remember that?'

'Don't complicate things. Children their age can't remember anything.' There is a pause. 'I've reminded you where we were, and now I'm going to tell the police.' The determined look on her face tells me not to argue with her. 'Carly, you can stop swearing now. Calm down.'

~ Rob ~

I move through what feels like a large version of a public school or an Oxbridge college. Past a chapel. A library. A fountain. Balanced Georgian buildings. Past the Great Hall, whose function I am not quite sure about. I turn right, past old brick and sleeping winter flowerbeds, which in summer must be a burst of colour. I know my plants. Delphiniums. Hibiscus and Hydrangeas. Daylilies. Candytuft. Brown Eyed Susans. Sunflowers. Marigolds. Ornamental grasses. Even today, with bare trees and depleted flowerbeds it is an oasis of peace trapped in a bygone age, the sounds of the city muted.

When I reach Mr Hockerman's chambers the door is wedged open. Hesitantly, I step inside and wind along a convoluted corridor, walls laden with modern art; splodges, splats and lines, until I reach the clerk's room. It is stark and utilitarian. Rows of black shiny suits are sitting at computers. One of them looks at me and smiles as I hover in the doorway.

'Dr Burton?' he asks as he abandons his computer and steps towards me. He smiles; I try to smile back but my mouth doesn't move.

'Mr Hockerman QC is in the conference room with your wife's solicitor.'

Along another rabbit warren corridor to a doorway in the furthest crevice of the basement area, where a man with dark hair and a fermented face is waiting for me, sitting at a circular plastic conference table that almost fills the room. He has papers spread in front of him; Carly's solicitor, Mr Ward, a sullen young man, with hair cut so short he must have pushed a number four hair clipper across his head like a lawnmower, sits next to him. Mr Ward's hair makes him look like a bouncer in an unruly nightclub, pugnacious and tough. That must be the look he is attempting to create. He sits next to Mr Hockerman QC as if he is guarding him. Mr Hockerman QC half stands as I enter, gesticulating for me to sit down at a chair opposite him. Mr Ward doesn't move. The clerk disappears like a ghost. I had imagined leather winged chairs and bookcases. This is disappointing. White walls. Plastic furniture.

Mr Hockerman leans forward to read a paper from the top of the pile in front of him, just for a few seconds, as if he is double-checking something. He has pubic sideburns and nasal hair that needs trimming. He looks up, eyes meeting mine over half-moon spectacles. Pale blue, watery eyes.

'Good morning, Dr Burton. Thank you for coming,' he says. His voice is educated. Long vowels. Clipped consonants. 'I know it was a terrible shock to you, Dr Burton, the news that your wife is being charged with the murders of Craig Rossiter and Anastasia Donaldson, as well as Jenni's.'

Shock doesn't even begin to capture what I've been going through. My life has become torture. Permanent hell. But I don't share that with Mr Hockerman, I let him continue.

'We have now received the evidence from the prosecution and we felt it is important to put you in the picture; keep you updated.' Mr Hockerman is stirring in his chair, bristling with energy. Mr Ward is as still as a Chinese terracotta soldier. Mr Hockerman leans back. His trousers ride up to display bright red socks. Very non QC. Very non Mr Hockerman.

'I want to reassure you,' he continues, 'that the evidence against your wife is flimsy. Let me show you – we've got a copy of the CCTV footage now.'

He fumbles about in his pocket, and soon he is looking directly at me, brandishing a memory stick. He pushes the stick into a portal of his computer.

'Stand behind me and look at this,' he instructs.

Mr Ward and I do exactly as we are told. He presses play and the CCTV evidence begins to roll. A chubby blonde-haired woman in a yellow dress is hobbling across the car park near Craig and Jenni's house. The footage is very dark, very blurred. She is on the screen one moment and then before my eyes can get used to what she looks like, she is gone, to be replaced by a woman in a baggy red raincoat. This time the picture is worse; even grainier. I blink and she too is gone.

'Let me show you again, in slow-mo.'

We watch again in silence. Mr Hockerman switches his computer off.

'So, Dr Burton, what do you think? Is it your wife?'

'I can't see it clearly enough to be certain.'

'Exactly,' Mr Hockerman snaps. 'No one can.' He pauses. 'Judges are not stupid. This evidence will go away. Which just leaves the handwriting travesty.' He takes a deep breath. 'How they've managed to contort this, we'll never know.'

Mr Hockerman's face is pinched inwards to express his disgust. He is pulling some papers towards him from the plastic table in front of him, snorting with indignation.

Mr Ward is watching him, shaking his head slightly. His lips have moved. A smile is attempting to play on his lips. It doesn't quite appear.

I close my mind to my surroundings. To Mr Hockerman and Mr Ward. To Mr Hockerman's energetic self-confidence. To Mr Ward's passive aggression. I need to concentrate. This is so different from how I imagined it. So different from Inspector Johnson's snarling condemnation of my wife when he came to tell me he she was being charged with Craig and Anastasia's murders. He made it sound as if the outcome was unquestionable. Or at least that's how I interpreted what he said. And I have been to hell and back. My wife, the woman I married, a serial killer. Not even prayers have helped. I have just been helping Heather look after the children, attempting to run the surgery, like a shadow of a person, not myself. Like a burnt piece of debris, floating on the wind.

I open my eyes. Mr Hockerman and Mr Ward are both sitting looking at me, frowning a little in concern.

'What do you mean, contort this? What's been happening?' I ask.

Mr Hockerman takes over again, a smile invading his lips.

'When Carly was arrested over Jenni's death, they reopened the two suicide cases. They had the handwriting on the suicide notes checked by a local expert who informed the police it looked a bit like Carly's. But I've never seen such a sloppy piece of work. Look at this, I'll show you.'

He hands the piece of paper he is holding to me. I sit deciphering it. Reading the curly lettered note. Reading Anastasia's less curly, more spidery. The curls of the letters are a bit like Carly's, but not the spidery ones. I look up.

'Well?' he asks, eyes pushing into mine.

'I'm not good with handwriting, but it doesn't look definitive.'

'Exactly. Not definitive. That's the point. You should have been a lawyer, Dr Burton.'

'That's what Carly says sometimes.' I don't tell Mr Hockerman that she means it as an insult, not a compliment.

Mr Hockerman continues, 'I've got our forensic handwriting expert to start looking at this. Melissa Barrington. She's got all the right state-of-the-art equipment. The woman is top notch. Apparently, the notes are obviously forgeries, but exactly by whom needs to be confirmed by more tests. So far they bear very little resemblance to Carly's stroke work.'

He beams at me. I didn't think his long thin face was capable of beaming. Mr Ward is grinning too. A grin completely changes the landscape of his face. He must only be about twenty-five. He's actually OK looking when he smiles; not such a hatchet-man.

'And finally,' Mr Hockerman taps his pen on his desk. 'We have your mother-in-law saying she was with Carly shopping on both the days in question, even though you can't back her up because you've misplaced your diary. So,' a flourish of his pen, 'a strong alibi, as well.'

He seems so confident, so bullish, but still I tremble inside as I contemplate what might happen to my wife, my family. About what has happened to Jenni, to Craig, to Anastasia. About where my diary is. About whether Heather is lying. About whether Carly is.

Carly.

I feel so low every time I think of her. As if I'm about to go in front of a firing squad or be led into an electric chair. Heavy with grief, because I fear my wife is lying. I don't trust her and yet I don't want to admit it. If Carly didn't do this, who did? Not Jenni. Jenni had the Lord in her heart. Jenni would never do this. My mind pushes back. I am standing in the coroner's court, holding two girls' trembling hands.

'But what about the coroner's ruling?' I ask.

'They had used a local handwriting expert who didn't even have an electron-microscope.'

Mr Hockerman raises his hands in the air. 'Anyone who

knows anything about this knows that this evidence is useless without that.'

'So how did the coroner's court get away with it, then?' I splutter.

'How do any of us?' he asks, standing up and leaning across the plastic table to shake my hand in dismissal. As far as he is concerned Carly Burton is dealt with for the morning. He needs to get on. He terminates our meeting with a smile. Mr Ward copies him. I try to smile back but I'm not sure that I manage.

I leave the conference room and move away, through the rabbit warren corridors, taking wrong turns a few times, but arriving back at the clerk's room, eventually, to find my bearings from there and escape into fresh air.

But fresh air does not help me feel any better. Nothing helps. I sidle back through Lincoln's Inn, across the manicured lawn, surrounded by antiquity, feeling as if I'm carrying the weight of antiquity on my back.

~ Carly ~

My time in here is suffocating me. The only time I am enjoying is association, when we are allowed to walk around the quad and chat. I like moving arm in arm with quirky, almost-pretty Sarah Jane. Even behind concrete walls decorated with hoops of barbed wire I can smell spring in the air, and it fleetingly reminds me of better times.

Better times, walking hand in hand along the riverbank, my husband and I. Head singing with happiness as we stroll along beneath the canopy of trees, dappled by sunlight. Pippa, roller-blading ahead of us, hair streaming behind her as she weaves gently between other people meandering along the towpath – families out for their Sunday afternoon constitutionals, elderly couples clinging on to one another, shoulders bent. Dog walkers, joggers. A cacophony of people enjoying the river; its slow-moving peace, the serenade of the river birds.

I remember Matt and John, ahead of us on their bikes. Making our way to the café by the bridge. The café serves a mean millionaire's shortbread. A perfect Sunday, walking along the riverbank, the sun metallic across the water.

Reaching the café by the bridge; iron tables and chairs

scattered across a flat piece of grassed land in front of it. Yew trees and pigeons. A stone statue of a colonial Indian General I have never heard of. The café's counter and kitchen are squashed into an archway in the bridge. Our offspring used to wait for us at a table near the statue, faces flushed with exertion, tea and cakes and my much-craved millionaire's shortbread in front of them. We would sit and drink, chat and eat. In my mind, the soft toffee of my shortbread cake clings to my teeth. I savour it.

But it is not like that in here. Jenni, you have taken my life away from me. Will I ever walk like that again, will I ever enjoy my family after what you've done to me? You have killed my ex-lover and his girlfriend, then set me up for their murders.

I see you in your cottage, crushing drugs into his wine. You know what you are doing with drugs, don't you, Jenni – look what you did to me! And now you are out and he is sitting watching TV and drinking your concoction. He didn't have a chance, did he? After all, you'd had a practice on me. And now I see you writing his suicide note. Why are you doing that? Just in case setting me up goes wrong?

I told the police what you did but they don't believe me. They think I'm a killer. They think I killed you on purpose, don't they? And even if I did, Jenni, wouldn't you think that it was fair enough, that eventually everyone would realise how dangerous you were, and that in the end I had to protect myself?

~ Rob ~

In life, I knew I would have to walk away from you. For the sake of my religion. For the sake of my marriage. And I was coming to terms with this. In death I cannot. I cannot walk away from you and the damage my wife has inflicted on you. I visit your grave every day to talk to you. Can you hear me, Jenni?

I go back to all our old places. The church. The river. Soft Sunday afternoon walks beneath dappled light. I visit Stuart and your boys. Your dad's a brick, isn't he? But then you always knew that. And now, continually restless without you, I have boarded a train to Cornwall, to Trethynion where you used to live, to feel closer to you there. As I step off the train you step towards me as you did last time when Carly and I visited, smelling of musk and patchouli oil. Embalming me with your eyes. I weave around your village of winding streets serenaded by the melancholy cries of seabirds, the salt air you used to breathe corroding my face. I move past your cottage. It is still taped off, Jenni. Tired blue police tape is still flapping in the wind. I move out of the village and up the cliff path.

Up the cliff path where you walked so often. Climbing. Climbing. Crumbling white cliffs and blue silken sea falling behind me. Up towards your church, to pray for you there.

~ Carly ~

I'm lying on my bed in my cell, trying to relax. Sarah Jane is listening to her iPod in the bunk above mine, its distant sound scratching towards me, when a screw knocks on the door. The door is opened, closed again. The screw, a young man in a grey uniform, stands in front of me looking severe.

'Carly Burton, come with me. Your legals want to see you.'

No warning. No time to think. No time to smooth out my answers. What do they want now? I run my fingers through my unkempt hair, trying to tame it a little with my fingernails, and push saliva around my mouth to freshen it as I follow the screw along the corridor. At least he hasn't cuffed me this time.

Mr Hockerman QC and my solicitor, Mr Ward, are waiting for me in the out-of-hours visiting room, a small room at the end of my cellblock. The screw lets me in to join them and locks the door behind us. Mr Hockerman and Mr Ward smell of the City, clean and smart-suited. I sit in the plastic chair opposite them, across a plastic table. I am out of my cell but still locked in this grey plastic world.

'Good news,' Mr Hockerman says. 'We came to tell you immediately.'

I feel the bag of cement that I had swallowed as I left my cell start to ferment and lighten.

'They're dropping the charges against you for the murders of Craig and Anastasia.'

My blood moves from the core of my body to its periphery. Dancing. Dancing. So much so that I feel as if I'm about to faint.

'What happened?' I ask, clinging on to the table in front of me.

'A proper forensic handwriting expert looked at the suicide notes. Melissa Barrington, far more experienced than the person the police first used. Internationally respected in her field. The writing in the suicide notes is completely dissimilar to yours. Her research had what they call a strong conclusion. She actually believes that Jenni wrote them both.' He pauses for breath and to give me a jubilant smile. 'And so the prosecution have dropped charges against you.' Another pause. 'You only have to go to trial for the fire.'

I inhale. I exhale.

'At last, someone believed me.'

Mr Hockerman takes my hand in his.

'I always believed you, Carly. We just had to wait until the police did.'

Tears well in my eyes.

'But what about Rob?' I ask.

Mr Hockerman does not reply.

~ Rob ~

I am kneeling by your grave, talking to you, praying for you. Can you see me? Can you hear me? Please, Jenni, please tell me the truth. Please tell me you didn't do this. That the police have made a mistake.

We all sometimes make mistakes, don't we, Jenni? Don't we?

~ Rob ~

Your trial starts today. So Heather and I are braving London together, to support you.

London. People are moving, shoulder to shoulder, speed walking in suits and trainers, rucksacks on their backs carrying their shoes. People eating on the hoof. People with their heads down, checking their emails as they move. Moving, moving, everything is moving. Except for the buses, gridlocked on Waterloo Bridge. The river. The clouds. The Millennium Eye. Moving. Moving. Moving.

At the bottom of Waterloo Bridge an army of bicycles is skipping the lights, protected by helmets and high-vis jackets; I have never seen so many bikes in my life. It takes ages to cross the road at the end of the bridge, but Heather and I stick together and eventually we manage. There is a bit more room on the opposite pavement, freeing us to turn down the Strand, and move at a normal pace towards Fleet Street and the Old Bailey. The Old Bailey. Portland stone pillars and majestic cupola. The gold figure of justice terrorising us from above.

I push my bag and my coat through the X-ray machine at the entrance. Heather follows me. Heather. The only person who knows where you were on the dates Craig and Anastasia died. Heather, do I believe you? Carly, do I believe you? Even though some of the charges against you have been dropped, I have continued to look and look for my diary to satisfy my own doubt. I can't find it anywhere, and suspicion towards you continues to incubate inside me.

Today I push through the security loop, an overweight guard eyeballing me. He lowers his eyes and waves me through. I grab my bag as it judders out of the X-ray machine on its side and stand and wait. Heather is frisked, arms splayed, legs apart, patted down by the gentle touch of the overweight security guard. She is released by a nod of the head, and we walk through the entrance hall of the Old Bailey together.

It is the modern entrance. Not the original entrance, the marble-floored palatial hall of the internet and BBC dramas, now only used for high days and holidays. We are ushered straight into the back of a courtroom, where a wigged and gowned Mr Hockerman nods at us to acknowledge our presence. The courtroom. Solid with silence. Heavy with self-importance. Lawyers arriving to greet each other with meagre smiles. Gowned court officials, pacing up and down. I am not sure who they are, or why they are pacing so self-importantly. The air presses down on me and stifles me. I feel as if I need permission to think, permission to breathe.

A door opens to the right of us, and we turn our heads towards the noise. A guard enters, a bull of a man, all torso and chest. You are handcuffed to him. Why? If you run away now, how far will you get? He uncuffs you and you sit down next to each other, in the area reserved for the defendant; in the middle of the court at the back, behind a glass screen. You are wearing a pink dress. You look thin and pale. Wide-eyed. Dusted with innocence. You rub your wrist where you were cuffed, as if the metal had been hurting you. When you finish making yourself comfortable, you look across, first at your mother, then at me. When our eyes meet, I silently ask you,

'Carly, was all this really necessary?'

You lower your eyes and look at your feet.

The judge enters from a door behind his seat at the front of the court. He sits high up in the middle, the focal point of the room. We all stand up as he enters. When he sits down, we all copy him. He looks across to the clerk of the court.

'Please bring the jurors in.'

I look across at you, Carly, watching the jury enter, eyeing them with a distant, diffident air. Running your fingers through your short wavy hair. You do not look afraid or intimidated. Just bemused. Interested. You have a calm surety about you which will take you a long way. As I look at you, sitting there in sugar pink, bathed in candyfloss innocence, I smell it all again.

The acrid smell of death that will never go away.

~ Carly ~

I spend hours layering my face with natural make-up. Mum has chosen me tasteful, low-key clothing; Brora, Monsoon, M&S. Nothing too flashy. Nothing too figure-hugging. Everything pastel. I sit in the dock, concentrating on the trial and on my facial expressions, my body language trying to remember what Mr Hockerman said about 'demeanour in the box'. Demeanour, typical Mr Hockerman, who uses a word like that these days? I sit, feet apart, hands in my lap, shoulders wide, flattened back. I do not glare. I do not frown. I do not put my hands to my mouth.

It is too hot in this court. Sweat pools at the base of my spine, behind my knees, on my forehead. Lakes and lakes of it. I cannot draw attention to it by wiping it away, so I must sit, shoulders back, allowing it to pour off me, embracing it as part of me. Part of my heat. Part of my energy.

I watch the judge sipping water from his glass, his Adam's apple descending as he drinks. He is flicking through the papers in front of him, boredom brushing across his face. Every time he speaks, the jury turn their heads towards him with staring eyes, heads stiff like a row of puppets.

Hours have melted into days.

Endless transportation between the Old Bailey and the holding jail they've put me in for the trial, rattling about cuffed in my cubicle. Endless time spent watching the jury; listening, fidgeting, yawning, taking notes. Their sharp intake of breath when they were shown your photograph, Jenni. Oh, the fascination of the charcoal crust of death.

The closer we are to the end of the trial, the more the hours are stretching. The tighter the knots in my stomach. The sweeter my smile. The more I mimic your cow eyes, Jenni. For they move towards me, still. I will never forget them.

~ Rob ~

You sit in the dock swathed in violet silk, your hands clasped in front of you. The jury are sitting, backs straight, eyes fixed on Miss Sally Jennings, the prosecution barrister who is about to sum up. The air is so heavy it presses against my lungs as I breathe. Sally Jennings is thin and aggressive, everything about her pointy and scratchy; her face, her fingernails, even her hairstyle. A chin-jutting, pugilistic woman who I know Mr Hockerman QC doesn't like.

'Carly Burton is very bright,' she starts. 'Very manipulative. Carly knew Jenni was dangerous when she invited her to the bonfire party. It seems she was the only one who did – it's fair to say that Carly was two steps ahead of everyone, even the police. And now it is known that Jenni did indeed kill her husband and his lover in a similar way to how Carly alleges Jenni tried to poison her. So Carly, a woman who hadn't been believed by the police, decided to take the law into her own hands and deliberately gave Jenni petrol rather than paraffin to light the bonfire. She then made herself scarce and waited for the flames to erupt. It is obvious that Carly wanted Jenni out of the way because she thought Jenni was chasing her husband,

Rob. The practice manager Sharon has corroborated in her witness statements that Jenni was indeed chasing Rob.'

I watch your face blanching at the mention of Sharon. Sharon giving evidence against you.

'So Carly had both motive and opportunity,' the silk continues. 'The only feasible verdict is guilty.'

'No,' I hear you articulate more loudly than you are allowed. But the judge shows you some mercy, he doesn't reprimand you in public.

Miss Sally Jennings sits down and Mr Hockerman stands up. He adjusts his glasses. Mr Hockerman swallows and turns his head to the jury, shoulders raised.

'The evidence shows that my client, Carly Burton, suffered acute clinical depression which wore her down and led to a sexual affair which she deeply regrets. She was thrilled to be reconciled with her best friend Jenni, and exceedingly supportive when Jenni's husband died last July. Carly is a loving nurse, wife and mother, who has been devastated by her friend's death. She made the fatal mistake of giving her dear friend petrol instead of paraffin to light the bonfire. The family were tragically storing spare petrol in the shed in a similar canister. Carly simply got the canisters mixed up. This is a mistake for which she has already paid dearly; she has paid by losing her best friend. By being away from her family for so long. It is a mistake that has cleft her life in two. It is the responsibility of the court to release this woman and give her back to her family, all of whom are longing for her to come home.'

You try to stop yourself from crying by biting your lower lip. You don't manage. A tear escapes and runs slowly down your right cheek. You flick it away with your fingers.

Miss Jennings and Mr Hockerman's words burn in my brain. Why isn't it obvious who to believe? How can truth be a compromise? Help me, Carly. Tell me the truth. Please.

~ Carly ~

Counsel have summed up. The jury are deliberating. My life will be decided by people who don't know me. I am sitting on a wooden slatted bench in a cell beneath the Crown Court, waiting. My whole family were in court today; Rob, Mum, Matt, John, Pippa. It was so good to see them that I didn't listen to everything that was being said. Most of the time I just sat watching them. Watching my mother trying not to stare at me for too long, smiling at me and telling me she loves me with her eyes. Watching Pippa holding Matt's hand. John and Matt, wriggling. Rob. Still and unresponsive. A cardboard cut-out of himself. A distant stranger I used to know.

As I sit on this solid bench, I feel as though time has stopped. Perhaps it is the end of my life. For my life to continue, for time to move again, I need to go home. I attempt to pray. To beg an unknown deity to help me. But I stop myself. I don't believe in God. I never have. I never will. All I believe in is movement and life. And that is what has been taken away from me. I close my eyes and attempt to float in the vacuum of my mind, slowing my breathing and preparing to die.

A noise breaks through the vacuum. A guard has opened the

door and is standing in front of me. The same guard that has been taking me up and down between my cell and the court all through my trial. Not that you'd know from any recognition or friendliness he shows me; there is none. No presumption of innocence with him. To him I am just a criminal. An invisible non-person, without feelings, without humanity.

We go up in the lift together. He hasn't cuffed me but his cuffs dangle in his right hand like a threat. Nausea swirls in my stomach. My hands tremble like feathers in the wind.

I am led into the dock. My family are all watching me, everyone but Rob. Mum gives me a tart smile. Pippa engulfs me with her eyes. Matt and John sit looking at me like a pair of bush babies. I want to take them in my arms and hug them. Rob fiddles with his iPhone, busy-thumbed – too intense with emotion to look up.

The judge enters and we stand and bow. He's a neat little man of about sixty with a clean-shaven face and pebbly eyes. He asks the clerk to fetch the jury. The clerk, who looks angular and well-meaning, nods his head and slips away. The judge sits down, but I remain standing. I stare at the back of Mr Hockerman QC's head, at his straight back, at his wig. Trying not to watch the jury coming in, I move my eyes down and focus on the floor. Thin blue carpet. A sweet wrapper. A plastic cup. One glance. I allow myself just one glance at the jury.

A middle-aged woman with frown lines. A young man with a shaved head.

Eyes back to the plastic cup. The plastic cup has a crack in it. If I were to drink out of it, I would scratch my lip.

'Have you reached a decision?' the judge asks, his voice humming in distant airwaves.

The foreperson, the middle-aged woman with frown lines, stands up. She has metal grey hair the colour of a pan scrub. She takes a deep breath and replies,

'Yes.'

'And is that the opinion of all of you?'

'Yes.'

'On the one and only count, do you find the defendant guilty or not guilty?'

Time solidifies. Like it did in the cell, only worse.

'Not guilty.'

My knees fold. The world is no longer the world, but rather slow-motion cinema photography. The police officer opens the door to the dock in quarter time.

'The defendant is free to go.'

Free to go. But my muscles have spasmed. For a second I have forgotten how to walk. Then, slowly, slowly, I move past the glass wall of the dock into the courtroom. Slowly, slowly, my family move towards me. My mother reaches me first and clamps me against her. Drowning me in the softness of her cashmere. Choking me with the strength of her perfume. Pippa and the boys are crushed against my legs. Mr Hockerman QC is approaching, his face split in two by a grin. Somehow through the body-blanket of my family I manage to shake his hand and thank him.

Through cuddles, kisses, smiles and laughter, through wondering how I get my possessions back from prison and whether they are even worth collecting, all I want to do is hold Rob.

'Where's Rob? Where's Rob?' My voice scratches in panic.

My mother unfurls herself from me and steps to one side. Rob is standing right behind her.

'Good to have you back, Carly,' he says. Politer than polite. As if I am a stranger. He pulls me towards him. His body is taut, ready to spring away. I rest myself against him, but I do not feel part of him.

We travel home on the train. It's a journey which passes in

442

a daze. A private journey held in public. A journey in which I wish to give nothing away. I sit limply next to Rob, allowing him to hold my hand dutifully, looking out of the window. Green trees and sunlight. Tower blocks. Litter and graffiti. My family must sense my mood. They do not push me to speak. They sit in silence too.

Back home, Rob and I hit the booze. Beer for Rob. Red wine for me. Heather makes herself a sandwich and a cup of tea, and orders takeaway pizza for the children. Now they stab me with questions. Question after question. So many questions that my throat is sore from answering. Questions about my cell. About my cellmate. The food. The bed. The washrooms. The activities. I am revelling in their attention. Far too hyper to calm down and take an interest in anybody else. Eventually, pizza demolished, my mother shuffles the children up to bed. After a surfeit of cuddles from our offspring, Rob and I are alone at last.

My mind is fugged with alcohol. The room is swaying gently around me. We're sitting together on the sofa, pouring each other another glass each.

'I told you Jenni was dangerous,' I slur.

The soft blurry colour of the room tightens around me. His face moves towards mine and sharpens. So close to me, his breath takes mine away.

'What happened to Jenni is far too serious for an "I told you so".'

'Come on, Rob.'

A long pause.

'You don't actually think I set fire to Jenni on purpose, do you?'

~ Rob ~

'You don't actually think I set fire to Jenni on purpose, do you?' you ask, looking at me as if you would like to annihilate me.

But Carly, I will not let you intimidate me. I do not reply. My whole life has become a lie. Staying married to you. Pretending you forced me to say I 'quite liked' Jenni, when Jenni had enthralled me for years. I stayed with you because of my Christianity. Oh, Carly, if I could turn the clock back. If only on that chilly night at the campsite in France, I had given a different answer. If only I had said, 'Carly, I will never love anyone else as I love you.'

Would that have stopped this chain reaction? One more lie and Jenni would have lived?

~ Carly ~

You do not reply.

Even tonight, when I've had so much to drink that my thoughts and my words are spinning in my head like tornados, I know from the twist of your face, the curve of your mouth, the flatness in your eyes, I know you do not believe me about Jenni.

'Please, Rob,' I beg. 'Please tell me why you won't accept the truth about Jenni.'

'I never said I didn't accept the truth about Jenni.'

'You don't need to. I can see it in your eyes.'

You are sitting looking at me sanctimoniously – taking a leaf out of her book.

I hate you, Rob. I hate you for not believing me.

'I didn't intend to kill Jenni,' I scream at you.

I lose control. I pummel you with my fists. I use all my energy to try and damage you, pulverising your arms, your stomach, your legs, with my fists. I hate you. I hate you. I hate you. I used to love you but there is a thin line between love and hate.

'And it's not just your attitude about the fire that cripples me,' I shout. 'It's the way you can't accept that Jenni was dangerous. The way you never believed me. The way you don't even believe the police about what happened to Craig and Ana. It's because you want Jenni to be innocent, not me. It's because you wanted Jenni, not me.'

You are backing away from me, cowering a little, using your arms to protect your body from my blows. From nowhere, you say,

'Carly, I never found my diary. Where did you put it?'

'I didn't put it anywhere, you bastard,' I shout.

You manage to overpower me. You hold my arms behind my back, and my body against yours.

'Carly, I'm sorry, let's stop this. It's out of control. Let's talk about it in the morning. We've both had far too much to drink.'

~ Rob ~

I lead you upstairs. Carly, you are very, very drunk. The drink has made you aggressive, even more volatile than usual, but you are calming down now. When you've slept off this poison, maybe then we can communicate. Find some peace between us. You are almost asleep as I undress you, slowly, slowly, carefully, carefully, splash your face with a little cold water and settle you into bed. I switch the light off and curl up beside you. Your breathing slows and deepens as you drift into a semi-comatose sleep.

Hours and hours pass. But my body can't relax and join you. Why are you lying to me? Where have you hidden my diary? My body is pumped up with alcohol and fury at the violence you have shown to me. I have looked everywhere for that diary, more or less ransacked the house. But whatever I do, after the way you have treated me, I want to find it now. My wakefulness is overpowering me. I feel so claustrophobic lying here, I need to get out of bed. I toss my covers away. I slip my feet to the floor and reach for my bathrobe, moonlight curling towards me from around the curtain edges. Carly, you are lying on your back, snoring gently. Sleep well. Sleep deep. It isn't going to be an easy conversation in the morning. Avoiding the second stair that creaks, I creep downstairs.

I crack the kitchen light on, and the familiarity of my family kitchen is illuminated in front of me, so still and dead in the middle of the night, like a stage set at the theatre waiting for the actors to walk across it and breathe some life into it. Pippa's pink hairband lying by the computer. A row of wellington boots by the back door. An empty coffee cup by the sink waiting to be washed. It feels so cold when no one else is here. I put the kettle on to make a hot drink to warm myself up. The kettle seems to struggle noisily; I eventually manage to make myself a cup of Nescafé, and then sit in a chair at the kitchen table sipping it, placing my mind on rewind. Rewind until I've found my diary. Rewind. Rewind. Rewind. What does Heather always say when the children have lost something? Her words rotate in my mind. When did you last see it? When did you last play with it, darling? Rewind. Rewind. Rewind.

A few nights before the fire. Before Carly was in prison. I was writing in it. I had a terrible headache that night. The pain in my temples was cracking and cracking. It was becoming volcanic. I was looking for pain relief. My doctor's case was upstairs and I didn't feel like fetching it, so I started fumbling in our medicine cupboard which we keep in the kitchen. The childproof jar of ibuprofen that we always kept there was empty. So I pushed to the back and found an old paracetamol packet. Not my favourite treatment for a headache, but I didn't want to wake the rest of my family up by rummaging about in the dark upstairs. So I swallowed some and hoped for the best. That was the last time I saw my diary. The night I developed that wretched headache. So, if Carly hasn't stolen it, it might still be in here. Here in our family kitchen.

Where to look? Where to look? It feels as if I've looked everywhere. I look everywhere again. Every pan drawer. Every cupboard. I even try the medicine cupboard. But the medicine cupboard is too small. I would never have put it in there. I push with my fingers, I shove, I bumble. Past old packets of aspirin, discarded blister packs that used to contain ibuprofen. I feel something smooth like leather. I clasp it in my fingers and pull.

My diary *is* here.

Carly Burton. Carly Burton Bright, I'll catch you now.

I sit at the kitchen table pelting through the pages to Heather's shopping dates, the dates in question. The ninth of July. The seventeenth of September. The dates I have always been so suspicious of.

9th July.
Quiet day at home. Raining. Shoved the children in front of a film. Updated twenty patient records, Carly defrosted the freezer.

Heather was lying to protect her daughter, but she didn't really need to. Carly wasn't in Cornwall.

17th September.
Carly shopping in Brighton with Heather and the kids. They had lunch at Pizza Hut. Matt made a pig of himself with the ice cream factory, apparently. Carly bought me a present. A pair of leather gloves.

So. They did go shopping. On the second Saturday – only half a lie then. All documented. In my diary. In my handwriting. Carly was never anywhere near the deaths in Cornwall. My heart stops.

Sorry, Carly. Sorry.

I know saying sorry can never be enough.

How could I have been so very wrong about you? About

the mother of my children? About my wife? Had Jenni so distorted my perception? I sit at the kitchen table, knowing that I need the help of the Lord. Lord, help me. Lord, help me forgive myself. Help Carly to forgive me. Help me make it right with her tomorrow. When I've had some sleep. Somehow, however difficult it is, with your help, Lord, I will find the right words.

I tiptoe upstairs. I open the bedroom door, slowly, and slip into bed next to my wife, who has turned on her side and stopped snoring. I put my arms around her and kiss the soft warm skin at the back of her neck. Even tonight after so long in prison she still smells of vanilla.

Carly. Carly. Carly. Wife. Wife. Mother. Mother of my children. I float towards the Lord, towards forgiveness, towards sleep.

~ Carly ~

I wake up, unsure for a second where I am. Slowly, I remember. Back home, in bed with Rob, mouth tasting of decomposition because I drank too much alcohol last night. I do not feel as I imagined I'd feel when I returned. Absolved. Innocent. Ready to start my life again. I always thought that if I won the case, I'd be jubilant. Like a teenager leaving school, life running in front of me in an endless river of possibility.

But I am dead inside. My life has stopped.

And then I remember why.

Rob.

The opinion of the jury is meaningless. Rob is the dissenting thirteenth man who doesn't believe in me any more. He has been telling me for a while. In the turn of his head. The pain in his eyes. The harder I try to get close to him, the more he pushes me away. The more he idolises the memory of Jenni. Once we were a couple, weren't we, Rob? We would wake up in the night and touch each other's bodies. We would chat about something and nothing, and everything, for hours and hours and hours. Do you remember, Rob? I don't know when you first started to pull away from me. Whether it was because

451

of Jenni. Whether it was because of my breakdown. Because I found being a mother hard to adjust to? Because I became too wrapped up in Craig? Whatever it was, I'm sorry, Rob. I've really let you down. And now I have let myself down by allowing Jenni to frighten me. From beyond the grave she frightens me, because I can never compete with her in your eyes. I cannot live with your disgust, your hatred. I cannot live without your trust. I'm not religious. I know that when I'm dead I will feel nothing. Oblivion will overcome me.

Oblivion will take away my pain.

I pad slowly out of the bedroom without switching on the light. I can see just enough because of the strips of moonlight pushing around the curtain edges. I grab my dressing gown from the hook on the door. I creep along the landing to the bathroom, step inside and lock the door.

~ Rob ~

I reach out for you, Carly, to tell you what I know you long to hear. To tell you that at last I believe you and that I'm sorry, so very sorry that it has taken me so long to realise. I reach out to hold your hand and pull you towards me. But I cannot find you. You are not here. Your side of the bed is empty. Cold and empty.

Where are you, Carly? Why aren't you here? I want to take you in my arms and hold you. I pad towards the bathroom. We were both so far gone last night, you must be unwell. The door is locked. I knock. No reply.

'Carly,' I shout.

There is no reply. Carly, don't give me the silent treatment. I push the door handle down as hard as I can and press my full body weight against the door, leaning into it with my shoulder. I hear the crack of splintering wood and the door gives. One step inside.

Your body is hanging from a beam above the bath.

Panic simmers inside me, white hot panic, tinged with numbness. Ice dead eyes hold mine. I cannot move. Eyes. Eyes. Eyes. Staring at me accusingly from beyond the coldness of death.

Eyes shouting at me. Eyes hissing. Eyes spitting. Eyes accusing me of not loving you enough to believe you. Eyes accusing me of not loving you enough.

Oh, Carly, if only I could turn the clock back. If only, on that chilly night at the campsite in France, if only I had said, Carly I will never love anyone else as I love you, would that have stopped this chain reaction? One white lie and you would have lived? One more lie, just one more lie, and both my girls would have lived. Sometimes, a white lie is all it takes.

Acknowledgements

First I would like to thank Phoebe Morgan, my editor at Avon HarperCollins, who it has been a pleasure to work with from start to finish. Thanks indeed also to my agent Ger Nichol of the Book Bureau for noticing my work and for believing in me.

Technical help. Thanks to: Charles Owens – police procedure; Lindsay Parr – medical; Carol Robson – pharmaceutical.

Thank you always to my family and friends who are the backbone of my life. My parents Shirley and Peter who I am so lucky still to have. My mother Shirley, my grandmother Marjorie (who died when I was twenty-one), and I have always loved nothing better than to have our noses in a book. This love of reading seeded the desire to write, so my mother and my grandmother deserve particular thanks. My husband Richard supported me wholeheartedly while I wrote this book. But then he is always there for me, and he always does. My sons Peter and Mark. Peter's partner Meg. My brother Chris who so often rings me for a chat at the end of a long day's writing and buoys me up. My brother-in-law John, who does the same. My friends, loved like family, take an encouraging interest in my work. In particular, Angie Fitzhenry, Jackie Westaway, Joanna Tempowski, Alison Buscaine, Rachel McCullock, and Gerry Fletcher.

I want to thank my chums in Sion Row Book Group with whom I enjoy spending so much time. Reading together for so many years has helped formed my taste and ideas about literature. Again dear friends who are like family to me.

Attending the 2011 Faber Academy novel writing course was a very special experience. My tutor Richard Skinner deserves much praise and thanks. He has a well-deserved first class reputation as a novelist, poet, and Director of the Fiction Programme at Faber Academy. He works a bit of magic I think. Check out his success statistics. They will make you blink. Friendships on the course also meant a lot to me. Tamsin Barrett, Julie Fischer and Colette Mcbeth in particular have encouraged me to keep going.

Finally further back, I would like to thank my English teachers, at school and at university. If only I could step back in time I would like to thank them and give them a big hug. In particular Paul Pascoe, my English teacher at Formby High school in the 1970s. If Paul or anyone who knows him reads this, please get in touch, I just want, very belatedly, to say thanks.